GW00890387

THE COMMERCIAL
by BARRIE JAIMESON

COPYRIGHT - BARRIE JAIMESON 2016

PROLOGUE

SEPTEMBER 1983

'Clear the floor please. Now!' The floor manager's voice cut through the silence. Gradually a murmur started up from several actors and extras as they started to make their way from the studio.

Only Greg Driscoll remained, standing alone and confused in the middle of the floor. He didn't really know what had just happened. One minute he was going through the scene, rehearse-recording, when out of the blue, Hermione Allen, the young actress he was acting opposite, screamed, smacked her hand hard across his face and ran from the studio.

'He touched me! He touched me! The bastard touched me!' Her sobs echoed down the corridor.

Greg was aware of many heads shaking and fingers pointing as the floor was cleared. He ran his hands through his thick curly brown hair and felt the heat from the side of his face where the slap had made contact. It was sore but Greg did not want to show it. The floor manager came up to him, clipboard in hand, listening intently to whoever was speaking to him through his headphones.

'Yes. OK. Will do. I'm with him now.' He turned to face Greg and sighed. 'You're to go to Room 1276 in half an hour,' he said before adding, 'thanks for being such a tosser!' He left the studio, shouting instructions to various technical people still waiting to be told what to do. Greg didn't hear what the instructions were.

Room 1276 was 'The Market' production office. 'The Market' was a daytime soap opera, filmed in Birmingham, which had been running for roughly six months. Twenty year-old Greg Driscoll, straight from three years at Drama School had landed what he thought was a dream job. He played Steve Willetts, a market trader. He dreamed of fame, fortune and all the good things that brings. Very soon, he was realising the realities of daytime soap. No fortune, very little fame and a lot of hard work. Tight schedules, little rehearsal time, poor scripts that were not easy to learn and a producer who made Genghis Khan look like a reasonable person. Len Allen was an ex-City trader, had made a pile when the Government sold off everything the country owned to balance the books, and started a production company. It was his company that made 'The Market' and Hermione Allen was his beloved daughter.

Greg stood outside Room 1276. He had knocked on the door and was awaiting a response. He knew this was going to be big trouble. It wasn't the first time Len Allen had had 'a word' with him but it was the first time he'd been summoned to the big office. The door opened and the floor manager walked out. He scowled at Greg. And stalked off down the corridor. Greg peered round the open door.

'Did I say you could come in?' Len Allen was sitting behind his large desk. He was a brute of a man, about six foot three tall and nearly as wide, shaved head sticking out above the thick neck squashed into a very expensive shirt, silk tie, all enshrouded in an Armani suit.

'Er...no.' Greg replied

'Then get the fuck out and close the door after you!'

Greg went back outside and leant against the wall. He felt like a schoolboy summoned to see the headmaster. Two or three people passed, secretaries mostly. Greg winked at a particularly pretty young girl who shook her head and looked at him as though he were something she'd found on the bottom of her shoe. Things were not looking good for Greg. He felt like something found on the bottom of a shoe.

The door opened suddenly and another lackey exited the room. Greg paused, not knowing whether to enter or not. His dilemma was answered by a loud roar from inside the room. 'Get in here now!'

Greg mooched through the door. The thin cord carpet he'd been standing on outside transformed to a thick pile, pure white floor covering. He looked around him. Room 1276 was a long bare oblong of a room. It was devoid of any warmth, white cold walls, naked, apart from a few pictures on the wall, a mixture of photographs showing the great man shaking hands with various luminaries and paintings of some sort. They could have been priceless works of art but to Greg's mind they were little better than the posters on the wall of his bedsit. His eyes lighted on a photograph of Hermione aged about eight, dressed in a pink frock, holding a large cup and smiling, showing her perfect teeth. There was an engraved plaque underneath with the legend 'Hermione Allen – Actress of the Year 1973'. Greg was disgusted. What was this man doing running a television production company? It was just a rich man's playground for his spoilt daughter. His thoughts were interrupted by Hermione's father.

'Who do you think you are, Driscoll?' Len Allen didn't look up from whatever he was studying on his desk. Greg resisted the urge to point out he'd just said who he was and muttered, 'dunno.'

'You don't know? You don't know? Well, shall I tell you? Shall I?' Len Allen lifted his eyes and glared at Greg. He remained silent.

'You are a bloody nobody! That's who you are.' Allen paused obviously expecting a reply. Greg's mind could not produce one at the moment. 'Do you have nothing to say for yourself, Driscoll?'

'Why am I here?' Greg queried.

'A question I've often asked since I agreed to you being cast in my programme.'

'I'm sorry, maybe I'm just being thick but I don't understand what I'm supposed to have done wrong.' Greg crossed to sit on the chair in front of the desk.

'You arrogant young man! Stand up when I'm talking to you.'

Greg remained standing.

'Do you know what I could do to you? I could ruin you. You're at the beginning of your career and you choose to openly cross me. Me, who has done everything to make you, boy.'

'I still don't know what I've done.'

Len Allen stood up and walked round his desk to where Greg was standing. Although Greg was average height – five foot ten – and build – about twelve stones, Len Allen made him feel like a small child as he towered over him. Allen put his face close to Greg's. He smelt of garlic and sweat. 'If you try and touch my daughter up ever again I will make it my business to cause you a very serious injury, Driscoll.'

'And when am I supposed to have committed this heinous crime?'

Len Allen's face went even redder than it already was. 'Don't try and deny it, I have it on film.' He went back behind his desk and pressed a button. A screen wound itself down on the wall behind Greg. He turned round as a projector flashed into life. On the screen appeared the scene they had shot that morning. There was a two-shot of the back of Greg's head and Hermione's face. She was beaming and looking straight at the camera, even though her dialogue was addressed to Greg's character, Steve.

"I think I'm falling for you, Steve. When I saw the way you helped that old lady who'd lost her purse, I knew you were a proper man."

"It's just what anyone would do."

"Kiss me, Steve."

At this point the camera pans out to show Greg take Hermione in his arms. Before their lips can meet, Hermione's hand slaps Greg across the mouth.

'There.' Len Allen pointed at the screen

'It says in the script that they kiss passionately. It doesn't say she slaps his face.' Greg was still looking at the screen.

'It doesn't say Steve grabs her breast, does it, you young pervert?'

'Look, I may be young to you but I'm not a pervert.' Greg's anger was rising. 'I have, believe it or not, been fortunate to have indulged in a number of passionate kisses and in nearly every one a certain amount of physical contact has taken place apart from the lips. I don't think it's very real for two people to kiss and not touch.'

'Get out of here, now, before I do something that we might both regret. I shall be in touch with your agent right now.'

Greg looked at the large man behind his desk, turned and walked out of the door, leaving it open. He realised he may have just walked out on what could have been a promising TV career but right now, he didn't care. He was trained as a classical actor, why was he wasting his time doing daytime soaps? He ignored the shouts of 'Close the door' and stalked off to the pub.

*

The Red Lion was situated on the corner opposite the TV studios and was used by the staff as a sort of green room. There was a room at the back, separate from the main pub and it was there that most of the actors and crew hung about after they'd finished for the day. There were only half a dozen people in there as Greg entered with his pint of lager. The conversation stopped. Greg stood there looking at them. He knew them all; he'd been working with them for six months.

'What?' he said.

Gemma Green, one of the cast, spoke first. 'How'd it go?'

'How d'you think? I got a bollocking. Apparently I touched up his precious daughter.'

'Is he gonna sack you?'

'Haven't a clue.' Greg went over to any empty table in the corner and sat down.

Gemma stood up and came over to him. The others turned their backs and continued their conversation. Gemma was twenty-five and had been in the business since she was a child.

'Look, Greg. It's probably not for me to say but you need to be careful. Len Allen's quite powerful. It's best to keep your head down and keep your job.'

'Bollocks!' Gemma stood by the table and leaned over towards Greg.

'Look, we know you didn't do anything wrong and I know you're not long out of Drama School but the business is very different from Drama School.'

'Really? Why did I bother then? Why did I learn about Shakespeare, Chekhov, Oscar Wilde? So that I could stand three feet apart from some talentless tart and pretend to kiss her? I'm not interested.'

'You're destroying yourself, Greg. Don't do it. And lay off the booze, that doesn't help.'

'What?'

Gemma pushed that morning's Daily Express in front of him. It was open on an inside page that showed a rather blurred picture of Greg Driscoll falling out of a nightclub in London, very obviously in a poor state. Underneath was written *'Minor soap star drunk again. Who does he think he is'* Nothing else, no article, no explanation.

'If the big man's seen that, which I'm sure he has, it's not going to make your life any easier.' Gemma went and joined the others leaving Greg on his own. He downed his pint and left, walked up the road to The Duke of Wellington, went over to the bar and ordered a pint of lager and a large whisky.

*

It was past midnight when Greg stumbled into the small one-bedroom flat the studio rented for him. He ignored the flashing light on his answerphone and fell asleep on the sofa.

At seven-thirty the ringing of the phone finally sank into Greg's brain and woke him. The angry voice at the other end of the line belonged to Denis Young, Greg's agent.

'What the hell have you been doing, Greg? I was trying to get hold of you all day yesterday.'

'I was busy.'

'Well you won't be busy for much longer. I've had Allen on the phone. He wants to sack you. I pointed out that he would find that difficult under the terms of your contract but he didn't seem to care. I'm hoping he's talked to his legal people and seen sense but I can't guarantee it.'

'I don't really care, Denis.'

'Well I do. I'm your agent, Greg, and I have a reputation I want to keep even if you don't want to keep yours. I want you to go in and apologise to both Allen and his daughter and try and keep your nose clean. And don't get drunk in London nightclubs!'

'I'm not apologising. I have nothing to apologise for.'

'Then find a new agent!' Denis hung up.

'Shit!' Greg hauled himself up and went into the small shower room. He stuck his head under the showerhead and turned the cold tap on.

Two hours later he arrived at the studio.

'Mr Driscoll? The boss wants you. Room 1276.' The receptionist pointed towards the lift.

'Yes, I know where it is, thanks.'

Greg trudged up to the first floor, he didn't take the lift. He stood outside the door and breathed deeply before knocking. The door opened and a man in a suit ushered Greg into the room. Allen was sitting behind his desk.

'Your agent and my legal man here suggest I can't sack you. What do you think I should do?' Len Allen was looking at his desk but Greg assumed he was the one being addressed.

'I think you should accept my apology.'

Allen lifted his head. 'What apology?'

'The one I've just given you.'

'Call that an apology, do you?'

'Yes, I do.'

The suit stepped forward and whispered in Allen's ear. He scowled at him.

'I'm taking you out of the next three episodes, Driscoll, which gives you two weeks to think about your behaviour. I'm having your part re-written so that he has nothing to do with Hermione's character. You've cost me a lot of money and the cast and crew a lot of time and effort. This is your official final warning. Now get out!'

As Greg turned to go, Allen thrust the previous day's Daily Express at him. 'And don't think of your suspension as a holiday. If I see any more of this sort of behaviour, you will not be coming back and I will be within my legal rights to tell you to fuck off!'

Greg sauntered back to his flat. He felt he had been unfairly treated. All he had done was to brush Hermione's right breast in a clinch that was scripted. At least that wasn't going to happen again. He was never going to have to do a scene with that soppy, spoilt, piece of wood ever again. He reached for the phone and dialled Denis Young's number.

'Hi Denis. I think I owe you a drink. I'm getting the 3.40.train.'

*

They avoided the usual places and went to a hotel bar near Denis' office in the West End. Denis Young was ten years older than Greg and considerably more level-headed. He never seemed to wear anything other than a smart wide lapelled suit with a shirt that usually had a shade of pink about it. Greg had never seen him without a tie. He assumed Denis was gay but didn't know for sure. He'd never seen him with any sort of partner. He had always been charming when introduced to any young lady Greg had happened to be around and never made any sort of pass at any of Greg's male associates. His hair was worn quite long and swept over the top of his head in a bouffant style falling down to the top of his collar.

The two of them sat a table by the window, Denis ordering a dry white wine for himself and a lager for Greg.

'You're really going to have to learn, Greg,' Denis was explaining. 'If you want a career in this business you have to play the game.'

'It's a shit daytime soap that about three people and a dog watch, Denis. It's not The Royal Shakespeare Company.'

'That's not what you said when you were offered the job.'

'That's because you said it was good for my career.'

'It could have been. A new continuous series could've led to all kinds of offers if you'd controlled your urges.'

'Urges? I was acting. That's what I was being paid for. And, to be honest, it was bloody good acting. I wouldn't go near that cow with a bloody bargepole if it wasn't in the script.'

'Keep your voice down, Greg. I believe you.' Denis ran his hand through his mop of hair. 'I didn't know it was going to turn out to be such a bad show. The problem is, now you're in it, you can't rock the boat.'

'I know, Denis. It's hell, though. I never thought acting would be such a terrible way of making a living.'

'It's not, Greg. You just can't always play Hamlet. Sometimes you just have to do as you're told. Your contract's up in a couple of months and I doubt they'll renew it, then you can find out what it's really like to be an actor – out-of-work; broke; homeless, unless you can find someone stupid enough to take you in. That's how most actors have to live. You were lucky, straight out of Drama School into a TV series with a regular monthly wage.'

'Not a very big one, though.'

'I didn't say big, I said regular. Be grateful.'

They sat in the bar, Greg drinking heavily, Denis drinking sensibly until ten-thirty when Denis called a cab and took Greg back with him to his flat, despite protestations from Greg that he was quite capable of visiting a club in the West End without disgracing himself.

*

A week later the new scripts for 'The Market' arrived at Greg's flat back in the West Midlands. He opened the envelope with trepidation and turned to the first episode. His character, Steve, had two scenes; the first in the market pub, where he sits in a corner drinking, the other people in the scene making comments and gradually ostracising him. Steve stands and walks unsteadily over to his friend Jim and offers to buy him a drink. Jim just looks at him and walks out. The camera closes in on Steve's face. The next scene is a police car drawing up beside a drunken Steve, lying in the gutter, dragging him roughly into the back of the car and driving him off to the cells. The next two episodes don't improve. Steve is gradually cut off from the rest of the market residents as he becomes more and more under the addiction of the alcohol and is admitted to a rehabilitation clinic.

Greg grabbed the phone and rang Denis. 'They're trying to write me out, Denis.'

'That's great. It means you won't have to do it anymore.'

'But they're making a fool of me, Denis. They're making me look like a drunk.'

There was silence from the other end of the phone.

'Denis? Did you hear me?'

'I heard you, Greg. What do you want me to say?'

'I want you to get them to give me my character back.'

'That's not in my jurisdiction, Greg. I stopped them sacking you, which would have been a blight on your career, I can't write the scripts for them. Just see it through for the next couple of months and leave with your head held high.'

'As a drunk.'

'As a working actor, Greg. Whether the world sees you as a drunk or not is completely up to you and how you behave.'

'Oh thanks for your support,'

'It is support, Greg. You'll see that one day, I hope. And a word of advice; steer clear of nightclubs or places where you might be seen pissed!'

Greg put the phone down and looked around his flat. If he was being forced out of 'The Market' that would mean he would have to leave this place, the flat was part of the package. He went out, bought some plastic storage boxes and started packing. He was starting to look on the situation as a positive. He could move back to London, find some decent acting work and start living his own life again.

*

Steve Willetts made his last appearance in 'The Market' a week before Christmas. The character himself didn't actually appear. His demise was reported in the market pub by his ex-friend Jim who entered the pub to tell the assembled cast that Steve had suffered a pulmonary embolism whilst undergoing detox and hadn't survived. There was a moment of silence before the script went back to the main storyline of Hermione Allen's character's appearance as a singing sensation at the pub's Christmas entertainment.

Greg didn't see the programme. By now his contract had expired and not been renewed, he had vacated his flat in Birmingham and returned to London. Finding somewhere to live had not been as easy as he'd expected. He'd stayed with Denis for a couple of weeks before being told emphatically that he had to find his own place. Denis had helped him find a small bedsit in a converted house. It wasn't great, he had to share a bathroom with the family who lived down the corridor, but at least he had his own space.

Finding work was proving even more difficult. Denis suggested it was very quiet at the moment but Greg suspected the great Mr Allen probably did have a bit more influence in the business than he had thought and was spreading rumours. It was over a month before he even had an audition and then it was for a fringe production of Lorca's 'The House of Barnarda Alba' with an all-male cast. Greg went for the audition, was cast but turned it down as there was no money and he thought it was a stupid idea to do a play that has only female characters in it with an all-male cast. Denis, although secretly agreeing with Greg, was forced to point out to Greg that work breeds work, whether it's good work, paid work, or rubbish work. Contacts were what this business was about. He'd already upset one eminent TV producer and it wasn't a good idea to be arrogant with up-and-coming directors who may not always be working on the fringe.

Greg consoled himself by visiting his new local pub 'The Welcome', and he was welcome. He had wondered if anyone might recognise him from his days on 'The Market' but couldn't find anyone who'd actually seen the programme. The landlord was friendly and they got on well. They would spend many a happy hour discussing the world over a several pints before Greg returned to his empty bedsit.

As time dragged on Greg became more despondent. He managed to pick up an odd day's filming and a TV commercial pilot that never quite made it to the screen but his funds were seriously low by now. He had his dole money but that didn't go much farther than over the bar at The Welcome. He was sitting alone at the bar one evening, it was the landlord's night off, when he became aware someone looking at him. He looked around to make sure he was the target of the pair of dark eyes situated under the long hair of the girl sitting on her own in the corner of the lounge bar. There appeared to be no-one else in view so he hopped off the bar stool and wandered over.

She spoke first. 'Hi.'

Greg smiled. 'Hi. Anyone sitting here?'

'Only you if you like.'

Greg sat at the table. The girl suddenly seemed bashful. 'I'm sorry,' she said. 'I don't usually invite strange men to sit with me.'

'That's OK. And I'm not really that strange.' Greg looked at the girl across the table. She wore jeans that had paint or something streaked down the legs. He wasn't sure if they were designed to look like that or whether they were actually dirty. A check shirt, not tucked in. covered her top half. She was quite short and had a round face with a hint of a blush on the cheeks.

'I think I've seen you on TV.'

Fame at last! Greg shrugged his shoulders. 'Maybe.'

'Were you in a daytime soap called Market something?'

'The Market. It was just called The Market. Yes.'

'It was shit.' She looked away again, her cheeks reddening more. 'Oh, sorry.'

'That's OK. It was shit. That's why I got out.'

'My boyfriend did a job for it.'

Her boyfriend! Greg heart sank. Just when he thought things were looking up.

'He's a scenic designer. Well, he makes scenery for TV, film, shows and stuff. He'll be here in a minute. I don't know your name, I'm afraid.'

'Greg. Greg Driscoll.'

'I'm Mandy.'

No surname. There was a silence. Neither of them seemed to know what to say next. The silence was broken by a tall man with shaggy blond hair who seemed to appear from nowhere.

'Picking up strange men in pubs again, Mandy?' He turned to Greg. 'Hi, I'm Andy.'

'Greg Driscoll.'

Mandy perked up. 'Greg was in one of your shows. The market thing.'

'The Market? What a pile of shit that was!' He turned to Greg again. 'Did you meet the Executive Producer?'

'Once or twice, yes.'

'What a tosser! That series was just a showcase for his precious daughter. Another tosser! The shit I had to put up with on that set.'

'I know. I had a few problems myself.'

'I bet. What are you drinking?'

Greg ordered another pint and Andy went off to the bar. Mandy smiled shyly.

'Sorry. Neither of us is being very complimentary about your show.'

'It's OK. Like I said I got out. Andy your boyfriend?'

'Yeah. Andy and Mandy. Sound like a kid's show, don't we?'

Andy returned with the drinks and the three of them spent the evening chatting about theatre, TV, all the stuff that Andy and Greg had done and wanted to do. Mandy was a model artist, which wasn't, as Greg suggested, someone who posed naked for life drawing classes but someone who makes set models etc. for scenic artists. By the end of the evening Greg had somehow agreed to give Andy a hand with a project he was doing for a music promoter, helping to build a set for a big tour. He had a studio in Wapping, an old warehouse, and was willing to pay Greg to bang a few nails in and screw a few screws and any time off for auditions would not be a problem. He was to start in the morning.

The next few years were to see Greg spending more time building sets than acting on them.

***

JULY 1993

CHAPTER ONE

Greg Driscoll dragged himself away from the warmth of the arms of the girl of his dreams and into the cold reality of his empty bed, it was 9.50am.

The telephone ringing had rudely interrupted his early morning fantasy. Ten to ten was very early when one had fallen drunkenly into bed at four in the morning.

'Morning, Greg. Feeling crapulent?'

'Crapulence is something I gave up feeling when I was a teenager, Denis!'

Denis Young was an old friend of Greg's. They had known each other for a good ten years, many of which Greg seemed to have been spent looking at the underside of barroom tables countrywide. He'd been a good friend to Greg, supporting him emotionally and financially when needed, boosting his confidence and cushioning the downs when his ego became too large for him to sustain.

He was also his agent.

'What the hell are you ringing me for at this unearthly hour? Are you into sadism now?'

'It's nearly ten o'clock, Greg'

'Thanks for the time-check. I might have missed opening time!'

'I've an interview for you.'

Greg still earned a kind of a living from being a member of The British Actor's Equity Association, which gave him the right to call himself a professional actor, but more accurately, he was by now a professional benefits claimant, painter and decorator, odd-job man, dreamer and drunkard. But, he believed, that tag could be attached to quite a lot of the members of Equity!

'Don't tell me you've actually been doing your job for a change? What's it for? Major feature film? West End leading role? Or something really good, like a beer commercial?'

'Close, but don't get excited. It is for a commercial but nothing to do with alcohol, I'm afraid. It's for margarine and only to be shown in Holland.'

'Oh great! That'll further my career.'

'Well, across the water, anyway.'

'Very droll! Oh well, it'll pay a few bills, I suppose.'

'Or your slate at The Suffolk Arms!'

The Suffolk Arms was Greg's local pub. A place he frequented daily, whether he had money or not, using his skills learnt from set building to do odd repair jobs and decorating for the landlord in lieu of liquid payment.

'That big a fee, is it?'

'Greg, it's just an interview. Let's talk about fees if you get the job.'

'When I get the job, you mean. Have I ever let you down before?'

'Me? Never. I'm not going to go bust if you blow another job. It's you you have to think of. Try and be sober, that's all I ask.'

Greg had always convinced himself that he'd never blown an audition because of an excess of alcohol but in brief moments of reality he knew it possibly could have hampered his chances. But they were all a long time ago before he could really handle the booze.

'Alright, Denis. What time, where and when?' Greg decided to ignore the abstinence remark.

'Today, 2.30, St James' Church Hall, Brixton. You're to meet a Rob Vanderlast. They just want a video of your face. Wear straight clothes, preferably clean. That's all I have on it. Must go, the other line's ringing. Just be there. Oh and good luck'

Denis Young hung up his phone.

Greg dragged himself across his bedroom towards the window, turned the handle that opened the venetian blinds and let in what light was seeping through the dank Hackney morning. Greg could never understand why he had blinds on his windows, he'd far rather have curtains but the powers that be in Hackney Council, who owned the flat, had decided to put venetian blinds between the two sheets of double glazing. The inside sheet opened to allow cleaning etcetera, not that Greg ever bothered. He'd lived in the flat for five years. It was a legacy from an ex-girlfriend, Julie.

They had met at a dinner party thrown by his scenery-maker friend Andy who Greg had been helping out more on than off for the last few years. It was an 'in-between' job, whilst waiting for Hollywood to call. Greg had been invited to the party to provide the entertainment as Andy put it.

'You're always good at a dinner party' he'd said. 'You keep the conversation going.'

Julie had recently been dumped by her long-term boyfriend and was in need of cheering up. Greg, feeling rather like a whore, agreed to be placed next to her and engage her in conversation. She was a key worker, a teacher, rather dowdy, Greg thought at first, reminding him of all the teachers he'd hated at school, boring, into themselves and their particular subject, in Julie's case economics – something which Greg had absolutely no knowledge of or interest in. However, as the evening wore on and the wine flowed more freely, Julie stopped talking about how to save the country from economic disaster and lightened up considerably. She'd spent some time freelancing as a journalist while she was at University and reviewed television shows, including the disastrous lunchtime soap

'The Market' starring none other than Greg Driscoll. She hadn't realised that Greg had even been in the series until he just happened to mention he had once been a household name. Obviously not in Julie's household, however, at least not until his very public sacking. Once she'd made the connection, Julie's whole conversation turned to Greg and the outrageousness of his dismissal. She understood how he must feel, somehow relating it to her own recent dumping by her boyfriend.

Greg and Julie agreed to meet again the following day. They went to Hyde Park, walked around, fed the ducks and had ice creams. It was the start of what they both hoped was going to blossom into a beautiful romance. In a way it had. They'd seen more and more of each other, Julie staying at Greg's little bedsit – she'd been living in a rented room in a house since her ex had thrown her out of his flat and no overnight visitors were allowed. In a matter of weeks they'd agreed that they should move in together. Greg's bedsit was too small and, according to his lease only one person was allowed to live there. It was Julie who had suggested trying for a council flat. Being a key worker meant she had lots of points and they hadn't been on the housing list for long when they were offered this newly renovated one-bedroom apartment. It wasn't a bad place at all. It was on the top floor of a four storey Victorian tenement block by Clapton pond.

Not that you could see Clapton pond from the windows, all you could see from the windows were the tower blocks of the large estate they'd built in close proximity during the 1960's.

Julie had furnished the place by taking out a store card. The coir flooring and bright orange sofa weren't really to Greg's taste but it was a great improvement on the bare floorboards they'd sat on for the first few weeks they'd lived there. Greg helped to pay the monthly instalments on the card when he was working. Andy's scenery business had moved up in the world and he and Mandy had emigrated to the USA, where he was doing some good work in the movie industry. Greg's career had also taken a turn for the better. He'd had quite a few jobs when they first moved in, a couple of small parts on TV as well as some decent work in repertory theatres. It turned out to be the downfall of the relationship, though. Julie didn't like it when Greg was away and she didn't like it when he was at home not bringing any money in. He'd taken her to the wrap party at the end of the last TV he'd done. The lead role had been played by some, supposedly up-and-coming young star; crap actor but very good looking! Whilst Greg had been off getting drunk (it was a wrap party after all and the booze was free!) it seemed Julie had been getting off with the leading actor. Greg only found out about this when he was away in Chester playing Osric in Hamlet at the Gateway theatre. He'd received his 'Dear John' letter just before the opening night. Julie had been due to come up and stay for a couple of days but it seemed she'd had other plans. When Greg arrived back from Chester at the end of the run, he was greeted by a completely empty flat. No orange sofa; no coir matting on the floor; not even a bed. Julie had taken the lot and moved in with 'Mr soon-to-be-massive-superstar'. Still, it turned out that his remarkably good looks weren't enough to compensate for his lack of acting ability and large ego and within a year, Julie had moved on to bigger and better superstars. Greg thanked his lucky stars he was not only out of that relationship but somehow had managed to hang onto the flat!

It had taken some time to re-furnish the place from local junk shops but, at last the flat had taken on Greg's personality. No coir matting on the floor, just strips of non-matching used carpet; no orange sofa, just a pair of old armchairs rescued from a skip. He had actually spent money on a fridge and a cooker and a kettle. He'd also managed to convince the local TV Rental shop to hire him a TV and video recorder.

Greg went through to the lounge and opened the blinds in there before going through to the kitchen to put the kettle on. He was more than aware that getting to Brixton from Hackney by public transport could take the best part of a whole day! That would cut into arrangements to repaint the back bar at The Suffolk Arms (a job he'd already been paid for – in kind!) Still there was always another day for that, after all he was supposed to be an actor by profession. Greg hated this feeling. It was a mixture of lethargy and intense nervous anxiety. He loathed interviews, he really just wanted someone to offer him a job without having to go through interviews but unfortunately his previous credits did not put him in that sort of league. To be perfectly honest, he'd have been far happier to go to the pub, have a few drinks, eat and go back to bed. However, that cost money, consequently he had to try and find work and a couple of days on a commercial for Europe must be worth at least as much as a couple of days painting and decorating.

So, after the obligatory three cups of coffee and four or five Marlboros, Greg dressed in his 'going for a commercial' outfit (about the only time he wore a tie) and set off for Hackney Downs station. It was noon and if the transport connections all fitted together, he could be in Brixton in time to find a local hostelry and get a couple in – just to steady the nerves.

Two and a quarter hours later, nerves steadied, Greg was standing outside St. James' church hall trying to discover which of the rooms held the Dutch margarine men by studying a small, yellowing typewritten notice encased in a paint-peeling wooden case with grubby, cracked glass doors, situated in the porch of the hall. It stated that the over 60's aerobics class would no longer take place on Fridays but the Saturday morning class would still take place and anyone interested in joining in this exciting fitness extravaganza should contact Madame Chevalier (R.A.D.) through the vicarage. The dog training class in the Howell Room was already in progress judging by the growls and howls coming from inside, unless, of course, the over 60's were attempting to carry on without the guidance of Madame Chevalier (R.A.D.)

Whilst contemplating this spectacle with amusement, Greg continued his search for something vaguely relating to Dutch margarine. He realised that Denis had not given him the production company's name, only that he had to see a Mr Vandersomething, a name he hadn't written down and couldn't clearly remember. Greg looked round for a phone box to ring Denis for more information and was confronted by an extremely tall person wearing a bright pink running vest above the tightest pair of cycling shorts Greg had ever had the misfortune to encounter.

'Mr Driscoll?' said the Harlequinade giant. He was at least six foot five, had short black hair, was anorexically thin and had the sort of nose that made him look like he should bend at the waist and dunk it a glass of water!

'Yes,' was all he could think of to safely say.

'Rob Vanderlast. Follow me, please.'

Greg followed in the wake of Mr Vanderlast to a small, wooden-floored room at the top of an extremely long flight of steep stairs where he was greeted by another character from the land of giants who introduced himself as Han Koolhaven. Greg nodded as he waited for his breath to catch him up. Han Koolhaven bore a remarkable similarity to Mr Vanderlast, except for a different colour scheme. His vest was light green and had a faded picture of Jimi Hendrix adorning the front. Mr Koolhaven's hair was long and blond and worn in a fetching ponytail style.

'Are you OK?' asked Han Koolhaven.

'Fine,' gasped Greg. 'Lot of stairs.'

'Yes. Well, if you're ready, could you sit on that chair and tell us a bit about yourself.'

Han Koolhaven pointed to a chair in the middle of the room. Rob Vanderlast had positioned himself behind a video camera set about three feet from the chair. Greg sat and started to go through his CV. He felt remarkably relaxed. Han especially seemed to be a very friendly and congenial bloke, the sort Greg would have enjoyed a pint or two with. They asked him if he'd ever been to Holland and whether he knew any of the language or customs. Greg confessed his knowledge of The Netherlands was confined to cheese, coffee and Grolsch lager, not necessarily in that order. They explained the commercial would be filmed on the boats and barges of the river Amstel in old Amsterdam. The three of them chatted for another twenty minutes or so; it appeared they had no-one else to see for the rest of that day. Greg didn't feel like he was in an interview at all and as the meeting drew to a close he even asked the two Dutch skyscrapers if they fancied a quick pint.

'Better not,' said Han. 'Work to do, you know. Just need to check you are available next Sunday and Monday?'

'I certainly am.' Greg was about to ask if that meant he'd got the job but thought better of it.

'Well, good luck, Greg. Hopefully we'll see you again.' Rob held out his hand. 'Bye.'

Greg left the church hall and went straight to the pub he'd left just over half an hour previously. He spotted some bottles of Grolsch in the fridge behind the bar and ordered himself one. It was expensive but Greg had already convinced himself he had the job and a couple of days filming in Amsterdam would be worth a few hundred pounds in expenses alone. Besides it was research, wasn't it? Had to get into the Dutch way-of-life!

However, as he drained the second bottle the doubts began to filter through. Why hadn't he said he'd been to Amsterdam as a student? He hadn't but they weren't to know and he did know several people who had travelled there in their youth. He could have mentioned Van Gogh, maybe said he'd played him in a production. Anything! Why did he always do this? One should always try and show some sort of interest. He could hear Denis' voice in his head. Cheese, coffee and Grolsch may have appeared a little insulting to the Dutchmen. Maybe they were laughing at him, not with him.

Greg's experience of filming commercials had not been all that successful – at one beer commercial, they had proffered free beer at eight o'clock in the morning and he'd ended up so drunk they had to cut any close-up of him. Apparently it's illegal to show anyone drunk in a commercial for alcohol. How stupid is that? Anyway, what did they expect when a poor chap is forced to drink from 8am to 7pm with only a break for lunch? It wasn't his fault! The commercial never made it to the screen.

The train back from Liverpool Street was busy. It was rush hour and it was full of suited, overpaid, bank employees from the city. Greg stood all the way, his nose too close to a stranger's armpits for his liking. His mood was deteriorating and by the time he alighted from the train at Hackney Downs, Greg had convinced himself there was no way he'd got the job and had resigned himself to continue painting the back bar of The Suffolk Arms to fund his meagre lifestyle. He was not feeling particularly jocular and contemplated whether to drown his sorrows in the bar but sanity overruled and he decided to get home for some food first. He could always go to the pub later.

The flashing light on his answerphone made Greg heart pound. '*Please let it be Denis saying I've got the job.*' That was about the nearest he got to praying these days.

Beep...You have two new messages...beep...First new message...Hi Greg, that's an awful message, you sound so depressed! Well, you don't need to be depressed. Come out for a drink with me tonight? Give us a ring. OK? Beep...second new message...beep...Greg! Sorry. Forgot to say that was me that phoned just now. I mean, Jenny, that is. I'm sure you knew anyway. Oh God! I hate these machines. Ring me. Please. Bye. Beep...End of messages...Beeeep.

That was it. Two messages from one of the last people he felt like hearing from when he was feeling depressed. Jenny was a young aspiring actress Greg had encouraged mostly because she was terribly attractive, in the vain hope she may show interest in him rather than his supposed ability to help her in her career. At the time it didn't work and she showed little or no interest in him at all but recently she had taken to phoning him regularly and wanting to meet up and chat about *his* career. He managed to put her off most of the time but the incessant phone calls were really getting on his wick. Somehow the tables had turned; she seemed to think she could help him! There had been a few times they had gone for a drink and, Greg had to admit secretly, they had had a good time. Jenny could be a good confidante, she understood what it was like to be 'between jobs' and although her advice could be naive, Greg had occasionally listened to her and felt better for it - plus she was stunningly good-looking.

At ten to six Greg was serving up his sausage, egg and oven chips. He would phone Jenny and make some excuse for not being able to see her tonight. He was sure she still thought of him as a great actor and an inspiration, someone to look up to. How could he see her when he'd just blown another audition and thought himself to be useless? The phone rang. He hadn't had time to think of a plausible excuse. He'd have to think on his feet.

'Hello, Jenny. Sorry….'

'…No, I'm sorry, Greg. It's only your boring old agent. Fancy a trip to Amsterdam?'

'What?'

'You got the ad. Fly out Sunday at 6pm. Overnight stay. Shoot Monday, maybe overnight stay Monday too, depends on the rushes or something. It's only an £800 buy-out, I'm afraid but there's £200 expenses and your air-fare and accommodation's paid for. So get your passport ready. It is up-to-date, I assume?'

'Hold your horses. You're supposed to ask me if I want to accept the deal or not.'

'Don't piss me about. I've already accepted for you. I got you £200 more than they wanted to pay. You should say 'Thank you, Denis''

'Thank you, Denis. You're still supposed to ask…'

'Look. I'd like to get away from the office tonight, just tell me it's OK and you're happy.'

'It's OK and I'm happy! Happy? I'll buy you a drink when I'm paid.'

'That'll be the day. By the way, there seems to be some chance of this becoming a series of commercials if this one goes well, so you could be in for a lot more money if you behave, if you know what I mean?'

'I hope you're not implying anything?'

'Just don't drink too much, Greg. Bye. And well done'

Denis hung up his phone. Greg didn't put the receiver down; he waited for the dialling tone and dialled.

'Hello? Jenny? Got your message, how are you? Working?...Oh well, never mind something will turn up, as Mr Micawber says….Me?...Yes, I'm about to do a series for Dutch TV. Look how about I buy you a drink or two tonight? Cheer you up a bit….Great, see you at 7.30.'

Greg smiled to himself as he replaced the receiver. He felt good. Who knows, maybe Jenny would show a bit more interest in him personally. Especially now he was working again. He went for a bath, just in case.

*

He met Jenny at a trendy bar in St Martin's Lane, her choice, called Green's or Brown's or some colour. He was early and felt very conspicuous amongst all the Friday night bankers and posh kids sipping champagne, which appeared to be the drink to have at this place – and it seemed you had to make sure everyone knew you were having it by shouting *'Who's for more shampoo'* very loudly every few minutes. Greg hated these places, they reminded him of his mother's boyfriend and he wished he was in the Suffolk Arms in Hackney.

Jenny arrived looking very attractive, as usual. She was wearing a long flowery shirt over tight black needlecord jeans tucked into cowboy boots. Her dark auburn hair was loosely tied into a pony tail. Greg ordered her a sparkling wine (not champagne) and himself another overpriced bottle of some Eastern European beer.

Jenny bought the next round before suggesting they went for a meal to celebrate Greg's new job. Greg had to point out that after an hour and a half in this overpriced shampoo shop he didn't have the ready cash for a meal.

'My treat,' said Jenny.

Jenny was the product of very rich parents. She'd never really gone into detail, not that Greg could remember anyway. He thought they'd lived in Mayfair or somewhere so were probably millionaires. They had bought Jenny her own flat in South Kensington but he had never been there yet, although ever hopeful of an invitation. Jenny didn't behave like a rich kid. Yes, she dressed in expensive clothes and could afford to go to expensive bars and eat out at restaurants but she never flaunted it like those oiks in the bar. Jenny's father was passed away some years ago and she never saw her mother – something else she and Greg had in common. She'd always hated being considered posh and was more than happy to agree to Greg's suggestion of going for a pizza rather than a posh meal so they headed off for a pizza round the corner in Coptic Street.

They sat at a table for two in the back room of the Pizza house. A candle flickered in a raffia bound Chianti bottle on a red check tablecloth, looking like a refugee from some nineteen-sixties cafe. They ordered their food, Greg an American Hot pizza and a bottle of Peroni beer, Jenny a salad nicoise and water. Greg looked at her, she was talking but he wasn't listening, he was studying her. He'd never really looked closely at her. She laughed and her little nose crinkled, dimples danced on her cheeks. No, not dimples, these indentations were larger, longer. They were deep laughter lines, full of joy, of happiness. Greg eyed her with envy. Here was a beautiful young girl, desperate to be an actress, yet currently temping in some Godforsaken office, probably being chatted up by the seedy suits. Greg considered he would have to change his opinion of Jenny, look further into her and get to know her better, instead of just thinking of her as someone to sleep with. She really was a beautiful person.

'...don't you think, Greg?'

'Sorry? What? I was miles away.'

'Somewhere nice?'

'Somewhere very beautiful and romantic, actually.' Jenny laughed again, her nose wrinkling. Greg smiled.

Greg drank more bottles of Peroni, Jenny more bottles of water. He held her hand across the table as they chatted about acting and theatre and Greg becoming a big star in Holland and before long they were the only two left in the restaurant. The waiter was hanging about trying not to look too irritated at not being able to go home.

'I think they want us to go, Greg.' Jenny whispered.

'I could stay here forever.'

'I think Mr Driscoll may have had one bottle of Peroni too many!' Jenny called the waiter over, paid the bill and they left. They held hands as he walked her to the tube at Tottenham Court Road. She gave him a peck on the cheek at the entrance to the tube.

'Thanks, Greg, for a lovely evening,' she said.

'No, thank you for buying me a meal and all those drinks. I'll pay you back when I'm famous. Or, if you'd like to come home with me I'll pay you tonight, if you know what I mean!' He tried to kiss her but she pushed him away.

'OK,' she whispered.

'Oh God! I'm really sorry, Jenny. That was horrible of me. I'm such a shit! Why would you want to come home with me? I'm so sorry, Jen. So sorry.'

Jenny was laughing. 'Greg. I said yes!'

Greg was taken aback. She'd said yes.

'But not tonight, eh? Let's wait till you're back from Holland and make a whole night of it.'

'Waiting till I'm famous, eh?'

'No, waiting till you're sober.' She gave him a kiss full on the lips. They stayed locked together like teenagers for at least a minute before she broke away and went through the gate to the escalator. Greg watched her disappear down the moving staircase, her hair blowing in the breeze created by the arrival of an underground train. Greg wondered if the auburn colour was natural or dyed. He smiled to himself, before almost running on air to catch the last train from Liverpool Street back to Hackney Downs.

***

CHAPTER TWO

Stansted airport at four o'clock on a Sunday afternoon was not the ideal place to be, Greg decided. His experience of jet setting was very limited and he was surprised to find the bars closed. He naturally assumed they'd be open all day at an airport, irrespective of the archaic Sunday licensing laws. What made it worse was the fact he had foregone his usual Sunday lunchtime session at The Suffolk Arms, afraid he might lose track of time and miss his plane. All this meant he now had time to kill in the sterile atmosphere of a semi-closed airport.

He'd had a bit of a fight with Denis, insisting he flew from Stansted instead of Heathrow. It seemed stupid to spend half a day getting right across London when he could get from Hackney to Stansted via Liverpool Street in less than an hour. Denis had said he didn't want to upset the Dutch people, they hadn't signed any contract yet and they could always find someone else. Greg, however, full of Dutch courage from the pub, insisted that his agent should put more faith in his client's esteem. Denis had countered by saying he was fully aware of his client's esteem and it wasn't exactly keeping his agency in business but he agreed to see what he could do about changing the flight. As it turned out Rob Vanderlast was more than happy for Greg to use Stansted and, in fact, he would meet Greg there and fly out with him.

Greg had discovered that once he was through the check-in he could go to the departure lounge where Sunday licencing laws seemed not to apply. The only problem was he couldn't go through until Mr Vanderlast arrived with his ticket and he wasn't here yet.

He sat on one of the cold plastic seats in the designated smoking area, his newly bought suitcase at his feet. He wondered what it would be like if and when he was famous. Did Stansted have a special VIP area? He supposed they must have. How famous did you have to be to get in there? He liked the idea of being recognised, overhearing people say 'Look! There's Greg Driscoll. What a fine actor!' Trouble is, these days, people are more likely to say how rubbish and overpaid they think actors are. If only they knew. He'd had this conversation with Jenny when they went for their pizza two nights ago. All she wanted was to be famous, to be recognised wherever she went. That would be the height of success for her, she'd said.

'What about the paparazzi? You'd never be able to go out without worrying who was snapping you falling over drunk. Believe me, I know.' Greg had pointed out.

'That's not really likely to happen, Greg, is it?' Jenny had replied, as she'd sipped her mineral water.

'But you couldn't even go for a meal without the public harassing you between forkfuls!'

'Greg, I'd just go to the posh restaurants where they don't allow the riff-raff in!' she'd laughed.

'I'd just like to be appreciated for my work.'

'Quite right! You should be, Greg. You are a very good actor.' She'd paused. 'Maybe you should think about how much you drink, though. That really could hold you back, you know.'

'I can think of several people it didn't. Being a Hell raiser used to be an asset, I don't know what's happening to my profession. Another water?'

Greg's star potential felt very much on the wane at the moment. It was nearing half-past four and there was no sign of Mr Vanderlast. He picked up his suitcase and went for another walk around the concourse in the hope he might see the tall Dutchman. There were a couple of shops open, selling newspapers and cigarettes but the bars were all closed up, peopled only by cleaners pushing oversized vacuum cleaners around, oblivious to the needs of travellers.

The airport was quite busy. Greg wondered where everybody was going. Families with young children. It wasn't the holiday period. There were teenagers, maybe students, reading trashy novels, older men being harangued by their wives. Everyone seemed stressed. Airline staff wandering around with clipboards, trying to keep everyone calm. Maybe they should open the bars, then! Apparently there had been a delay at some foreign airport causing a backlog for the planes waiting to take off. Greg looked around in vain for Rob Vanderlast before wandering back to the smoking area and lighting yet another Marlboro. He was running out but knew he could buy some duty-free once he was through the check-in.

'Greg! Hi!' Rob Vanderlast put his hand on Greg's shoulder. 'I am so sorry I am late. The taxi was delayed on the M11. They do so many roadworks here in the U.K. don't they?'

Greg thought about saying he should have come by train, like he'd had to but instead replied, 'Yes, bloody nuisance, isn't it? Still, I bet you could do with a drink after all that?'

'On the plane, maybe. There's not really time before we board.'

'OK. That's fine with me,' Greg lied. They went to the Air UK check-in and duly checked in.

Champagne was not a drink Greg indulged in very often, it reminded him of those yuppies. However managing half a bottle on the short flight to Amsterdam was an enjoyable and not unpleasant experience to cope with, as he told his travelling companion more than once, eager to show his gratitude and willingness to accept any further perquisites his director's expense account cared to put his way.

They chatted vaguely about the shoot they would be doing the next day and Rob gave Greg a script and a shooting schedule. There was hardly any dialogue in the script and what there was would be dubbed over in Dutch at a later date. From what Greg could see there weren't any problems, it was a straight-forward scenario, if, perhaps, a little bizarre.

It appeared that Greg's character was on the run from two rather unsavoury villains. The scene opens in a brown café in Gravenstraat called De Drie Fleschjes which apparently means 'The Three Bottles', with Greg sinking a small beer – all very good so far. He spots two people standing at the bar, a look of horror appears on his face and he leaves the beer (what!) and nonchalantly makes his way to the lavatory, leaps through the window and out into the street. The villains notice his absence and follow. The pursuit takes us to the canal and across the barges moored on the bank. As the villains close in on Greg, they both slip off the side of the barge and are picked up by a Police launch that just happens to be passing by. Greg points out that, somehow, he has managed to smear the deck of the barge with Poepjes Melkboter Margarine. This was followed by the slogan 'Poepjes Melkboter Margarine verspreidt zich gemakkelijk op bijna alles' which apparently means Poepjes Melkboter Margarine spreads easily on almost anything! Greg asked how to pronounce these words of wisdom but the only bit he could make out when Rob told him was the first word which sounded like Poopies! Rob explained that Poepjes was quite a common surname in The Netherlands and that this was the name of the person who started the company. Greg was slightly worried if this was the client's name. He wasn't sure he could keep a straight face if he was introduced to a Mr Poopies!

'It's OK, Greg. We do understand that in English Poepjes sounds amusing but don't worry,' Rob assured Greg, 'the client is called Peiter Wiersma.'

Greg pretended to study the script. It was certainly not the best advert he'd ever imagined but he wasn't about to say goodbye to a contract that paid the best part of a grand.

The plane landed at Schiphol Airport at 7pm local time and, after going through customs, made their way to the pick-up area where Han Koolhaven was waiting in a rather old and battered looking Mercedes. After brief re-introductions Han and Rob suggested Greg checked into his hotel room and then meet them in the bar at about 9.30 to go for a meal.

Han's driving left a lot to be desired. The tiny streets of Holland's ancient capital city were not built for high-performance motor cars. Han, however, seemed to be blissfully unaware of this fact, weaving in and out of back streets, hand on horn, at a speed more appropriate for a Monaco Grand Prix than just a traverse from Airport to hotel.

'You English are far too timid and polite on the roads. That is why you have more jam-ups than over here.'

Greg had his doubts about the truth of these words of wisdom and clung tightly to the litre bottle of duty-free whisky and the two hundred Marlboro he'd purchased on the plane, wondering whether he could light up one of his duty-free cigarettes in the car. He had just about summoned up the courage to ask when Han screeched to a halt outside the hotel. Having deposited their passenger on the pavement, Rob and Han sped off reminding Greg to be in the bar at 9.30. The hotel was called The Convent Hotel. It was one of the many tall buildings lining the canals of Amsterdam and used to house two monasteries in the 13th & 14th centuries as well as a printing house. Greg wasn't at all sure a hotel called The Convent would even have a bar! However on entering the rather grand reception area, Greg soon realised he was in a rather posh 5 star hotel. There were bookcases lining the walls filled with very grand looking volumes with leather bindings, large wingback chairs, standard lamps and a deep-pile scarlet patterned carpet. It looked like the interior of a posh gentleman's club, Greg imagined, never having been in a posh gentleman's club. Rob and Han had left without checking him in so he approached the reception desk very tentatively, quite expecting to be ejected and told his hotel was next door or something but, on giving his name, the staff could not have been nicer. A young man in livery even offered to carry his luggage to his room. The key was a piece of plastic about the size of a credit card with holes punched in it. The porter put the key in a slot on the door, removed it and pushed open the door. Putting the suitcase on a sort of trestle table by the wall, he then handed Greg the piece of plastic and stood there.

'Thanks,' said Greg. 'I can manage from here.'

With a slight nod of his head, the young man turned and walked off.

Greg checked the room – mini bar – (good but probably not included in expenses so avoid!), kettle, tea and coffee, a few smelly bits in the bathroom, shower and bath but no free bathrobe to nick. Never mind! He took the glass from the bathroom and poured himself a large scotch from his duty-free whilst his bath filled.

At 9.15 he was in the Duke of Windsor bar ordering a glass of Kroon Pilsner as recommended by the barman. It was described in the very helpful tasting notes as having 'a hint of tobacco, pepper, vanilla and butter aroma; bitter taste with grass, citrus and fruit aromas; bitter finish with grass and tobacco; very good hop aroma and quite full-bodied for a Pils.' Greg was tempted to ask if it tasted of beer but the barman seemed very proud of his description so he thought better of it and went off to find one of the plush leather sofas to sit on.

Ten minutes later Han and Rob arrived and took him down the road to Humphrey's.

'This is a good restaurant, Greg,' said Han. 'I think you'll like it. Try the hare stew, it is very good.'

Restaurant Humphrey's was situated just off Dam Square in the centre of the city and looked rather small and tacky from the outside. It had a white painted frontage with a black and white painted sign swinging from a bracket situated above a blue canopy. However, going through the door opened a completely different world. The first room consisted of a large brick-walled bar where aperitifs were taken, before entering the long dark wood-lined room with chandeliers hanging from the ceiling where they were to eat. More bookshelves, filled with more leather-bound books, covered one wall and row upon row of jars containing a wide variety of nuts and pulses on glass shelves butted onto the side of them covering another wall. The restaurant staff all seemed to know Han and Rob who introduced Greg to them. Everyone shook hands and laughed a lot. Greg was already enjoying his time in the Dutch capital and was hoping that there would be more episodes of the commercial in the very near future.

Greg acquiesced over the hare stew and actually enjoyed the meat dish served with mashed potato, roasted Brussels sprouts with hazelnuts, thyme and a game sauce along with a very nice red wine which he followed with apple crumble with brown sugar and cinnamon. He got on really well with Han and Rob. They chatted about the commercial a bit but more about the state of the industry and why they were doing commercials instead of the 'real art' they'd all set out to do years before. Greg also found himself talking quite a lot about Jenny Gulliver for a reason he could not fathom. She seemed to be on his mind since they'd gone for their drink last week. They finished off the evening with large cognacs in the hotel bar. Greg still felt the need for an unnecessary whisky nightcap in his room before falling into his large comfortable bed and descending into a deep sleep.

***

CHAPTER THREE

The telephone rang at six-thirty the following morning.

'Hello, Greg? Rob here. Are you ready?'

Greg shook his head. It hurt. 'Give us five minutes, Rob. Almost ready.'

Greg rushed to the bathroom, found his bottle of 'Cleereye' eye drops and squirted enough into each eye. This was a trick he'd learned years ago, watching an 'old pro' making up for an early morning shoot on a TV he'd had a small part in.

'Essential part of an actor's make-up, dear boy. Soon gets rid of the hangover red-eye.'

He'd never travelled without a bottle since.

It was ten minutes before he raced to the reception where Rob was waiting.

'You haven't had breakfast?'

'No. I'm not bothered, though.'

'It's OK. I want you to meet the clients.'

Rob and Greg went through to the restaurant where Han was sitting with a rather overweight pin-stripe suited man with a large walrus moustache and a spiky-haired young lady. Han stood and introduced Peiter Wiersma and Marjan Smits. Greg politely shook hands with Mr Wiersma and turned smiling to Ms Smits. As she was extremely attractive,

Greg decided a kiss on the cheek would be quite correct. As he leaned towards her she turned her face towards him and they kissed lip to lip. Greg blushed and Marjan winked as she sat down. This job was getting better all the time! Greg wasn't sure whether Peiter Wiersma spoke English but he didn't show much interest in Greg as Rob joined in the conversation with Han. It turned out he was the German owner of a large supermarket chain and grocery manufacturer in Europe. He also seemed to have set up a production company specifically for this advert. His suit was expensive, as was the gold jewellery on his fingers. He was in his late fifties, Greg surmised and not very tall but he was very wide with a fat gut. If his suit had been white he would have been a dead ringer for Sydney Greenstreet in The Maltese Falcon. He didn't carry a fly swat but did look overhot. He kept wiping his face with his silk handkerchief every five minutes. His large walrus moustache wriggled on his top lip as he spoke. The top of his head was covered with what could have been a toupee, it was evidently a very expensive one, and it matched the rest of his hair but didn't seem quite natural to Greg. He wasn't speaking English so Greg turned to Marjan asking if she would like more coffee.

'I'm fine, thank you.' Marjan's English was perfect. She was from the Netherlands and was wearing clothes that emphasised her lithe young body. She worked as a P.A. for the production company. Her hair was very blonde almost white and obviously dyed as her eyebrows were dark. There was a thin covering of downy hair on her top lip which was barely noticeable unless you looked closely. Greg found himself looking rather too closely at Marjan which she obviously noticed.

'I am 28 years old, I don't have a boyfriend, I don't have time. I rent a very nice flat on the third floor of a house overlooking one of the canals. I earn a good living and enjoy my life. Anything else you need to know?'

'More coffee?'

'I already said no, thank you. Too much coffee is very bad for you.'

'Depends how much you've drunk the night before, I find.' Greg muttered.

'Drinking before an early shoot is not the best way of preparing, really, is it?' Marjan stood up and rallied the rest of the party in Dutch before turning back to Greg. 'Ready?'

Greg swallowed the last of his coffee and stood up.

Greg was pleased to see a taxi waiting outside. He hoped the taxi driver may not drive like Michael Schumacher but was disappointed. It seemed that everyone in Amsterdam thought the streets were built for them alone and anyone else was just in the way. A matter of minutes later they were standing beside a remote part of the canal where several barges were moored. Han started to go through the script with Greg while a number of burly men clambered over the barges with Rob carrying lights and other bits of metal equipment.

Han wanted Greg to try saying the Dutch tag line so they could synch the words to his lips later. Then into make-up – the back of a truck parked nearby. No-one seemed to want to speak English, so Greg just sat there being smeared with liquid and powder to try and cover the blemishes on his skin. Costume was in the back of the same truck and he slipped into a pair of trousers and a shirt, neither of which looked like offering much protection from the rather cool breeze that was blowing down the canal.

The morning went slowly. Greg tried to convince himself that every time they had to re-shoot a scene it really was because there was a 'hair in the gate' and not because he had not done what was required. He only had a small glass of wine at lunch to show he was taking his job seriously, Denis' 'don't drink too much' echoing round his head. They were shooting out of sequence so the first part of the commercial in the brown café was shot after lunch. A good idea as that meant they could stay in the café after shooting and have a good old drink. The inside scenes went a lot smoother than the morning's session and they were finished by 6 o'clock but instead of staying at the café Han and Rob took Greg by taxi back to the hotel, his clothes and the stuff he'd left in the make-up truck had been delivered and were waiting in reception.

'You go up and change, Greg and we'll see you in the bar in ten minutes or so just to talk about the day. OK?'

Greg took his clothes back to his room. He'd have liked a shower or even a bath but thought he'd better get back to the bar ASAP. Besides while Han and Rob were there they would buy the drinks and he could keep his expenses!

Over a small beer in the bar Han and Rob told Greg how pleased they were with him and blamed the tech crew for the day being so long and tedious for him.

'No worries, guys,' assured Greg. 'It's barely 7 o'clock. Plenty of time for a few in the bar before dinner.'

'Er...yes.' Rob paused and looked at Han before carrying on. 'Look, Greg. This is completely up to you. If you want to, you can stay another night and get a flight back tomorrow but there's a flight tonight at 10 o'clock and...well...you could do us a great favour. We've still got some background shots to do and some wild-tracking for the sound. The problem is we'd like to get the films we've shot today back to London as soon as possible. I know it's an imposition and, like I say, it's completely up to you but if you could take them with you tonight and drop them into a studio in Dean Street tomorrow morning, first thing, everything will be ready for us by the time we're back in the evening.'

'Well,' said Greg, who was looking forward to another night in the five star hotel. 'It's a bit of a responsibility. What if something happened to the films?'

'Nothing will,' butted in Rob rather hastily. 'Just keep them in your hand luggage. Don't put them in the hold because of the temperature change. There's two hundred pounds extra travelling expenses in Sterling, cash, for you if you take them.'

Two hundred pounds! That seemed a lot of money to Greg. More than they'd spend putting him up in the hotel (even including his bar bill!)

'Tax-free?' he said

'It's cash, Greg. Whether you declare in or not is up to you.' Rob winked.

'Well, OK. If it'll help you out.' Greg decided to push his luck. 'My agent mentioned something about this possibly becoming a series of commercials. What form would the other adverts take, I mean, would they be based round my character or would they all have a different cast?'

'Glad you mentioned that, Greg.' Han handed him another small beer. 'This is why it's so important to get the rushes back to the UK as soon as we can. Peiter and Marjan have approached a few companies for ideas and so far they like ours best but this is a kind of test shoot. If they like the finished product they'll give us the whole contract. And, yes, they would all be based around your character with you, obviously, playing that character. We're very pleased and, between you and me, I don't think we'll have any worries. Marjan particularly mentioned that you were a very good actor. Trouble is, though, like all business people, they're very impatient and if they don't like it, for some reason, they'll have to start again from scratch which is expensive and time-consuming. So if we can get it finished really quickly and it's all processed by the time we get back to the UK tomorrow, we can get on with the editing and stuff. This could make us all quite rich, you know. The plan is for the product to go world-wide in the next couple of years.'

'Well, I'd better get your film back quickly, then. The sooner we convince Peiter and Marjan that we're a winning team, the sooner we'll all be laughing.'

*

Greg packed his bag, grabbed a couple of miniatures from the mini bar and went downstairs where Rob handed him his plane ticket and two hundred pounds in nice new twenty pound notes.

'Han's in the car with the film cans. They're already in a holdall and a customs slip made out. Don't let the films out of your sight and, whatever you do, don't open them or allow them to be opened. There shouldn't be any trouble.

Good luck and hopefully we'll see each other again, soon. I'll be in touch with your agent. Bye.'

After another hair-raising drive through the back-streets of Amsterdam, Greg was sitting at the bar at the airport, downing another small beer waiting to board his flight to Stansted. He had already decided to go and see Denis Young in the morning after delivering the films to the address in Dean Street that Han had given him in the car. His agent's office was only round the corner in Oxford Street so he thought he might surprise him with an early morning visit for coffee (with a slug of office brandy, maybe). After all, he could be about to become one of Denis Young's most valuable assets! He'd have to convince Greg he could handle it or he may have to look for a bigger agent. There'd be personal appearances, supermarket openings, chat shows. Who knows what? Look at Captain Birdseye!

'Greg Driscoll?' The Basso-Profundo voice quickly brought Greg back to reality. 'Brian Carter. Chester Gateway theatre, nineteen hundred and way back when. Remember?'

Greg did remember. They had both been in a production of Hamlet, Brian playing the First Gravedigger and Greg giving an extremely camp Osric. It had been a toss-up as to who had received the better notices. All the local papers mentioned them both, much to the annoyance of the old reppy actor giving his Great Dane. '*For this relief, much thanks!'* headlined the Liverpool Evening Post. *'Brain Carter is the most disgusting specimen to crawl from any grave and the way he spoke the Bard's lines probably had the great man turning in his! Greg Driscoll's Osric makes Larry Grayson look positively butch. However at least these two gave me some amusement in one of the dullest evenings I have ever spent in the theatre'*

'Well met, old friend! What bringst thou to Old Amsterdam?'

'Oh, business, Greg. You?'

'Just a bit of filming, you know.'

'Still doing it, then? The acting lark?'

'Oh yes. Doing quite well, these days. What about you?'

'No, not me. Couldn't cope with living below the breadline all the time. Got myself a proper job now.'

'Very sensible.' Greg always felt a certain pride when he heard of people leaving the profession. At least he was still doing what he was born to do! Although there wasn't a great deal else he could do. Even his painting and decorating exploits were not good enough to earn him a proper living.

'I joined the Old Bill, mate'

'You're joking!'

'Afraid not.'

'Bloody hell! Are you on duty now?'

'Sort of. Why? Not on the run, are you?'

'Don't be stupid! I was going to buy you a drink.'

'I think I can probably allow that, sir. Are you on the Stansted flight?'

'Yes.'

'In that case why don't we wait till we're on the plane, it's boarding now.'

Greg wanted to point out that, although still overpriced, drinks were cheaper in the bar than the aeroplane but, instead, thought of the extra expenses in his pocket and decided to be generous for once.

'You're on the same flight, then? Excellent.'

With a little negotiation and a flash of his police ID card, Brian managed to get them adjacent seats by the centre exit doors.

'Extra leg room, you see.' Brian needed the extra leg room. He was tall, well over six feet and Greg thought he could have done with extra body room in the seat; his wide girth was trying to invade Greg's personal space!

Joining the Police had done nothing to stem Brian's thirst for alcohol. They had enjoyed many a drunken night together in Chester. Brian explained he'd joined the force not long after their Chester exploits.

'I did a training film for the Met and became totally obsessed. I signed up for the course almost there and then.

Went through the course, did my time 'on the beat' and eventually trained as a detective.'

'I thought you had to be an uneducated gorilla to work for the Metropolitan Police. You're reasonably intelligent and aesthetic. Why on earth did you do it?'

'Don't believe everything you see on the telly, Greg. We're not all yobbos. Most of our time is spent chasing paperwork rather than criminals and, as well as having top physical education teams, we also top the pub quiz league.'

'Only because they let you win.'

'Not at all, Greg. Most people seem to think like you about police officers. We're only appreciated when you're in trouble.'

'OK, that's me told. I'll salute my local bobby next time I see him in the street, if I ever do. So, what are you working on in Amsterdam? Murder? Political intrigue? Or just increasing your trivial knowledge of Europe for the next pub quiz?'

'Well. I can't really go into detail, of course. I'll just say narcotics. What about you? I suppose you're starring in some major feature film?'

'Close. In my bag here I may just have the key to my fortune!'

'What?'

'It's top secret!'

'What do you mean?'

'It's a product you're going to see all over the world and I am the man who is going to sell it to you!'

'Oh, you're a Sales Rep. Thought you said you were still acting.'

'I am, you fool. This here is a new series of commercials, going worldwide and starring yours truly.'

'And that's going to make your fortunc?'

'You just wait and see. Call the stewardess and get the drinks in.'

*

It was raining as they disembarked at Stansted. Brian asked if Greg was declaring anything.

'Only my destiny. These are my Dutch masterpieces.' Greg pointed to his holdall

'Come with me, then.' Brian flashed his card again and he and Greg walked straight through the customs.

'Wait a minute,' said Greg. 'I'm supposed to show this customs slip.' He took out the form Rob had given him.

Brian gave it a cursory glance and said, 'I wouldn't bother, if I were you. Red tape, it'll only hold you up.'

Brian had explained to Greg that he was now married to an ex-WPC and had two young sons. This meant that he couldn't stay for a quick drink at Stansted as he had to get home. Besides, it looked like they were about to close anyway but it would be good to meet up soon. So they exchanged phone numbers saying 'get in touch' but Greg knew that the odds on that happening were very long. It was something about the theatrical profession. For the few months you work with someone you're the best of pals then as you part say we must keep this up at home. It rarely happens; you don't see each other for years but seem to pick up just where you left off without the need to see them again for years. It had been good to have a travelling companion but Greg wasn't sure he wanted to hang around with a policeman much. He caught the train to Liverpool Street and then managed to get a train to Hackney Downs without a great delay. He'd decided to see if the lights were still on at The Suffolk Arms. As it was off the main streets, there were often afters served there but it was a Monday, he reminded himself. So he was very relieved when he turned the corner and spotted a light from underneath the front door. A tentative knock saw him soon sitting at the bar with the landlord regaling him with anecdotes of his Dutch exploits and tales of fame to come.

He staggered into his flat at three the following morning. As he manoeuvred round the usual debris that cluttered his bedroom floor his foot caught on a pile of books he'd always meant to read and tipped him headlong onto the floor, catching the end of the bed in the process. Greg still had the films in their holdall slung around his neck and he landed heavily on top of them, the film cans taking the full weight of his fall.

'Shit! The films!'

Greg carefully opened the holdall and looked inside. It appeared that film cans were made sturdily enough to withstand drunken bodies falling on top of them. He took each can out and examined it. Barely a dent in either of them. As he was returning one of the cans to the holdall he noticed a small trickle of white powder seeping under the tape sealing the can. He picked the can up and shook it. Either the film inside was very soft and covered in talcum powder or it wasn't a film. He shook the other can. The same. A soft thud against the inside of the can. Greg himself now started to shake. He was suddenly very sober. Instinctively he reached for the card that Brian Carter had given him at the airport and dialled the number.

'Greg Driscoll? Do you know what time it is? I'm a married man with a job to keep up, you know, not a layabout actor with no responsibilities! What the hell do you want?'

'Can you come to my flat in Hackney, sort of now?' Greg was still shaking.

'Is this some kind of a joke, Greg? Why the hell would I want to come to some Godforsaken part of London at..' he looked at the alarm clock by his bed..'three fifteen in the morning!!!'

'Well. I can't really go into detail. I'll just say narcotics.'

***

CHAPTER FOUR

Brian Carter arrived at Greg's flat just after 4am. Greg showed him the holdall which Greg had thought contained his masterful piece of acting.

'It's high-grade cocaine alright,' said Brian having rubbed a small amount of the powder onto his gums. 'Tell me again exactly what happened and who's running this so-called film company.'

Greg went through the details of his filming in Amsterdam and then his late-night exploits in the Suffolk Arms that had led to him falling onto the film cans and exposing the cocaine.

'So, do you think there may be a chance of doing another one of these commercials, Greg?'

'You must be joking! There obviously is no commercial. It's just a cover for a drugs racket.'

'Possibly. But presumably they did shoot the commercial and still have that in their possession, so they still could put that out on TV and you wouldn't have any suspicion. They don't know you've already discovered the drugs. So, if they think they've been successful this time, they could keep recording commercials using you and have you run endless supplies of coke into this country.'

'But they haven't been successful!' Greg protested. 'I've reported them to you, the police'

'Have you told anyone other than me?'

'No. I thought I'd let you sort it all out. I don't want anything more to do with this. I don't want them to find out and come looking for me.'

'Good. As I see it, the best way to play this is for you to let them think they have succeeded.'

'What do you mean?' Greg was starting to fell distinctly uncomfortable.

'Do you have any coffee, Greg?'

Greg led Brian through to the kitchen and switched on the kettle. He put spoonfuls of coffee into two mugs. Brian sat at the kitchen table.

'No milk, I'm afraid,' he said, looking in the fridge.

'That's OK. I take it black anyway.'

Greg brought the coffee to the table. He was suddenly feeling exhausted as he slumped into the chair. He put his head on the table. Brian looked at him, reached out and put his hand on his shoulder.

'You're supposed to deliver the film cans later this morning, right?'

'To a photographic studio in Dean Street, yes, but you're not expecting me to do that now, are you? There's no way I'm walking through central London with film cans full of cocaine under my arm, thank you very much!'

'You are, I'm afraid, Greg.'

'No, Brian. Why can't you just go in and arrest the people in Dean Street. They're obviously involved. Just go in and pick them up.'

Brian shook his head.

'They'd be no point. It's the people at the top we want. Higher even than your Dutch friends. I'm sorry, mate, but you've got to help us. We've known there's been a ring working out of Holland for some time. That's why I was there yesterday. This could be the lead we've been waiting for.'

'What about Peiter and Marjan, the so-called clients for the ad? They looked like villains to me. Go and pick them up.'

Brian took a sip of his coffee.

'Greg, look. You don't understand how these things work. I also don't think you quite realise your position in all this. If you don't deliver the goods, they will come after you without a doubt. Even if we arrested everyone you've mentioned, there will still be others and they'll know who shopped the rest of them. It's actually safer for you if you just go along with what they want and play innocent. Come on. You're an actor, just look on it as another part you're playing.'

Greg sat silently. He held his mug in his hand and swilled the dark brown liquid round and round. He felt sick. He was aware that he was shivering as the cold reality of his situation hit him. Brian watched him, weighing up whether Greg would be capable of doing what he needed him to do.

'Well, Greg?' he said breaking the silence. 'The decision has to be yours. We need your help but we can't provide any protection for you if you don't co-operate.'

'I'm frightened, Brian. I don't really have the bottle for this. It's not like another acting part. If you get shot on stage you get up and go home at the end of the evening. I don't want my career to end at the bottom of a canal in Amsterdam.'

'If you help us you'll get all the back-up you require. Look, just make the drop this morning. Who knows? Maybe that's all you'll have to do. They may not risk another run through the 'commercial' route, and then you're safe. However, if they want you to do another ad, we'll want you to go ahead as if everything was normal.'

'This is anything but normal to me, Brian.' Greg stood up and tried to stretch the tension from his arms to no avail. 'What exactly do you mean by back-up?'

'You won't spot them yourself but there'll be plain-clothes coppers with you every second of the day.'

'And at night?'

'Someone will be posted outside your door.'

Greg was silent for a moment. 'Any chance of a nice young WPC inside my door?'

Brian smiled at his erstwhile colleague.

'That's more like the Greg Driscoll I know!'

*

There was a light rain falling as Greg's rather shaky legs took him up to the photo lab in the attic of the tall Victorian building half way down Dean Street. Greg had been violently sick after Brian had left his flat earlier that morning. He hadn't bothered trying to get any sleep. Brian Carter had successfully convinced him of his dire position; he basically had no option other than to carry on as an unwilling courier for the Dutch connection. He'd been sworn to secrecy about his part in the cocaine trail. He was not to report to the police directly, only to Brian. There was a paging number for Greg to ring and leave the message *'meet Larry for a drink'* –a reference to Sir Laurence Olivier. This code, Brian assured him, would keep Greg's involvement secret. He was then to go to The Princess Louise public house in High Holborn. This was a busy West End pub but Greg's suggestion of meeting somewhere quieter was put down by Brian explaining that two people talking together in a crowd was far less conspicuous than two conspirators plotting in a quiet corner of some country inn.

On his journey from his flat that morning Greg had kept a look-out for his minders. If they'd been there, Brian had been quite right that he wouldn't notice them. Greg had kept his eyes peeled but no-one appeared to be tailing him. He had the film cans, now securely re-taped by Brian, safe inside the holdall. At the top of the fifth flight of stairs there was a door with a sign saying *'The Dean's Photographic Laboratories.'* Greg entered to be greeted by a shapely blonde secretary who took the holdall from him, smiled and thanked him.

'I'm supposed to hand them to a Mr Simmons,' Greg muttered.

'That's OK. I'll make sure he gets them.' The secretary smiled. It was a practiced smile. No warmth. 'He's in the dark room now, so I can't disturb him. They are expected and I'm to thank you for your help. However, if you'd like to wait...?'

'No,' Greg replied a bit too hastily. 'It's OK. I'm a bit busy this morning. It's non-stop when you're in demand.'

The girl looked at him, gave him the practiced smile again and carried on reading the magazine in front of her.

Outside in Soho the rain was still drizzling. Greg found a phone box that hadn't been vandalised and left his coded message on Brian Carter's pager.

The pub didn't open until eleven o'clock which meant Greg had at least an hour and a half to fill in before he could meet Brian. He considered calling in on Denis for some office brandy but he would be bound to ask about the commercial shooting and Greg wasn't sure what he could tell him. Brian had made it clear that he should talk to no-one about it but him and Greg was sure he wouldn't be able to hide his anxiety from his agent.

Instead he chose to wander through Soho Gardens. It never ceased to amaze him that in the middle of one of the most built-up cities in the world that there were these little green paradises hidden away behind the high-rise offices and houses. This square had been there since the seventeenth century and, as Greg sheltered in the wooden gazebo from the increasingly heavy rain, he tried to imagine the fine ladies promenading around the gardens. However all his eyes saw today were a group of tramps resting on the benches getting wet and several suited people racing past under the sanctuary of their umbrellas.

He was outside the Princess Louise as the staff unlocked the doors and he hurried through into the warmth and dry of the bar. By the time Brian arrived, Greg was beginning to dry out with the help of a couple of large brandies. He'd been promised an expense account from Brian to cover any essential extras he had to pay for. Brandy seemed an essential to Greg. He'd never had an expense account before and, under the influence of M. Remy Martin, was beginning to relish his part of undercover detective. Besides, the immediate danger, i.e. the delivery of the merchandise, had passed without incident. His head felt heavy, the lack of sleep the night before was beginning to tell and the brandy wasn't doing its job of waking him up.

'You look like shit!' Brian brought a couple of lagers over to where Greg had situated himself. 'How did it go?'

'No problems. Delivered package to secretary, got thanked and left. Mission accomplished, sir.' Greg saluted.

'Excellent. Now all we have to do is wait for them to be in touch and hopefully offer you another commercial.'

'Or not, as the case may be. I think I've had enough excitement for the time being. I'd rather get back to a low paid but comparatively safe job in the Great British Repertory Theatre, thank you.'

There had been no developments from Brian's side, so, after finishing their drinks, they went their separate ways, Brian saying he'd expect a call from Greg soon. Greg hoped he meant a social call but feared he might be wrong.

Greg hovered briefly outside his agent's office before deciding it would be better not to talk to Denis just yet. He still wasn't sure how much Brian would allow him to say. For similar reasons he avoided The Suffolk Arms too and went straight back to his flat. He had an important secret assignment to consider. He needed to do a lot of thinking. What if he was offered more commercials from Rob and

Han? What would he say to Denis then? He'd have to do the commercials; obviously, Brian had made that quite clear. He was over the proverbial barrel, play innocent or die! Maybe he could get another job and not be available for the commercials. That would be a way out. He made up his mind to write to every theatre company in the country, found his slightly out-of-date copy of Contacts and opened the page at Theatre Companies. Five minutes later his head dropped onto the kitchen table and he fell fast asleep.

The ringing of the phone roused Greg. It took a few seconds for his head to clear by which time the answerphone had picked up. His heart started beating heavily as he heard his agent's voice.

'Beep...Greg...Denis here. You old bugger! I've just had Mr Vanderlast on the phone raving about you. Apparently they've got the whole series of commercials and he wants you to be the main man....We're talking big money here....Ring me as soon as you get this so I can finalise the details...See you, Rockefeller...beep'

Greg sat back in his kitchen chair. For the first time in his life he'd been offered what looked like a great job. But he knew it wasn't! He knew he was about to get himself into the biggest pile of shit he'd ever known. He decided to come clean with Denis and get him to say he wasn't available. He went towards the phone in the hall. As he reached for the receiver the phone rang. Greg jumped, let it ring, let the answerphone take it.

'Beep...Greg? Han. Super news. Peiter and Marjan loved you...Oh, thanks for delivering the films, they've been done and they look great. You look like a million dollars. There's going to be a whole series...shooting all over the world and we're the team. Rob, me and you. I'm so excited...Rob's rung your agent but I just wanted to ring you and talk to you about it but you're not there....Ring me soon. I'm at the London office....Bye for now...beep'

Greg sat down and poured himself a very large duty-free whisky. What was he to do? He had to tell Denis. He had to get out of it. He leaped up and grabbed the phone as soon as it rang.

'Hi, Denis?..'

'No Greg, just Jenny, I'm afraid. How did it go? Were you a massive success? I'm sure you were. Thanks for the other night, it was a really good night. Are you around for a drink this week?'

'Er…not sure about that, Jenny.'

'Have you gone off me? If it's something I said, tell me.' Greg could imagine her pouting her lips, her eyes laughing. He wanted to see her but it would have to wait.

'No, of course not, I'm just busy. It seems they want me to do more of those commercials.'

'Fantastic. I knew you'd be brilliant. Let's have drink. What about tonight?'

Everything in Greg's body wanted to say yes, to be with Jenny, holding her, loving her, it was what he'd wanted for ages and she had promised to spend the night with him when he returned from Holland. It was what he wanted but he knew he couldn't have it. Not now.

'No, I'm sorry, Jenny. I really am busy. Have to talk to my agent and things, you know. Look I'd love to talk and we will have a drink soon. I'd really like that. OK?'

'OK. Don't forget me when you're rich and famous.'

Greg put the phone down. Jenny had sounded disappointed. That was a bonus in a way, it meant she wanted to see him and she cared. Don't forget me when you're famous? Don't forget me when I'm sitting in a prison cell or worse! He downed the rest of his glass of Scotch and poured himself another before picking up the phone again. He listened to it ringing at the other end of the line ready for the moment Denis Young answered.

'Denis, listen. There's something I have to tell you.'

'Don't say you won't do the commercials as I've already accepted them for you..'

'You had no right…'

'I'm your agent, Greg. You signed your life over to me ages ago and now I'm hoping to cash in. What do you want?'

'Well,' Greg hesitated. What was he supposed to say? Everyone seemed to be so happy that he was about to make them all rich. No-one was taking into account the risks he was taking. No-one seemed to know.

'Come on, Greg. Busy, busy, busy! Have a client with me. I'll be in touch soon with the details of the commercials. First one's in Holland again flying out Friday, filming Saturday. After this one the world's your oyster apparently. Everything OK?'

'Yes, Fine. Ring me later. Please. I do need to talk to you about this.'

'Nothing to talk about. Leave it all to me. I'll make sure you do very well out of this. Don't worry. Bye.'

Denis hung up. What was going on? Why did Greg feel like he was being bulldozed! Everyone had it sussed, didn't they? How many of them knew what was really going on? Han? Rob? Peiter and Marjan, obviously. Denis? Did he know? He didn't want to talk as he'd already accepted the job. He'd never done that before. The phone rang again as Greg poured his third large scotch. It wasn't Denis.

'Any news for me, Greg?' Brian was cool and collected. Doing his job.

'They want me to do more commercials.'

'Great news. I'll be over this evening to discuss.' Brian hung up leaving Greg holding the receiver in one hand and his glass in the other. He finished the scotch in one before he replaced the phone, went back to his kitchen and poured the remainder of the bottle into the empty glass.

***

CHAPTER FIVE

The meeting arrangements for the commercial were similar to the previous job. Greg had spent Wednesday and Thursday in a bit of a stupor. He was almost hiding from the world. He didn't leave his flat other than a quick trip to the corner shop for milk and a cheap bottle of whisky. The phone hadn't rung which was good There was no way he could talk to anyone at the moment, not his agent not Rob or Han, not even Jenny, though he wanted to. He'd even picked up the phone to ring her a couple of times but couldn't. What would he say? Once this commercial was out of the way, maybe he could get back to his normal life.

So it was that he met Rob at Stansted Airport just after four o'clock on Friday afternoon. The airport was even busier than the last time he'd waited for the Dutch director but the bars still weren't open so he couldn't have a drink before Rob arrived. They travelled to Schiphol, Han drove like a madman to the Convent Hotel, Greg freshened up and they went off for hare stew at Humphrey's. They discussed the script, which just seemed to be a very slight variation on the previous commercial. This time he had to escape from the villains up a ladder, smearing Poepjes Melkboter Margarine over the rungs below him sending them slipping to their doom once more. Greg couldn't show any enthusiasm, knowing it was just a cover for drug smuggling.

Rob seemed to notice as he gave Greg a lot more direction this time and there seemed to be more takes than on the previous shoot. Greg decided he ought to pull his socks up and concentrate. He didn't want to be discovered.

The filming finished, though, in plenty of time for Greg to get a plane back to Stansted that evening, surprise, surprise!

'I suppose you'll want me to catch the evening plane and take the rushes back, like last time?' Greg said.

'Oh, there's no hurry this time, Greg,' replied Han. 'We've got the contract now so we can take the films back at the weekend. Stay and have a few drinks, go back in the morning. We have your hotel room booked anyway.'

Greg felt uneasy. He'd arranged to meet Brian at Schiphol Airport.

'Er, it's no bother, honest,' said Greg, trying not to sound too desperate. 'I've a meeting I'd like to go to tomorrow in London anyway. I'll be going past Dean Street early in the morning, so I may as well take them in for you. It'll be a help, won't it?

Greg thought the whole point of him doing this commercial was so he could courier the drugs back to the UK. If not, why was he here? Did they know he knew what they were up to? Had he been discovered? What would they do to him if he stayed overnight? Greg was starting to sweat.

Rob was talking quietly in Han's ear. What was he saying? Greg looked for an exit, in case he had to run. Han turned back to Greg. He seemed to be angry.

'Rob appears to now think it would be good if you did take the cans back again. I don't see why, to be honest. I think it's unfair to use an artist as a courier. We employ you as an actor. It pisses me off that Rob seems to think you can just do what he wants. I don't like taking advantage of people's good nature, Greg.'

'Hey, it's not a problem, Han. Like I said, I'll be passing Dean Street in the morning anyway and I do really need to be at this meeting so it'd better for me to get home tonight. Is it Mr Simmons again?'

'I guess so,' said Han, 'you'd better ask Rob.' Han went back to the bar and ordered himself a drink as Rob came over to Greg.

'Hey, thanks for this, Greg,' he said. 'I'll get you a cab when you're ready.'

Greg went to his room. He hadn't bothered to unpack so he just picked up his case and went downstairs. Rob already had the films in an identical holdall to the one Greg had been given before. He handed them to Greg.

'Don't worry about Han. He's a bit stressed at the moment. Nothing to do with you. I'll go and order your taxi.'

I bet he is stressed, thought Greg. Not half as stressed as I feel, though.

*

Brian Carter was waiting for Greg in the bar at Schiphol Airport.

'Thought you weren't going to make it, buddy.'

'They didn't want me to take the cans back,' explained Greg. 'I don't know what's going on!'

'You have got them, though.' Brian looked anxious.

'As it happens, I have.' Greg tapped the holdall slung across his shoulder.

*

The flight back seemed to take no time at all. Brian had been quiet which pleased Greg. His mind was preoccupied. Greg only had one scotch during the flight. He'd been terrified when he thought he had been rumbled. He hadn't spoken to Denis before he started this job. Greg was suspicious and had become more convinced that Denis knew what this was all about. He'd have it out with him in the morning, straight after he'd delivered the drugs.

As they disembarked the aircraft, Brian said he needed the loo and disappeared. Greg said he'd meet him at the baggage carousel.

'Mr Driscoll?'

Greg turned to face by a large customs officer flanked by two policemen.

'Yes. Have you been sent by DC Carter?'

'Who's that, then, Mr Driscoll?'

'He's just gone to the loo; he'll be here in a minute.'

'Will he? We'll make sure he finds you, then. Would you come this way, sir?'

'Yes, of course,' replied Greg. He assumed this was some sort of undercover operation set up by Brian and that he would be waiting for him wherever he was being taken. They went into a small room at the customs section and the officer locked the door behind them. Greg noticed there were no windows and no Brian!

'May I look in your bag, sir?' said the large officer, standing a little too close for Greg's comfort.

'Of course,' replied Greg, adding with a smirk, 'it's full of cocaine.'

The customs officer appeared to have no sense of humour. He put on a pair of rubber gloves and removed the cans from Greg's holdall and opened the first one. To Greg's surprise a long ribbon of film unravelled itself onto the floor. The second can was opened with the same result. The officer searched the remainder of the now visually empty bag before taking a knife and slitting the lining at the bottom of the holdall.

As Greg stared open-mouthed at the debris on the floor and the table, there was a knock on the door. Instead of Brian Carter entering, as Greg had expected, a young customs officer entered with what looked like the remainder of his suitcase. The large officer took the case and held up it in his gloved hands.

'Is this your suitcase, Mr Driscoll?'

'Well, it looks like it used to be once. What happened to it?'

'Are you aware of the law regarding possession and importation of narcotics into the UK, sir?'

'Of course I am. I think. The drugs should be in the film cans, sorry. I don't know what's going on. What's happened to my suitcase?'

Greg was now feeling angry and confused.

'Mr Driscoll, during a routine check of the luggage on your plane, one of our dogs discovered this in your suitcase.' He put a small orange plastic bag on the table in front of Greg.

'The bastards!' Greg exclaimed. 'You mean they put it in my suitcase this time? Why? My suitcase is ruined now.'

'So you admit to possession of this?'

'It's not a very big quantity, though, is it? Hardly seems worth it.'

'Would you like to speak to a lawyer, Mr Driscoll?'

'No I wouldn't! I'd like to speak to DC Carter. Right now! Where is he?'

The officer looked enquiringly at one of the policemen leaning against the wall. The policeman shook his head.

The officer looked Greg in the eye. 'I'm afraid we don't know of any DC Carter, Mr Driscoll.'

Greg looked back at the officer, expecting him to start laughing, one of Brian's practical jokes, meant to frighten him. He looked towards the policemen who were no longer leaning against the wall but standing staring back at him. One of them took a step towards him.

'What are you going to do?'

One of the policemen read him his rights, charging him with possessing and importing heroin, whilst the other brought Greg's hands behind his back and clamped handcuffs round his wrists.

'I'd like to make a phone call, please.'

***

CHAPTER SIX

Denis glared angrily at Greg Driscoll.

'What I don't understand is, if you knew what was going on, why didn't you let me know and why did you let me accept the second commercial?'

They were sitting in a pub in Chelmsford, Essex. To say Denis was staggered by Greg's phone call telling him he'd been arrested for drug smuggling would be more than an understatement. They'd often talked about drugs and how many of their friends and associates had seen their careers go AWOL because of the amount of stuff they'd put up their nose. He knew Greg was very anti-drugs. He didn't even smoke grass.

Greg had spent the night in the cells at Essex Police Headquarters in Chelmsford before Denis had raised the money for the police bail. He'd had no doubts that Greg had been set-up but couldn't believe he'd been taken in by the phoney commercial company himself.

'I tried to tell you, Denis.' Greg protested. 'You were always too busy. You kept saying you'd phone, you never did. I suppose you were having dinner with an important client or whatever you call it these days.'

'Enough of the recriminations, Greg. We've a lot of thinking to do.'

'I'd rather do a lot of drinking, thank you. I'd like to forget about the last couple of weeks, if you don't mind.'

'I don't mind, Greg, but it's a bit more complicated than you think. Do you know a Jenny Gulliver?'

'Jenny? Yes I do. Why?'

'I'll get some more drinks.'

Denis went to the bar leaving Greg mystified. Why was Denis talking about Jenny? Had she had an accident? His heart sank. Oh God! Don't tell me she's involved in this. He'd been shouting his mouth off to her when he got the first commercial. Was she in on it? Straight-laced Jenny working with drug dealers? Surely not. Greg felt he couldn't trust anyone these days.

Denis returned with two lagers and whisky chasers.

'Whisky this early in the day? This is bad news you're about to tell me, Denis, isn't it?'

'Jenny Gulliver rang me. She said she was a friend of yours, an actress, no agent. It turned out that she'd been offered a job and wanted me to handle it. I told her I didn't normally take people on just because they had a job but as a friend of yours…'

'…what sort of job. I only spoke to her a couple of days ago. She didn't have a job then. To be honest she seemed on the verge of giving it all up.'

'It's a commercial for Germany. She reckoned they must have got her name from Spotlight.'

'She's not in Spotlight. Said it was a waste of money and had never got her a job so she stopped putting her photo in there.'

'I know. I checked.' Denis paused then sank his whisky in one go. 'How well do you know her, Greg? I mean, are you in a relationship?'

Greg looked at his agent. Denis was usually the sort who tried to stare deep into one's soul. He considered it an essential part of his job to assess people's personality as completely as possible. Now he could only stare into his beer.

'Why are you asking me all this, Denis?'

Denis continued staring into his glass.

'It's the same people you've just been working for. I'm afraid I've taken Jenny on and accepted the job for her. But now...' He looked up at Greg. 'I mean, after what you've told me about this shower of bastards...do you think....?'

'Do I think what, Denis? Do I think you've pushed a young girl into a very dangerous situation? Yes I do! Do I think you perhaps should have spoken to me first? Yes I do! Do I think they'll get her running drugs? You bet your arse! What the hell were you thinking?'

'I didn't know, remember. You didn't tell me. I thought I was doing you and your girlfriend a favour. And

I'd keep your voice down, if I were you. You are on bail, you know. Shouting about drug running in a pub won't help you.'

Greg sipped his whisky. It tasted sour. A cheap whisky poured into a branded bottle most probably. Was no-one honest anymore? He was confused. How was he supposed to feel about all this? Jenny wasn't his girlfriend but she was a friend and, recently in her company he had come to realise that more and more he would like to be in a relationship with Jenny. Maybe settle down, who knows? He was angry that a young girl aspiring to be an actress, trying to eke out a meagre living from her chosen profession was being used to line the pockets of racketeers. What made him angrier was that was exactly what had happened to him. An easy well-paid job, he thought. An ego-boost. He'd been bragging about it to anyone who'd listen, when all he'd been, in fact, was just a glorified errand boy.

'What should we do, Greg?' Denis sounded worried.

'Well you'll have to stop her doing the job.' Greg looked at his agent. 'It's too late, isn't it? When did she go?'

'This morning.'

'Bring her back. Phone them. Bring her back.'

'I can't, Greg. She's on location somewhere in Germany. Oh God! I wish you'd told me about all this.'

'Brian Carter said it had to be kept under wraps. Have you found him, yet?'

'No. That number you gave me is unobtainable. The operator suggested someone hadn't paid their bill but couldn't, or wouldn't, check it for me.'

Greg had given Denis the number Brian Carter had given him at the airport, when he phoned from the police station, and told him to get hold of him quick. Greg considered it Brian's fault that he was in this predicament. He thought he was doing undercover work for the police and therefore the police should be helping him not arresting him. This had been met with only laughter at the police station the night before.

'The CID doesn't reveal their cast lists,' Denis continued. 'They wouldn't say whether they had anyone called Brian Carter on their books.'

'Well somebody must know him! He's definitely in The Met, I saw his badge.'

'Have you ever seen a Met Police badge before, Greg?'

'Are you suggesting I'm wrong?'

'Wouldn't be the first time.'

'Are you going to help me find Brian or not. He's the solution to this problem you've got me in.'

'Me?'

'You got me the job. We need to find Brian and tell him about Jenny. He'll know what to do.'

Denis wasn't so sure. The last time Greg had seen Brian he'd done a runner. Now he couldn't be found. He finished his beer and studied the empty glass.

'Should I try and get hold of this film company and see if they know where Jenny is? We could warn her.'

'No.' Greg was emphatic. 'We need Brian first. We could put Jenny in more jeopardy by alerting them. They must already know I've failed to deliver. Don't go any further with this until I say, Denis. Brian reckons it could be very dangerous.'

Denis agreed. He didn't like the faith Greg was putting in his so-called friend from the Met.

'It still sounds very fishy to me,' he added.

'I think smuggling cocaine and heroin is more than fishy, Denis.'

Greg stood up.

'Where are you going?'

'I need to find Carter, somehow.'

'Don't forget you're out on my bail money.'

'Don't worry I'm not going far.'

*

By the next day it was Greg that was worried. Very worried. He'd left his message on Brian's pager and sat in the Princess Louise for four hours. Carter never showed up. Three times he'd left the message with no response. Denis had employed a solicitor, Graeme Ford who had managed to get some co-operation from the Metropolitan Police. He had asked Greg for descriptions of Brian and of the badge Greg had seen him flashing. It seemed there had never been a Brian Carter or anyone answering his description in The Met, nor had he been to their training school. Enquiries were now under way with Scotland Yard to see if he could be traced to any other police force. Greg's description of the badge brought nothing more than jollity from the police. Whatever it was it certainly was not a police badge. Greg had wanted to point out that it had also fooled the customs people at Stansted but Graeme had hushed him.

Greg was back in his flat. Jenny had been on the answerphone four times, telling him about her exciting new job and wanting him to ring her before she had to leave for Germany. He would have if he hadn't been in the police cell. Poor Jenny. For someone who didn't like answerphones she sure phoned his a lot. He listened to her messages again. His heart sank deeper and deeper as he realised what she was getting herself innocently involved in.

The phone rang. Please God, let it be Jenny. Greg was praying a lot these days.

'Mr Driscoll?' It wasn't Jenny. 'Graeme Ford here.'

Denis' solicitor sounded calm and business-like.

'Scotland Yard say there has never been a Brian Carter with your description in any police force in the last five years. However, they do want to talk to you and I think you'll be treated with a bit more respect this time. There has been an influx of drugs coming from the continent recently and they haven't been able to trace the source. They want your help, which can only be in your favour. They're not dropping charges or anything but I have an inkling they believe your story. I've arranged an interview for 11.30 tomorrow morning. Does that suit you?'

'Yes,' replied Greg. 'What will they want me to do?'

'Give a few descriptions, I suppose. You know the people you were dealing with in Holland.'

'I didn't deal with anyone, Graeme.'

'Well, strictly speaking, you did. On the second trip you were expecting to carry drugs back into the country in the film cans. That could go against you if you don't co-operate.'

'I was under the impression that I was helping the police by doing the smuggling.'

'Yes but you didn't tell anyone except this Carter chap. You really should have checked him out first, you know.'

'Oh come on! If someone shows you a police ID card and talks about undercover work you don't go and check with Scotland Yard.'

'A Mickey Mouse ID card!'

'Well, I didn't know. I've only seen them on TV. It looked authentic to me.'

'Anyway, the police don't think Carter, or whoever he is, is very important. They think he's likely to just be another pawn. He could even have been sacrificed by now, unless you were meant to be caught, of course.'

'Why?'

'I don't know, Mr Driscoll. I suppose it's part of my job to find out. But first let's get this interview sorted out tomorrow. Why don't you come to my office for 10am and we'll go through the procedure and don't be late.'

Greg agreed to be at Graeme Ford's office at 10 and hung up the phone.

He went to bed early hoping to feel bright for the morning interview with Scotland Yard but found sleep elusive. He dozed on and off, looking at the clock every half hour or so, longing either for deep sleep or the morning to arrive.

Just after he'd seen his clock display 03:00 he thought he heard a noise in the living room. Wide awake, he listened very carefully but could hear nothing above the pounding of his heart. He lay for what seemed like hours but was barely minutes, working out how best to deal with any intruder. He kept an ancient iron golf club next to his bed. Living in a council flat in Hackney he had picked up several tips about self-survival from some of his neighbours, and slipping silently from under his duvet he took hold of the worn leather handle. As he approached his open bedroom door he heard a footstep ahead of him. His leaden arms swung the club out in front of him with all the might they could muster. The club connected with something and he sprang through the door expecting to find the sprawled bleeding body of the intruder. There was nothing. He went to switch on the light. As he did he felt a heavy dull thud between his shoulder blades and finally darkness and a deep, deep sleep did come upon him.

***

CHAPTER SEVEN

'Operator, can you please check the line again. It can't still be engaged, surely?'

'I can only suggest that the party you are trying to reach has left the phone off the hook, sir.'

Denis was more angry than worried. He was angry that Greg had obviously been drunk again the night before, knocked the phone off the hook and passed out. It wouldn't be the first time. The problem was it was now 10.30 and Greg had still not shown up at Graeme Ford's office. Graeme had been on to Denis because he couldn't get hold of Greg, Denis was now shouldering the responsibility and he didn't relish having to tell the CID that his client had slept in due to an excess of alcohol the night before. It didn't show Greg to be a very responsible source of information about drugs rings! His last-minute attempt to avoid having to get a cab to Hackney and physically drag Greg out of bed had not worked so he locked the office and ran out to Oxford Street to grab the nearest taxi.

As Denis' cab approached Greg's block of flats he could just see the ambulance through the crowd of onlookers. Two policemen were taking statements from a couple of vociferous old women in housecoats standing outside on the pavement. One of the policemen broke off from the interviews to apprehend Denis as he hurried towards Greg's flat.

'Where do you think you're going?' he said, rather aggressively, Denis thought.

'I'm here to pick up my client who has an important meeting with your bosses at Scotland Yard.'

'Really. What number?'

'30.'

'You'll be lucky, mate. He's in there.' The policeman pointed to the open doors of the ambulance. 'What was this important meeting about?'

But Denis had already gone towards the ambulance, ignoring the shouts of '*Oi, You!*' arriving just as the paramedics were closing the doors.

'What's happened? Is he bad?' Denis implored the green jacketed young lady trying to restrain him.

'Are you a relation, sir?'

'No, I'm a friend. Well, I'm his agent. What's happened?'

The lady smiled. It was a false smile, probably learned at some training session and put her hand on Denis' shoulder.

'I'm sorry, sir. We have to get to the hospital as soon as possible.' She turned to get into the front of the ambulance.

'Which one?'

Denis just about heard 'Homerton' before the sirens started and up and the ambulance sped away.

The policeman was back.

'Now, sir. If I could just take a few details from you. You say you're his agent?'

'Yes. Look, if you want to interview me, here's my card. Right now I need to get to this hospital. Homerton, is it?'

'I wouldn't know about that, sir. I'll need a statement before you go.'

A taxi with its yellow light on was slowing down to see what was going on. Denis leapt into the back and told the driver to go to Homerton hospital as fast as he could. They were on their way before the policeman could stop him. He didn't really seem to care and went back to interviewing the other bystanders.

'He didn't look good. Skull split open, I reckon.' The taxi driver said over his shoulder, almost relishing the gory details.

'How do you know? You didn't see him. You'd only just arrived!'

'I'd been round the block, mate. Love a bit of gore, meself.'

'That's a friend of mine in there.' Denis felt like hitting him.

'Sorry, mate.' The cabbie turned back to look at the road. 'Anyone know what happened?'

'I don't know. I didn't know anything had happened till I arrived five minutes ago.'

'Probably drugs. Lot of that in those flats. Was he mixed up in drugs?'

'Are we nearly there? Can't you hurry up?'

'Can't go faster than the traffic.' The driver muttered, adding something about bloody druggies.

Denis sat in a cold sweat. The cabbie was right. Greg was mixed up in drugs. Whoever had done whatever to Greg had probably been sent by the drugs ring to silence him. He could be dead. Denis didn't know.

'Are we nearly there?'

'Just round this corner. Waiting for an ambulance to come out. Don't want to get in the way of the dying.'

Denis threw a ten pound note at the driver and got out. He could see the hospital ahead and ran towards it.

He wasn't allowed to see Greg, who was now in the safe hands of the NHS, he was told. If he wasn't a relative he wouldn't be allowed to see him anyway and was told he might as well go home. A young policeman overheard his conversation and took him to one side and started asking him questions about Greg. He didn't seem too interested in what Denis had to say and he couldn't give Denis any details, it just seemed like a routine robbery with violence. Denis asked to speak to a superior who could get him in touch with Scotland Yard.

The Policeman smiled condescendingly. 'I don't think Scotland Yard will be interested in this, sir,' he said.

'Oh I think they will.' Denis spotted a payphone by the entrance and went over to ring Graeme Ford to explain as much of the situation as he could.

Graeme Ford picked up the phone after the first ring. 'Where the hell is he?' He thundered.

'Homerton hospital, Hackney. It seems someone didn't want him to go to Scotland Yard today,' replied Denis.

'What! Is he alright?'

'Don't know. They won't let me near him. I think he might be in intensive care. The cabbie said it looked like a split skull. I'm really worried, Graeme.'

'Hang on there. I'll get hold of Scotland Yard and be right with you. I could be about an hour or so. Don't let him speak to anyone!' Graeme hung up leaving Denis wondering how he could stop Greg from speaking to anyone when he wasn't allowed near him. If he could speak. If he was still alive! Denis sat on a red plastic chair in the reception area and waited wondering what to do next. Jenny Gulliver! Shit! He hadn't tried to get hold of her yet. He only hoped they really were just shooting a commercial and not getting her involved in the drugs running. He feared it was a forlorn hope.

*

Jenny's flight had been fun. Of course, she'd flown to more exotic places than Germany with her parents as a child but this was her, on her own, doing a job. She felt good. An adult. The brief for the commercial was to play an 'English rose' type with a touch of comedy. This meant Oscar Wilde to her and she carried with her a copy of 'The Importance of Being Earnest' which she devoured on the plane. Studying classic drama reminded her she was an actress, even though she'd been tied to a word-processor for the last two years. In fact she'd never had more than two lines in a play as a professional but this was a feature for her. There was no-one else in the commercial. It was fantastic!

She exited customs to be met with the usual row of taxi drivers in the Arrivals lounge, holding up signs for their clients and nearly missed the tall dark-haired man holding a sign saying 'Jenny Gulliver'.

'Oh! That's me!' she blurted out. Then felt very foolish and uncool as the other passengers stared at her. The tall man walked towards her, offering his hand.

'Hello, Jenny. Rob Vanderlast,' he said. 'I'm so pleased to meet you. We are very glad you accepted this job at such short notice. You came with a very good recommendation. I hope we find it very exciting working together.'

'I'm sure we will,' said Jenny. 'I'm really, really looking forward to it.'

Jenny smiled in a way she hoped made her look like an 'English rose'

'Such a beautiful smile. You are even more attractive than your picture, Jenny. I love your auburn hair, almost Pre-Raphaelite. The car's this way; I'll take you to your hotel.' Rob Vanderlast took Jenny's suitcase from her and led her to his car.

***

CHAPTER EIGHT

Graeme Ford arrived at Homerton hospital at midday. He had two policemen with him. Denis, looking haggard and worn out, was still getting no information from the hospital. Now the doctors explained to the police that there seemed to be no sign of Greg regaining consciousness at present although he was not in intensive care and they weren't showing any particular sign of concern. It turned out that whoever had attacked him knew exactly the point between the shoulder blades where a heavy blow would put Greg out for a long time.

The police had a report from Greg's flat. They were looking at it being a burglary; video, TV etc. appeared to be missing. Denis agreed to go with the police to check if anything else had gone as soon as he knew whether Greg was going to be OK.

At around one-thirty the doctor came through to the waiting room and informed Denis that Greg was awake and asking for a Mr Young. The police wanted to talk to Greg but the doctor would only allow one person into the room. Denis insisted that as Greg was asking for him, he should be the one to go in. The police didn't seem that bothered and Denis was given five minutes and told not to excite the patient.

'This has got to be the worst hangover I've ever had,' groaned Greg, trying to smile. He'd heard it took fewer muscles to smile than to grimace. Right now he didn't believe it, smiling was hurting so he tensed back into a grimace. 'This is all a bit heavy, isn't it, Denis?'

'Try not to worry. The police think it's a burglary.'

Greg tried to laugh and pain shot through his chest and back. He grimaced again.

'Have you any idea what happened, Greg?'

He considered shrugging his shoulders but thought better of it.

'Someone tried to help me get to sleep,' he said.

'Yes, well, perhaps you need some more sleep now. I mustn't excite the patient, I've been told. Doctor's orders! I have to go and check your flat with the police but I'll be on my pager if you need me. Get the hospital to page me if you want. Should I tell anyone?'

'Could you call in on Olive next door? Apparently she found me and called the ambulance. Buy her some flowers or something.'

'Family?'

Greg just glared at him.

*

Denis knew Greg hadn't spoken to his family for years. He'd told him one night as they sat in a pub. Greg had probably had one too many and Denis had probably asked him once too often.

'I was eleven when they split up,' he said, focussing on the rim of his pint glass. 'There was no warning. We were just an ordinary middle-class family. My father used to come home from his job around seven. My mother would have the dinner on the table in the kitchen and we'd all sit round it and eat. They didn't go out much, didn't drink a great deal. They appeared to be a perfect couple, at least to me. They never argued, never raised their voices,' he took a swig of beer and looked at Denis over the top of his glass. Denis smiled in what he hoped was a sympathetic manner. Greg took another swig.

'So you had a normal family? Lots of normal families split up.'

'That's ok, then.' There was a pause. 'One day my father was late, like very late. My mother wouldn't let me eat at seven and I suppose I whined and moaned and eventually I ate my warmed up dinner at about eight o' clock. There was still no sign of my father. My mother was quiet, I kept asking her where he was and she just shrugged her shoulders. It was nearly nine o'clock when he turned up. He'd been drinking. I'd never seen him drunk. I was watching something on television; I don't remember what, just sitting on the sofa. He flew into the room and told me to get out. I suppose I cheeked him, I don't know, but he came over and clouted me with the back of his hand. He'd never hit me before. I went to my room, lay on my bed and sobbed. Like a baby – he yelled after me as I ran up the stairs. He was like another person, someone I'd never met.'

Denis reached out and put his hand on Greg's arm. Greg glared at him. 'Don't touch me,' he said quietly. Denis withdrew his hand. Greg picked up his pint glass and drained the contents.

'Do you want another?' Greg was silent, focussed on the table. Denis took the glass and crossed to the bar. Greg didn't move. He was still staring at the table when Denis returned with a full pint for Greg and glass of wine for himself. He put the glass next to Greg, sat down and waited. It was a full minute before Greg picked up the glass and took a drink.

'I lay in my room listening. They were rowing downstairs. I could hear my father. He was yelling at my mother. Jezebel; whore; adulteress. Words I'd never heard my father say about anyone. Yelling them at my mother. I should have gone downstairs, confronted him but I didn't. I just lay there, listening.'

Denis looked at Greg. He could see Greg's eyes filling up but he didn't say anything, didn't touch him. He just sat and waited. Greg drank some more lager.

'Anyway, after a while the door slammed and I never saw my father again!' he looked at Denis and smiled but his eyes were still watery.

'Why?'

'Didn't know where he was! Apparently he went out to Spain or somewhere. Packed his job in and just left! Could be dead by now for all I know!'

'Don't you care?'

'Do I care? I don't know. I don't know if I care or not. I don't think about it.'

'And your mother? You never mention her either.'

'Darren!'

'What?'

'She's with Darren, I suppose. I don't really know.'

'Who's Darren?'

'The adulterer. The one who caused it all – along with my mother, of course.' Greg drank his pint. He drank it in great gulps, quickly, nearly a full pint and stood up. He swayed only a little. 'My round, I think.'

Denis looked at his half full wine glass. 'I'll get them,' he said, rising from his seat.

'No! It's my round, I said. I'll get them.' Denis sat down. 'Lend me a tenner,' Greg held out his hand. He was being quite aggressive, unusual for Greg. Denis reached into his jacket pocket, pulled out his wallet, extracted a ten pound note and handed it Greg.

'Thanks, add it to the next commission you take from me.'

Denis sipped the remainder of his wine. He wished he hadn't asked Greg about his family. He still didn't understand why he had never been in contact or even tried to find where his father was. He looked over to the bar. Greg was downing a small glass of what looked like whisky before bringing the pint of lager and the glass of wine back to the table.

'Darren moved in barely a week after my father left. He was a bastard! Did something in the City. Had loads of money which he thought made him better than other people. People like our neighbours, people who lived in their modest middle-class houses, people like me. My mother started going out with him a lot in the evenings, leaving me on my own. So I started going out too. Mixing with what she used to call 'the wrong sort' getting up to mischief. I suppose I was looking for attention. In vain! All her attention was reserved for Darren. We never had dinner at the table. I don't think they ever ate at home. I survived on a diet of pizza and microwave meals. They drank a lot too. The fridge was always full of Champagne and there was a new cupboard that doubled as a bar, packed with spirits. I suppose that's where I got my taste for alcohol from. Home alone, curious as to what these bottled coloured liquids were. Nobody cared.' He took another long drink. 'Anyway, they decided to move after a few years. Darren couldn't stand living amongst the plebs any longer. Darren, the barrow-boy's son made good and now making even more money under the benevolence of Mrs Thatcher. He wanted a country pile! A mansion to show off his wealth. I was coming up to sixteen. I'd put up with this man for long enough. I refused to go with them. Darren couldn't hide his delight at getting rid of me. I heard my mother saying something about me only being a child and him replying that at my age he'd been working the market, out in the real world, which was why he was successful and I'd always be a loser. My mother didn't argue. Obviously she thought the same. Anyway, the upshot was, my Grandmother stepped into the breach – which was odd. It was my mother's mother. She hadn't really had anything to do with us since the marriage break-up and now suddenly there I was living in her house. She spent all her time belittling my mother. The name Jezebel came up again! I was no longer allowed out to mix with 'the wrong sort'. I stayed in, doing homework, studying for exams that would supposedly make me a better person. My grandmother lived nearer town than we had and I soon discovered there were things to do in the middle of towns. Pubs, for instance. Grandmother wanted me join the local church youth club – that was never going to happen – but there was an advert in the local newspaper for a youth theatre and I chose that. Grandmother was unsure but her local vicar had told her it would do me good, help me to express myself so she agreed. What she didn't know was that after every session we adjourned to the pub next door. I discovered all sorts of things at the youth theatre. Girls, expressing myself, girls, drinking pints and a seeming ability to act. Exams didn't matter anymore. I didn't need exams to be an actor! I became immersed in The Drama! For the first time in my life everything came easy.'

'And your mother?'

'Went off with Darren to somewhere. Probably living in some exotic country by now – and before you ask, no, I don't care. I don't care a fig for my mother or her fancy man.'

'What happened to Granny?'

'She died while I was at Drama School. No-one told me. I went home one weekend and she wasn't there. The vicar tried to take me in, give me a load of doctrine, telling me everything would be alright. I went back to London on the next train and never returned.'

'So you have no wish to find out where your parents might be?'

'Do they care where I might be? No, Denis. I have no wish. As far as I'm concerned I'm Little Orphan Annie!'

'As long as you don't think of me as Daddy Warbucks,' said Denis, trying to lighten the mood.

'That's an interesting concept. Get the drinks in, Daddio.'

'Don't you think...?'

'...no I don't think I've had enough!'

Denis sighed and went to the bar.

*

'Does Jenny know?' Greg asked.

Denis looked away. 'I haven't spoken to her.'

'You haven't spoken to her? Not at all? Did you not get her back from Germany?'

'Greg, it's all being taken care of, don't worry. It'll be alright'

Greg looked at Denis and could see it was anything but alright. His head felt very heavy and was throbbing. His eyes were starting to close and he felt extremely tired.

'I think I do need some more sleep, Denis, you're right. I think they must have pumped me full of drugs or something. Drugs, eh? Who needs them?'

Denis stood by the bed and watched his friend and client drift off to sleep. He leant over and took his hand.

'Don't worry, Greg. We'll sort these bastards out somehow.' Denis wasn't sure whether Greg heard him or not but convinced himself that Greg's hand returned his squeeze.

A nurse entered and started to take Greg's pulse. She was a large woman originating from the Caribbean. She smiled at Denis.

'He'll be alright, don't worry.'

Denis went back to the waiting room to find the police had left. Graeme Ford explained that they had something 'more important' to do. Denis and Graeme headed off to Greg's flat.

*

'That's great, Jenny. We just need one more take on that last shot. Not your fault, problem with the sound. Just smile your beautiful smile and do exactly the same as last time.'

Jenny Gulliver's first experience in front of the camera was not as enjoyable as she had expected. She'd had very little sleep the night before and the taxi had only stopped at the hotel long enough for Jenny to leave her bag. She hadn't even checked in. She'd then been taken straight to the location, not even time for a shower. Something to do with the light being just right apparently. Something to do with saving money, Jenny thought was more accurate! And taking advantage of her inexperience! There didn't seem to be a lot of natural light anyway, only great big lanterns everywhere. It was overcast and drizzly. The last thing she wanted to do was sit on the bonnet of a car in the middle of a market square, wearing only a bikini eating ice-cream and trying to smile!

Han Koolhaven had been very nice in the taxi. He appeared to be genuinely upset that Jenny had not been told all the details of the commercial shoot. He'd insisted that if she didn't want to do it in a bikini he could arrange to alter the shot and she could wear shorts and a tee-shirt if that made her feel more comfortable. Embarrassed, Jenny tried to explain it wasn't just the costume that was the problem, more the content of the script – or rather the lack of content. She didn't realise that people still did car commercials with girls sitting on the bonnet in a bikini – or a tee shirt and shorts! Han tried to explain it was supposed to be ironic but Jenny knew they really wanted her to be a sexy dumb blonde (even though she was a redhead!) When they'd arrived at the shoot she was whisked into a porta-cabin and told to put the bikini on anyway, they didn't have a tee-shirt and shorts and they were losing the light. Desperately wanting to cry and run away, Jenny had had to 'pull herself together' and get on with it. It took her back to her boarding school, a time she'd hated. Constant bullying! She'd asked her parents to remove her from the school but her parents chose to believe the school's stories that she was disruptive and told her to 'pull herself together' and do as she was told.

It had been a long day. She was cold and wet from the drizzle, even though the very nice make-up girl had ensured she had a dressing gown to wear between takes, and she was tired physically and emotionally. She was very thankful when Han called out 'That's a wrap' and she could get into her own clothes and get back to the hotel. She was longing for a hot bath and a long drink.

*

In Greg's flat, Denis was clearing up the debris left by the burglary. Graeme Ford had returned to his office, having informed Denis that the police would like a call from Greg as soon as possible so they could close the case. They didn't hold out any hope of catching the burglars. Graeme was intending to update Scotland Yard regarding the possible real reason for the intrusion. As far as Denis could tell only the TV and video were missing but the place had been ransacked. Seemingly indiscriminate destruction had taken place. Books strewn all over the floor, chairs turned upside down, broken bottle of scotch. The bedroom was a similar scene of chaos and in the kitchen there didn't seem to be an item of crockery left unbroken.

Denis was sure, in the back of his mind, that this was not just a burglary. Why had they smashed the place up? Was it some sort of warning? Were they looking for something? More to the immediate point, would they come back? Denis felt a shiver as that thought crossed his mind. He checked the lock on the door; it didn't seem to be damaged. He wondered how they'd entered last night. Maybe they had keys? Maybe they'd made copies of Greg's keys while he was away from the hotel shooting the commercial. Denis told himself to try and control his imagination. Perhaps it was a coincidence. Perhaps this was just a random burglary. Whatever it was, Denis wanted to clear up the flat as quick as possible and clear out!

There was a knock at the door. Denis froze. Another knock followed by 'is anyone there?'

It was a woman's voice with a Caribbean accent. Denis went towards the door and opened it slightly.

'Oh, hello. Who are you?' Standing the other side of the door was a tall black woman. She was looking suspiciously at Denis.

'I'm a friend of Mr Driscoll's,' he answered. 'Who are you, pray?'

'My name's Olive,' she replied. 'I live next door.'

Denis opened the door wider. 'I'm so sorry, Greg asked to me to call in on you. You found him this morning, I believe.'

'Is he alright? He looked a right mess.'

'He's at the hospital. I've spoken to him. I suppose we'll just have to wait.'

'Anyone know what happened?'

'I was hoping you could throw some light on that, Olive.'

'I feel so guilty. There was a hell of a rumpus going on in the early hours.' She looked over Denis shoulder at the still untidy flat. 'Did he have a fight or something?'

'The police think it's a burglary.'

'Highly possible round here. I was just going to work and I saw his door open. When he didn't reply I went in and there he was on the floor. I've had the police round but I can't tell them anything.'

'You didn't think to see what was happening in the early hours?'

'You don't interfere round here.'

Denis stood at the door. This woman was irritating him. He wanted to finish clearing up. She was just being nosy. 'Well, I'll give him your best when I get to see him, Mrs...?

'Just Olive. Thank you.' She went back to her flat.

Denis turned and looked at the mess, sighed, found a bin liner in the kitchen and started to fill it with the bits of Greg's broken life.

*

'Hallo, Jenny. I'm sorry it's been such a long day. Let me get you a drink. My name's Marjan, by the way, I'm the sort of production assistant, well, I work for Mr Wiersma, general dogsbody really.'

Jenny looked at the blonde spiky-haired girl who had just sat down opposite her in the reception of the hotel. 'Sorry, who's Mr Wiersma?'

'He's the client. The man with the money. Peiter Wiersma. He owns a load of supermarkets as well as this production company. Look, I'm sorry I couldn't be with you earlier; I had some business to clear up this morning in Holland. Still, that all seems to be have been sorted out quite nicely now. You must have been freezing today. I hope they looked after you OK?'

'Yes. They did all they could. I wish I'd known I was going to have to wear a bikini, though.'

'Didn't anyone tell you? That's terrible! I'll have a word. I'll get you some more money.'

Jenny sighed. 'It's not about the money. I just...well... you know, it's more about my female dignity. I'm not a feminist or anything...'

'I understand,' said Marjan, taking Jenny's hand, 'I told them about that when I saw the script. These men just don't get it. Let me fetch you that drink.'

Jenny ordered a whisky and ginger ale. She'd had a bath but was still feeling a bit chilled. More than anything she was disappointed. She'd so wanted her first proper job to be the sort of job she'd dreamed about watching Audrey Hepburn and Ingrid Bergman on TV as a girl, trying to hide away from the realities of boarding school life. Coming to terms with the fact that a lot of acting was really just about doing a job and lacking in glamour was not easy. This job certainly hadn't increased her confidence in the way she'd hoped it would. At least Marjan seemed nice. Jenny watched her as she stood at the bar. She appeared confident and chatty. I bet she wouldn't have worn a bikini and sat on the bonnet of a car without kicking up a fuss.

Marjan came back to the table with the drinks.

'I got you a large one.' Marjan handed Jenny her drink and sat down.

The two of them chatted amicably together. Jenny liked her. Their upbringings couldn't have been more different; Jenny with her big house and private education, Marjan brought up by her single mother in the Dutch equivalent of a council estate, but within half an hour one would have thought they'd been best mates at school. When Han arrived he could see the intimacy that had developed between them and almost felt embarrassed as he took the two of them into the hotel restaurant.

*

Denis had all but finished clearing Greg's flat and was just making a last minute check. Something caught his eye as he switched off the bedroom light. Something green was flashing under the bed. He stooped down and pulled Greg's answerphone out. Greg's answerphone had two functions. As well as taking messages from incoming calls, there was a memo function to use 'as a personal electronic notepad to exchange messages with family members or associates.' It was this green button that was flashing. Denis pressed the button. After a short pause the tape inside rewound and delivered its message.

"Crackle...Get

Carter...crackle...Cartmel...Crackle...Chase...Roger"

It was a very staccato voice and very faint. Denis had to listen to the message several times in order to interpret it. It wasn't Greg's voice. It sounded like it was coming through some sort of walkie-talkie, except for the name Roger at the end which was loud and clear. It was followed by the sound of footsteps and then silence. What did it mean? Carter was the name of the supposed DC that nobody admitted to knowing. Who or what was Cartmel? A person? A place? A building? Was it where Carter was? Was it a message from him? How did he leave the message? To use this function you had to record it onto Greg's machine.

Denis took the micro tape from the machine and put it in his pocket. He phoned Graeme Ford's office. His secretary answered and informed Denis that Graeme was in a meeting and couldn't be disturbed. Denis hung up. His instinct was to take the tape to the police but to whom? The local police who were dealing with the burglary or straight to Scotland Yard? He fingered the tape in his jacket pocket. He wanted to ask Greg what he wanted to do. It was his flat, his tape, his message presumably. He was most involved. It had to be his choice.

Denis locked the flat and checked his watch. It was late. He decided to go back to his own flat. A visit to Homerton hospital could wait till morning

**

CHAPTER NINE

After a good night's sleep in the hotel followed by hot coffee and croissants, life seemed much more rosy for Jenny Gulliver as she sat in the foyer waiting for the car to take her to the airport. The previous evening had seen Jenny, encouraged by whisky and wine in more quantity than she was used to, pouring her heart out to Marjan and Han about the trials and tribulations of being an aspiring actress. Han had been particularly encouraging and, although agreeing he hadn't actually seen her doing any real acting yet, he could tell by instinct and the way she behaved for the camera her potential was immense. She could rest assured that if he ever had a suitable part in the future she would be his first choice. She'd heard that before, of course. Greg Driscoll had implied something similar as he tried to seduce her when they'd first worked together. She was wiser now but when you are desperate to be a working actress you are ready to believe anything. The strange and, to be honest in her rather drunken state, ultimately disappointing thing was that Han didn't seem to be in the least interested in seducing her. Having been defensive against such actions at the beginning of the evening she ended up giving Han the most blatant signs. Even after Marjan had left early (a meeting in Holland first thing being the excuse) Han hadn't even as much as brushed her knee with his hand. However he had massaged her ego which in the cold light of morning was far preferable to the embarrassment she could have faced this morning.

She felt a slight touch of anti-climax but was more positive than she'd been for months. She'd done her first commercial; she had an agent; almost the promise of a job from Han; a chauffeur-driven car to the airport and money being paid to her for working. Yes! Things were definitely on the way up for Jenny Gulliver.

*

Things were on the way up for Greg Driscoll too. He'd spent a quiet night, been woken at six-thirty for what the NHS considered to be breakfast and now sat comfortably if not expectantly in his bed awaiting luncheon. His headache had all but gone and, apart from a stiffness between his shoulder blades, appeared to be suffering no serious ill-effects from his ordeal. The doctor was 'pleased with him', a statement that made him feel like a schoolboy receiving a good end-of-term report. Not that he'd ever received a good end-of-term report himself. One of the nurses, one of the very attractive nurses, had even asked for his autograph (in case he ever became famous!) and but for her having to work the night-shift for the foreseeable future, would have eagerly taken up his dinner-date invitation he was sure.

He was about to ask her to make it a lunch date instead when he saw Denis approaching. The nurse smiled and left.

'Leave her alone, Greg, you're supposed to be convalescing.'

'I don't know what you mean,' smiled Greg.

'I've known you long enough to recognise that look on your face. You must be feeling better. We all thought you were a goner!'

'Thanks! It takes more than a blow on the head to stop Greg Driscoll, you know.'

'Good.' Denis sat down next to Greg's bed and looked at him. 'How are you feeling really?'

'I'm OK, I suppose. A bit stiff across the shoulders. Doctor says he's very pleased with me!'

'Have the police spoken to you yet?'

'Oh yes. First thing this morning. Couldn't tell them anything, of course. They suggested I called in at the station when I'm released from here, which, incidentally, could be this evening.'

'Really? So soon?'

'According to Matron, sorry Ward Sister, they don't like being called Matron anymore. Something to do with Hattie Jacques!'

'When will you know?'

'In about an hour or so after the doctor's seen me.'

'Great I'll come and pick you up if they let you go.'

'Excellent. I'll even let you buy me a drink.'

'Is that sensible?'

'I've had all the sense knocked out of me. How would I know?'

Denis laughed, then sighed heavily. Greg could see he had something to tell him and he guessed it wasn't going to be good news.

'Have you checked out my flat?' he asked. Denis nodded. 'Everything as I left it?'

'Not really. I tidied up a bit.'

'And?' Greg tried to look Denis in the eyes but he turned away.

'And what?'

'And you obviously have more to tell me. Spit it out.'

'It was a bit of a mess, things smashed up. Perhaps you'd better stay with me if you're out today. Do you know anyone called Cartmel?'

'What?'

'Cartmel.'

'No. I know Cartmel race-track but not anyone called Cartmel. I knew a girl called Carmen once. She was Spanish. That any good?'

'Where is Cartmel race-track?'

'Up North somewhere. Why? If you're thinking of taking me racing I'd rather go somewhere nearer. Sandown or Kempton, maybe?'

'We'll see. Look I'll come back at about five. See if you're being let out. Bye.'

Denis stood up and left. Greg was feeling confused. What was all that about? The nice nurse came back with two cups of tea.

'Oh, has your friend left,' she said. 'I've made him a cup of tea.'

'You have it,' replied Greg. 'Take the weight off your feet. Now about this dinner date, why don't we make it a lunch date if you're on nights?'

Denis hurried from the hospital and went into the Ladbrokes shop across the road. Sure enough, there was a race-track at Cartmel. It was just south of the Lake District. The next meeting was Saturday, three days away. He thanked the red-jacketed girl who had supplied him with the information and went back to his office. He did have other clients than Greg to look after, he made a few calls, typed a couple of suggestions to casting directors and made a note that he must try to see the first night of one of his clients' West End debut. He then put Greg's micro-tape into his own machine and replayed the message.

"Crackle...Get Carter...crackle...Cartmel...Crackle...Chase...Roger"

It still didn't make any sense. Was Carter going to be at Cartmel races? Was he trying to get in touch with Greg? If that was the case, why send someone round to smash up him and his flat? Or was it Carter himself who came round? That was possible. No-one in the police force seemed to have heard of him. Maybe Carter was involved with the drug smuggling. He certainly knew a lot about the enterprise. If Carter thought Greg had realised his involvement, he would assume that Greg would tell someone and would have to shut him up. So why not finish him off properly? Whoever attacked Greg knew exactly how far to go to scare him.

*

'Miss Gulliver? Your car has arrived, madam.'

Jenny walked over to the desk and thanked the man at reception and went with the driver to the waiting Mercedes. The driver put her case in the boot and opened the door for her.

As she sat back in the leather seats Jenny allowed herself a look back at the hotel.

So! Sneaky old Marjan, she thought. There was obviously no early meeting in Holland. Marjan could be seen quite clearly through one of the bedroom windows talking to a very prosperous-looking gentleman in a smart suit. She must have spent the night with him. Well, why not? She didn't have to lie, though. She waved at Marjan but she looked too busy to notice her.

Had the car not pulled off at that moment, Jenny might have noticed that the discussion Marjan was having was anything but loving. It was a heated and animated argument. She might also have noticed Peiter Wiersma hit Marjan hard across the mouth and leave the room, locking it behind him.

*

Jenny Gulliver's knowledge of the road networks of Germany was very limited. In fact it was non-existent. However her sense of time was not lacking at all and it seemed to her that it was taking her a lot longer to get to the airport than it had to get from it the previous day.

'Excuse me?' The driver looked at her in the rear-view mirror. 'Are you sure we're going the right way? Only it does seem to be taking a long time and I do have a plane to catch, you know?'

The driver just kept his eyes on the road.

'Excuse me? Erm….Do you speak English?'

The driver looked in the mirror again but did not reply.

Jenny was getting worried; she studied the driver's face in the mirror. It was quite expressionless but didn't look menacing. She tried again.

'We are going to the airport, aren't we? I mean, you've got the right pick-up? Jenny Gulliver going to the airport.' The man in front of her was silent. 'Will you please speak to me!'

The driver maintained his silence but Jenny became aware of the car slowing. It pulled over and stopped by the side of the road.

The driver undid his seatbelt and turned to look at Jenny. 'I am sorry, my English not good. You are Jenny Gulliver.'

It was a statement, not a query. He opened his door and stepped out of the car. The door closed behind him with a quiet click as he crossed the road and disappeared into the bushes. Jenny sat in the back of the car confused and quite frightened. She assumed the driver had gone into the bushes to relieve himself and didn't feel she should follow him. There was no telling what result that might bring! She looked out of the window at the bleak surroundings – just fields surrounded by hedgerows for as far as she could see. She sat for what seemed like ages wondering what she should do. The driver was taking a very long time. There was no way she was going to catch her plane at this rate. She made up her mind. She would risk going over to the bushes and if the driver had done a runner she'd walk as far as she had to till she found a phone. This was ridiculous. She pulled at the door handle only to find the door locked. She leaned across the front seats and tried the driver's door. That was locked as well. All the doors refused to open. Panic was setting in. Why had she been left locked in a strange car at the side of the road in a strange country? Jenny looked for the window handle but there wasn't one, all the windows were electric. She started banging on the window hoping to break out but she just hurt her hands. She was in the front of the car now, searching through the glove compartment. What for? A spare key? There was nothing but a few tissues and an old pair of gloves. She heard the driver's door open and felt the breeze in her hair, sensed the cloth over her face, smelt the musty odour and blacked out.

*

'Han, it's got to stop! You can't do this! She's just a kid! She doesn't know anything! It's gone too far!'

Marjan was beating her fists against the tall Dutchman's chest. He took hold of her and shook her. She then received the second slap across the face that morning. She dissolved onto the bed in a fit of uncontrollable sobbing. Han sat down next to her and hugged her.

'Marjan, pull yourself together, you're hysterical. What's all this about?'

Han had just been leaving the hotel to return to Holland, when the receptionist called him to the phone in the foyer. Marjan had always seemed a sensible and together sort of girl, a business woman. He wasn't prepared for the hysterical outburst that came from the other end of the phone. He had sent the chambermaid away as soon as she'd let him into Marjan's room. Marjan had gone straight for him. He took her head in his hands and looked her in her eyes.

'Now, Marjan. Tell me slowly. What's happened? I thought you were in Holland.'

The sobbing slowly subsided. Marjan looked at Han.

'You…you don't know?'

'Know what?'

'That girl. Jenny. You must have… You must have realised. Why Han? What can we gain?'

'You're not making any sense, Marjan.'

Marjan broke away from Han and moved to the other side of the room. He must know what's going on. Peiter had never told her how many people knew but surely Han and Rob must be in on it. She turned to Han who was still sitting on the bed looking perplexed.

'Han, you've got to be honest with me, please. What are you doing here?'

'You asked me to come here. You're upset.'

'No! Not here in my room. Why are you here in Germany?'

'We're making a commercial, Marjan. What's the matter with you? Do you want me to call a doctor?'

Marjan sighed. She could fell the tears starting to choke her again. 'What are you going to do with me?'

'Do with you? Nothing. I just want to make sure you're alright.'

'Like Jenny?'

'Look, what is all this about? Was Jenny upset or something? Was it about wearing the bikini? I told her she didn't have to. Rob was supposed to have told her all about it in the breakdown. I don't know how she didn't get that information. I'm sorry. She should have said.'

Marjan looked at Han. 'You really don't know what I'm talking about, do you?'

'I do try to understand. I know I'm only a man. I didn't choose the costume.'

Marjan wanted to laugh. She'd obviously credited Han with more intelligence that he warranted. It appeared that he really did think he was actually shooting commercials.

*

'How long has this been going on?

Han and Marjan had checked out of the hotel and were now sitting in the airport bar waiting for their flight to Schiphol. Marjan was filling Han in on the real business that Peiter Wiersma ran under the cover of his supermarket chain.

'The drugs have been run to the UK for some time. I became involved several months ago. I was stupid! I unwittingly carried a package for Peiter on the ferry. I thought they were proofs for a campaign. Peiter only told me when I got back. He paid me a big bonus and explained the whole set-up. I did a couple more drops before he asked me to…well…become more involved was how he put it. There was a lot of money to be made and if we weren't doing it someone else would be. I had big ideas about starting up my own advertising agency, so I could do this for a couple of years, maybe and get out with enough money.' Marjan sighed, tears welling up again. 'You don't think of the consequences when someone offers you a seemingly easy way to fulfil your dreams.'

Marjan paused, reflecting that her dream at best was never likely to materialise and, at worst, most likely to become a nightmare. She looked at Han. He was glaring at her.

'So all the adverts are really just a cover?' He was trying to control himself. His first reaction to Marjan's revelations had been incredulity but slowly, as his own position became clear to him, he passed through fear to resentment and anger.

'I'm sorry, Han. I thought you knew. It was you who encouraged Greg Driscoll to take the cans back early.'

'Hey! Hold on a moment. Is Greg Driscoll involved in this?'

'He is now. Did you really not know, Han? No. I don't think you did. I'm so sorry, I think you've been taken for a bit of a ride.'

'A bit of a ride?' Han was shouting, now and people were looking over at the two of them.

'Han. Now it's your turn to calm down. People are looking. How long have you been working with Rob Vanderlast?'

'Rob? I've known Rob since film school ten years ago. You're telling me Rob...?'

'How long have you been working with him?'

Han paused. 'The Amsterdam commercial was the first time I've actually worked with him, I suppose, since film school.' Han admitted. He had thought it a bit strange when Rob had rung him up out of the blue with the job. They hadn't been in touch for years.

'Rob's been with Peiter for two years,' Marjan continued. 'He knows what's going on obviously. That's why I thought you must as well.'

'So is that how it's done? Taking the stuff back in the film cans?'

'That's one way. Greg didn't know what he was doing, Han. He didn't do it very well, either. That, apparently, is why we now have Jenny in the position she's in.'

'What do you mean?'

Marjan sighed again. 'Peiter seems to think that Greg might have worked out a bit too much of the business. He's got him watched in the UK. He thinks he may have gone to the police.'

'And Jenny?'

'She's some sort of girlfriend of Greg's.'

'That's why Rob wanted her. I didn't audition her; Rob just said he knew the right girl for the job. At least she'll be back home now.'

'I don't think she is.'

'Then where is she?'

'Han. I don't know. What are we going to do?'

Han stood up and picked up his bag. 'For a start, we change our flights.'

***

CHAPTER TEN

Greg wasn't released from the hospital until Thursday afternoon. He had been dismissed by the hospital on the understanding that he stayed with Denis for a few days. He was not to drink or smoke and was to go straight to the doctor or the hospital if he starting getting headaches or started shaking.

Greg had wanted to go straight to a pub near the hospital but Denis persuaded him it would be better to get away from the hospital as he wasn't supposed to be drinking and they took a cab to a wine bar in the City. Greg, not being a big fan of wine, had ordered an overpriced bottle of continental lager, not Grolsch – he'd gone off Dutch lager after his recent exploits. While Denis was at the bar Greg went to the cigarette machine and purchased an extremely over-priced packet of sixteen Marlboro. Denis' reminder that he was not supposed to smoke or drink and seemed to be doing both was met with a report from Greg that after two days without alcohol or nicotine he was more likely to get a headache and start shaking unless he topped up his levels.

'Carter didn't know about the drugs until I rang and told him about breaking open the film cans.'

'But Carter did say he worked in narcotics, which doesn't seem to be true,' reminded Denis.

'I know. He behaved like a policeman, though.'

'How many detectives do you know, Greg?'

'OK! I don't know any but he played the part well if he wasn't in the force and he was never that good an actor. Maybe the police do know who he is but aren't letting us know.'

'Unlikely, I think. He talked about a drugs ring in Holland, so he knew something. He must be involved in some way.' Denis was getting exasperated with Greg's defence of Carter. 'What about the next day, him making sure you delivered the consignment, making you do the second commercial, making sure you didn't tell me or anyone else. It's all very fishy, if you ask me. And why do a runner when you arrive at the airport unless he knew you would be caught. And why plant such a small amount in your bag? They just wanted you out of the way. Carter must have got worried.'

'Whoa! Slow down, Denis. I'm only just out of hospital, my head's spinning, I can't take all this in.' Greg took a slug from his bottle – they didn't seem to do glasses for beer in this pretentious bar. 'If you're sure Carter's involved on the wrong side, what does this Cartmel message mean? Why is he leaving me coded messages?'

'That's what we need to sort out. Perhaps we should give it to the police. Let them do the work.'

Greg drained his bottle. 'I have to see them on Monday. Maybe I should take it in but...I'm not sure. I don't know who to trust anymore. Let's see if we can work out what it means first. It's your round, by the way, I've just cleaned out what little I had on these.' He held up the red and white packet of cigarettes. Denis gave him a dirty look. 'All the rest of my money was in my flat.' Greg smiled at his agent.

Being in the City, the wine bar decided to close early which they seem to think of as their prerogative in that square mile in the heart of London, and would not serve Denis any more drinks. Denis had booked a room at The Mad Hat Hotel, which was far enough away from the archaic City customs, had an on-site pub and stayed open later. They took a cab and settled into the bar.

Denis had brought his memo recorder and was quietly replaying Greg's tape over and over.

'Get Carter – Cartmel – Chase Roger. What does that mean? Is there someone in Cartmel waiting for me? Someone called Roger? For what? To finish me off? They could have done that in my flat. What's your take on it Denis?'

'If your friend Carter is involved it could be some sort of scare tactic.'

'That doesn't make sense. I can't be sure that's Carter's voice anyway. It's so blurry, could be anyone. If it is Carter he might need my help.'

Greg and Denis paused while the table was cleared. Denis went to the bar and ordered more beers. Greg listened once more to the tape, the battery was starting to run down and the voice was becoming more blurred. Greg switched it off and sat back in the chair trying to work it all out. Denis returned with the beers.

'Get Carter was a film with Michael Caine, wasn't it?' he said putting the drinks on the table.

'I don't think they're taking him to the pictures, Denis.'

'I know but what was the film about, can you remember?'

'What time is it?'

'Nearly six.'

'Right, give me a tenner and order me the speciality pie and mash with beer, I won't be a minute.'

'Where are you going?' Denis took a ten pound note from his wallet which Greg grabbed.

He didn't answer Denis' query and walked out of the pub, leaving Denis to wonder if he should go after him, he was supposed to be in his care. By the time he'd thought,

Greg was out of sight and Denis decided, against his better will, he'd have to trust him and went to order the food.

Greg hurried round the corner. There was a bookshop selling remainder books he'd spotted from the taxi. He entered the shop, noting the expression of the man behind the counter who obviously had wanted to close up. There were hundreds of books on shelves and in piles on the floor, there didn't seem to be any order to them.

'Do you have a book on films?' he asked the man.

He raised his eyes and said, 'Have you tried the film section?'

'I'm not sure where that's supposed to be,' replied Greg looking round at the piles of novels and books about sex.

Reluctantly the man left the stool on which he was ensconced, and pointed to section of shelving which had a small hand-written sticker saying 'entertainment'. Greg thanked him and started looking through the titles.

'We're about to close,' said the man. 'Looking something specific?'

'I want a book that tells me the plots of films.'

'What films?'

'A film called Get Carter.'

The man reached up and took down a thick paperback and handed it to Greg. The cover had a picture of Michael

Caine and was entitled 'The films of Michael Caine'. Greg opened the book and searched for Get Carter.

'You can't read it here. Either buy it or put it back.'

Greg handed the man his ten pound note and left the shop. The man didn't bother to call him back for his change and pocketed the seven pounds that should have been Greg's, or strictly speaking Denis's.

The pie and mash was on the table when Greg returned. He sat next to Denis and flicked through the pages until he came to Get Carter.

'What's that?' said Denis between mouthfuls.

'It's a book, Denis. You may have something with the Get Carter film. Do you know what it's about?'

'It's a long time since I saw it.'

'Well, listen to this: Jack Carter is a gangster in London; he goes up North to meet an old acquaintance for information. He goes to a racetrack, Denis. It's Newcastle not Cartmel but it's a racetrack. Are you with me?' Denis nodded. 'Someone wants to get rid of him and he comes across a businessman who's a crook and he tries to get Carter to kill another villain who's trying to take over his patch. There's a chase along a beach – is Cartmel near a beach? – where he kills the villain and then is shot himself. It all fits, Denis. Well done.'

Denis was looking at Greg in disbelief. 'Are you seriously suggesting that these people are about to play out the plot of an old film? For what reason?'

Greg was quiet for a moment. Denis was right. What reason would they have? 'There are some co-incidences though,' he said.

'Eat your pie before it goes cold.'

'How can I check whether there was racing going on at Cartmel two days ago when I was knocked out?'

'There wasn't!' said Denis smugly. 'I followed that line of investigation. There's no racing at Cartmel until Saturday.'

'This Saturday coming?'

'Yes.'

'Like the day after tomorrow?' Denis nodded. 'Right! I'm off to bed, I'm knackered.' Greg stood up and made for the hotel rooms.

'Wait! You haven't eaten your food' yelled Denis. 'You can't just walk away. What have you discovered?'

Greg turned back to Denis. 'Nothing, I'm knackered, that's all. Pay the bill, there's a good chap and I'll see you in the room.'

'Greg, I insist on knowing what's going on. I'm supposed to be looking after you, remember? You know what happened last time you left me in the dark!'

'Denis, I'll go to the police station in the morning first thing. I'm not leaving anybody in the dark so don't worry. Good night.'

Greg was asleep by the time Denis had settled the bar bill and arrived at the room. He lay on the bed and worried for the rest of the night.

*

Friday morning saw Greg Driscoll up very early. Before breakfast he had visited the local newsagent and bought a copy of 'The Sporting Life Weekender' a thick racing paper showing all the race cards for the following day.

Following their hearty breakfast, Denis had to go to his office but agreed to meet Greg for lunch at 12.30, having ascertained he would be alright visiting the police station on his own.

Greg sat in the wood and metal surroundings of the bar of The Mad Hat. It wasn't open for alcohol, so he satisfied himself with a pot of coffee. He turned to the Weekender. Something convinced him that the answer to the riddle left on his answerphone lay in Saturday's race card at Cartmel. He wasn't a regular race-goer. He had been known to put a few quid on some horses if the racing was on TV and he was bored. He turned to the pages showing the runners and riders for Saturday's meeting at Cartmel on Saturday.

*

Denis was late getting to the bar where he'd agreed to meet Greg.

'Sorry, Greg. Had a client on the phone complaining about her digs in Peterborough. What does she expect me to do about it? I didn't sort them out for her. Anyway, sorry. How did you get on at the station?'

'There's a train leaving Euston at half past three this afternoon. We need to be on it.'

'What are you talking about? I meant the police station.'

'Fine.'

'Really?'

'Yes, Denis. They accept the possibility that my being hit over the head could be connected with my bringing drugs into the country.'

'And…?'

'And nothing. I still have to see them on Monday morning under the conditions of my bail, even though it's a Bank Holiday, so the weekend's all my own. Close the office, put the answerphone on and get packed. We're going racing.'

***

CHAPTER ELEVEN

Cartmel is a village on the southern edge of the Lake District. It has an ancient priory founded by the Augustan monks in 1190. The village itself consists mainly of an historic market square surrounded by centuries old houses and inns. The nearest train station is Cark, a couple of miles from the village. Greg and Denis had caught the 15.30 train from Euston to Oxenholme Lake District station where Greg had made Denis hire a car. They travelled down the side of Lake Windermere to Newby Bridge where Greg had booked a room (in Denis' name) for the two of them. Newby Bridge was about six miles from Cartmel and, as the proprietor of the three star (and quite expensive) Newby Bridge hotel pointed out, was usually where all the racing folk liked to stay prior to the next day's racing. They were lucky to pick up a cancellation made only that day, otherwise the hotel would have been fully booked.

Denis had quizzed Greg all the way up from Euston. They had found, much to Denis' disgust, a smoking carriage near to the restaurant car. Due to some idiosyncrasy the usual licensing laws not allowing one to purchase alcohol in the afternoon didn't apply to moving transport. Hence Greg sat back in his seat armed with a couple of cans he'd got Denis to buy in the restaurant car bar.

Greg pointed to his copy of The Weekender. 'As I see it the solution to the riddle on the answerphone is contained somewhere in this masterpiece of sporting journalism.'

Denis shook his head. 'I think that bang on the head you sustained has knocked what little sense you had out of it.'

'I didn't get banged on the head! Look, there's racing at Cartmel tomorrow. There's not a lot else at Cartmel other than the racetrack, so if we assume that the Cartmel in the message is to do with the racing, then I think Carter will be there. There might be some clue in the runners and riders, I don't know.'

Denis sat back in his seat and sipped the gin & tonic he'd bought himself. 'So, basically, this could all be a wild goose chase. I'm spending a fortune pandering to a whim? There may be no connection to Cartmel at all. Is that what you're saying?'

'No. Listen.' Greg was hunched over the paper that lay on the Formica-topped table that was in between him and Denis. 'There's a horse here in the fourth race called Abrogate.'

'And?' Denis was getting seriously worried about Greg's mental state.

'It's from Germany.'

'What is?'

'The horse – Abrogate.'

'So what?'

'It's owned by...' he pointed to the owners name in the paper.

'Bloody hell, you're right.'

The horse was owned by Wiersma Lebensmittel.

'I don't like this, Greg. Shouldn't we tell the police or something?'

'Tell them what, though, Denis? I think we need to find Carter and see what's going on. My guess is he'll be in one of the bars at Cartmel. He must know something and is there undercover.'

'Then he should deal with it. It's nothing to do with us.'

'I'm under suspicion for drug running. It has everything to do with me. If you want to go home, that's fine but I'm going to find Carter. By the way, did you get hold of Jenny?'

'No. You wanted to get Carter first you said.'

There were still a good couple of hours to kill before Oxenholme. Greg went through to the restaurant car and ordered a couple of cans of Stella and set off back to his seat, completely unaware of the man in a suit who had been watching him. The man smiled to himself and set off in the opposite direction.

*

Han Koolhaven and Marjan Smits had arrived at Heathrow airport early on Friday evening. They had had to wait for an available flight from Germany for two hours, Marjan getting more and more agitated as the time went by. They tried phoning Denis Young but had only got an engaged signal. Marjan had tried again just before they went through to departures but, although no longer engaged, there was no answer.

*

Jenny sat up slowly. She was cold. Her arms were sore and her head ached as if she had a heavy cold or flu. Her hands were tied and attached to something above her head. She was naked and uncovered.

'Oh, please God, no,' she tried to say but the words did not get past her sore, sore throat.

Something stirred in the shadowy corner of the room. She tried to move away from the advancing figure but it appeared her feet were also tied to the bed, her legs splayed. She looked around in a blind panic. She was evidently in some sort of room with painted un-papered brick walls. A warehouse or an old empty office. She tried to scream but, once more, the muscles in her throat refused to co-operate.

'So the sleeping beauty has awaked.' The voice was deep and had a German accent. Jenny did not recognise it. It wasn't the so-called taxi driver she was sure. She peered through the gloom but was unable to make out a face. A pain shot through her head as a very bright light was suddenly switched on. Jenny tried to cover herself by bringing up her knees as close to her chest as they would but it was pointless. Her feet were tethered.

'What's the matter, little one? Gone all shy? You weren't shy on the front of that car in your bikini, were you? Or last night.' He let out a deep guttural laugh. 'Oh no you were not shy at all last night or the night before.'

'Who are you?' Jenny's voice croaked into life. 'Where am I? How long have I been here? What have you done with me, you bastard? I'll kill you. I know a lot of people, you'd better watch out.' What was she saying? I know a lot of people? Why didn't she just shut up, take what was coming and get out alive.

'You are not in a position to be telling anyone anything and as for killing me…? Have a go, my dear, have a go.' As the figure leaned towards her Jenny brought her knee up sharply as far as the ropes on her ankles would let her. It caught him somewhere and made him gasp, followed by the deep guttural laugh again. The next thing she felt was a thud to the side of her head and the light went out again.

*

Han and Marjan were standing outside Denis' flat. They had been ringing Denis' office since the previous night. The answerphone had picked up the call and gave his home number for emergencies. This was certainly an emergency! There had been no reply at the home number either. They'd tried both number this morning with the same result and Han and Marjan spent some time searching through all the D. Young's in the London Telephone directory until they found the address that corresponded to the number and taken a cab straight there.

'He's not going to be in, otherwise he'd have answered his phone,' Han had protested.

'He may just have been at the shops. We have to try, Han.'

They had spent the previous evening in a hotel near Marble Arch. They'd sat in the hotel bar trying to work out some sort of campaign. They had to let Denis know that Jenny was in trouble. Quite what they expected him to do they weren't sure. It had been a spur-of-the-moment decision to fly straight to London. Marjan was worried about her own position, after all she knowingly helped Peiter Wiersma run his business and she knew what he was up to.

It was now just after 10 o'clock on Saturday morning, there was no reply from Denis' doorbell as there had been no reply from his phone.

'What are we going to do, Han? We can't just stay here. I dread to think what danger Jenny's in.'

Marjan's concern was genuine. Apart from the guilt she felt at helping to get Jenny into this mess, she had a feeling of affinity with her. They had chatted for a long time in the hotel bar in Germany and for the first time in many years Marjan had felt she could open up and confide in Jenny a little. She'd never spent much time getting to know people well. She'd convinced herself that personal relationships of any kind only hampered the road to success and success was what she wanted more than anything. Standing in this suburban street in London she was starting to doubt her conviction and starting to re-evaluate the consequences of achieving her goal. Marjan leaned on the doorbell marked Young again.

A window opened on the first floor above them.

'Can I help you?' A middle-aged woman in a housecoat and wielding a yellow duster was glaring at them disapprovingly.

'Hello. Yes, we are looking for Mr Young,' said Han.

'He's not in.'

'We're aware of that. Do you know where we could get hold of him?'

'I'm only the cleaner.'

Han could not see the relevance of that statement but continued with the questioning.

'Do you clean for Mr Young? Did he say when he'd be back?'

'He doesn't tell me anything. How am I supposed to know when he's going off gallivanting? He won't give me a key and yet he expects his place to be clean. What am I supposed to do? And I've got a bad back.'

Marjan decided to take over from Han who was looking totally bewildered.

'Do you have any idea how we could reach Mr Young? It's very important. A friend of his is in trouble and we must reach him somehow.'

'Trouble? What sort of trouble? I don't want no trouble.'

'It's to do with his work.'

'Oh, is it an actress? Surprise, surprise! I can guess what sort of trouble she'll be in then. He's a nice man, Mr Young, but he cares too much for the people he gets involved with. I've told him before he ought to settle down at his age.'

'It's not that sort of trouble, Mrs..?'

'I don't give my name to strangers.'

'It's to do with a contract abroad. It's very important we get hold of him as soon as possible.'

'Well, I don't know where he's gone. You could try Helen at number forty-two,' she pointed across the road. 'She works in his office sometimes but I don't suppose he'll have told her anything either.'

'Thanks very much, we'll do that. Sorry if we've bothered you.'

'It's no bother to me, dear. Put me a bit behind but I'll just have to stay a bit longer. I don't suppose you'll find him, though. I'd try his office after the Bank Holiday he doesn't usually miss out on his work.' She closed the window but Han and Marjan were aware of her watching them as they crossed the road to number forty-two.

Helen Clarke was an actress in her mid-twenties. She had been blessed with a baby son eighteen months previously. The boy's father had left just under two years ago but Helen was a stubborn girl and determined to bring up the child on her own, without help or contact from the boy's father. Denis, being 'a nice man' and also needing someone to help out on an ad hoc basis in his office had come to an agreement with Helen that suited them both and the social services didn't need to know about. Partly because of this, two people turning up unannounced on a Saturday morning made her suspicious and not very communicative.

'Can I see some sort of identification, please,' she said as she answered the door to Han's knocking.

'I'm, afraid we don't really have any. Oh, I have my passport somewhere. We need to get hold of Denis Young, very urgently.'

'Well, I'm sorry I can't help you. I only see him very occasionally and then usually just to wave to across the road.'

Han was getting impatient. 'I thought you worked for him.'

'Who told you that?'

'The cleaning lady across the road.'

'Oh, did she? She doesn't declare that work, you know and she's on the dole.'

'I really don't care! Can you help us get in touch with Denis or not?'

'No! I'm sorry, I can't.'

Marjan stepped in front of Han just as Helen was about to shut the door and handed her a piece of paper she'd been writing on.

'Helen, here's where we're staying. Please if you hear from Denis tell him to get in touch with us. It really is very important. Someone could be in serious trouble.'

Helen closed the door.

*

'Jenny? Jenny?....Wake up, Jenny. How are you, Jenny? Wake up now.'

Jenny's eyes slowly opened and came to focus upon the puffy face of a large man sporting a huge walrus moustache.

'How are you Jenny? Are you feeling better now?'

'Who are you?' she croaked.

'My name is Peiter Wiersma, my dear. I run the company you've just been working for.'

Jenny looked around her and saw she was still in the same room and in the same bed but she was now wearing her long thick woollen sweater and her hands and feet were no longer tied. She also had her knickers on but no jeans. There was a blanket on the bed.

'What's happened? Where am I?' Jenny's voice sounded as though she'd just smoked forty cigarettes consecutively.

Wiersma smiled at her. 'You seem to have had some sort of accident, Jenny. You were found wandering around by the side of the road. You've been asleep for nearly three days. I thought you were never going to wake up. And I was hoping you could tell me what happened but there's no rush, you have some more rest if you need it.'

'Where am I? In hospital?'

'Yes. A sort of hospital, you'll be well looked after.'

'Who took my clothes?'

'You are wearing your clothes, Jenny.'

'No. Earlier I wasn't, and I still don't have my jeans.'

'Your jeans were badly torn, Jenny. Anna here has got you something else, it's OK.'

Jenny thought it was anything but OK. She was confused and frightened and yet, somehow seeing Peiter made her feel slightly safer. Marjan had said he was basically a good man even if he was ruthless when it came to business.

The room was well lit now. It was small and, apart from the bed had just a small table and chair upon which sat a woman in a nurse's uniform. The walls were painted in semi-gloss magnolia paint. It looked cold and uncomforting but clean. Very clean. There did not appear to be anyone else in the room. Jenny turned towards Peiter Wiersma. Her body still ached.

'Who was it that…that was here earlier?'

'There's been no-one here but the nurse since you arrived. Has there, Anna?'

The nurse stood, almost to attention. Jenny expected her to salute but she just said 'that is so' and sat down.

Jenny looked at the nurse who smiled back. She had a kindly face but, Jenny felt, not a friendly one. 'There was a man here earlier. I didn't have any clothes on. And there was no blanket on the bed. There was no light and it was cold.'

Anna stood up and went over to Jenny's bedside. She was carrying a long skirt with a flowery pattern on it 'You've had a fright, Jenny, and you've been dreaming. You were thrashing about all over the place. Here, put this on, you'll be more comfortable.'

'There was a man here. You weren't here. He…he attacked me.'

'Jenny. You've had a trauma. You're bound to think the worst. It is very common to feel like this.'

Jenny sat up in the bed. Her head was throbbing but apart from her aching limbs she felt OK physically. Anna helped her put the skirt on. It came down almost to her ankles and looked stupid. It was made from a flimsy material and Jenny suspected it was see-through. She straightened it over her legs as best as she could.

'Can I go home now, Mr Wiersma?'

'Not yet, Jenny. I've let your agent know and he's coming out to get you. You're safest here until he arrives. Get some rest. He's on his way as we speak.'

*

Jenny's agent was not on his way to Germany, he was sitting in the small bar of the paddock enclosure of Cartmel racecourse. He and Greg Driscoll had tried in vain to get into the members' enclosure but were told, rather rudely Denis thought, that there were no daily tickets for the members' enclosure today, not for love or money. Denis was short of both at the moment anyway. The Bridge Hotel was quite a high-class hotel and consequently had quite a high tariff. On top of that he'd had to pay for two entrances to the racecourse, race cards and several drinks. Greg pointing out that he hadn't been paid for his commercials yet (and was never likely to) didn't help Denis' mood.

Greg was in an excitable mood and feeling rather smug. He'd thought through his theory and convinced himself he was right about the meaning of the answerphone message. He was standing at the bar, next to Denis, looking round eagerly at the sparse crowd of punters gathered in the room. Greg and Denis had not seen any races, they'd spent the afternoon searching bars for the promised arrival of Brian Carter. It seems they were going to be disappointed.

'What does he look like, Greg?' Denis was getting impatient.

Greg ignored him.

'Come on, Greg. Admit it. This is a complete waste of time, not to mention money!'

'I'm not leaving, Denis, until I see Carter. I know I'm not wrong about the message. Can you explain…?' He was cut short by the sight of a man in a deerstalker and cape striding towards him. The man prodded Greg in the chest.

'Are you Driscoll?'

'I might be. Who's asking?'

'I'm a very busy man, Mr Driscoll. I'm Colonel West, a steward here and I don't take kindly to having mine and the committee's time being wasted.' The man thrust a piece of paper at Greg, turned on his heel and left the bar.

'What is it, Greg?' Denis was at Greg's elbow looking at the piece of paper. It was a sheet from a memo pad with 'While you were out' printed in black at the top. Underneath was scrawled: *message for Greg Driscoll in*

Paddock Bar: *GET OUT IF YOU KNOW WHAT'S GOOD FOR YOU'.*

Greg went after the caped steward but as he got to the door and looked out the steward was nowhere to be seen. Denis caught up with him.

'What does it mean, Greg?'

'It means, my dear friend, that despite your protestations to the contrary, I was right.'

'Was that Carter? Is he here?'

'No, that was Colonel West. He's a steward here.'

Denis looked at his race card. There was a list of stewards for this meeting. Colonel West's name was not there.

'He's not a steward here, Greg.'

Greg looked at his agent, smiled and shook his head. 'Really, Denis? You do surprise me. I wouldn't have thought stewards had anything better to do just after a race than to run messages!'

'This isn't the time for sarcasm, Greg. Let's get after him.'

'No. Let's have another drink.' Greg walked back to the bar and ordered a bottle of Pils. He knew there was no point in trying to catch the bogus colonel. He hadn't seen his face and undoubtedly the cape and deerstalker would no longer be adorning the mystery messenger. Greg looked at the message again as Denis joined him at the bar. 'Pay for the drinks, Denis, there's good chap.'

Greg took his drink over to a table. The third race was starting so the bar was quite empty. Denis brought his own bottle of Pils and sat down next to him.

'We really ought to leave, Greg. You can't have a clearer message than that. I think we should get the police involved now, don't you?'

'No I don't, Denis. Abrogate runs in the next race. There has to be a link. Where's my drink?'

'There!' Denis pointed to the bottle on the table. Greg picked it up and poured most of the contents down his throat.

'Quick then. Set 'em up Joe. The third race has just finished there'll be a queue at the bar in a minute.'

Denis thought about protesting but the doors to the bar opened and people started pouring in to either celebrate their luck or drown their sorrows, so he rushed to the bar and ordered two more bottles, and returned to Greg at his table.

Greg was looking at the open newspaper in front of him. 'Abrogate in the Longdell Chase, a two mile five furlong...'

'What did you say?' Denis seemed suddenly excited.

'A two mile...'

'No. Before that.'

'Abrogate in the Longdell Chase?'

'The Longdell Chase, yes. Greg, There's a hotel…No, that's silly. I'm getting as bad as you.'

'What hotel?'

'The Longdell Chase is a hotel on the banks of Lake Windermere.'

'As well as the name of the fourth race on a Saturday afternoon's race card at Cartmel, you mean?'

'Do you know what abrogate means, Greg?'

'It doesn't mean anything, does it? It's a horse's name.'

'Abrogate means to rub out or cancel.'

'Sorry, I didn't have a university education.' Greg thought for a minute before slowly adding, 'I think I see what you're getting at. Rub out Carter at the Longdell Chase. No. It's ridiculous.'

'There must be other words in the message that we can't hear for the crackling.'

'Get Carter – that's clear enough. Then there's a crackle and Cartmel – well, that's the racecourse. Crackle then Chase. That could just be the name of the race the Longdell Chase.'

'Or it could be the name of the hotel.'

'And who's this Roger chap?'

'I think that might be the recognised code for received as in Roger and out.'

Greg nodded. He felt a bit stupid.

'What do we do now?' said Denis.

'Lend us a fiver. I'm going to have a bet.' He picked up Denis' bottle. 'And don't drink any more, you're driving, remember?'

*

Abrogate won the Longdell Chase at 13-2. Greg picked up his winnings, waited until the bar started to clear for the fifth race and headed for the exit. Denis had hoped that something would have happened at the racecourse, Carter turning up, having a drink and explaining everything. No rubbing out, no abrogation, no more trouble with the police. Denis' hopes had faded along with all the punters who hadn't backed Abrogate in the Longdell Chase.

Three-quarters of an hour later Denis and Greg were driving alongside Lake Windermere, heading towards the Longdell Chase Hotel. Denis had managed to book a room for them from the phone-box in the paddock area. Apparently they too had just had a last-minute cancellation so they could fit them in.

Denis wondered how often people cancelled a booking just before someone else was about to ring a hotel. Greg had wanted Denis to ask if a Mr Brian Carter was staying there but Denis pointed out that, if he was, he probably wouldn't use his own name.

*

The phone rang in Marjan's room just after five o'clock. She and Han had spent the day at the hotel trying to work out what to do next. Their decision to try and find Jenny in Germany was desperate to say the least but it was all they could think of. The phone message gave them an excuse to throw that idea out of the window.

'Phone call for Miss Smits,' the receptionist said.

'Thank you. I am Miss Smits. Hello?'

There was a pause at the end of the line followed by a quiet voice. 'Hello. I don't know if I should be doing this or not. It's Helen Clarke. We spoke earlier. At my house.'

'Yes. Hello, Helen.' Marjan tried to sound encouraging. Helen was obviously nervous; Marjan didn't want her to hang up.

'I'm sorry I was a bit rude earlier. I've had a stressful week. Look, I went shopping this afternoon and when I got back there was a message on my answerphone. You said you wanted to talk to Denis. Can you tell me why?'

'It's a very long story, Helen, but basically one of his clients is in trouble out in Germany and we want to see if we can help.'

'And who are you?'

'I can understand that you feel protective towards Denis. We are trying to help, believe me. We work for the production company that his client is working for and there are a few contractual problems that have to be sorted out.'

'Is this the job Jenny Gulliver's on?'

'Yes it is.'

'There shouldn't be any contractual problems. I was in the office when the contract came through. I typed her commission slip. She should be back home now. What's happened?'

'There's a problem. She's stuck out in Germany. I can only explain to Denis, you must understand. Do you know where he is?'

'Well, he left a message saying he might not be back in time to open the office on Tuesday morning, so could I do it. Apparently he's in the Lake District.'

'Do you have a number?'

There was a long pause.

'He's staying at the Longdell Chase Hotel in Windermere.'

'Thanks, Helen. You've been a great help.'

'I hope everything's alright. I'll be in the office on Tuesday morning if you need me. I hope Jenny's OK. This is the first job we've sent her on, you know. You can't tell me anything more, I suppose?'

'I'm sorry, Helen. We must speak to Denis. I'll try and call you.'

'It'll have to be at the office on Tuesday.'

'OK, Helen. Thanks again, Bye.'

*

Greg and Denis arrived at The Longdell Chase at half-past five. There seemed to be some sort of wedding reception going on. A lot of attractive young ladies in long dresses. Denis dragged Greg away to the reception desk and checked in.

'I think this was a good idea, Denis. I sort of hope Carter's not here so we can gate-crash that wedding party. Very nice hotel, isn't it?'

'Very expensive hotel, Greg. Now. What do we do next?'

'Dinner?'

'I do have a limit on my flexible friend, you know.'

'I'll pay you back, one day. Look, if we sit in the restaurant we'll be less conspicuous and we can watch to see who's around. Look for Carter or anyone else I might recognise.'

'Who are you expecting to recognise?'

'Who knows, Denis? Who knows?'

Less than an hour later, Greg and Denis were in the bar at the Longdell Chase, observing. Denis had had to fork out more money to buy Greg a shirt and tie, trousers and a jacket from the hotel shop. There was a dress code. He was going to have to work really hard when he got back to his office to recompense himself. Only some of this could go down to essential business expenses! A man in a black tailcoat with a white waistcoat, black bow tie, grey pin-striped trousers and shiny patent leather shoes approached them. He had a white cloth over his arm so Greg assumed he must be a waiter or something. He turned to Denis.

'Mr Young, there's a phone call for you. You can take it at reception or I can have it put through to your room.'

'Thank you. I'll take it at reception.' The waiter left.

Greg stood up to go with Denis but was promptly told to sit down.

'It's not for you. It'll be Helen from the office, I phoned her earlier.'

'How did the penguin know you were Mr Young?'

'It's that sort of hotel, Greg.'

'It could be a trap to lure you away.'

'You just sit here and carry on observing. After all, I don't really know what I'm looking for.'

Denis went off to reception leaving Greg to pretend to study the menu. He didn't know what he was looking for either. The more he thought about it the more ridiculous it all seemed. He had convinced himself that something was meant to happen and was meant to happen in this hotel.

When Denis returned his face was pale.

'What's the matter? You look dreadful.'

Denis sat down, he couldn't look at Greg. 'It's Jenny. It seems she in some sort of trouble. That was Han Koolhaven on the phone. He and Marjan are in the UK looking for us. They've hired a car and are driving up here now. We're to wait till they arrive.'

'What's happened to Jenny?'

'Han couldn't say much, he said he'd explain when they got here.'

'If you've got Jenny in the shit, I'll….'

'…If you'd told me what was going on this wouldn't have happened.'

'Hang on. It's a trap.' Greg looked at Denis. 'Han and Marjan? Who both work for the company that employed me – and now Jenny – to run their drugs? Why are they coming here? How did they know we were here? What the hell is going…'

'I told Helen we were here. I thought she might need to know where I was as she might have to open the office if we're not back. She told Han.'

'Oh great! Why not put a big sign up with a pointy finger saying 'here they are, come and get 'em''

'I'm sorry, Greg. I don't think they're involved. They sounded worried about Jenny.'

'I bet they are. I saw that Marjan with Wiersma. Thick as thieves – or drug runners! Did you tell them why we're here?'

Denis was silent.

'You did, didn't you?'

'I told them we received a note and we worked it out but I didn't give any details.'

'You didn't need to.'

'Mr Driscoll?' A porter with a silver tray was standing next to Greg. He leaned over and proffered the tray towards Greg. On it there was an envelope with Greg Driscoll printed on it. Greg looked at the porter. 'Who gave you this?'

'It was left at reception for you, sir. I'm afraid it's been there since this morning. We didn't realise you were booked in in Mr Young's name or we would have delivered it to you on your arrival.'

'How did you know I was here now?'

The porter moved a little closer to Greg. 'We've just changed the shift, sir and the assistant manager blew his top when he saw your envelope sitting there. The receptionist looked through all the names in the registration book. It should have been noticed when you checked in. I'm sorry, sir, it's very bad service. The manager asked if you would like a drink on the house.'

'What all night?'

'No, sir. Just the one each. I'll come back and take your order when you've finished your current drinks. Will that be all for now, sir?'

'Erm…Has anyone else asked if I was staying here at all?'

'No, sir.'

'Thanks. Get yourself a drink.' Greg put a pound coin on the silver tray. The porter looked at it and tried, unsuccessfully, to conceal his disdain. 'We've finished these drinks, could you bring a very large scotch for me and a very large G & T for my friend.'

The porter nodded and went over to the bar as Greg opened his envelope. A shiver ran through his spine as he read the contents.

***

CHAPTER TWELVE

'What does it say?' Denis stared at Greg's face. The colour had drained completely and his mouth was gaping, his eyes glazed. He handed Denis the printed card he'd revealed in the envelope. It was black-edged invitation card.

YOU ARE CORDIALLY INVITED TO MR BRIAN CARTER'S FAREWELL PERFORMANCE IN THE BOAT-HOUSE AT 8PM. BLACK TIE WOULD BE APPROPRIATE.

Greg was up and moving before Denis had finished reading the card. He followed him out of the bar and caught up with him at the reception area.

'Who left this for me?' Greg was almost shouting at the astonished young girl behind the desk and waving the envelope in her face.

'Greg! Wait!' Denis pulled Greg away from poor girl. 'I'm sorry, my friend has just had some rather distressing news.'

The man in the tailcoat came over. 'Is there a problem, sir?'

'Too right there is!' replied Greg. 'Who left this for me?' He waved the envelope again.

'I'm sorry, sir. It was just left at reception. I don't actually know who left it, there was a note asking for it to be delivered to you.'

'Hand-written note?'

'No, typed, sir.'

'Don't you check these things? Shouldn't you know who you're delivering messages from?'

'We operate a strict code of confidence and privacy, sir. It's not our job to delve into people's private correspondence.'

'Well, you should…'

'It's alright,' Denis butted in. He could see Greg was getting out of control. 'It was just a bit unexpected.'

'Is there anything I can do to help at all, sir?' The penguin had somehow managed to move Denis and Greg to a quiet corner of the reception area.

'Yes. Is there a boat-house somewhere near here?'

'We're at the side of a lake, sir. There are many boat-houses.'

Greg was getting fed-up with this supercilious toff. 'Well, thanks for your help,' he said and turned to go.

'There is what we call our boat-house, of course. We let it as a luxury self-contained cottage.'

'Why didn't you say that in the first place?' Greg turned back to face the penguin. Denis stepped between them.

'Could you let us know if it's booked at the moment?'

The tailcoat went to the reception desk, Denis following in his wake. He flicked through the registration book, shut it and said 'yes. If that will be all I'm quite busy.' Denis nodded and the penguin waddled of to his station with his nose in the air.

'Stuck-up twat!' Greg said almost too loudly. Denis took him to one side.

'Let's go back to the bar,' he said.

Denis guided Greg past the tailcoat and led him to the bar. He ordered more drinks.

'We have to assume the boat-house on the card is the one in the hotel. What are we going to do, Greg?'

Greg stood up and headed for the door. 'I know what I'm going to do.' He strode to the reception desk and aware of the penguin's beady eyes asked who was booked into the boat-house.

Denis hurried after him and intervened. 'I'm sorry, my friend is a little agitated. We've had an invitation to the boat-house this evening.' Denis leaned forward and whispered, 'Mr Driscoll is an actor, he's in the middle of a big film and we want to make sure this isn't a scam by the paparazzi.'

The receptionist looked at Greg in the hope that she recognised him. She gave him her best smile, just in case, then wrote something hurriedly on a piece of paper and handed it to Denis.

'I'm not supposed to do this,' she whispered. The penguin was on his way over, Denis quickly pocketed the note and said loudly to the receptionist. 'Thank you very much for your help,' and then to the penguin, 'excellent service. That girl is very good, look after her.' He grabbed Greg and walked out onto the terrace behind the bar. The man in the tailcoat looked quizzically at the receptionist before returning to his post.

There were metal tables and chairs on the terrace and Denis forced Greg into one of the seats overlooking the grounds of the hotel. Greg was still agitated, he stood up again and was about to return to the reception but Denis grabbed hold of him. 'For God's sake! Sit down and calm down for a minute.'

'I want to know who's in that boat-house.'

Denis reached into his pocket and read the note. 'Oh God!'

Greg stopped and looked at him. 'What?'

Denis handed him the note which he took one look at and sank back into the chair.

'Rob Vanderlast! Bastard!' Greg knew Rob must be involved in some way. Was he the 'big man' the police were after? Perhaps he should ring the police now and tell them what was going on. But what was going on? What was going on in that boat-house this evening? He stood up and beckoned to Denis.

'Come on. We've a farewell performance to attend.'

'You're not serious? Don't you think we should wait?'

'Wait? What for?'

'Greg, we know it's Vanderlast down there but we don't know how dangerous he is. Let's wait for Han and Marjan to arrive and check it out then.'

'Good idea! Han Koolhaven and Mata Hari Marjan. They won't be in on it, of course. They're not colleagues of Mr Vanderlast or anything. Why do you think they're coming up here? Do you think they're the cavalry come to rescue us? I think it more likely they're making sure the job is finished properly this time unlike at my flat!'

'No. I spoke to them on the phone, remember. They are really worried. I don't think they know what's going on.'

'Like hell!' Greg strode towards the steps at edge of the terrace. 'It looks like this leads down to the lake. That must be where the boat-house is. Are you coming?'

'Greg!' Denis tried to protest but his friend and client was off down the path towards the lake. He sighed and followed him down the steps. He caught up with him at the end of the long sloping lawn that ran down to the water's edge. Greg was standing looking at a brick built folly resembling a tiny castle next to a jetty that ran a few yards into the lake. It was a two story building, the lower half being open at the water's edge where small sailing dinghy were kept next to a launching ramp, the upper half had been converted into the luxury self-contained apartment rented out by the hotel.

'Is that the boat-house, do you suppose?' said Denis catching his breath.

'Must be.' Greg didn't take his eyes off the little house.

'Shall we go in, then?'

'No. I'll go in. Your name wasn't on the invitation.' Greg started to walk towards the boat-house. Denis grabbed his arm.

'If you think I'm letting you go in there alone, you're very wrong.'

Greg stopped and looked at his friend. 'I don't know what I'm going to find in there, Denis. I suspect it's not going to be particularly pleasant. If there's danger there, I need someone out here to get help. Give me five minutes, if I don't wave to you from that window up there, you can come in and get what's left of me.'

Denis was about to speak but Greg put his hand up and hushed him. He turned and went towards the steps to the upper level of the folly without looking back. Denis found himself a position where he was out of sight yet could still see the window in the upper chamber.

Greg paused at the top of the steps. The door to the room was open and the lights were on but he could not see anyone inside. He put his head round the door and called. 'Brian? Brian it's Greg?' There was no reply. He tried again. 'Brian? Brian Carter?' Nothing. 'Rob Vanderlast? Are you there?' Greg listened. There was no sound. He took a step inside. The place looked empty and apart from the lights being on it didn't look like it had been occupied in the recent past. It was cold. He stepped out onto the top of the steps again, looking for Denis. He couldn't see him. He wished he'd agreed to let him come up with him now. He could see the wedding party having cocktails on the terrace. It was like a scene from a Noel Coward play. There were dresses which were open at the back almost past the line of decency, dinner suits as black as pitch with knife-edge creases. All that was lacking was the long cigarette holders but smoking was no longer de rigueur among society. Standing looking at this scene, Greg thought that was about all that was different. They were all living there in their own little world completely unaware that a few hundred yards from them there was a very frightened man about to enter somewhere deeper than hell. He had an invite with black edges more usual for a funeral. Was that where he was going? Whose funeral was it, though, that's what worried Greg most? He took a deep breath and walked straight into the main living room. There was no-one there. There was a mock-Turkish rug covering most of the floor, a table and two chairs next to a window overlooking the lake and a long sideboard running down the length of one side of the room. Above, there was an open-plan mezzanine floor with a double bed. Greg stepped into the middle of the room and looked around. He went to the table and chairs and looked out at the lake. He was struck by the beauty of the sun setting over the water. He resisted the urge to sit and just look at the lake.

'Greg! Greg! Are you there?'

Denis' voice made him jump. He turned to where he was standing in the doorway.

'Have you found something? What's the matter?'

'You didn't wave.'

'Oh God! What's the matter with you? I've only just got in here. It's empty. This is just a wild goose chase. Come on.' Greg moved towards the door. Denis had entered the room and was surveying the scene.

'It's nice here, isn't it? Wonder what it costs to rent it?'

'I really don't care, Denis. Come on.'

Denis started back towards the door. As he passed by the sideboard he noticed an envelope perched against a clock. It had Greg's name on it.

'Is this the envelope you were given at hotel?'

Greg looked at the envelope. It was unopened. He slid a finger under the flap and tore the envelope away from the card inside. It was another black-edged invitation.

JOIN ME IN MY BOAT. WE'RE GOING FOR A BLOW ON THE LAKE – BRIAN

Greg went back to the window. He couldn't see a boat. Presumably Brian was waiting in the boat-house area underneath them. He raced to the door, leaving the card on the sideboard. Denis picked up the card, read it and hurried after Greg.

'Greg! Wait!' he caught up with Greg. He was standing looking at a man lying in a small boat with an outboard motor at one end. Denis took Greg's arm. 'Who's that?'

'It's him, Denis. It's Brian Carter.'

'Is he alive?'

'Of course he is.' The man in the boat was wearing a light blue summer suit and dark glasses. His legs were crossed and he seemed to be listening to a personal stereo through large headphones. His head was leaning back on the prow of the boat and he looked very relaxed. He looked like a man waiting for his friend before going out on the lake. There was a case of beer and a bottle of scotch on the wooden seat next to his legs.

'I don't like it, Greg. Let's go,' he whispered.

'No. Maybe Brian can explain what's been going on, where he's been hiding, what his involvement, if any, was with the drugs ring. Basically what the hell's going on?'

'It's got to be a trap, Greg.'

'What sort of trap?' Greg looked around him. 'There's no-one else here.' He went towards the boat.

'Call out to him first.'

Greg turned to Denis. 'He's got headphones on. Look. Brian? Hello?' There was no response. 'Go away, Denis. I want him to think I'm on my own'

'I'll be right behind the boathouse. If you need me, yell.' Denis walked round the corner of the building. Greg took a step towards Brian Carter. He could suddenly see Brian's face clearly. It was grey and lifeless.

It all happened very quickly. Greg could not explain what made him throw himself face-down into the shallow waters at the edge of the lake in front of him. Maybe it was Denis shouting or did that happen later? Maybe it was fear; bottling out. Maybe he saw the puff of smoke escape from the personal stereo hanging round Brian Carter's neck. Whatever it was, it saved his life. There was a blinding flash of light followed by an ear-splitting explosion. The water around Greg seemed to boil for a split second and then turned icy-cold. Something wet hit the back of his neck. It was a piece of the very ex DC Carter. Greg had dragged himself from the water and was throwing up when Denis reached him.

The wedding party had been brought to an abrupt halt and a number of well-dressed young men were to be seen racing across the well-groomed lawns towards the banks of Lake Windermere, which was now rippling gently, as if nothing had happened.

'Greg, are you alright?' It seemed a stupid question to ask but was all Denis could manage to say.

Before Greg could answer, a burly figure ran towards them and grabbed both of them by the collars, dragging them roughly towards the oncoming stampede of wedding guests.

'Get back! Get back! Keep away, it's not safe!' The man was pulling Greg and Denis who were half-running, half-stumbling in his clutch. A few of the guests paused not knowing whether to attack or obey the charging bull-like figure coming towards them.

'Please! Get away! Let us through! Keep away from the water!'

The suited mob gave way and followed the odd threesome back to the steps of the terrace. Several of the female guests and the bride were screaming hysterically and were vainly being comforted by the few men not brave, or perhaps foolhardy, enough to run from the relative safety of the terrace towards the explosion. Members of staff were appearing on the terrace trying to restore some sort of calm.

The man threw Greg and Denis onto the terrace steps. 'What the hell do you think you're playing at Driscoll?'

Greg looked at the angry face glaring at him from above. It was not a face he recognised.

'Who are you? How do you know my name?'

The crowd of onlookers was increasing; they seemed to be surrounding Greg, closing in on him, smothering him. He could hear sirens in the distance. His head was swimming and his body decided to switch off, he closed his eyes and fell limp.

*

Han and Marjan arrived at the Longdell Chase just after 9pm. As they pulled into the drive Marjan grabbed hold of Han's arm. There were police cars all over the car park. A young man in uniform came up to the car window and explained that no guests could be admitted at present, there had been a fire or something but temporary accommodation had been arranged for anyone booked into the hotel at the Wood Hotel further up the lake. Han spoke to the constable.

'What is the problem, officer?'

'It's not anything to worry about, sir. There's been an incident and no-one's allowed in at present. I'm sure everything will be back to normal by the morning.'

'Did you say there was a fire or something,' asked Marjan leaning over to the open driver's window. 'Was anyone hurt?'

'There haven't been any casualties reported, madam, as far as I know. If you could move along now, please, the Wood is expecting you.' The policeman moved away from the window and directed Han towards the exit.

Han doubted the Wood would be expecting them as they hadn't got a booking at the Longdell Chase but there didn't seem any point in arguing. He waved a thank you to the officer and headed out of the drive. He turned right and went back the way they came.

'Where are we going, Han?'

'I saw a sign for a country hotel just back here, I think. Ah yes.' He took a right turn down a winding road towards the lake and turned into The Crag Country House Hotel. The middle-aged woman behind the reception desk looked at them rather sniffily as they asked if there was any chance of a room for the night.

'Are you married?' she said

Marjan was about to ask what the hell that had to do with anything but Han butted in with an affirmation that they were. Marjan glared at him. The woman looked like she didn't believe them. 'We only have a four-poster room left,' she said. 'And they're expensive!' she added as if they looked like they couldn't afford to stay at a hotel like this.

'That's fine, thank you for your help,' said Han and handed the receptionist his gold American Express card.

*

Greg woke up in his hotel room. He was in bed wearing only his damp boxer shorts. Someone was at his bedside and he could sense more people over by the window.

'He's coming round.' It was a gentle voice, light but definitely male. 'How are you feeling, Greg?'

'What am I doing here? Who are you? What happened?' Greg's head was heavy as if hung-over.

'That's what we're here to find out.' A tall man broke away from the window group and approached Greg's bed. Recollection forced its way into Greg's dulled thought patterns. Of course. The explosion. Is this the police? Or one of Vanderlast's mob?

'Detective Inspector Milne.' The tall man had his hand held out as he introduced himself.

'Yes,' croaked Greg. 'We spoke in London, I remember.'

'Are you up to answering a few questions yet?'

The young man by the bed interceded. 'I'm not sure he should be disturbed just yet,'

Greg interrupted the kindly-voiced man. 'It's OK, doctor. I'm getting used to this.'

'I'm not a doctor, I'm a nurse. The doctor will be back shortly. I think we should wait and let him look you over first.'

'It's OK.' Greg insisted. He wanted to know what was going on as much as the police. 'I get knocked about all the time these days, don't worry.'

'Well, you're not my responsibility so don't blame me when the doctor comes in and gives you a good ticking off.'

Greg smiled, which hurt the sides of his face. He must remember not to try and be jolly. 'I won't blame you, my friend, I assure you. Thanks for looking after me.'

The nurse sniffed and sat back in his chair at the side of the bed. Greg looked round the room. Apart from the DI, there was the burly man who'd pulled him from the lake, the penguin and a young man with short hair in a light blue shirt – a policeman, definitely. There was no sign of Greg's agent.

'Where's Denis? Is he OK?'

'He's in another room, Mr Driscoll, answering a few questions as well.' DI Milne sat on the edge of Greg's bed. He added, as if it were an afterthought, 'he's fine, by the way.'

Greg pointed to the burly man. 'What's he doing here? And how did he know my name?'

'Sergeant Murray? Come here Sergeant.' The burly man came over to the bed.

'Sorry if I seemed to be a bit rough with you, sir. I had to get you away from the scene in case there was another explosion. There often is, in my experience,' he said.

DI Milne dismissed Murray with a wave of his hand, 'Now, Mr Driscoll, perhaps you could let us know what you think's been going on here and, more to the point, what the hell you think you're playing at?'

*

Han and Marjan were in the small wood-panelled bar of the Crag Country House Hotel. They had a good range of malt whiskies but they both settled for a small glass of very expensive white Burgundy. The other guests in the bar were talking about the fire at the neighbouring Longdell Chase. They were saying it had started with an explosion and there were all sorts of rumours going round, ranging from a terrorist bomb attack to the bad management of the archaic heating system.

Han went over to the barman. 'Anyone hurt, do you know?'

The barman shook his head. 'Don't think so. A couple of blokes were messing about near the boathouse apparently, when it just went up. More likely to have been kids. There'd be fuel and stuff in the boathouse. Dropped cigarette, something like that could send it up. They don't take much care, that place.'

186

'I heard it was a bomb.'

The barman laughed.

'We have a friend staying there. Any idea when we'll be able to go and check it out?'

'Not tonight, that's for sure. Bobbies all over the place. Seems a bit over the top to me.' He leaned towards Han conspiratorially. 'Unless they know something.' He tapped his nose.

Han wasn't sure how to react so he just nodded and went over to where Marjan was sitting.

'He doesn't seem to think anyone was hurt and he laughed at the suggestion of it being a bomb but he thinks there's too many police there.'

Marjan sipped her wine. She was worried. 'You don't think Peiter would try anything, do you?'

'I do, I'm afraid. I don't trust that man at all after what you've told me and, like our friend at the bar, I don't think the British police force would waste so many man hours on a heating malfunction, do you? If it was a bomb, it would be a bit of a co-incidence for terrorists to decide to bomb the same hotel Greg and Denis were sent to by some coded note, unless your friend has links with terrorists, of course.'

Marjan face reddened. 'He's not my friend, Han. Peiter is just someone I worked for, just like you did.'

'Except I was working in good faith. You knew his real business.'

'Do you think I don't regret that now? I know I was stupid and naïve. I didn't think it would be like this. I'm sorry.' She tried to brush away the tears that were welling up but the force was too strong and she burst into uncontrollable sobs. The hubbub in the bar went quiet for a second whilst the other guests looked at her disapprovingly before returning to their previous conversations.

'Crying isn't going to help us Marjan!' Han tried to sound comforting but somehow couldn't find the right words. 'What we have to decide is what to do next.'

Marjan was embarrassed and cross with herself. She'd been in control up to this stage. Whether it was the wine or seeing the police cars or Han berating her she couldn't tell. She clenched her fists and bit her lip. 'You said the barman laughed when you mentioned a bomb. It must just be a fire. It is a co-incidence, Han. It has to be. I can't believe anything else. I won't believe anything else.' The tears filled her eyes again and she turned away. Han looked at her. Much as he was angry with her for helping Wiersma, he realised he was as involved, really. He hadn't seen through him. He put his hand on her arm.

'You go up to the room. You need some rest.' He stood up.

'Where are you going?'

'I'm going to try and find out a bit more, if I can.'

Marjan grabbed Han's hand. 'No, Han. Wait till morning. There's no point in antagonising the police. Whatever's happened, you're not going to be able to talk to Greg and Denis, are you? How are you going to explain your presence to the police?'

Han sat down again. 'I feel so impotent just sitting here.'

Marjan gripped his hand and bit her lip again to stop the tears.

A middle-aged woman in a tweed suit crossed behind Han and touched him on the shoulder. 'That's better, now, isn't it? You make it up to her young man. No point in arguing. My honeymoon was a strain too, they all are. Make it up to her.' She smiled at Marjan and left the bar. Han and Marjan looked at each other. Marjan's tears turned suddenly to laughter.

***

CHAPTER THIRTEEN

Sergeant Murray was leaning on the window-sill of Greg's room looking at the view across the lake. There were worse places to be dispatched to, he supposed. He was listening to DI Milne asking Driscoll what he'd been up to. Murray could tell him exactly what Greg had been up to for the last forty-eight hours. He had been detailed to follow him wherever he went. He'd caught the same train from Euston to Oxenholme, hired a car and followed them down to Newby Bridge – slept in the car as the hotel was full!- gone to Cartmel, nearly lost them when they slipped out of the course but picked them up on the road along Windermere, ending up at The Longdell Chase. Here he'd telephoned Milne to ask for some relief as, if he had to spend another night without sleep in the back of his hire car, he wouldn't be much use to anyone. Milne hadn't been happy and decided to come and relieve Murray himself. Except he hadn't been relieved. Milne arrived after the explosion and there was no way he was going to be allowed to get any sleep now. The DI was sure Driscoll was making contact with someone in the drugs ring and was using Greg as a rabbit to flush out the leaders of the ring. He didn't believe this cock-and-bull story about being duped into drug-smuggling. Murray turned and looked at Milne leaning over the bed like some pathetic 1970's TV cop.

'Who is your contact, Mr Driscoll? I think we've taken this far enough now, don't you? Or perhaps you want to get yourself killed. Who was the man on the boat? Was he your contact or was he in a rival gang? Bit of double dealing? You're mixing with some very nice people, aren't you, Mr Driscoll? What was his name? Are you going to try and convince me that you didn't know him? I don't think you'll find that easy. I can be very stubborn if I want to be, can't I, Sergeant?' He turned to check Murray was still awake.

'Oh very, sir.' he agreed.

Greg was sitting propped up on several pillows and cushions on the bed. It wasn't the room they'd checked into, it was much bigger. There must have been another cancellation! He didn't know what time it was, there was no clock in the room but it must have been around dawn judging by the light coming through the window. He was tired. He'd explained to Milne over and over that he wasn't involved in any drugs ring. The man in the boat was Brian Carter. Brian Carter was the man he'd told Milne about when he interviewed him in London during the week. The man who'd told him he worked for the Met. Why was he going over it again and again? Why didn't they chase up Rob Vanderlast and Peiter Wiersma? Or Han Koolhaven and Marjan Smits? The reason he'd come here was just a hunch he'd had, now proved right surely, based on a message on his answerphone. Yes he did realise that withholding evidence was a serious crime, he hadn't realised he had withheld it, he thought he must have told them about it, he'd told them everything he knew at the time but he had been knocked out so could have been muddled. That was not true, of course. He knew he hadn't told them about the tape. He thought it better not to. They didn't believe Carter existed. He wanted to speak to him himself. However, the way he felt right now, he wished he had told the police everything but he'd needed to know more before he dared trust even the police. Sometimes he could be very stubborn, too.

Denis was not having an easy time of it, either. He was in the room they had originally checked into. He was being grilled by a keen young detective. Denis did not take to him well at all. The fact that he kept being told he would lose the bail money he'd put up for Greg because the bail conditions had been broken, didn't endear him to the detective. If there was anything sure to piss him off it was telling him he was going to lose money. As far as he knew Greg hadn't broken his bail conditions. They were going racing as a weekend break to get away from the stress. He didn't know Brian Carter and was positive that Greg couldn't possibly be involved with any drugs ring but was sure he'd been set-up. He'd never met Rob Vanderlast or Peiter

Wiersma, he'd only dealt with Vanderlast on the phone and, as far as he was concerned, he was a film producer. He'd never heard of Mr Wiersma before all this happened.

He thought Han and Marjan would have some more information but he wasn't going to tell this to any stuck-up young detective. Like Greg, he wasn't sure he was ready to trust them with any information that they could turn to use against them. He was starting to get annoyed.

'Am I under arrest?'

'No, sir. You're just helping police with their enquiries.'

'Well, I've decided to stop being so helpful. I'd like to phone my solicitor, I think.'

*

Han and Marjan discussed the situation throughout the night. Han had offered to sleep on the sofa, giving Marjan the four-poster bed to herself but she told him not to be so silly and the two of them had sat on the large bed all night. Neither of them had slept really. Han had still been keen to go to the Longdell Chase that night but Marjan had persuaded him to wait until morning when they would both go.

'But the police will want to talk to us and I'm not sure they'll take kindly to your involvement with the ring, Marjan.'

'I know, Han. But I might have vital information as to how to find Jenny. They need to know, I'll just have to take the consequences.'

Han sighed. 'I'm not sure, Marjan. I think the best way you can help both Jenny and Greg is to keep away from the police, for the moment. If you tell them about your involvement with Peiter Wiersma, they'll just lock you away while they carry on their enquiries. We need you to help us find Peiter and you can't do that if you are locked up. I'm going to the hotel first thing in the morning on my own. If I'm not back by, say, noon, check out of this hotel and make your way to Heathrow and book into the Hilton Hotel near Terminal 4. If I don't contact you there, stay overnight and fly back to Amsterdam in the morning. Stay at my flat until you hear from me. Here's the key, you know the address.' He gave Marjan the keys to his flat and went over to the kettle. 'Coffee?'

'No! Aren't you being a bit overdramatic, Han? Look. I won't come to the other hotel, if you don't want me to, but why can't I wait for you here?'

Han poured his coffee. 'I hope I am being over-dramatic, Marjan, but after what I've heard from you in the last twenty-four hours I think we should take every precaution. If this fire was directed at Greg, then we have to know if it was successful or not.'

'The policeman said no-one was hurt.'

'As far as he knew. The point is if someone was detailed to harm or even kill Greg and they haven't succeeded, they're likely to try again. This is dangerous, Marjan. I don't think you should be anywhere you can be found at the moment. You know more than Greg, so if they're trying to wipe him out, what chance do you think you stand?'

'We don't know anyone was trying to wipe Greg out.'

'It was just a coincidence the hotel blowing up, was it?'

'There was a fire, Han. That's all. You're tired and letting your imagination run away with you.'

'I'm confused and not sure what is right and until I can find out what's going on, I need to know you're safe. Please do as I say.'

Marjan was tired too. She could feel tears welling up again. The thought that Greg could have been hurt or even killed, had been kept firmly in the back of her mind, she couldn't bear to think about it. But she knew it was Wiersma's intention to get rid of Driscoll. He'd told her as much. Why hadn't she stopped him? There was some sense in Han's plan. Maybe it was best for him to try and find out a bit more before going to the police but all the while she didn't know what was happening to Jenny. She looked at Han.

'OK. Please be back soon, I don't want to be sitting in Heathrow or your flat without knowing what's going on.'

Han arrived at the Longdell Chase just after 7.30am, went straight to the reception desk and asked for Denis Young. The assistant manager, who thought he should be doing something more important than looking after reception, glared at Han.

'Who wants him?' he asked

'Me.' Replied Han.

'It's been a very long night, sir. I don't know if you know but we had an incident here last night.'

'I had heard. Mr Young?'

The assistant manager took Han's name and told him to take a seat.

Ten minutes later a young constable came up to Han and asked him to accompany him. They went to room 206, Denis Young's room. Inside the room were four people, Denis, DI Milne, the young detective who had been questioning Denis and a constable was standing on guard by the door. Han was ushered into the room and the door shut behind him. Milne was the first to speak.

'Come in, Mr Koolhaven. Sit down,' he said.

Han walked towards a high wing-backed chair by the window and sat down. He looked at Denis who was still wearing the clothes he had worn the night before, his trousers were covered in mud and he had not had a shave. He looked a mess. This was the first time Han had seen Denis, every contact up to now had been over the phone and this did not look like the sophisticated theatrical agent he had negotiated with. This looked like some sort of tramp. He smiled at Denis but he just stared back at him.

'What's going on here?' he said.

Milne interjected before Denis could answer. 'Mr Young tells me you're involved in a production company that makes television commercials for the continent, Mr Koolhaven. Is that true?'

'Yes. I am a film director in the Netherlands. Can you tell me what's going on here?'

'There's been an incident here, sir, and we need to question everyone in the hotel. May I ask what your business with Mr Young might be?'

'I need to talk to him about an on-going contract with one of his clients. Should I come back later?' Han stood up.

'I think I'd like you to wait here for a little while, if you don't mind. You may be able to help us with our enquiries.'

'I don't see how I can help if I don't know what's going on.'

DI Milne took a few paces towards the door. Leaned against it and turned to Han with a weary expression on his face. 'Mr Koolhaven, does this client of Mr Young's happen to go by the name of Greg Driscoll, by any chance?'

'Yes. Has something happened to him?' Han held his breath.

Milne studied Han for a moment before answering, 'An attempt was made on Mr Driscoll's life last night. He seems to think it may have something to do with a commercial he was making for you.' He studied his notes. 'Do you know a Mr Peiter Wiersma?'

'He's the client we're making a series of commercials for. I don't know him intimately, why?'

'What sort of man would you say he is? Honest? Trustworthy?'

'I've always found him so.'

'Not the sort to deal with the criminal element?'

'I don't know what you mean.'

Milne walked slowly over to Han and stood just a little too close to him. Han stood up. Tall as DI Milne was, he still only came up to just above the Dutchman's large nose. 'Well, Mr Koolhaven, our friend Mr Driscoll has made some pretty serious accusations about Mr Wiersma. According to our enquiries Mr Wiersma is a respected member of the Dutch business community. I was wondering if you could give us any clue as to why Mr Driscoll might think differently?'

'I have no idea, officer.'

'I'm a Detective Inspector, Mr Koolhaven. Thank you for your help. Are you staying at the hotel for a while?'

'I shall stay here until I can speak to Mr Young about my business.'

'Oh yes. The commercials. They are for some sort of food product, I believe. That must be a very interesting job. Being a film director, I mean. I envy you, Mr Koolhaven. I'm sure Mr Young will be available for you very shortly. In the meantime please have some breakfast on us for your trouble. Constable Bennett will take you through to the breakfast room. I'd be grateful if you could make yourself available to us later, should we need to speak further. Thank you.'

Han looked at Denis. Never having actually met him, he had no proof that it was Denis Young sitting on that bed. As he reached the door he turned and spoke to Denis.

'Is it possible for me to get hold of Greg at the moment, Denis?'

Denis raised his head and glared at Han. 'I have no wish to speak to Mr Koolhaven at the moment, Detective Inspector. I would like him out of my room.'

The voice was gravelly, smoky but did sound enough like the person Han had spoken to on the phone for him to believe it was Denis Young on the bed. But why did he not want to speak to him?

'He's had a shock, I'm afraid. Mr Driscoll is not available to be spoken with but is perfectly safe. Have some breakfast Mr Koolhaven.' DI Milne ushered Han out of the door that Constable Bennett was holding open for him, adding to the PC, 'keep your eye on him.'

It seemed PC Bennett had decided that that meant part of his job was to join Han for breakfast. He was happy to be out of the stale atmosphere of room 206 and he was starving. Breakfast was about the last thing Han wanted, on the other hand, and if he had he would not choose to eat it with a British Bobby. Denis had looked a mess. What had happened here last night? He was still none the wiser. He needed to talk it through with Marjan. Try and decide what the hell was going on.

'Am I allowed to make a phone call, Constable?'

Bennett laughed. 'Of course, sir. You're not under arrest or anything. You can make as many phone calls as you like.' He was looking through the breakfast menu. 'Shall I place an order for you?'

'Just some coffee for me, please.' Han walked towards the public telephone in the reception area. Bennett could still see him so he was keeping an eye on him and didn't need to follow him. He ordered a full English with extra toast.

When Han got through to the Crag Country House Hotel he was told that his wife had checked out just after 7.30am and left the hotel. She didn't say where she was going.

*

Whilst Han had been at the Longdell Chase, Marjan had made her way down into Bowness-in-Windermere. This was a small town on the edge of the lake. She couldn't bear to sit in the hotel room any longer. She'd been there all night trying to sort out the mess inside her head. She couldn't just sit and wait for Han to get in touch. She needed to think and, sitting in a small café at the water's edge, thinking was what she was doing. She was thinking about Peiter Wiersma and Han and, most of all, Jenny. Poor Jenny. What on earth was happening to her?

*

At this precise moment, nothing was happening to Jenny. She was lying on the bed safe in the knowledge that Peiter had been in touch with Denis and he was on his way to take her home. She hoped he hadn't told her mother, she wouldn't be able to cope. Her mother was an ill woman and she didn't approve of Jenny being an actress. This sort of thing would only go to prove her point that it was a dangerous profession for a young girl.

Anna was sitting at her desk by the door quietly dozing. She hadn't had much sleep recently. After Mr

Wiersma had brought that man in on the first night and then Jenny had told her about his behaviour, she had not let anyone else take over from her. She was a nurse and took her job seriously. Her job was the welfare of her patient. What Jenny was doing here and what Mr Wiersma's intentions were, was none of her business and she didn't want to know. As long as her patient was not bothered again was all that was important. She was just doing her job. The only sort of job she could get these days. Cash jobs. No questions asked jobs.

In the small room next to Jenny's a lot was happening. Peiter Wiersma was shouting into the phone. *'If you do not find that bloody girl you will not have a minute's peace for as long as you live – which won't be very long!'*

'She's gone to England with Han. I told you we shouldn't have trusted her. If you hadn't left her in that hotel room we wouldn't be having this trouble. Why couldn't you take her with you? You don't usually want to let her out of your sight. What do you want me to do? She could be anywhere. Do you want me search the whole country for her?' Rob Vanderlast was a worried man. Peiter Wiersma was not a man who liked to be crossed. He got what he wanted and he didn't care who got hurt in the process. Everyone was expendable in his eyes.

'Why don't you start in the English Lake District?'

'What makes you think she'll be there?'

'Maybe she went to look for Carter and Driscoll.'

'Why should she want to find them, Peiter? What's going on here? Is there something you're not telling me?'

'Get on a plane, go back to the UK and find her! And use a false passport. If she's talked they could be looking for your name' Wiersma hung up the phone. There was a lot Rob Vanderlast didn't know. He didn't need to know. He didn't know about the demise of Carter, Peiter hadn't let anyone who didn't need to know about that. He was putting too much trust in his employees. Carter had given too much away, so had that smart-alec actor Driscoll. They were out of the way now. Marjan Smits was next along with Koolhaven. He'd been careful not to tell Marjan too much but she knew enough to cause him and several other people a lot of trouble. If it came to her word against his, he had enough dirt on Marjan Smits to discredit her but if anyone were to more than scratch the surface of his legitimate business there was a distinct possibility that his own good name could be exposed as disreputable, to say the least. He had a certain amount of insurance in as much as he would take several eminent names with him if he had to but that didn't make him feel any better right now. The Smits girl had to go. She was ruthless, he'd known that from the start, that's what he'd found attractive in her. He could recognise some of his own ambition in her, the drive, the desire for money, not caring

how she came by it or who got hurt. Until now. Her stupid infatuation with the Gulliver girl. The whole point of using Driscoll's girlfriend was insurance against Driscoll telling anyone what he thought he knew. Was it the knowledge that he was going to get rid of Driscoll anyway that had caused her sudden pang of conscience? Peiter was normally very careful of what he spoke about in bed. He was aware of the danger of giving information away whilst in the throes of sex, better men than him had been caught that way. But they were emotionally weak. Peiter never relaxed. Sex was just another way of having power over people. A release of physical tension, maybe but not the mind. The mind had nothing to do with sex as far as Peiter Wiersma was concerned. It had been a mistake telling Smits about Greg, though. It was a moment of weakness. He wanted her to share the thrill he felt after arranging an execution. It increased his enjoyment of sex, thinking of sending someone to their death whilst indulging in an act that was designed to bring people into the world. Marjan had gone cold, though, turned off. She wanted to know why, if they were getting rid of Greg, they were still hanging on to Jenny. Why not let her go now before she realised any connection? Peiter had accused Marjan of being a little too interested in Jenny. Was that why she was worried about her? Did she want to get into her knickers? It had been intended as light-hearted and he didn't expect the reaction it had brought. Marjan was strong, she had fought, scratched, kicked and punched before Peiter finally managed to overpower her. He wasn't sure why he hadn't quietened her more permanently then and there. Maybe he thought she'd see sense.

Anna knocked gently at the door and entered. 'She's awake, Mr Wiersma and asking for you. What shall I tell her?'

'Tell her nothing. Give her something to put her out for a long time.' He glared at Anna as she paused in the doorway. 'Just do as you're told, nurse. It's why I pay you.'

Anna went out of the room leaving Peiter wondering what he'd done to be so pestered by women. He picked up the phone and booked a flight to the UK.

***

CHAPTER FOURTEEN

It was nearly midday by the time Greg was allowed to emerge from the room the police had held him in. Milne had left him to stew in the early hours of the morning. Murray was still there, dozing in a chair. The nurse had been replaced by someone else. Milne had returned at about nine to see if Greg had come up with any sort of confession yet. He'd tried everything legal he could think of. He had a lot of experience dealing with stubborn suspects who were far more professional than Greg Driscoll. Breaking him should have been a piece of cake. Unless there was nothing to break. Doubts were staring to creep into Milne's mind. Driscoll was frightened. He looked like the sort that, if he was being threatened by the villains, would turn himself in to the police and try and get their protection. Milne knew that sort well. He detested them. He had a kind of grudging respect for the hardened criminals, they were a challenge and, let's face it, without them he'd be out of a job. Driscoll was very small-time, mixed up with something that had got out of hand, too big for him. Or had he? Had he just been an unwilling patsy who'd become an irritability? Denis Young had nothing to do with anything, he was convinced of that. Having assured him he was not under arrest and didn't need a solicitor, Denis Young had given him names. Names he already knew. He had no information that could be of any help. Carter he knew about but he wasn't important. He was another patsy and anyway he couldn't question him now, he was in bits across Lake Windermere. He'd been duped into helping someone. But who? Koolhaven? Milne didn't think so but he needed to be watched, he had some involvement. Rob Vanderlast? Possibly. Milne hadn't got a hook on him yet. Interpol would be on the lookout for him but there had been no sign of him. A minor film producer in Holland, worked with Koolhaven, old pals. Marjan Smits. Who was she? Assistant to the producers and to Mr Peiter Wiersma. Peiter Wiersma was a big shot, yes but a big shot in wholesale foods. He had money, a lot of money, enough to finance a drugs ring if he wanted to. DI Milne thought it unlikely. Interpol had nothing on any of these people. They'd almost laughed at the idea of Wiersma being involved. Apparently he owned one of the biggest supermarket chains in Europe, a sort of Dutch Mr Sainsbury – clean as they come, gave to charities. What's more one of the charities he supported dealt with drug rehabilitation. However, everything that Greg Driscoll and Denis Young said came back to these five names. Wiersma was the only one with the right backing. The idea was clever, running drugs in film cans, using dumb actors so desperate to work they wouldn't question anything out of the ordinary. But what about Driscoll? Was he just a dumb actor who discovered something by mistake as he claims or did he know more? There was nothing to be gained by holding him any longer, they'd learn nothing more from him locked up. They might just find something out if they keep him under observation. They'd have to wait and see.

*

Greg joined Han in the bar just after noon. He accepted a lager with derisive thanks. Like Denis, who had refused to speak to him, Greg was not feeling kindly towards Han Koolhaven at the moment. If he had never met this man he wouldn't have been arrested, hit over the head or nearly blown to pieces. Probably more importantly, a sweet, young, inexperienced actress wouldn't be gaining the sort of experience no-one wanted to gain. Han invited Greg out to the terrace where he'd been sitting all morning at a white wrought-iron table overlooking the lake. The normally beautiful view was stained for Greg, not only by his recent experience but by the occasional sight of a police frogman and a lot of blue and white tape blowing like bunting in the wind. It was not cold but Greg was shivering. He stood up and walked back to the bar area and found a seat inside. Han followed.

'I'm sorry, Greg. That was a stupid place for me to sit. I was finding it oppressive in here under the constant watch of PC Plod over there.' He nodded towards the young plain-clothes policeman sitting reading The Sun in the corner.

'Where's Jenny?' Greg enquired

'I don't know, Greg. Marjan said Peiter might have taken her as insurance. He thought you knew too much and holding her would keep you quiet.'

'I didn't know what was going on, Han! You did! Why didn't you tell me? Were you waiting to see if I'd been wiped out first? Is that why you couldn't get here any quicker? If anything's happened to Jenny, I'll kill you – and Wiersma and anyone else that's touched her!'

The policeman looked up from his copy of The Sun.

'Greg, calm down.' Han turned his back on the PC. 'There's a lot you need to know and I can't tell you here. What you must know and believe is that I'm on your side. The first I knew about any of this was yesterday morning when Marjan told what had been going on.'

'Oh yes. Marjan! Where is she? Reporting back to base? Mission not accomplished?'

Han was silent. He couldn't answer that. He didn't know where Marjan was or what she was doing. It was possible that she was indeed doing exactly what Greg suspected. He hoped not.

'Well?' Greg glared at Han. There was a distinct possibility he might smash this Dutchman's head into a pulp, constable watching or no constable watching.

'I can't tell you, Greg. I wish I knew myself.'

'What!'

'I left her in a hotel up the road but she seems to have checked out. I have an arrangement to meet her in a London hotel this evening. I'm sure she'll be there.' Han wasn't sure, not sure at all. He wasn't sure about anything anymore. Why had Marjan told him so much and then run out on him? Was he to be bumped off too? Han was frightened, more frightened than he'd ever been in his life. Who could he trust? Where was Marjan? Why was Greg being so hostile to him? He knew the answer to that. Greg felt the same as him, in Limbo, trusting no-one. With good reason. Han hadn't been attacked yet. He needed Greg as an ally. 'Look, Greg. I know you're not going to trust me at the moment but if we're going to get to the bottom of this and help Jenny, you must listen to me, please.'

Greg folded his arms and leaned back in his seat. 'Go on, then.'

Han looked over his shoulder at the young policeman. 'Not here. Meet me tonight at Heathrow Airport.'

'Oh yes, lovely! I've just had my passport confiscated and I've promised to be a good boy. It'll look really good, heading off to Heathrow Airport, won't it? Where are we going to go? Acapulco? Or is that old hat for villains these days?'

'We're meeting at the Hilton Hotel. We're not going anywhere else. Just ask for me at reception. And please get Denis to come with you. He won't speak to me. Don't be foolish, Greg, we have to work together.' Han stood up and walked out of the bar leaving Greg totally bewildered. He stood up to follow but caught the eye of the constable who had also stood up and was looking to follow Han. Greg sat down and let him go. He ordered another beer from the waiter who came to clear the empty glasses from his table.

'Oh, and waiter? Is it possible to get a message to Mr Young in room 206 and ask him to join me here?'

The waiter smiled and said he'd see what he could do.

*

Peiter Wiersma hired a car at Gatwick Airport and drove towards London. He had business to do. He could no longer trust anyone to do this for him. The exchange was due to take place at Maldon on the Blackwater estuary in Essex later that evening. He would supervise this himself and then cool the operation for a while. For months if necessary. A holiday would not go amiss, get away from it all, maybe take Marjan – maybe not. He needed to find somebody else. Somebody not involved. Maybe leave the whole business behind. He had money. He still had one of the biggest supermarket chains in Europe. The drugs business was starting to bore him. He didn't need it. It didn't thrill him anymore. It wasn't an easy way to make a quick buck anymore, customs were tightening up everywhere. His only problem would be convincing the other syndicate members. That, and finding Marjan before she dropped him in deeper. His portable phone rang as he turned off the M23 onto the M25.

'Peiter?'

It was a familiar voice. One that Peiter had been waiting to hear.

'Where are you? I tried your office, no-one knew where you were.'

'I'm in England. On my way to London. Where are you?'

There was a pause before the voice answered.

'Meet me at the Heathrow Hilton as soon as possible.'

'I'm not going anywhere near Heathrow, I'm afraid. Where are you?'

'I'm in England. Tell me where I can see you.'

Peiter checked his notes. 'I'm staying at The White Boar Hotel in a place called Maldon in Essex. You know why I'm here. Come to me before it's too late.' He switched off his phone and turned to look over his shoulder. 'It seems we're going to have company, my dear.' Smiling he carried on towards the Dartford tunnel feeling pleased with himself.

In the back seat Jenny didn't answer. Her head ached and the excruciating pain in her stomach was increasing. She wanted to cry, to scream but all she could do was to clench her hands and pray.

*

Marjan Smits hired a car at Heathrow Airport and headed off round the M25 towards Chelmsford, Essex. She pulled off at the South Mimms services and headed to the public telephones. Ten minutes later she was back on the M25 consciously keeping her speed just below seventy. The last thing she needed was to be picked up by the police. She took the A12 towards Chelmsford and then the A414 to Maldon. As she reached the small Essex town she looked at herself in the rear-view mirror. She looked calm. She looked collected. She felt terrified.

*

'I'm not sure I want any more to do with this, Greg. Can't we just leave it to the police this time?' Denis was sitting in the front seat of the hire car feeling thoroughly drained. Greg was driving. Denis had tried to persuade Greg not to drive, pointing out he wasn't a named driver and therefore wasn't insured but he needed sleep and wasn't prepared to argue. The last hour and a half had been a harrowing experience for him. One he never wanted to repeat. And yet, here he was heading to another four-star hotel, rapidly reaching the end of his tether and his credit card limit. Greg looked briefly at Denis before returning his eyes to the road. Denis sighed and closed his eyes. He woke to the sound of aeroplanes very close to his ears.

Han came out to meet them as Greg parked the car in front of the hotel entrance. He'd been sitting in the bar looking through the window at every car arriving. There had been no certainty that Greg would turn up, it had been a risk walking out of the hotel in Windermere before Greg could reply to the invitation but it appeared the calculation had been right. He opened the driver's door.

'Greg, thank God!'

Denis looked at Han across the car. He turned on Greg. 'You didn't tell me we were fraternising with the enemy.'

'Would you have come if I'd told you we were meeting Mr Koolhaven?'

'I certainly would not. I think I would have gone straight to the police. In fact, that's exactly what I think I will do.'

'And tell us everything this time, I hope, Mr Young.'

Detective Inspector Milne stepped out of the shadows. Greg looked towards Han who shrugged his shoulders.

'It's alright, Mr Driscoll, Mr Koolhaven and I have had a nice long chat. Apparently I already know more than either of you. Let us repair to the hotel. I have procured a room for us.'

*

Milne had followed Han from the Lake District. It had been a bit of a whim, a hunch. He knew there was a link that needed following up. He couldn't arrest Han; he'd done nothing illegal, as far as Milne could prove. He could invent something like a driving offence or something, he didn't seem to be the most careful of drivers but he needed his co-operation and there was no point in antagonising him. There had been a moment of panic when Milne realised Han was heading for Heathrow, he didn't want him to leave the country, so he was relieved when he checked into the hotel.

Han had asked at reception if there were any messages for him but there had been no word from Marjan or anyone else. He had booked a room from the Crag Country House Hotel when he went to check out and he went to his room and dumped his bag. He was about to go down to the bar when there was a knock at the door. Expecting to see Marjan, Han got a shock to see DI Milne on the other side of the door. His immediate reaction was anger towards Greg. Why had he told this detective about their meeting? Well, maybe he was right. Maybe he didn't want any further risks. Han had accepted Milne's invitation to join him in the bar for a drink and a chat but was wary of Marjan turning up. He didn't think Milne would take a very kind view of her involvement. But where was she? There had been no message at the Crag and no message here. Maybe she'd done a runner, gone back to the Netherlands. Maybe she'd gone to the police, maybe that's how Milne had found out about Han being here. Han had sat by the window in the bar so he could keep an eye on cars turning up, preferably one with Greg or Marjan in. Milne brought the drinks over and said, 'Mr Koolhaven, I think I need your help.'

They were now sitting in a conference room in the hotel. Milne had arranged for drinks and coffee.

'I told you we should have left it to the police, Greg.'

'Very sensible, Mr Young. However, as you didn't, what we have to decide now is what we do about all this. Mr Koolhaven seems to think we should all work together. I think I'll need a bit of convincing, personally.'

The atmosphere in this room at the Heathrow Hilton was very different to the one at Longdell Chase. Although it was more sterile in its furnishings neither Greg nor Han felt the animosity from Milne they had earlier. They were almost relaxed, Greg nursing a beer, Han a cappuccino. Milne was at a desk by the wall making notes. Only Denis Young felt uncomfortable. Both Greg and Han felt safe in the knowledge that Milne needed their help and was coming round to the idea of them all helping each other.

'The most important thing for me, Inspector, is to find Jenny and get her home safely,' said Greg, adding quietly, 'if it's not too late.'

'I agree, Mr Driscoll. If what Mr Koolhaven has told me about Mr Wiersma is true, she could be in real danger but we don't actually know where she is. I don't want to put anyone's life at risk but if he is the head of this drugs ring I can't jeopardise the whole operation by alerting him at all. I have to tell you that my superiors are not at all keen on me letting you help in this operation. They want me to come up with a result as quickly and cheaply as possible or they will remove me from the case which will not be good news for any of you, believe me. I'm risking a lot here; the force does not view wasting police time very favourably in the current economic climate.'

Denis stood up and walked towards the window. He watched a 747 take off from the nearby runway and wished he was on it, wherever it was going. 'Aren't the police wasting their own time and money by sitting here in this hotel talking to us? If you suspect Mr Wiersma why don't you just find him, arrest him and let us all get back to our lives.'

'I understand your agitation, Mr Young, but you must remember that Mr Wiersma is a very well respected member of the European Community. The last thing we want is a diplomatic situation on our hands. We have to catch him doing something illegal, preferably handling or supplying illegal drugs. And I also have to remind you that the only persons who have been caught doing something illegal so far are sitting in this room!'

'I do understand that. I'm not completely stupid. I just don't want this involvement. I'm a member of the European Community myself, you know.'

Greg nearly choked on his drink. What was Denis trying to do? Get us all locked up?

'I'm serious, Greg. I deal with companies across Europe and the USA.'

'Oh, come on, Denis. You're a theatrical agent. The only effects of you being involved in a bit of espionage are going to be good for your business. Think of the rights when they make the movie!'

Denis took a step towards Greg. He couldn't understand how he could be so flippant. Milne stepped between them.

'I can't force you to help us, Mr Young, if you don't want to but you have, by your own admission, withheld evidence from us.'

Denis went back to his place by the window. Another plane was taking off. He was hoping that this was all some sort of dream and that he would soon wake up, probably with a massive hangover, and it would all be over. He knew in reality that was extremely unlikely. Never had he wanted to get to the quiet of his office so badly and get his head into work.

Han Koolhaven shifted in his seat. He was feeling uncomfortable now, he could understand Denis' frustration. He too wondered why they were all sitting around a table seemingly doing nothing.

'What do you propose we do, Inspector? I've told you all I know. If I knew where Marjan was, that would help. She was supposed to be here but she's not. Can't we find her somehow? Are there alerts at the sea and airports?'

'That all takes time and money, Mr Koolhaven.'

The phone in the conference room buzzed loudly. Milne went over, picked it up and handed it to Han. 'It's for you.'

Han listened to the voice at the other end. It was the hotel receptionist.

'I've just received a message for you, Mr Koolhaven. The lady wouldn't give her name or wait to be put through. I hope I did the right thing.'

'What was the message?'

'Well, all she said was, 'Wait for me. I'm going to Maldon. Don't follow.' That's all she said. I hope that makes sense to you, Mr Koolhaven.'

'Did she say she'd phone again?'

'No, sir, that was all, like I told you. Will you be requiring dinner?'

'No.' Han replaced the receiver and turned to the assembled company. 'I've had a message from Marjan. She's on her way to somewhere called Maldon. No explanation, just that I shouldn't follow her.'

DI Milne picked up his briefcase and took and out a pocket sized road map. He looked up Maldon in the index. There was more than one, a New Malden in Surrey, Maldon on the Essex coast and a village in Bedfordshire called Maulden. 'Did she give any indication where this Maldon place was?' he asked Han.

'I don't think so. The receptionist just said going to Maldon.'

'Why would she be going to this Maldon place?'

'I've no idea. She didn't tell me anything about going anywhere.'

'If you were delivering an assignment would you choose a built-up urban area or a small coastal town?'

'I don't know. If the assignment was coming in by sea…?'

Denis interrupted. 'What assignment? What is this?'

Milne turned to Denis. 'If Ms Smits is meeting someone in this Maldon place then we need to know who and why. My hunch is that she is meeting an assignment coming in to this country.'

'What?' Denis turned from his plane-spotting at the window. 'Why would…'

'…And if she is and it's who I think it is she's meeting, she could be in real danger.' Han stood up.

'Do think she's meeting Wiersma, Han?' Greg's heart started beating faster just at the mention of the fat German's name.

'Could be.'

'Then he'll know where Jenny is.' Greg stood up and put on his coat. 'Come on! What are we waiting for?'

'What if it's a trap? Ms Smits has not been helpful so far.' Denis was feeling panicky. Something was not right, he couldn't explain what, he just knew that this Maldon place was not a place he wanted to visit right now.

'Mr Young is right. Ms Smits has not been too reliable. She may try and get hold of you here. We don't know why she's going to Maldon yet, do we?' Milne scratched his head.

'She did say not to follow.' A request Denis had every intention of agreeing to.

Greg started towards the door. 'She didn't ask me not to follow.' Milne put his body in between Greg and the exit.

'Wait, Mr Driscoll! Maybe someone should stay here and forward any message that may come through.'

'I agree,' said Denis who was keen not to put himself in any more danger, 'I'll stay here.'

'I think it has to be Mr Koolhaven. She may want to speak personally and if she finds out anyone else knows, she may do a runner.'

Greg looked at Milne. 'Why don't they both stay here, Inspector, and you and I go together? Surely the less people turning up in Maldon the better.' Greg opened the door.

'You're right, Mr Driscoll. If it's OK with everybody else we'll try and find Ms Smits. I have a radio in the car and Constable Graham here will be able to contact me via that.' He indicated the police constable standing to attention outside the door.

Denis told Greg to take care.

'Don't worry about me, Denis. You just try and find me another job. This one has cost us a lot so far and I can't see us getting paid from Mr Wiersma's company.'

Milne was at the door. 'Come along Mr Driscoll.'

Greg turned to go. 'Inspector, if we're going to be spending any time together can we drop the Mr Driscoll. Call me Greg.'

'Certainly, Greg. And you can call me Inspector.'

The two left the room.

***

CHAPTER FIFTEEN

Peiter Wiersma checked into The White Boar hotel in Maldon. He had booked a double room in the name of Muller. It was an alias he used regularly. Marjan would know it but no-one else. Jenny felt in a daze, her head was spinning, her stomach churning and she needed a toilet desperately. She noticed the receptionist looking at her strangely and Jenny wanted to cry out to her, ask for help but she knew it was pointless besides her throat felt like it would never utter a sound again. She wanted to see a doctor; someone to tell her she'd be alright. Her legs felt weak and she felt faint again. Peiter put his arm round her. She tried to pull away but could not move an inch, his grip was tight, almost suffocating her against his fat sweaty body.

'Come along, my dear,' he said, adding for the benefit of the receptionist, 'she's a bad flyer, I'm afraid. We've just arrived from Germany. She'll be OK in a little while but we'd appreciate not being disturbed if that's possible. Oh, unless a Miss Smits asks for me, I will be available for her. Thank you, we can make our own way to our room.'

Jenny and Peiter entered the room. Released from his grip Jenny fell to the floor writhing in pain.

'I need the toilet…Please!' Her voice was hoarse.

'Of course, my dear. Come with me.' Peiter took Jenny to the en-suite bathroom and closed the door behind them. Jenny stood holding on to the wash basin waiting for him to leave. It was evident he was not going to.

'Please leave me,' she pleaded. 'Leave me some dignity.'

'You will show me nothing I have not already seen, if you remember. Of course maybe you don't remember but I do, my dear. I have many pleasant memories of our time together.' He smiled. Jenny felt sick. She did remember lying naked in the 'hospital' in Germany. What did he mean about many pleasant memories? The thought that that fat slob had been on top of her was realising her worst nightmares of the last few days. What did anything matter now? Dignity? She had none left. She pulled her flowery skirt down over her knees and dropped her knickers. There was blood on them. The pain in her stomach was intense. As she went to sit on the toilet, Peiter crossed to her, picked her up and placed her, quite gently, onto the bidet, like a parent putting a child onto a potty.

'In there, my dear,' he said.

Jenny felt the cold porcelain against her thighs. Why was Peiter making her go in the bidet instead of the toilet? Pain and nature took over before she could think any further. She screamed involuntarily as she felt like she was splitting in half. The smell of excrement was pungent. She fell forward onto her knees. Peiter picked her up and carried her through to the bedroom. He laid a towel on the bed and put Jenny on top of it. She lay with her knees up, tired, still feeling the pain in her stomach and back. Peiter removed her shoes and socks. He put his hand on her forehead and smiled. His other hand moved down her body to her stomach and rubbed in a circular motion.

'There, is that better, my dear?' His hand moved further down her body and then up her naked thighs. Jenny closed her eyes and choked back the tears. She felt wasted, drained, like a piece of meat on a butcher's slab. She had no resistance left and succumbed easily to the pressure from Peiter's hand, letting her thighs open and fall to the bed. Peiter stood back and looked at her. Jenny opened her eyes and saw his face, eyes glazed, a crazy grin on his face, almost in a trance, just staring at her.

Abruptly he turned and went back into the bathroom. He ran a cold tap and sluiced his face. Sexual gratification would have to wait; he had more important business right now. He went to the bidet and turned the taps on. As the remains of Jenny's faeces flushed through the stainless steel grill in the bottom of the bidet. Peiter Wiersma picked out four condoms. Carefully washing them under the tap he could see the white powder wrapped in its soft polythene bags inside the pink latex. Four. Not a bad return but it meant there were still four inside Jenny's body. He would have to wait. But for how long? It could be days. Some inducing may be needed but he did not want to risk damaging the condoms. If he wanted Jenny out of the way there were cheaper ways than giving her a huge internal overdose of pure, high quality cocaine. The problem was he had to make the drop in a few hours. He carefully dried the four condoms he had, wrapped them in tissue paper and placed them in an embossed leather case intended to hold cigars. He put the case in his jacket pocket and returned to the bedroom. In his suitcase he had a small bottle of chemical liquid which worked as an emetic and a laxative. He didn't care which end they came out as long he could get the condoms before eleven. That would give him time to get to the drop, make the exchange and leave considerably richer.

A knock at the door caused him to replace the bottle in his suitcase before he could give Jenny the mixture. He looked towards her, she had turned over and seemed to be asleep. He wrapped the towel round her legs and crossed to open the door. Marjan burst into the room and threw her arms round Peiter. She sank to her knees and started sobbing.

'Peiter, I'm so sorry. I've been so stupid. Please don't throw me out. I need you. Please take me back in. I'm so sorry.'

Peiter was silent for a moment, then took Marjan by the arms and gently lifted her to her feet. He kissed her hard on the mouth, she responded and they stood there kissing and embracing for fully five minutes.

*

Detective Inspector Milne had a list of all the hotels in Maldon. Fortunately there weren't many. Certainly not of the class he would expect a man like Peiter Wiersma to use.

There had been a slight complication when Milne had reported back to base that he was on his way to Maldon in Essex. The young detective manning the phone at HQ had pointed out there was a Malden in South London and a village in Bedfordshire with a similar name and was he sure he was going to the right place? Arrogance was something Milne detested in others whilst failing to recognise it in himself. Only now, as they were by-passing Chelmsford in Essex did some doubt start to filter into his mind. He had convinced himself that a late-night coastal drop was the most likely reason for Ms Smits to be going Maldon but then South London was notorious for the number of opportunities for drug deals. It depended how big the drop was going to be. If there was going to be a drop at all! He has no proof, just a hunch and some information from sources that had not been over-reliable in the recent past.

Greg sat silently in the unmarked dark green Rover. His thoughts were on Jenny and what he was going to do to Peiter Wiersma. His heart was beating faster than it ever had, even on the first night of a production. He feared his chest would burst before they reached their prey. In the back of his mind he was trying to store this feeling so he could reproduce it on the stage or screen should he ever have to play a character in this situation but he knew that was ludicrous. If he tried to reproduce this feeling he'd never be able to speak! No! This was real! Not the sort of reality one saw on the TV. Acting was definitely not reality, of that he was certain.

DI Milne had decided that the first place to try was The White Boar hotel. A check had been done on hire-car firms at Stansted, Gatwick and Heathrow and Luton airports and he was waiting for a response. He assumed that Wiersma would have hired a car at the airport and the plan was to reconnoitre the car parks and look for the hire-car. It was a bit of a long shot but better than alerting Wiersma by asking at every hotel. They had nothing definite to pin on him and they didn't want him to get wind of them and flee the area. Milne wanted to catch him exchanging drugs and was sure that if they could find him and follow him, that is exactly what they would do.

The radio crackled into action.

"We've got a positive, sir. A grey Mercedes was hired at Gatwick by a large German gentleman this afternoon. He used a driving license in the name of Muller but he answered the description you gave us. He had a young woman with him."

Greg, acting as Milne's assistant, took down the registration number. All they had to do now was to find the car and wait. Greg's heart was beating even faster as they pulled into the White Boar hotel.

*

Inside the hotel, Jenny was feeling ill again. She had been woken by the bouncing of the bed caused by Peiter and Marjan. Her stomach was still on fire and her nausea was only increased by the proximity of the copulating couple writhing within inches of her. She caught Marjan's eye as she pulsated underneath the sweating mass of Peiter's body. There was a look of pity in her eye that made Jenny feel more like throwing up. There was no look of enjoyment in Marjan's face but Jenny understood. Peiter was her boss. You had no choice with him. There was something about him that made you do what he wanted when he wanted. What was it? Fear? If it was it was a new kind of fear for Jenny. It wasn't the fear she had had of her father or her teachers at school. It wasn't the sort of fear she had auditioning for a director with a reputation or first-night nerves. She couldn't explain it but she understood. She closed her eyes again and waited in pain for Peiter to finish before summoning up enough strength to roll off the bed onto the floor. Peiter withdrew from Marjan. He pulled up his trousers, picked Jenny up and carried her to the bathroom, placing her once more on the bidet. He closed the bathroom door.

Marjan wiped the tears from her eyes. She didn't want Peiter to see that she'd been crying. 'Poor Jenny' she thought as she pulled on her corduroy jeans. They'd used the condom method to transport drugs before; in fact Marjan had swallowed some herself on an earlier mission, so she knew what Jenny must be going through. The pain was extremely unpleasant. She sat on the edge of the bed waiting for the sobbing coming from the bathroom to subside. Peiter burst out of the bathroom pulling Jenny after him. He threw her on the bed next to Marjan.

'You talk some sense into her Marjan. There's still one inside she won't let go of.'

'I'm sorry, really I am. I can't do any more. Please. I need to sleep.' Jenny croaked between sobs.

'You will sleep, young lady, for a very long time if you do not do as you're told!'

'Leave her, Peiter. I know what it's like, remember. You can't rush it. Let her rest.' Marjan smiled at Jenny. Jenny would have spat in her face if she had had any fluid left in her body. She just closed her eyes. 'Let her have some water, Peiter. That might help.'

'Get her some then and I hope you're right. I need that condom by eleven-thirty at the latest.' Peiter went into the bathroom.

Marjan followed him, returning with a glass of water. She leaned over the washed-out figure on the bed. 'Jenny? I know what you're going through, I've been there myself.' Jenny lay still, her eyes closed. Marjan leaned closer to her and kissed her gently on the cheek. She whispered in her ear. 'Jenny, it's going to be OK. I've left a message for Han. He should be with Greg. They'll come to help us, don't worry. Drink some water.'

Jenny slowly opened her eyes. What did Marjan mean by help us? Help us with what? Whatever was going on here she felt sure that Greg Driscoll would not want to be involved.

Marjan had climbed onto the bed next to Jenny. She lifted her head and put the glass to her lips. Jenny took a few sips,

'How are you feeling, Jenny?' Marjan was very close to Jenny. She put her arms round Jenny's shoulders.

'What's going on, Marjan?' Jenny's voice was barcly audible. 'Why am I here? What do you want me to do?' Jenny was prepared to submit to almost anything.

Marjan took Jenny's face in her hands and looked her straight in the eye. She leaned forward and kissed her fully on the lips. Jenny felt Marjan's tongue part her lips. Her immediate revulsion turned to a warm relaxed feeling that overwhelmed her. She tried to put her arms round Marjan but found she couldn't lift them from the bed. She lay back and closed her eyes. Neither Jenny nor Marjan noticed Peiter come out of the bathroom and leave the room.

*

Greg's adrenalin level increased rapidly. There, brazenly parked in the middle of the open lot, stood the grey Mercedes. Greg checked the number with the one he written down earlier. It matched. Peiter Wiersma was in this hotel. DI Milne drove through the car park and parked the unmarked Rover into a space in the far corner. There were only three other cars in the car park. Milne's car was behind a red Granada. He switched off the engine.

'What now?' Greg was exited. He wanted to go in and confront Wiersma but Milne sat still, resting his chin in his cupped hands.

Eventually he said 'I'll go and check at reception. You sit tight and don't let anyone see you, OK?' He opened the door, got out of the car and headed towards the hotel. A well-built man in a grey suit was coming out of the main door as he entered. Milne stood back and let him pass. The man thanked him. His voice was strong and had a trace of a German accent. Greg, watching from the car, was about to run out and attack the man. He needed to let Milne know who he'd nearly bumped into. He also needed to be sure that if he got into his grey Mercedes he was kept in sight. The whole thing could be wrecked if Milne didn't return immediately. Greg realised that if Wiersma saw him sitting in the Rover that would wreck everything too. He lowered himself in the seat, adjusting the rear-view mirror so that he could still see the parked Mercedes. He was lying flat in his seat for what seemed like ages. He couldn't see Peiter Wiersma in the mirror. The car was still there. Slowly Greg edged himself up in the seat and peered out. Wiersma was standing just a matter of feet from the Rover. Greg threw himself flat on the seat again, his heart pounding. Had Wiersma seen him? Had he blown it? He checked the mirror again. Peiter Wiersma moved into view. He stood next to the Mercedes for a short while before opening the driver's door and sitting down behind the steering wheel. Greg kept his eye on the reflection in the mirror. Where was Milne? Why didn't he come back? Peiter Wiersma leant over to the passenger side and appeared to be opening a large suitcase. He sat up and dialled a number on his portable phone. Greg switched on the police radio in the Rover and started frantically turning the tuning knob. The radio crackled and whistled as Greg tried in vain to tune into Wiersma's portable telephone. He kept desperately turning the knob backwards and forwards along the dial. There was no telephone conversation coming over the speakers. Greg suddenly became aware of footsteps travelling towards the Rover. He checked the mirror but couldn't see Wiersma. The footsteps stopped at the driver's door. He held his breath and turned to face...what? The barrel of a gun? The blade of a knife? Whatever it was it was not likely to be anything nice. He heard the door handle being lifted followed by the click of the latch opening. He clenched his fists and cowered.

'What the hell are you doing?' DI Milne stood outside the car looking in at the quaking figure lying hunched on the floor in front of the passenger seat.

'Get in and shut up,' hissed a slightly relieved Greg Driscoll.

DI Milne thought about mentioning insolence and the fact that he knew what he was doing here. He was the professional and would not be told what to do by an amateur. However, one look at Greg's demeanour changed his mind and he got in and sat in the driver's seat.

'Put that radio back in the glove compartment!'

'Peiter Wiersma is sitting in the Mercedes,' whispered Greg.

Milne turned in his seat and looked towards the hire car. 'There's no-one in the Mercedes, Greg.'

Greg edged up and checked the mirror. 'Damn! He was there. He was on the phone to someone. I tried to tune into his call on the radio.'

'You need a short wave radio for that. Full marks for trying, though.'

Greg swallowed. 'There's no need to be condescending.' If they were to get to Wiersma and help Jenny he was going to have to try harder to get on with this arrogant Detective Inspector. 'Well, what do we do now?' He resisted the temptation to add sir and salute!

'Nothing,' came the reply.

'Nothing? Why can't you go in and find him?'

'We sit here and wait for him to come out again. Don't worry, Greg. I've done this sort of thing before, you know. Put the radio back in the glove compartment'

*

Marjan and Jenny were sitting on the bed in the hotel room when Peiter entered. There were tears on Jenny's cheeks. She hadn't bothered to try and wipe her eyes. They were like a tap, dripping constantly. Marjan had her arm round her, comforting her like a lost child.

'Has she delivered?' Peiter wasn't looking at them. He was standing by the dressing table packing a small holdall.

'No, Peiter. She will. Give her time.' Marjan tried to smile.

'That is the one thing we have very little of. Time. The delivery is expected at eleven-thirty. I've spoken to our contact, he is going to keep a lot of the money back if the consignment is not complete. Maybe she needs a little help.'

'No, please! Let me see what I can do.' Marjan took Jenny into the bathroom and closed the door. Jenny was bewildered. She no longer knew what was going on. She had heard a lot about rape. She had expected to be raped for the last few days. She may have been. She didn't fully know what had happened during her drugged imprisonment. She remembered being left naked for long periods. But this time she had been awake, tired, exhausted even but aware of what was happening. Then again, had Marjan raped her? Was that rape? No-one ever seemed to talk about girls being raped by other girls. What's more, it didn't feel like she imagined rape to feel. It had been tender, caring. Jenny looked into Marjan's eyes. They seemed to hold a lot of pity. She moved towards Jenny and knelt down. She put her hands on Jenny's stomach and rubbed gently in a circular movement.

'Come on, Jenny. Try and get rid of it. Peiter will be much rougher than me.'

Jenny stood there immobile. Peiter opened the door and walked in and indicated to Marjan to leave the room. She stood up and looked at Jenny. A tear rolled down her cheek as she went back to the bedroom.

Jenny could hear Peiter talking to her but couldn't understand what he was saying. She didn't know what was wanted of her. What was she supposed to get rid of? She didn't know where it was, whatever it was. Peiter was shouting at her. The tears were streaming down her face now. Marjan re-entered the bathroom. She was carrying a small black shoulder bag. Marjan opened the bag and gave Jenny an embroidered handkerchief. She could smell Marjan's perfume on it and it gave her a strange comforting feeling. She sat on the toilet seat and tried to stem the tears.

'Leave us, Peiter. She can't do it if you're shouting at her!'

Peiter Wiersma stormed out of the bathroom. Marjan closed the door behind him. She took a small leather pouch from her handbag. Inside was a foil package which she tore open to reveal a pink condom. She unrolled it and held it between her finger and thumb. Her other hand delved into the bag and took out a coloured cardboard tube. It was a travel size container for talcum powder. She prised the top off and emptied the contents into the condom.

'I'll never get away with this,' she whispered to Jenny, 'but I think it's probably our only chance. Talcum powder can look like cocaine through a condom. We just have to hope they don't undo this one before we manage to come up with the goods. Peiter doesn't know what I'm doing, by the way, so keep quiet or we're both done for.'

Jenny didn't have the faintest idea what Marjan was talking about.

*

Denis was in a panic. Han had received another message from Marjan and had spent the last hour trying to get the police to contact DI Milne. An hour that had proved fruitless. It appeared that Marjan had information as to the exact whereabouts of Peiter Wiersma and was currently going it alone pursuing him. Denis knew that this put his clients in grave danger. Nevertheless, despite his protestations, he now found himself sitting in Han's hire car heading towards Essex.

'Where exactly are we going, Han? Do you know?'

'Not exactly, no. Marjan was heading for a place called Maldon. Once we get there we'll have to think again.'

'Great! Milne told us to stay where we were. He's already gone to Maldon with Greg. Why are we following?'

'There's no way I can sit in that hotel waiting.'

'Great!' Denis kept his thoughts to himself. What if they were on the wrong track and Greg and Milne were trying to get hold of them at the hotel? They had no means of contact with them. Worse, what if they were on the right track? What could they expect to find when they got to this place called Maldon? This was not what Denis had entered the theatrical profession for. If he'd wanted action and adventure he'd have joined the Army! Never again would he complain about sitting in his office waiting for the phone to ring. Suddenly that life did not seem at all boring!

*

DI Milne and Greg sat in their car waiting. What they were waiting for, Greg didn't know. He wanted to go in and bust Wiersma. Milne told him he'd been watching 'The Bill' too much! They had to let Wiersma make the first move, besides it wasn't just Wiersma that they wanted. They had to catch him doing the deal and take as many of the ring as possible with the proper back-up. He had arranged over the radio for a number of police cars to be standing by in the area. Confirmation for an issue of arms was expected shortly.

'Greg, I think you should get into the back of the car and lie down. There's a travelling rug on the back seat. Get on the floor and put that over you. If Wiersma sees you we're sunk. He has already seen me. It's probably best if he thinks I'm a travelling salesman on my own, OK?'

Greg reluctantly slipped out of the car and onto the floor in front of the back seat. He wanted to know what was going on, get involved, play the big hero and find Jenny but he knew in reality that he was not even a novice at playing Starsky and Hutch roles and was likely to do more damage than good. He pulled the rug over his body. It smelt of cigarette smoke and reminded him he wanted to smoke. He pulled back the rug, reached up and tapped Milne on the shoulder.

'Can I smoke?'

'Get down! I think we have some action.' Milne reached over and took a briefcase from the back seat as Greg covered himself up again. He put the case on the front seat, took some papers out and pretended to study them.

Peiter Wiersma preceded Marjan out of the front of the hotel. Marjan was supporting Jenny with both arms. Jenny was pale and weak-looking. They went towards the Mercedes and Peiter opened the door. Marjan and Jenny settled themselves in the back seat. Instead of getting in the car, Wiersma closed the door and locked it with the remote control key. It was DI Milne's turn to feel his heart race as Wiersma started towards the Rover sitting at the side of the car park.

'Keep quiet, for God's sake. He's coming this way.'

Greg tried not to breathe under his blanket. His talent for mime did not quite run to looking like a set of luggage under a rug but he did his best. He had managed to get his left leg into a very unnatural position and it was starting to protest. Cramp was setting in. His calf muscle screamed for release from its captive position. Greg gritted his teeth and told it it would have to wait. He tried every relaxation exercise he wished he'd taken more notice of at Drama School but without a great deal of success. He waited in silence for the door to open; waited to feel the barrel of a gun at his head; waited for Peiter Wiersma to tell him to get up. That would be very difficult at the moment. Greg was wondering if his left leg would ever let him stand up again. The pain was excruciating. He could hear footsteps on the gravel outside. They stopped next to his left ear. He heard a knock on the window. He wasn't sure whether it was the front window or the back. He lay still. He heard the whirr of the electric window and felt a distinct draught even under his rug.

'Hello? Are you looking for someone?' It was Wiersma's voice. The sound of it filled Greg with a feeling of both malevolence and nausea. He wanted to leap up from his hiding place and confront the bastard but fortunately realised his cramped leg would restrict him so he lay still and let the nausea override the sense of revenge.

'I'm waiting for a colleague. I was supposed to meet him in the foyer but it looks like he's late, as usual. I hate hotels, don't you? I'd far rather sit in the car. Are you in the selling game?'

There was a pause. Wiersma was looking round the inside of the car, Greg was sure. He held his breath.

'Yes I am, in a way. Sorry to have bothered you.' Greg heard the feet turn and start to walk away. They stopped and came back to the car.

'I'm sorry, have you seen anyone else hanging round the hotel. I, too, was expecting somebody.'

'Not a soul,' said Milne sounding extremely calm to Greg. 'I was just thinking what a nice quiet place this is. A good place to do all sorts of business, if you know what I mean, I must remember it. Do they have conference facilities here, do you know?'

There was no reply from Wiersma. Greg listened to his footsteps once more retreat across the car park. He heard a car door open and close, then an engine roar into life. The Merc was pulling out of the car park! Why wasn't Milne following? He'll lose him!

'Follow him,' Greg hissed from under his rug. 'What do you think you're doing?'

'Be quiet! I can't let him know! He'll be expecting us to follow him.' Milne retrieved the radio from the glove compartment and contacted headquarters. They already had a description of the Mercedes. The radio crackled and informed the inspector a car was tailing the Merc out of the town centre at that very moment.

'What do we do, then?' Greg enquired extricating himself from the rug and trying to stretch his left leg. 'Just sit here and wait again?'

'For the moment, Greg. Don't be impatient. You'll be there soon enough. You'll probably wish you weren't then, believe me. It's not a game, you know. And cover yourself up!'

'I've got cramp, can't I get up and walk it off?'

'No! Stay under cover. Move to a more comfortable position but keep that rug over you.'

Greg shifted his weight and slightly relieved the cramped leg. A horrible thought crossed his mind. Could he trust Milne? Why did he want to keep him under the rug? Is someone else in the car? Is someone else coming to get in the car? Wiersma? Were they in cahoots? Don't be stupid! Greg had heard the police radio. He was in the hands of the British Police Force. Safe and sound! Nevertheless, Greg lifted a corner of the rug and had another look around the car, just in case. Milne was talking quietly into the radio transmitter. There was no-one else in the car, Greg slipped back under the rug and tried unsuccessfully to relax. His body was jolted as Milne suddenly started up the car and released the handbrake.

'OK, Greg. We're on our way. It seems like we're off to the river. How are you're sea-legs?'

Greg was trying not to think of legs at that moment.

***

CHAPTER SIXTEEN

Han Koolhaven was feeling a bit despondent. They were driving into the small market town of Maldon on the Blackwater estuary.

'What exactly are we looking for, Han?' Denis was annoyed. Annoyed and worried. He really should not be sitting in this car with the man who had put his clients in the precarious situation they were now experiencing.

'I don't know,' replied Han. 'Boats, I suppose?'

'Boats!' What the hell for?'

'If Milne thinks Marjan is going to a drop delivered by sea then there must be boats around.' Han was scanning the streets, driving very slowly. An old Ford Fiesta with an open bore exhaust roared up behind them blowing its horn. Han pulled over and let the carful of youths zoom past each occupant waving two fingers out of the windows. The noise from the 200 Watt speakers made the hire car vibrate as they drove past. Denis covered his ears.

'Bloody hooligans!' he yelled.

They were approaching a small bridge over a river. Han suddenly stopped and pointed across Denis, sitting in the passenger seat. 'Look! Boats!' He exclaimed.

'Oh, very good, Han. It's a river, there's bound to be boats!'

He pulled off the bridge onto a concreted area beside the river and parked the car. He opened the door.

'Where are you going?' Denis grabbed his arm.

'To see what I can see.'

'Just stay in the car, Han. If there's a drop happening we don't really want to be anywhere near it, do we?' Denis was pleading more than asking.

Han ignored him and got out. There were a few narrowboats moored by the bank that were obviously occupied and a couple of masted boats. Han didn't know what sort of boats they were but they looked like they'd been there for some time and had seen better days. Denis reluctantly followed him out to the side of the river. A small door at the front of one of the narrowboats beneath them opened and a woman thrust her head out into the gathering gloom.

'That's private property you're on! What you wanting?'

Han leaned over. 'Is this like the only place in Maldon where there'd be boats?'

'Boats! Maldon's full of boats! And this isn't Maldon, it's Heybridge! You want The Hythe. That's what you'll be looking for. The bloody Thames Barges. Take up all the moorings, they do!'

'Thanks,' said Han. 'We'll go and have a look there. Can you give us directions?'

'Up Market Hill, turn left at the top, follow the High Street down again till you come to St Mary's church. It's there.' She went inside, slamming the door behind her.

They went back to the car and got in. Han started the engine and swung the car round heading up the steep hill in front of them. A dark green Rover flashed past them going at some speed in the opposite direction.

'They drive like bloody maniacs round here!' said Denis, gripping the dashboard in front of him. Han hadn't noticed anything out of the ordinary. He thought the British drove rather too carefully!

They reached St Mary's church in a little under five minutes, drove down past it to a wide paved area. The sun was setting and the sky had turned blood red across the mud flats creating an eerie backdrop to the five large boats moored two deep on the side of the quay.

'They'll be the barges, then, I suppose,' mused Han. He pulled into a parking bay by the side of the road and switched off the engine.

'What exactly are we doing here, Han?' Denis was tired and miserable.

'I don't know, Denis. Something tells me this is where we ought to be. We know she was heading to Maldon to contact someone and I have a feeling this might be the place, I don't know why?' Han looked at the disbelief on Denis' face. 'I know it's a long shot. I'm just…well…I don't know. Maybe you're right. Maybe we should have stayed in the hotel at Heathrow!'

Han was realising the folly of his rash decision. Where were they supposed to look? Denis, never having heard of Maldon, assumed it must be one of the many small villages on the east coast of Essex that originated out of trade and fishing routes long since made surplus to requirement by technology, better roads and the demise of rivers and canals as means of transportation. Denis had been almost right. Maldon had a small fishing industry, mostly based on oysters and a boat-building trade mostly dealing with renovation or the recreational side of sailing. There were several sailing clubs and Maldon was a town rather than a village, the population consisting of a mixture of affluent people moving out from London and an indigenous number of local tradesmen and women.

They now just sat in silence on The Hythe beside the five Thames barges, remnants of the past trading that Maldon enjoyed, now employed mostly as pleasure boats for cruises and wedding receptions. It was nearing eleven and apart from the juke-box sounding out from the bar of The Happy Sailor behind them the night had become overcast, dark and quiet.

The street lighting on the riverside was inadequate and the whole overlying mood was depressing.

'How long do you envisage sitting here, Han?' Denis turned to look at the silent figure sitting next to him. There was no reply. 'Well, I don't know about you but I'm not staying here all night.' Denis opened the car door and started to get out.

'Where are you going?' Han asked quietly.

'To the pub. The old Happy Sailor there just happens to be advertising accommodation and I'm booking in for the night. At least it should be warm in there.' He pulled his astrakhan coat round his shoulders and set off for the pub.

'Hold up, Denis. I might as well come with you.'

*

The radio was keeping Milne and Greg informed of developments as they made their way from the White Boar out of Maldon, over the river to the far side of town.

"They've stopped, sir," the constable on the other end of the radio crackled. "They're parked in the industrial estate and they're just sitting there."

'Thank you. Keep me informed of any movement.' Milne sat back in his seat. They were parked near to what looked like an old disused railway station. 'Are you alright, Greg?'

Greg stirred under the rug on the floor of the car. 'Yeah. I'd feel a lot better if I could see what was going on, though. What are the chances of you turning the heating down, it's blowing right up my back.'

There were two police units in the industrial area behind the station keeping Milne informed via the radio. One unit consisted of PC Otley and his partner PC Melbourne inside an unmarked Ford Escort, the other PC Weston and WPC Raynor on foot further into the Industrial area. Each had observed the grey Mercedes arrive and park on the far side of the disused red-brick building that had once been the main railway station for the town of Maldon before Dr Beeching decided Maldon no longer needed a railway line.

*

In the back of the stationary grey Mercedes, Marjan was holding Jenny's hand and squeezing it tightly. She was scared. Not so much for herself but for Jenny. She was praying that somehow Jenny would pass the last condom before Peiter made the exchange. There was no telling the lengths he'd go to to recover it when he found out, and find out he would, Marjan was sure. It had been a stupid idea to fill a condom with talcum powder. They weren't dealing with kids on the street here. These were big time drug dealers – dangerous people. They would surely do a test on each packet.

'What are we waiting for, Peiter?' They had been sitting there for nearly half an hour and Marjan was hoping they'd missed the drop or that there had been some kind of problem that was going to cause a delay. Another day and, surely, Jenny would pass the condom, then they could do the complete drop and… and what? What was she intending to do after the drop? Go off quietly with Peiter again? What would happen to Jenny? He wouldn't let her go. Not now. Not alive. She knew too much! Oh God! Why did she feel this way? How did it all get to this? Why hadn't she got out earlier? If only she'd just left when she had the chance, gone to the police. Prison must be preferable to this. Whys and ifs! They were going to be a part of Marjan's life forever now. She choked back the tears. Don't cry! Not now!

'Peiter? What happens now?'

'We wait!' He was looking towards the river at the far end of the industrial estate. It was a dark black night and he could only just make out the dim bobbing lights on the horizon and the faint sound of an outboard motor gradually getting louder.

*

DI Milne was waiting too. Greg wanted to get on with it but Milne knew the importance of being patient. He told Greg to remain out of sight, there would be action soon enough.

The radio came to life once more. "There seems to be some movement, sir, I can see someone getting out of the car. One male followed by two females."

Greg sat up quickly, throwing the rug from him. 'Two females! Who the hell are they?'

'I'm not sure, Greg. They left the hotel with him.'

'Get a description, quick! One of them might be Jenny.'

Milne spoke into the radio. 'Can you give me an ID on the two women?'

"I'm sorry it's too dark from here, sir."

'OK. Keep them in sight and let me know where they head.'

"They seem to be entering the old station, sir. The man has a pair of cutters and is cutting through the wire fence. Do you want us to go in and pick them up now, sir?"

'No! Wait where you are until I tell you.'

Greg opened the car door and rolled out onto the cold pavement.

'Where the hell do you think you're going?' snapped Milne.

'If one of those women is Jenny I'm going to get her out now!' he set off towards the railway station.

Milne threw the radio handset onto the passenger seat and leaped from the car. He caught up with Greg after a few yards, grabbed him round the neck and threw him onto the floor. He grabbed his arm and twisted it behind him. He put his knee in the small of Greg's back, took hold of his hair and pulled his head up from the floor, grazing his nose and chin.

'I've just about had enough of you, Driscoll. Just try and remember you are not a detective, not a vigilante, not a member of the SAS, you are just a member of the public, a busybody, someone who gets in the way of me doing what I am trained to do and paid to do. This is a straightforward job for me. There's no excitement. It's not an episode of Inspector Morse. You are here to help me. If you can't manage to bring yourself to do that I shall have you arrested and taken as far away from here as possible. Do you understand that?' He let go of Greg's hair and his face hit the cold concrete again. Milne kept hold of his arm and left his knee in Greg's back.

Greg turned his head and spat out some blood. 'Let go of me!' he panted through his anger. Milne released his arm slowly but kept his knee in place.

'What's the decision, Driscoll? Do you stay and help or do I call someone to remove you? If you stay you do exactly as I say and when I say. If I have to get someone to take you away it means I have less cover to help me release your girlfriend – if it is her! Think about it!'

Greg thought about it. He had had enough of being treated like a criminal. He was here to help, he just couldn't stand sitting around waiting. But Milne was right. He had no sort of training for this but of one thing he was sure; there was no way he was leaving now. If that was Jenny with Wiersma he wanted to see him brought to justice and Jenny safe. If it wasn't Jenny he wanted to know exactly where she was. He'd have to comply with Milne for now.

There was a voice on the radio. "Come in, sir. They're at the door of the station…Sir?…Sir?"

'Well, Driscoll?' Milne picked Greg up by the scruff of his neck. He was very strong and Greg found he had no resistance.

'OK I'm sorry. Just make sure Jenny's alright.'

Milne kept hold of Greg's jacket collar as they made their way back to the car. He picked up the radio handset and pressed a button on the side. 'OK. I'm here. Wait where you are.'

*

The bar of the Happy Sailor had closed and Denis and Han were sitting in the small room they had booked for the night. It was a very basic room with twin beds, an old dressing table with a kettle and two mismatched cups and saucers. The bathroom was on the next landing up. They had managed to procure a very expensive bottle of Teacher's whisky from the weary landlady. They had poured one glass each. The two glasses sat forlornly on the bedside cabinet barely touched. Neither of the men felt in the mood for drinking. Denis lay back on the bed and closed his eyes. Han stared moodily out of the window. From where he sat he could see large warehouse buildings on the far bank of the river through the furled red sails of the Thames barges. They looked dark and grey, dead buildings desperately trying to be kept alive by injections of new enterprises.

*

Outside one of the dark, dirty red-brick, boarded up buildings, Marjan and Jenny stood watching as Peiter took a small jemmy from his inside pocket and started to force a side door into what had once been the station waiting room. Once open he pushed the girls in first. Taking a torch from his pocket he checked out the inside of the empty building. What had once been a two-storey building now consisted of one large room with the remains of floorboards and joists jutting out from the walls about half-way to the dripping roof. The concrete floor was covered in rubble, plastic bags and puddles of water. Gingerly Marjan stepped forward into the gloom, followed by Peiter dragging Jenny behind him. They made it nearly half-way across the room when Peiter grabbed hold of Marjan and stopped her. They didn't speak. They made their way to the side wall and stood silently waiting. Neither of the girls had heard a sound nor seen a thing but something made them both follow Peiter's wordless commands. At the other end of the empty room something scuttled across the floor, making its way to where they were standing. Jenny stifled a scream as she felt the wet fur across her ankles. The rat scuttled away back in the direction it had come from. Jenny's eyes, starting to become accustomed to the lack of light, tried to follow it to the far end of the large room. There was nothing to be seen. She felt ill and tired, head spinning, pain in her stomach returning, sharp, twisting pains followed by a sensation of someone beating a drum deep inside her. She started to feel faint, the floor seemingly dissolving below her. Peiter's grip tightened round her wrist, he jerked her up and held her flat against the damp, slimy wall. The spinning in her head slowed but the pain inside increased. Finally the nausea achieved its victory and Jenny convulsed forwards and was violently sick. The vomit was projectile, landing with a heavy splatter a fair distance away on the dank floor.

Marjan went to her side and held her. 'Are you OK?' she whispered.

Jenny answered with another flow of vomit. There were chunks of red in it. The pain increased yet again. Jenny started to slip down the slimy wall.

A small beam of light flashed out from the far end. Peiter started to walk slowly towards it. As he neared the far end the torch shone again. This time it remained on, aimed at Peiter's face and moving slowly to meet him. The girls could just hear a low greeting as they watched the two torches conjoin. There were two dark figures apart from Wiersma.

They appeared to sit on something in the far corner of the room, near a pair of large double doors. Marjan took hold of Jenny's arm and tried gently to move her towards the group.

*

Milne drove round to the other side of the station. Having ascertained that Wiersma had not left anyone guarding the Mercedes he drove slowly towards the entrance to the waiting room. The pot-holed lane to the side of the station led downhill and Milne switched off the Rover's engine and coasted to a position a few yards from the forced door through which Wiersma and the girls had entered.

'OK, Greg,' he whispered. 'I want you to do exactly as I say. Wait in the car but keep your eyes and ears open. I'll blow on this whistle if, and I hope to God I don't, I need you. Listen for two short blasts.'

'A whistle! Is that the best you can manage in this age of technology?'

'It serves its purpose, it's small and it always works, OK? Besides you don't have a radio. Now do as I say. I can't tell you how dangerous your intervention could be.'

Greg thought he knew how Moses must have felt in sight of the Promised Land and not being allowed in. He watched as Milne silently and stealthily made his way to the waiting room door. He saw him talk quietly into the radio attached to his collar.

On the far side of the industrial estate Greg could see several shadows moving swiftly through the darkness towards him. He sank down in the seat and reached for his security blanket.

*

Marjan watched in terror as the two men seated with Peiter on pieces of old, fallen masonry, carefully took and opened the black leather pouches he had given them. The elder of the men, he looked in his mid-fifties, sneered in the direction of Wiersma.

'You could have removed the packaging.' He had a deep guttural voice. His dark eyebrows seemed to be set in a permanent frown.

'I told you there wasn't time,' Wiersma snapped. 'Give me the money and let's get out of this stinking rat-hole. It might be a desirable residence for the likes of you but my constitution is a little more delicate.'

The younger of the two, a gross shaven-headed man in his late teens, started to rise from his concrete block, his fists clenched but was stopped by the older man raising his hand.

'It's OK. He feels inferior. He's a foreigner. He likes to pretend he has a bit of class.'

Peiter glared at him 'The money!'

'All in good time, my friend. First we must do a quality control check. We're not complete imbeciles, you know, Mr Kraut!'

Marjan's heart sank as the older man threw a condom to his accomplice. The young man took out a small set of electronic scales and placed them carefully on the concrete block he had been sitting on. He opened a flick-knife with a six-inch blade and made a small slit in the side of the condom.

Marjan was still holding Jenny's hand but her attention was directed towards the activity going on in the far dim corner. Suddenly she felt Jenny's grip loosen as she staggered into the middle of the room. She was spinning round slowly, her arms reaching out sideways as though looking for something to take hold of. The three men in the corner started to stand as Jenny made a low groan followed by an unearthly scream that split the silence and echoed round the empty ex-railway station. The vomit was projectile again, this time a dark red in colour. Blood red in fact. It seemed to tear itself from Jenny's throat like an animal freed from a trap. The noise was ghastly. The guttural groans from Jenny mixing with the splattering of the vomit hitting the floor and walls of the vacuous room.

*

The scream had reached the ears of Greg lying in the back of the Rover. DI Milne was speaking into his radio, instructing his men to hold their positions and remain silent when he became aware of a figure running towards him. It flashed past where he was standing by the open doorway. Milne held out a hand but Greg pushed him away and ran into the room screaming like a lunatic. He made straight for the forlorn figure of Jenny, now in a crumpled heap on the floor. He took her in his arms and held her.

The paralysis that had overtaken the occupants of the room was broken first by Peiter. Grabbing the black leather pouches from the concrete block in front of him he ran towards Marjan, seized her by the wrist and took her off in the direction of the door. Milne entered as Peiter and Marjan reached the door. Wiersma swung Marjan round and ran full-pelt towards the double doors at the far end of the room. Without stopping his shoulder collided with the old wooden doors set into the wall. The ancient wood splintered around the mortise lock and gave way as if they were cardboard. The swinging, splintered doors struck two of the police officers holding their ground outside. Wiersma's elbow took care of a third as he dragged Marjan half-running, half-sliding down a muddy slipway leading towards the river.

Milne, running after them, was yelling at the stunned police officers. 'Shoot the bastard!' the other two men in the corner ran towards the door, the younger, still carrying the condom was waving his flick-knife in the general direction of Milne. As they reached the breached doors they were set upon by two of the recovering officers who proceeded to take revenge for their dented pride by piling an array of blows on the two. The younger's knife flying through the air into the river. Milne raced past them in pursuit of the other officers who, in turn, were pursuing Wiersma and Marjan.

Swimming and messing about in boats had never appealed to Peiter Wiersma but right now that was exactly what he intended to do. Still dragging Marjan behind him he plunged into the river Blackwater and swam towards one of the tenders dangling from the back of one of the larger boats moored in the estuary. In no time he had sliced through the painter and started the outboard motor. Behind him came shouts ordering him to stop. He ignored them. Turning his tender directly towards the two police officers wading out towards him, he headed straight for them. As he was about to make contact he veered sharply. The tender barely slowed as the propeller cut cleanly through the back of PC Weston. WPC Raynor halted her pursuit and took hold of PC Weston. There was blood oozing from PC Weston's back and mixing with the dark oily waters of the River Blackwater. She slowly made her way back to DI Milne on the bank of the river supporting the heavy weight of PC Weston; Milne came towards them and shone his torch. Weston's body was bent over showing two deep wounds, one at the waist the other across the shoulder blades. The bleeding was now surprisingly slight but the cuts were very deep, deep enough to sever the spinal column and extinguish the life of PC Weston. Milne swung his torch round to where the noise of the outboard motor was diminishing into the distance. There was no sign of Weston's murderers.

Inside the old railway station, Greg was still hunched over Jenny. She was quite silent. Greg was sobbing. Milne walked slowly into the room and looked at Greg and Jenny. Tempering his anger he crossed towards the two of them and put his hand on Greg's shoulder. Greg didn't move. The sound of sirens announced the arrival of a couple of ambulances followed by three police cars. Milne helped Greg to his feet as the ambulance staff entered carrying a stretcher. He let Greg help them lift Jenny onto the stretcher and watched them leave for the local hospital. He then turned to the six policemen standing in the doorway. They were wearing dark blue combat jackets and holding handguns.

'You're a little late,' was all he could say as he returned to his car. He sat quite still for a few seconds as though trying to come to a decision before starting his car and driving towards the hospital, leaving several confused police wondering what they were supposed to do. Not for the first time, DI Milne was wondering why on earth he ever wanted to be a member of the British Police Force.

***

CHAPTER SEVENTEEN

There was a lot of activity in the section of the bar set aside for breakfast in The Happy Sailor public house. Han and Denis had been up for most of the night. They had heard the sirens that belonged to the police cars the night before. They had watched helplessly from their bedroom window as the car headlights came and went on the other side of the river. Han had wanted to get involved, to rush across the river and catch Wiersma red-handed. Denis' sensibility had prevailed as he pointed out they wouldn't be allowed anywhere near the scene. Besides it might have nothing to do with Peiter Wiersma. It could just be an ordinary, run-of-the-mill break-in. Neither of them believed this!

'Did you hear? There was a big drugs raid in the old railway station last night!'

'Hundreds of police swarming all over the place.'

'Did they get them?'

'All but one apparently.'

'There were several people killed, I heard.'

Han and Denis sat quietly at their table listening to the gossip. The news that several people had been killed filled them with apprehension. Why hadn't they stayed in their hotel in Heathrow? They might know what had happened by now. What were they supposed to do? Han had been out already, he'd phoned the hotel in Heathrow but there was no message for either of them. He'd walked back up the High Street, back down Market Hill, over the bridge and back to where they'd first stopped on their entry into Maldon. They'd been no more than a couple of hundred yards from where the previous night's incident had occurred. He tried to get to the old industrial area where he'd seen the activity taking place the night before from across the river at The Hythe but they were not letting anyone any nearer to the old buildings, blue and white plastic tape stretched across the road reinforced by a number of police making sure no-one could get close. There was one Outside Broadcast van with a large satellite dish attached to the top at the end of the road and alongside the river a couple of reporters standing in front of cameramen interviewing the local residents and telling the world that there was nothing to report. Han spotted the woman from the narrowboat he had spoken with the night before and thought it prudent to steer clear. Nobody could give him any information whatsoever.

Han and Denis decided they wouldn't show any extraordinary interest in the previous night's events. Don't draw attention. Don't cause any suspicion. Act normally. Have breakfast and leave. Then what? Han still thought the idea of going to the police was a bad one but Denis was starting to take charge. He'd had enough of undercover work. After all, where had it got them so far? While all the action was taking place they had been stuck in a room in a public house. Han gave in reluctantly and following a breakfast neither of them were inclined to eat, was in their car heading for the local police station.

What worried Denis more than anything was the rumour that people had been killed. Where had Greg been during all this? Was he at the old station last night? Was he one of the ones who had been….it didn't bear thinking about! Denis tried hard to convince himself that Milne would never have let Greg anywhere near such a dangerous situation. He was not having much success. His only crumb of comfort was that sober Greg was a coward not a hero and the chances of Greg having got hold of any alcohol in Milne's company would be thankfully slim. He drove in silence to the police station still wishing that this would all be revealed as a bad dream.

*

At the Accident and Emergency Department of Broomfield hospital in Chelmsford, Greg was sitting in the waiting room nursing a cold cup of coffee. He'd been there all night. He'd held onto Jenny's hand all through the interminable journey from Maldon to Chelmsford. Milne had insisted that Greg be allowed to travel in the back of the ambulance, along with a policewoman and a female paramedic. Jenny seemed to be in a coma. To Greg she hadn't appeared to be breathing at all, although the bleeps coming from a machine with a small screen were telling that her heart was still beating. Once she'd opened her eyes and seemed to smile ever so slightly before drifting back into the safety of oblivion. She'd looked terrible nothing like the beautiful young girl he'd been having pizza with less than two weeks previously. Her face was drawn with sunken cheeks; her auburn hair dull and matted; her skin grey, like an old woman.

Greg was tired. His arms and legs were heavier than lead, his head ached, his heart was working hard. His eyes wanted to sleep but his mind was stubbornly awake. His grazed nose and chin had been cleaned up and he'd been offered some pills of some sort that he'd refused. He needed to be awake. His body picked itself up and pricked his ears at the slightest sound of footsteps. His mouth asked anyone in a white coat for a progress report. He was trying to piece together the last few horrendous hours. All he could remember was that awful scream from Jenny and the next thing being next to her holding her seemingly lifeless body in his arms. Milne had tried to explain a bit of what happened, how three of his officers were injured, one fatally – a PC Weston, married with two young kids. Whether Milne had meant to or not he made Greg feel totally responsible, not only for Jenny's situation but for the failure to catch Wiersma and, more significantly, the death of PC Weston.

The whole situation was unbelievable. Greg's head felt like it was filled with cotton wool. The WPC who had travelled with them in the ambulance brought another cup of coffee. He thanked her and put it next to the two half-filled cups on the floor next to his chair.

'I'm sure she'll be alright, try not to worry.' She smiled kindly at Greg, he smiled back at her. They always say that. What else could she say? She's going to die and it's all your fault. You worry, boy. That's the least you can do.

'I understand you're an actor. Have I seen you in anything?'

Greg resisted the urge to ask her if she ever went to a provincial repertory theatre or whether she thought actors only worked on TV and just said, 'I don't suppose so.'

'I wanted to be an actress, you know, when I was a little girl. I was turned against it by my school and my parents, though. They said I should get a job with more of a future. Silly really, isn't it? I think you should be allowed to do anything you want to do, as long as it's legal, I mean. You've only got one life, after all.'

Greg looked at the plump young girl in uniform sitting next to him. What was she? Twenty? Twenty-one? Not much more. He wanted to laugh. He was sure she didn't realise she was adding to Greg's agony. One life? How poignant! What sort of future was there for Jenny? Come to that, what sort of future was there for PC Weston. He didn't think the police force offered a very secure future.

'I'm sorry about your colleague,' he said.

The girl's eyes filled with tears. 'His poor kids.' She took a hanky from her sleeve and stood up. 'Excuse me,' she blubbed and walked off towards the Ladies.

*

Han and Denis, having spent the best part of an hour at Maldon police station trying to convince the duty sergeant that they had to speak to Detective Inspector Milne regarding the incident last night and weren't prepared to give a statement to anyone else, finally arrived at the Essex police headquarters in Chelmsford at ten-thirty. DI Milne had set up an incident room there, having been told that Maldon didn't have the facilities he required. He looked weary and appeared to Han and Denis to have aged several years since they'd last met, the day before. He invited them into a small office and asked them to sit down.

'I'm sorry I didn't get in touch with you at your hotel, I really didn't have much time.' Milne had his head in his hand and his elbows on the desk in front of him.

'That's OK,' replied Han before Denis could say that they had been in Maldon the whole time. 'We thought we ought to try and find you this morning and see what's been going on.'

'How did you know about the incident last night?'

'Well, we didn't really,' lied Han. 'We knew you were on your way to a place called Maldon so we tried there first. They eventually sent us here. There were no more messages from Ms Smits.'

'No. There wouldn't have been. She was here with Wiersma.' He paused, lifted his head and looked at the two men in front of him. 'I suppose I may as well fill you in a bit but I don't want you to involve yourselves in more than an information capacity. I've seen enough heroics for the time being.'

'What do you mean, Inspector?' Denis tried to keep the trepidation from, his voice.

'Your friend Driscoll screwed up a very expensive operation last night trying to rescue his girlfriend.' Milne gave Han and Denis a brief rundown of the previous night's events. Denis' face went from pale to white as the story unfolded. It recovered a slight hue as he heard of the relative safety of Greg and Jenny at Broomfield hospital.

'Can we see Greg and Jenny, Inspector?'

'I'm waiting to hear from the hospital when Miss Gulliver is in a fit state to talk to us. I shall take you with me if that is in the very near future. In the meantime I shall require you to remain here, if you don't mind. Coffee?' Milne poured them all some very black-looking coffee from a glass jug into plastic cups that started to expand with the heat.

*

Greg's coffee was cold again and barely touched as the nurse called the young policewoman over to her desk. He watched as they whispered to each other. The nurse pointed to Greg and the WPC shook her head. She crossed back to Greg and took his hand. 'It won't be long now, she's doing fine. Please don't worry.'

Why had she said please? That seemed an odd thing to say. It made Greg worry more.

'Is she awake? Can I see her?'

'She is awake, Mr Driscoll, yes but I'm afraid you can't see her just yet. She's very weak and the Inspector has to see her first. I'm just going to phone him now. Will you be OK for a minute?'

'Yes, I'll be fine, thanks.' Greg watched her leave with the nurse. As she turned the corner, Greg got up from his seat. He walked slowly towards the corridor the nurse had come from. He walked down the corridor looking in each room as he passed. He turned the corner and saw a room with a constable sitting outside trying to tackle the crossword puzzle in the 'Sun'. He looked up from his puzzle as Greg neared.

'Are you Mr Driscoll, sir?' he said.

'Yes, I am.' Greg waited for some sort of reaction from the constable. He was sure the constable would be blaming him for the death of his colleague.

'It seems like she's going to be OK. Don't worry, sir.'

Greg wished people would stop telling him not to worry. He stood outside the door. There was a curtain stopping him seeing inside the room. He took a step towards the door. The PC stood up.

'Can I go in and see her, please?'

'I'm sorry, sir. No-one's allowed in at present. You can sit here if you like. Paper?' He thrust the 'Sun' at Greg.

'No thanks. I'll...er...I'll go and sit back in the waiting area.'

'OK. Won't be long now, sir. Don't you worry.'

Greg thought about what the sentence would be for grievous bodily harm on a police constable as he returned to his seat in the drab waiting area of the Broomfield hospital and worried.

***

CHAPTER EIGHTEEN

Marjan knew that a description of her and Peiter would be circulated by this morning. Things had happened so fast the previous night. She had been in the back of the small tender before she'd realised. If she'd had time to think she would have given herself up to the police there and then but Peiter's might had forced her into the boat and out towards the sea. She had not seen the result of PC Weston's encounter with the outboard motor but had felt the jolt the boat had made as it cut through him. The force of the jolt had not done a great deal of good for the steering mechanism of the boat. As a getaway vehicle it was less than perfect anyway, being intended only as a means of getting between a moored yacht and the shore, not something one necessarily had to do in a hurry. As the tender had rounded the last mooring in the estuary, Peiter had turned hard to starboard and entered a little creek where some shabby boats were harboured. The boats all appeared empty, many were evidently not seaworthy as they rested on dry land with various parts scattered around them. They had made their way by foot to one of the most dilapidated and, forcing a hatch without much difficulty, made themselves a shelter for the night. Peiter had released some of his excitement and tension by forcing himself on Marjan. She hadn't resisted.

Before first light they were out of the boat and heading through the hedgerows. They came out on an unmarked road on the outskirts of town. There was a farmhouse a few hundred yards to their left and a country bus stop just beyond that. At the bus stop was an old red telephone box. Making Marjan stay out of sight, Peiter headed for the 'phone box.

*

Rob Vanderlast had spent a very fitful night. There had been no contact from Peiter. He should have received a call around midnight. Just a short message to tell him which plane to meet. Rob had sat in his flat in Amsterdam all night waiting, willing the phone to ring. He didn't like it. Something was wrong. It was to do with Marjan, of that he was certain. Peiter had told Rob to fetch her from some hotel in the English Lake District. Then he'd called saying not to worry, everything was OK now and he was fetching her himself. And why was Peiter doing the exchange in England anyway? He never did the exchanges himself he always left anything risky to his minions. Rob wanted to know what was going on.

The ring of the telephone interrupted his thoughts. He leapt from the chair and picked up the receiver. Peiter's voice sounded panicky.

'There's been an almighty cock-up. Get me two passports, fly to London Stansted Airport, take a taxi to a hotel called The Saracen in Great Dunmow and ask for Mr Morris.'

'Wait! What's going on? Two passports? Who for? In what name?'

'One for me, one for Marjan. In any name. Get here as quickly as possible. I will have the photographs.' Peiter Wiersma hung up the phone.

*

The shop assistant looked strangely at the young girl with the short bleached blond hair. She thought she knew everybody who lived locally and in a town the size of Maldon she probably did. Beautiful though the area was it didn't attract so many tourists to make a difference. Besides, she didn't look like a tourist, there seemed to be something odd about this girl. She was behaving furtively in the assistant's opinion. The establishment advertised itself as selling 'everything for the household'. It was an ironmongers, a stationers, a boutique (though not a very fashionable one) and an electrical shop. The girl was carrying the wire basket over her arm and appeared to be shopping with some haste. She had entered the shop as the assistant was unlocking the door that morning. Maybe she was going on holiday and needed a few things before rushing off for the plane? Most of the items in the basket seemed to confirm this to the assistant. An electric shaver; a couple of tee-shirts; a pair of jeans and some corduroy trousers; two pairs of canvas sailing shoes; two sweaters; some hair spray; a hair brush and a pair of nail scissors. Maybe she was running away from an abusive husband or maybe she was pregnant and her abusive father was about to lock her in her room while he arranged for the baby's father to be done away with. The girl paid in cash, smiled and left the shop leaving the assistant thinking she should stop watching so many soap operas and get a life.

The shop was in a small arcade off the High Street in Maldon. Two doors from the 'Sell-everything' shop was a novelty shop selling jokes and had fancy-dress costumes for hire and for sale. The blond girl went in and asked the man behind the counter if she could buy a long black wig for a party she was attending. Following a brief discussion where the shop-owner tried to persuade her it would be cheaper to hire a full-length witches outfit, the girl left with an overpriced, jet-black, waist-length nylon wig – 'guaranteed to look like genuine human hair when worn'.

Outside, the arcade was all but deserted except for a middle-aged woman indulging in a spot of gossip with a young mother. After all, it wasn't every day there was a drugs bust and people killed in Maldon. The two ladies were just bidding each other goodbye and going their separate ways as the girl left the shop. The young mother, pushing her pram ahead of her nearly collided with her. The baby cried and the two females exchanged apologies. It was over an hour later that the mother of the baby discovered that her purse was no longer in the top of her handbag.

*

Jenny Gulliver was not really aware of the questions that DI Milne was putting to her. What happened between her being taken from the car in Germany and put into the hospital, or whatever the place was, and waking up here in this hospital were a complete blank. She vaguely remembered Marjan as if she were part of a dream but everything else had been wiped from her memory. Being told about swallowing condoms would normally have made her giggle and blush. What a ludicrous thing for anyone to do! She found the mention of contraceptives by a senior policeman extremely embarrassing and she turned her head away. Her head throbbed. She had a drip in her left hand and a pain in her side. She slid her right hand under the bedclothes and could feel a large bandage attached to her right side with sticking plaster. The pain was increasing and she was finding difficult to focus. She laid her head back on the pillow and closed her eyes. She may have heard the doctor say something to Milne about exhaustion before the world went dark and she fell back into a deep sleep.

DI Milne detailed the young constable outside the room to let him know when the doctor thought he could ask

Miss Gulliver some more questions and made his way to the hospital tea-bar where Greg Driscoll was waiting. Greg had his head on the table and looked as though he had fallen asleep. Milne went up to him and lifted his head by the hair.

'You look bloody awful! Go and get some sleep.'

'I thought you'd want to question me, lock me up, keep me out of your way, that sort of thing.'

'It's a bit late for that now! I tell you, I wish I'd done exactly that before I let you...' he paused and looked a Greg. 'Well, before that fiasco last night. Did you see that agent of yours?'

'Yes. He and Han are going back to Denis' flat, I think. They told your constable. They said they'd be back soon but I doubt it. They looked so tired, I suspect they'll have a lie-down first.' Greg paused, as though he didn't dare ask the next question. 'How's Jenny?' he said eventually. His finger traced a pattern of the Formica table-top.

'She's a bit tired. The doctors say the prognosis is good, though, considering…'

Jenny had been operated on as soon as she arrived at the hospital. Her stomach had been opened up to reveal the final condom of cocaine. Apparently there was some deterioration starting in the rubber and if Jenny hadn't been operated on immediately it was almost certain the condom would have burst and she would have died from a massive overdose. Milne had asked if that was what had made her throw up so violently in the old railway station but the doctors assured him that if any cocaine had seeped from the condom she wouldn't be here now. The cocaine would have shot round her blood stream so fast she would have died almost instantly. There was evidence of internal bleeding which could have been caused by the vomiting. The doctors could give no definite reason for the violence of the vomiting other than it being a mechanism of defence by a body crying out for help and that there were still a lot of things we didn't know about the workings of the human body. Milne wasn't sure whether that gave him much confidence in the National Health Service or not.

Milne bought two cups of strong black coffee and sat down opposite Greg. He was still unsure what to do about Greg's intervention at the railway station. He knew that if Greg hadn't rushed in, Jenny would now almost certainly have been dead. He'd have to give his chief a full report and he knew disciplinary action could well be taken against him as well as Greg. After all, he was the one who'd let Greg come on the mission, which was breaking all the rules. He knew he should have waited for the armed support to arrive. He could have kept his superiors more informed but he was a superior officer himself, surely he could make decisions without being castigated. It was police bureaucracy that had held up the armed officers. Not his fault.

He offered Greg the coffee. Greg looked up.

'Do you have a first name, Inspector?'

Milne smiled. 'Roger. It's Roger, Greg.'

'Well, I'm sorry, Roger. It's all my fault, I know. I could have killed Jenny – like I did that constable.'

'You didn't kill him, Greg. He was killed in the pursuit of his duty. And you may just have saved Jenny's life. My only regret is that we didn't catch the bastards! I'd like to string Wiersma up by the balls!'

*

Peiter Wiersma was sitting in the back seat of a hired Ford Grenada. He was trimming his moustache with a pair of nail scissors prior to shaving it off with the electric razor Marjan had bought earlier. Marjan was in the front seat, driving. She was wearing the black wig. She had cut it so that the hair fell on top of her shoulders and styled it with the hair spray and brush into a sort of bob. She was wearing jeans and a sweater. Peiter was wearing the cords. Marjan was driving in the direction of Great Dunmow.

Taking purses from people's bags had been an easy way to make a sort of living when she'd been a kid in Amsterdam. Tourists were often careless and often quite flush. Rich pickings if you were skilled enough and Marjan had been. She hadn't picked anyone's pocket for a long time before that morning. She'd forgotten the thrill it gave her as she'd slipped the wallet or purse into her own pocket. She smiled to herself. The pickings that morning had not been rich. Twenty-five pounds in notes, not a lot to Marjan but probably enough to make a deal of difference to the young mother she'd stolen it from. However, without the two credit cards and the driving license in the purse, Marjan would not have been able to hire the car. She'd picked Peiter up from the phone box where he'd been waiting. He'd been pleased with her ingenuity in acquiring the car but Marjan felt no satisfaction from his praise. They drove through Great Dunmow town centre, stopping at the local supermarket and picking up passport size photos of each of them in their new identities from the self-service photo booth. Marjan dropped Peiter off at the front of the Saracen Hotel before parking the car in a side street roughly half a mile away and walking back to the hotel. Peiter was in the bar waiting to be served with morning coffee. Marjan sat next to him and he leaned over to whisper to her.

'I've booked a room. I've told them you will pay with your credit card. The room is in my name, which is Morris. You are my secretary.'

Marjan went to reception and, ignoring the smirk on the receptionist's face, checked into the room with the stolen credit card. She was shown up to the first floor room by a young man who also smirked when Marjan told him her bag would be arriving later. She closed the door in his face.

Suddenly, having stopped racing about, a tremble came over her whole body. It wasn't cold in the room but she hugged herself and lay down on the bed. The telephone ringing made her jump. It was Peiter insisting she joined him for coffee in the bar. Wearily she got up from the bed and looked in the mirror. She laughed to herself. She looked like a re-incarnation of her younger self, before she got mixed up with the wrong crowd, as her mother had called them. The black wig made her look homely, almost prim, she thought. Her eyes started to fill with tears and she turned away. Not now. Don't cry now. There'd be time for tears later – she hoped. Marjan left the room, went down to the bar and sat down next to Peiter.

'What do we do now?' she asked him as she poured the coffee.

'Sit and wait for Rob,' came the reply.

'Here in the bar? Shouldn't we keep out of sight?'

'Why arouse suspicion? No-one knows us here. Just relax, it'll all be over soon, I promise.'

'One way or another, I suppose you're right,' said Marjan, sitting back and sipping her black coffee.

Peiter was reading a copy of the Daily Telegraph he had picked up at the reception desk. Marjan looked at him over the top of her cup. He was calm, almost smiling. His face was transformed without his moustache. Marjan had never seen him with no facial hair. He didn't look any better. His top lip had a scowl that seemed to be a permanent feature, even though the rest of his body was relaxed. He looked just like someone waiting for a colleague. Marjan thought she must look like anything but his secretary. She had a feeling of self-loathing. How did she let herself get into this? Peiter put his newspaper down on the table in front of Marjan and sipped his coffee. He leaned towards Marjan and spoke quietly to her.

'The English are so stupid!' He leaned back and drank some more coffee, smiling as he eyed Marjan. She averted her eyes to avoid his gaze. They fell on the newspaper Peiter had left on the table. There was a picture of the old railway station at Maldon and what seemed like a short article running to two columns. She picked it up and started to read. '*A police officer was killed and two more seriously injured in an incident at a disused railway station in the Essex town of Maldon last night. Police stated that a shipment of narcotics was being delivered and, acting on a tip-off, a small force successfully recovered a small quantity of cocaine. They managed to capture several of the gang. The police officer who was killed has been named as father of two, Mark Weston, who has been recommended for a bravery award. He was killed trying to arrest two of the gang as they escaped in a small motor-boat on the Blackwater Estuary. Police are looking for a well-built middle-aged man, possibly of German origin, with a large walrus-type moustache accompanied by a girl in her early twenties, possibly Dutch, with short blonde hair. Police are waiting anxiously by the bed of one of the captives, a young girl, who is presently in Broomfield hospital in Essex. DI Milne, in charge of the investigation told our reporter: 'This young girl seems to have been duped into carrying condoms full of cocaine in her stomach. Whether she was forced to do this or not we are waiting to find out if she recovers. It appears, unfortunately, that one of the condoms may have burst inside her and she is now in grave danger. We should know in the next few hours whether she will pull through or not. At the moment it seems unlikely she will survive the night.' Police are hoping the young girl will recover and be able to give them vital information concerning the possible whereabouts of the missing members of the gang.'*

Marjan had turned very pale. She felt sick. Her hand was shaking as she reached for her coffee and drained the cup. Peiter smirked at her.

'Don't worry. I don't think Miss Gulliver will be telling the police anything. I don't know why you pretended to me that she had passed the condom. You should have let me help her to pass it but don't feel guilty, I know you were only trying to help her.' He sat back in his seat, picked up the paper and resumed his reading.

Marjan sat very still. She didn't know what to do next. Peiter was right she had been trying to help Jenny, she had a good idea what Peiter's methods of help would consist of, but all she seemed to have done was push her towards a painful death. It amounted to murder, which, with that poor policeman, meant she had now been an accessory to two murders in the last twenty-four hours. Maybe the report was wrong, maybe Jenny was alright really. They were wrong about recovering the cocaine. Marjan knew that Wiersma had picked the cocaine-filled condoms up as he ran towards the river because he had given them to her and they were sitting in their leather case in her handbag. Maybe they were not telling the truth. Maybe.

Rob Vanderlast came into the bar of the Saracen and looked around before recognising Peiter and Marjan. He went over to their table. He was tired and he looked it. He also looked worried. His head drooped between his shoulders making him look a lot shorter than his six feet five inches. His demeanour made him look like a schoolboy summoned to the headmaster.

'Drink, Rob?' Wiersma appeared icy cool.

'What's going on?' said the Dutchman.

'Have a drink.' This time it was an order, not a request.

Marjan stood deep in thought at the bar, waiting for the drinks. There was an embryo of an idea hatching in her mind. It was an idea that might not do her any good but it was an idea that more and more she felt she had to go through with. Her frame of mind was more relaxed as she returned with a large brandy for Peiter, a bottle of Pils lager for Rob and a mineral water for herself. She needed to keep her wits about her for the next few hours at least.

*

At Broomfield hospital Greg Driscoll was drowsing on his brown plastic chair in the area set aside for friends and relatives. He hadn't slept properly for forty-eight hours and was feeling completely done in. DI Milne had gone home and another young constable had started his shift, sitting outside the private ward on which Jenny Gulliver had been installed. There had been little news throughout the time Greg had been there apart from the fact that she was drifting in and out of consciousness, which was apparently completely normal for someone in her state! Milne had tried to get Greg to go home and get some sleep, all to no avail, especially when Greg pointed out that his home did not seem very welcoming to him at the moment. He hadn't spent a night there since the intruder had left a large bruise between his shoulder blades a week ago. So much had happened since then, none of it encouraging him to return to his lonely council flat in Hackney. Gravity pulled his head hard enough to wake him from his slumbers. He rolled his head and stretched. It was still light outside which appeared odd to him. It felt like three o'clock in the morning. He hadn't realised that it was possible to feel as though one had such a massive hangover when one hadn't touched a drop! A drop is what he wanted now, though. A very large drop. About the size of a bottle! National Health Service coffee was not what the doctor ordered. Certainly it wasn't doctor Driscoll's prescription. He stood and stretched his legs. He noticed one of the nurses smiling at him. She was leaning against the corner by the receptionist's window. He smiled back and she moved towards him. He didn't really feel like any more small talk at the moment but didn't have the energy to resist.

'Hi. You're still here then?'

Greg resisted the obvious and replied that he was.

'Do you fancy a decent cup of coffee or maybe a drink? I've just knocked off and I've a bit of time before my bus. How about it?'

'I'm sorry. Believe me, in other circumstances I wouldn't think twice but…well…I think I ought to stay here. Thanks.' Greg was tempted, he was definitely tempted.

'Look,' said the nurse. 'I know it's none of my business but I don't think your friend is going to worry about you having a quick drink. I think she'll be asleep for quite a while yet. She's been through a lot, you know, physically and mentally. There's nothing you can do to help her by sitting here, you know. When she comes round properly she'll want to see you all refreshed. Come along. Come with me now.'

Greg was too tired to even try to disobey and let himself be led to the exit.

*

The taxi pulled into the drop-off point outside the terminal at Stansted airport. Three people got out. The taxi driver watched them as they walked through the glass revolving doors and went towards the check-in desks. Something made him feel suspicious. It wasn't just the twenty pound note they'd given him for the seven pound fare, he often had large tips from foreign visitors on their way home. No! It was something about the girl. She seemed to be nervous as if she was being taken somewhere she didn't want to go to. The two men had talked in a language he didn't understand, could have been German he wasn't sure. He'd never done languages at school. The girl had sat quietly, not responding with more than a nod or a grunt when addressed by the others. He left his car and walked towards the entrance to the terminal. A policeman with a gun came up to him.

'You can't leave your car there.'

'I'm sorry. I'm a taxi driver and I've just dropped some people off and I think they're a bit suspicious.' He suddenly felt very stupid. Why hadn't he just driven away?

Why was he letting his imagination take over? He wanted to go back to his taxi.

'What made you think they were suspicious, sir?'

'Well, it's difficult to say, really. They just looked shifty, if you know what I mean.' He desperately wanted to run away now. 'Look, it doesn't matter. Just my imagination. My wife's always telling me I think too much. I'll move the car.' He went back to his car and drove off.

'Bloody nutter,' the policeman said to his colleague and they carried on discussing the tactical differences between Manchester United and Tottenham Hotspur.

Rob, Peiter and Marjan had checked in for their flight. Rob had delivered the passports and they'd pasted the new photos in them up in the room at the hotel. They were in the names of Alec Astrop and Mary Briggs. Rob also had a false passport under the name of Dennis Page. He wasn't sure whether the police knew his connection yet but they certainly would before long. He was not taking any chances. They had timed it well, the last call for passengers was just going out over the Tannoy. There should be no problem getting straight onto the plane and taking off to the relative safety of home. As they neared passport control, Marjan took hold of Peiter's sleeve.

'I still have those condoms. I can't take them through.'

'Where the hell are they? Why didn't you do something with them before?'

'It's OK,' whispered Marjan. 'I'll just go to the toilet and dispose of them there.'

Wiersma grabbed hold of her arm. 'No you bloody won't. Swallow them,' he ordered.

'What! After what's happened to Jenny?'

'You should have thought of that before. Go now. We will wait here for you.'

'No. You go through. I'll see you on the plane.'

'Come on,' said Rob. 'The plane will leave without us and I, for one, want out of this country as soon as I can.'

Wiersma hesitated. 'Make sure you're on that plane, my girl. You are not safe without me, don't forget that.' He let go of Marjan and she turned to go to the Ladies. Peiter watched her. He was worried but like Rob he needed to get out of the country – with or without Marjan. He handed his false passport to the official. Much as he had expected, when the plane finally took off fifteen minutes later, the seat next to him was empty. The stupid girl! He didn't know what she thought she could gain by not coming with him. He could have offered her a rich life, all she had to do was stay with him. He hadn't expected her to be faithful; just to be there when he wanted her. He felt a pang inside him. He wasn't sure if it was anger or what; it certainly wasn't jealousy, he wasn't the jealous sort. He didn't give a toss what Marjan did when he wasn't with her but he expected her to do as she was told when he commanded. He had commanded now and she had disobeyed. She was bringing trouble on herself. He ignored Rob Vanderlast and didn't speak a word on the whole flight.

In the Ladies toilet at Stansted airport, Marjan had locked herself in one of the cubicles. She sat down on the toilet seat and slowly took each rubber package out of the pouches and laid them on her thighs. She looked at them with loathing. Such a small amount of illicit drugs was causing such huge problems, not just for her but for Greg, Han and, above all, Jenny. She wished she could turn the clock back; back to before she met Peiter Wiersma and all his promises. Her tears dripped onto her jeans next to where the condoms lay like deflated balloons. She sniffed and tried to pull herself together. Not much longer now. She could hear over the loudspeakers the last call for passenger Briggs – her pseudonym. The plane was about to take off. She looked up. Someone had scratched *'You'll miss your plane'* on the door. She smiled. She certainly hoped she would. She sat still for nearly half an hour, occasionally wiping her wet cheeks. When she was sure the plane had taken off without her, she took the condoms in her hand and stood up. She took the nail scissors from her bag and carefully cut the tied ends off the condoms. Removing each tied up piece of rubber and peeling back part of the plastic wrapping, she licked her finger and put it into the white powder. Tasting the first one she felt a tingling sensation on her tongue. She repeated this with a different finger on the second and third condoms. The contents of the fourth left no tingling. She tried again and felt nothing but a chalky taste. 'Good,' she thought. 'That's the talcum powder.' Her head was very clear. She had stopped crying. She took a large pinch of cocaine and put it on the back of her left hand. Closing her left nostril with her right forefinger, she took a deep breath, feeling the powder shoot up her nostril. She opened her eyes wide and repeated the act for the other nostril. She emptied the remaining contents of all but one of the condoms into the toilet pan and flushed it. She watched as the water foamed slightly as the cocaine and talcum powder were washed away into the sewage system of East Anglia. The last unopened condom of cocaine she replaced in one of the leather pouches, depositing that pouch in her bag, leaving the empty pouch on the floor. She opened the cubicle door. The room was empty. Quickly she went to the wash basin, put her hand under the cold tap and switched it on.

*

Greg was sitting quietly nursing his pint. Sitting on the other side of the table was an extremely attractive young lady prepared to give him her full attention, a situation Greg would normally only have dreamed about. She had been talking cheerfully ever since they left the hospital. She'd hailed a taxi waiting outside the main entrance and taken Greg to The Blue Angel, a pub about a mile down the road towards Chelmsford. It was a great looking pub with good beers. The nurse's name was Cathy Brown and she lived in a small flat in Chelmsford with two other nurses, both of whom worked at the Broomfield hospital. She was twenty-five and single, having recently split from a four year relation with an accountant. Accountants were not boring, she insisted, at least not the one she'd been involved with. Turned out he was 'a bit of a lad' who couldn't keep his hands to himself. Cathy had finally got fed up with his infidelity and kicked him out. At first she'd regretted it, feeling lonely and insecure but was completely over him now. Most of what Cathy had said had just drifted through Greg's mind and floated off into the haze of the bar at The Blue Angel.

'What about you?' Cathy poked Greg's arm.

Greg looked up from his glass. 'I'm sorry?'

'You haven't been listening to a word I've said, have you? It doesn't matter. I do tend to rabbit a bit sometimes. Come on. Tell me a bit about yourself. I know you're an actor and that I don't think I've ever seen you on TV. Tell me about you, you know, what you do when you're not working, that sort of thing.'

'Oh, I don't know. Get drunk, get depressed, that sort of thing.'

'Do you want another drink, your glass is empty?'

'Look, I'm sorry. I'm not very good company. Perhaps I'd better get back to the hospital.'

'Not likely! There's nothing you can do there apart from get in the way. I think your girlfriend would rather see you looking healthier than you do at the moment. She'll need you to be strong for her for a while, you know.'

'And drinking's going to help me look healthier is it?'

'It might help you relax a bit. I'll get you another pint.' Cathy picked up Greg's empty glass and went to the bar. Greg watched her. She was very attractive. What was she doing here with him? Did she fancy him or something? She'd called Jenny his girlfriend. Was she? He didn't know, he didn't think so. They weren't going out or anything. What about this Cathy? Normally he'd be thanking his lucky stars or whatever but with Jenny lying in that hospital bed… He took a deep breath, sighed and rolled his shoulders. He was tired. He had always hated hospitals, they made him feel nauseous and he seemed to have spent a lot of time in them recently. He hadn't eaten for ages. He went up to Cathy at the bar.

'Get a couple of packets of crisps or something, please. I'm going to the loo and, by the way, Jenny's not my girlfriend she's just a friend who happens to be a girl.'

Cathy smiled as she watched him head off to the Gents. There was a flutter in the pit of her stomach that she hadn't felt for some time. The barman cleared his throat to attract her attention.

'Three pounds twenty, please, love.' He winked at her as Cathy handed him the money. 'First date, is it?'

Cathy smirked. 'You never know,' she said. 'You never know.' She went back to the table to wait for Greg.

In the Gents toilet Greg washed his face and wet his hair. He looked for some sort of towel only to realise that there was just a machine that blew hot air in the general direction of where he stood. There was a metal tube on the front that swivelled. He turned it towards his face and pressed the 'on' button. Hot air blew at him for a few seconds and then cut out. He pressed the button again and it roared into action once more. He could never understand who thought these machines were a good idea. Who was it that decided how long you needed to dry your hands or face? Obviously not someone who'd tried to use one for that purpose. However, eventually his hair was only damp. He ran his fingers through it, trying to flatten the bits that were sticking out, before going back to the bar. He was feeling slightly more human than when he came in. He could see

Cathy looking into a small hand mirror, sneaking a bit of lipstick onto her lips. She was very attractive. Greg went to the cigarette machine, bought sixteen Marlboro and went back to sit opposite her. She was right. There was nothing helpful he could do for Jenny right now. It would be better for him to relax for a bit. He tried to convince himself it would be what Jenny would want him to do. He doubted it but smiling at Cathy he put his doubts to the back of his mind for the present.

*

Marjan stood at the roundabout just off junction nine of the M11. She had walked from Stansted airport, about two and a half miles. As she had no money left and had disposed of the stolen credit cards, there was only one way she could think of to get to her destination. She had to hitch a ride. It had been a long time since she'd stuck her thumb out in front of passing cars. It used to be exciting, the sense of danger, not knowing who might pick you up, who you might meet, where you might end up. She used to like the freedom. She'd travelled across Europe this way in her youth. She'd even been to the States once, with no money. She'd taken a job as a courier carrying document across the Atlantic for the price of a return fare. Now, though, thumbing a lift was a chore! There was no thrill in her present journey apart from the danger of being recognised as one of the drug dealers being sought by the police. She didn't want that yet. She didn't care about what happened to her but she had something important to do first and she knew she had little time left.

***

CHAPTER NINETEEN

Jenny Gulliver was completely unaware of the fact that she was surrounded by several doctors and nurses. According to the bank of machines at her bedside, Jenny had been aware of very little for some time now. The medical staff were beginning to get concerned. When she had first been brought in she had been unconscious but stable, no sign of her slipping deeper into a coma. She had gained consciousness and spoken briefly to the doctors as well as the Police Inspector. She had given Greg Driscoll's name as her next-of-kin.

Jenny was the only child of mature parents. Greg had joked that she must have been a mistake and certainly a shock to them. Her father ran some sort of big business, she'd never say what sort of business, if she knew and her mother was a society lady. A lady who lunched! Jenny had been a spoilt child. Anything she wanted she got. Until she was at school. Her schooling at a private boarding school had not been enjoyable. Jenny always felt she didn't really fit in to this world of debutantes. She also hated the fact that her parents were so much older than her friends' parents. Her parents couldn't understand her problems as she was growing up, she couldn't talk to them, especially her mother. She'd wanted her mother to be a friend, someone to confide in as some her friends did with theirs. Her parents' attitude to any problem was 'you sort it out. That's what life's like.' Her father had passed away during Jenny's last year at school and her mother went into decline. Her way of dealing with her husband's death was to look deep into the bottle. She'd been used to drinking, she'd had to do enough of it at her husband's business dinners and at society parties but she had always been able to handle it. Not now. She had spent time drying out in a private clinic in the USA. Jenny had been banned from seeing her whilst she was in the sanatorium. She left school, no longer feeling the need to carry on her education at some finishing school in Switzerland, defying the wishes of her mother's solicitor who was handling her affairs. She received an allowance from the solicitor but she didn't want to live the life of a rich kid. She paid for typing lessons and found she had an aptitude for it and had signed on with a temp agency. She enjoyed the jobs the agency put her up for. The people she was working with were ordinary people not the snobs she been bullied by at school and she had soon become friends with one of the girls in the agency office, Paula Hawkins, spending a lot of their free time together. Paula was a stalwart in her local amateur dramatic society and encouraged Jenny to go along and join in. This was a revelation for Jenny. Suddenly she realised what she wanted to do with her life. This was it. Acting! There was nothing to stop her; no-one to stop her. Her mother would not have approved but right now her mother didn't even know what day it was. Before long she was playing leading roles for the drama group and applied for several Drama Schools, being accepted at The Central School of Speech and Drama in London. When she first met Greg, he had said she had been accepted because they knew she could pay the fees but Jenny said she didn't care. She'd been through Drama School and was now working as an actress. She was glad they'd kept in touch after that first job. Paula had married an Australian and had emigrated to his country so her only contact these days was the odd Christmas card. Greg had been her only semi-constant companion for the last few years. Her mother had stayed in America, in and out of institutions. Greg was the only one she felt she could really trust. That's why she'd put his name as next-of-kin.

*

Cathy's flat was on the first floor above a small electrical shop. There was a steep staircase leading to a narrow corridor with four doors leading off it. One door had a plastic plaque screwed onto it bearing the legend 'Yer tis' which was presumably the bathroom. The others were numbered one-to-three. Cathy's room was number three. It was a bed-sit really with a lounge-cum-dining room-cum-kitchen and a reasonably sized double bed behind a floor-length curtain. Jenny's trusted next-of-kin trudged wearily up the flight of stairs and followed Cathy into the living area.

They had taken another taxi from the Blue Angel. It wasn't something Cathy did often on her nurse's wage but this actor looked like he was interested in her and she was definitely interested in him. Not because he was an actor, more because he looked lost, needing taken care of – at least for tonight.

Greg sat on the seventies-style sofa. He felt very tired. Tired and old. Not long ago he would have been in his element, chatted up by an attractive nurse, almost press-ganged into going back to her flat for coffee, an invitation that could be extended to more than a second cup it seemed and yet all he felt was weary. He'd only had two pints of lager in the Blue Angel, Cathy three glasses of wine. He'd pretended to be jolly and he could tell she was getting tipsy as she became more amorous.

She brought the coffee over. A cafetiere which she placed on the coffee table in front of Greg, giggling as she shuffled up next to Greg.

'How are you feeling, Greg?' she asked, putting her arm round his shoulders.

'Fine thanks, Cathy,' he replied, not knowing quite what else to say. He sipped his coffee. It was hot.

'Would you like some Scotch in that?' she said, rubbing Greg's right shoulder. Greg nodded. He felt in need of some Dutch courage. He wished he'd stayed at the hospital, he knew he shouldn't be here. Alright, Jenny wasn't exactly his girlfriend but he remembered the parting at Tottenham Court Road tube station: *'Wait till you're back from Amsterdam and let's make a whole night of it!'* He was sure she hadn't meant spending the night in a hospital. He accepted the slug of whisky that Cathy poured into his coffee with gratitude. She sat next to him, pulled her legs up under herself and leaned against Greg. Her hand brushed his chin.

'Sorry, haven't had a shave for a while,' he said.

'It's OK. I like it.' She reached up and kissed him on the cheek. His hand involuntarily twitched, spilling a small amount of coffee onto his leg. Cathy took the coffee from his hand and put it on the table without taking her eyes from his. She brought her hand up to his right cheek. Her hand, still warm from the coffee mug, pulled his face towards her lips. Her breath was warm and smelled of white wine. The weight of her body increased against him as she leaned closer. Her lips brushed his. Greg closed his eyes and opened his mouth slightly, Cathy needed no more encouragement.

*

Marjan had been given a lift in a silver-grey Jaguar. The driver was a middle-aged man who told her he ran a small business in Huntingdon. He chatted all the way to Chelmsford. A lonely man, on the road trying to keep his business going and trying to keep up appearances with his flashy car. Marjan was as reticent as she could be. She told him she was originally from Holland and worked for a small firm in the UK as a secretary. She'd just been home for a holiday and had run out of money which was why she was hitching. The man offered to give her some cash but she refused before he could suggest what he would like to buy from her. He dropped her off on the outskirts of Chelmsford and, following some directional questions to passers-by and a long walk, she eventually walked into the reception area of Broomfield hospital. There was a sign indicating Ladies and Gents toilets and she turned and went directly into the Ladies.

Five minutes later she emerged and crossed to the main desk. The receptionist paused and looked closely at her when she asked if she could see Jenny Gulliver. 'I'll just see if she's taking visitors at the moment,' she said, picking up the internal telephone. 'Can I take your name, please?'

'I'm just a friend,' Marjan replied, thinking how stupid that sounded. 'I mean…she might not remember me…I read in the paper…I'm sorry. I'm a bit upset.'

'That's alright.' The receptionist sounded sympathetic. She knew Jenny Gulliver's name had not been mentioned in the paper and had been told how to behave if this situation occurred. 'I have a visitor for Miss Gulliver,' she said into the telephone.' There was a pause while she listened to the instructions coming through the receiver. 'Alright, thank you.' She replaced the receiver and turned to Marjan. 'If you'll just take a seat, someone will be along to see you in a moment.' She pointed to the brown plastic chairs that Greg had vacated a few hours earlier.

Marjan thanked her and walked slowly to the chairs, sat down and sighed heavily. She put her head in her hands, ran her finger under the elastic at the front of the black wig and pushed up and backwards. Her short bleached-blonde hair sprang upwards as the wig fell backwards off her head and onto the floor behind her seat. There was a middle-aged woman sitting two or three seats away watching as the wig fell off. She blushed, embarrassed by what she thought was the accidental depilation of the poor young woman who had obviously had some sort of operation causing her hair to turn prematurely white.

Marjan was not embarrassed at all, nor had it been accidental that the wig had slipped to the floor. Marjan didn't want to play any more games now. There was no point in hiding any longer. She sat and waited with her head down. She didn't hear anyone approach but felt the weight of a body lowering itself into the chair next to her.

'Are you Miss Smits?' It was a female voice that spoke to her. Marjan didn't look up but gently nodded her head. 'Would you like to come with me, please?' The WPC took Marjan's arm and tried to get her to stand. Marjan pulled away.

'No. I wouldn't like to come with you. I'd like to see Jenny Gulliver.'

'I'm afraid that's not really possible at the moment,' said the policewoman, taking Marjan's arm in tighter grip. 'Come on! Don't make a scene!'

'Where's the Inspector in charge. Let me speak to him.'

'You'll see him soon enough, don't you worry.'

Marjan stood up and shook the woman off her. All eyes were on the two of them, expecting a fight. 'I want to see him here and now! Do you hear?' Marjan was backing away. There was a wild look in her eyes. The receptionist picked up her phone and pressed two buttons. Marjan dashed across reception and grabbed the receiver from her. 'Hello? This is Marjan Smits. I want to see the Inspector in charge of Jenny Gulliver. I will not leave here until I have!' There was a pause before a voice answered.

'Wait there, Ms Smits, I will be with you shortly.'

The WPC was standing next to Marjan as she replaced the receiver. Marjan apologised to the receptionist and thanked her for the use of her phone. She turned to the policewoman and smiled.

'I believe the Inspector will be along in a minute. Shall we sit down and wait?'

The WPC was quite young and not very experienced. She wasn't sure how to react to this person. Marjan smiled at her. 'It's OK. I'm not going to run away. Let's sit, yes?' Marjan made her way to the brown plastic chairs and the policewoman followed meekly.

DI Milne strode into the reception area. The WPC stood up and tried to pull Marjan up with her.

'It's alright, constable, I'll take over now.' Roger Milne sat down next to Marjan Smits.

'I'm not going anywhere until I've seen Jenny, Inspector. Let me do that and I'll tell you anything I can.'

'We don't do deals, Ms Smits. Come with me now, please.'

Marjan stood up again, her eyes flaring.

'I'm not leaving!' She shouted.

'No you're not, 'Milne agreed. 'I have an office here. Come with me and we'll have a talk.'

Roger Milne led Marjan into a small room which he had commandeered as a temporary office. There was one desk, two chairs, one telephone and a large number of box files stacked up against the wall. The room appeared to have been some sort of storeroom hurriedly converted for Milne's use. There was a constable stationed outside the door. He stood up as Milne approached. The DI nodded to him and told him to wait outside. Marjan sat in the seat Milne offered her inside the room. She was tired now, wanting to just get it all over with. Milne looked at her and said nothing. He had time. He could wait. Marjan sat with her head drooped. It was five full minutes before she lifted her head and returned Milne's gaze. Neither of their faces showed any sort of emotion. Eventually Marjan turned away and muttered under her breath. 'How is Jenny?'

Milne said nothing and continued his stare. Marjan looked back at him and repeated her question louder.

'She's in a coma at the moment, probably dying.' Milne did not take his eyes from Marjan's face.

'I tried…' Marjan began, her voice quiet and strained. Milne stared. She took a deep breath and sighed. 'Can I see her, please?'

'Why?'

'Because…I…need to.' Tears were starting to well in her eyes. She swallowed hard.

Roger Milne looked at the pretty young woman sitting opposite him wondering how someone like her got herself involved in something like this. She was evidently intelligent, had the ability to 'get on in the world'. Milne decided he hated this job. There was no satisfaction in seeing someone like Marjan Smits sitting opposite him in a genuinely distressed manner. He wanted to talk to people like her, to try to understand what it was that made them turn from a normal life to this. A normal life? What was that?

And had this woman ever known such a thing? What did he know about her background? Even after all these years he knew no more about the criminal mind than when he started. The evidence showed that there was a criminal mind sitting on the other side of this small desk in this hospital storeroom. What about PC Weston? She'd been there in that boat that had been driven cruelly straight at him. What about Jenny Gulliver, who was lying, most probably dying, just a few yards from where they were now? Marjan had been with her, certainly since the White Boar in Maldon. Why did she want to see her now? To make sure she never came round? To make sure she didn't speak to the police? To finish off the job properly? Roger Milne hardened his heart and kept up his stare.

'Please can I see Jenny? I'll help you in any way that I can.' Marjan's voice sounded pathetic.

'Tell me about Peiter Wiersma.'

'What do you want to know?'

'Well, where is he? That might be a good start.'

'Let me see Jenny and I'll tell you anything you want to know.'

'Where is he?'

'Let me see Jenny and I'll tell you.'

Milne sat back in his uncomfortable chair and sighed. It looked like he could be in for a long night.

*

It was eleven-thirty pm when Greg woke. For a moment he wasn't sure where he was. The surroundings were unfamiliar, the paint on the walls was pink, the duvet cover flowery. He blinked and shook his head.

'Coffee?' Cathy stood by the curtain in front of the bed, smiling. The bed area was dark but there was an aura of light round Cathy's head coming from the living area. 'I left you sleeping, you looked like you needed it.'

'Thank you. Thanks very much, Cathy, for everything.' Greg did feel grateful to her. She had helped him relax and put the last few days to the back of his mind.

'No sugar, I'm afraid,' said Cathy as she walked over to the bed with two mugs of coffee.

'That's OK. I'm sweet enough.'

Cathy laughed and handed Greg his mug. She was wearing a light blue kimono-style dressing gown and wore nothing on her feet. Greg suspected she had nothing on at all apart from the kimono. She sat with her knees up on the bed drinking her coffee. She leaned over and pecked Greg on his cheek.

'How long was I asleep?'

'Not long, a couple of hours maybe.'

'I'm sorry, not very polite of me, was it?'

'Don't worry about it.' Cathy smiled and kissed his forehead. She took his mug and put it down on the bedside table, followed by hers and taking him in her arms, snuggled down under the duvet.

*

The consultant knocked on the storeroom door where Milne still sat with Marjan. It was past midnight, he was tired and wanted to go home, his shift had supposedly finished. He entered without waiting to be asked.

'You wanted to know if there was any change in the condition of the patient, Inspector. I'm afraid it's not looking very good,' he informed the Inspector.

Marjan stood up. 'What's happened?' she demanded.

The consultant looked towards Milne.

'This young woman was with the patient at the time of her…er…accident, doctor.'

'Could you bring her along, Inspector? She may just help jog the memory. We really have to try anything we can at the moment to try and get her out of this coma.'

'I'm afraid that's not possible. This young lady is helping us with our enquiries.'

'Am I under arrest, Inspector?' Marjan was still standing.

'Not at the moment, Miss Smits, but something could be arranged.'

'If I can help Jenny in any way you have to let me go to her.'

'I don't have to do anything, young lady!'

Marjan looked at the consultant. 'Do you think I would be any help, doctor?'

The consultant looked towards Milne. He didn't like the presence of police in his hospital. The most important thing to him was to try and save people's lives irrespective of what they may have done or were suspected of doing. 'I don't know,' he said. He turned back to Milne. 'I can't see it doing any harm, you will be with her if you're worried, Inspector.'

Milne was in a quandary. Obviously he needed to do all he could to save Jenny, yet how could he give in to Marjan's demands to see Jenny. He'd said there could be no bargaining and Marjan had not been forthcoming with any information he did not already know. Maybe now he needed to review that situation.

'If I let you into Miss Gulliver's room, I shall ask you to wear these handcuffs and stay by my side. I shall then ask you to accompany me to the police station and be interviewed on tape. I shall expect you to give me all the information I require. Do we understand each other?'

Marjan stared directly back at Milne. 'I think we do, Inspector.'

The sight of Jenny lying in her bed with tubes projecting from all parts of her body made Marjan's knees start to give way. She turned her head and took deep breaths until the strength returned to her legs. She was handcuffed to DI Milne by her left wrist. She took a step towards Jenny and looked at the consultant standing on the other side of the bed. There were two nurses standing behind him next to a bank of monitors all showing Jenny to be in a deep, deep sleep.

'Can I sit on the bed?'

The consultant checked with Milne before nodding. Marjan sat down gently on the edge of the bed, her left arm attached to Milne held out behind her in an uncomfortable position. Slowly she reached out with her right hand and took hold of Jenny's. It was warm but that was the only sign of life. Marjan squeezed slightly, DI Milne moved closer to the bed, easing Marjan's left arm. She turned and smiled, a tear finding its way onto her cheek and running down to her shoulder. She turned back to look at Jenny. She leaned forward, as close to her ear as her handcuffed arm would let her.

'Jenny? Jenny? It's me, Marjan?' she whispered. 'Jenny, please wake up. Jenny? I'm sorry. I tried, I really tried.'

There was no response. Marjan sat looking at Jenny. There was a feeling deep inside her, a feeling of loss. She could not think of anything to say, her mind was numb, she was weeping openly, not even trying to hold the tears back.

The consultant and the police Inspector exchanges glances. The consultant shook his head.

'Come on, Miss Smits,' said the Inspector. 'There's nothing you can do, I'm afraid.'

'No!' Marjan grabbed hold of Jenny's hand again and squeezed tighter. 'I'm not going, Jenny. They want me to go. I won't go. Wake up Jenny. I love you, Jenny Gulliver. I love you.' Marjan was almost screaming. Her tears were choking her, making her words blurt out in short staccato bursts. One of the nurses had come and put her hands on Marjan's shoulders. She shook her off.

'Come on, it's time to leave her now,' the nurse said gently. With Milne's help the nurse managed to get her to stand but Marjan would not let go of Jenny's hand. As the nurse reached to take Marjan's hand away from Jenny's, Marjan let out a gasp.

'She moved! She gripped my hand!'

Milne looked towards the consultant who shook his head again.

'She did! She gripped!' Marjan looked at Jenny through her tears. 'Jenny, Please. Show them, Jenny. I love you!'

Suddenly the noises coming from the machines changed their pitch. The beeps seemed louder, more rapid than they had been. The nurse let go of Marjan and hurried back to the machines at the other side of the bed. The consultant took Jenny's wrist and measured her pulse. Marjan prayed out loud. 'Please God, Please.'

Jenny's eyes flickered and her lips moved slightly. She looked straight at Marjan and appeared to smile. Marjan fell onto Jenny's face and kissed her on the lips before anyone could stop her, Milne almost falling onto the bed as his arm was forcefully pulled forward. Jenny looked into Marjan's face and her eyes followed her as Milne pulled her into an upright position, still sitting on the bed.

Just as suddenly the noises from the machines changed again. This time, though they turned into one continuous tone. Marjan was taken from the room by Milne as the medical team went into emergency action.

A few minutes later, the consultant came out of the room. 'I'm sorry. There was no more we could do. I'm afraid she's gone.'

'Was it my fault, doctor,' stammered Marjan.

'No,' he said kindly. 'I don't think Jenny wanted to stay with us anymore but I know she was happy to see you. I'm sorry I have to go, now. A nurse will stay with you and there's a chapel across the quadrangle if you want go there.'

Marjan sat on a plastic chair in the corridor outside Jenny's room and tried to put her head in her hands. Milne reached over so that the handcuffs did not restrict her. He felt embarrassed. He wanted to take the handcuffs off. He knew she wouldn't try to escape and yet procedure would not let him. So he sat, taking care not to put his hand on Marjan, leaving his arm floating in limbo by her left ear. Marjan was sobbing. She had loved Jenny. She hadn't known or admitted it before and now it was too late.

*

Greg was asleep in Cathy's bed. He was exhausted. Cathy had made love to him earlier which should have been a wonderful experience for both of them but the knowledge that Jenny was lying in her hospital bed hung over Greg's head like a dark cloud. Cathy was in the kitchen area making herself some more coffee. She had a sense of guilt. Although Greg had said there was nothing between him and Jenny she could tell she meant a lot to him and maybe she had been wrong to take him away from the hospital and take advantage of him. He had looked so lost, so needy. The phone rang. It was two in the morning. The only people who rang at this time were the hospital if there was an emergency and they needed everyone to come in immediately. Cathy picked up the phone and listened. It was ten minutes later that she went towards the bed and put her hand on Greg's shoulder. He was in the slumbering state between sleep and wakefulness. It took a few seconds for him to fully come to. For some reason he blushed when he saw Cathy. She smiled.

'Hi,' she said. 'How are you feeling?'

'Er…fine, I think,' muttered Greg. 'You?'

Cathy sat on the bed and took his hand. It wasn't the first time she'd had to tell someone of the death of someone close to them and yet it never got any easier and the previous night's events only complicated this situation. 'Did you hear the phone, Greg?' He shook his head. Cathy took a deep breath and put her other hand on top of Greg's. 'It was the hospital. I'm afraid Jenny died about an hour ago. They've been trying to get hold of you. One of the nurses knew I had taken you for a drink and…well…they rang here.'

Greg sat still, stunned for a short while and then stood up and left the room. Cathy heard the bathroom door shut and the bolt being drawn across. She went into the kitchen area and looked for some sugar while the kettle boiled. She found some honey and used that to make a cup of hot sweet tea. She took the mug to the bathroom door and knocked gently, softly calling Greg's name. She could hear the tap running and waited. Greg slid the door lock back and opened the door. His face was wet and his mouth was hanging open, his shoulders hunched and his hands clasped together. Cathy offered him the tea but he seemed not to notice. She reached past him and put the mug by the side of the sink and took hold of him by the arms. His head fell onto her shoulder and he sobbed loudly as Cathy closed the door and enveloped him in her arms, hugging him as if he were a child.

By the time they reached the hospital, Greg had more or less accepted the situation. He had wanted to go straight there and see Jenny but Cathy managed to convince him that they wouldn't let him do that and made him sit down and drink his tea. They had talked about Jenny, his relationship with her, his feeling of betrayal, his guilt over what he saw as his leaving her to die alone. Cathy had listened to him, held him, cried with him. At four am she ordered a taxi and went with him to the hospital. He felt slightly numb and his legs went weak and he stumbled slightly as they entered the reception area. Cathy held his hand.

DI Milne met them and took them to the storeroom which was his office. He looked terrible, drawn, dark bags forming under his eyes. Greg sat quietly, his eyes lowered as Milne went through the previous night. He looked up briefly when Milne mentioned Marjan but said nothing.

'Where is she now?' he said when Milne finished speaking.

'She's been taken to a local police station for questioning. I'm about to go along there now.'

Greg smiled and sighed. 'I meant Jenny,' he said. 'Can I see her?'

'I'm sorry Greg. I'll have a word with the doctors but I'm not sure…'

'It's OK,' Greg interrupted. 'I just wanted to apologise to her but I don't suppose there's much point, is there? I guess she'll know already if...well...you know.' There was an awkward silence. 'Will you be needing me for more questioning?'

'Not at the moment, Greg, but, please, no running away this time, OK? I will need to see you at some time so let me know where you are.'

'Sure.'

Greg hadn't thought about where he was going. Back to his flat in Hackney? He thought probably not. Back to Cathy's? No. Definitely not there. He went back to the reception area and crossed to the public telephone. Cathy was standing by the desk with a number of other nurses. She was in her nurse's uniform, ready for another day on the wards. He waved to her and put his thumbs up. She smiled and started towards him but one of the nurses took hold of her arm and whispered in her ear. She nodded, waved at Greg and left reception. Greg picked up the telephone receiver and dialled Denis' number.

***

CHAPTER TWENTY

Marjan had been taken to the police cells to await questioning. The cell was small and smelt faintly of urine. The green metal door had been firmly closed and locked behind her. The small metal hatch in the door, about two-thirds of the way up had also been bolted shut leaving only a small round spy-hole between her and the duty police outside. She had been searched by a young policewoman, not too thoroughly, before being 'banged up' in the cell. A couple of constables who just happened to be hanging about the station had made some rather lewd comments about her as she went down the corridor to the cells but she hadn't really heard them. Her mind was cloudy. It was as if her brain was shutting off, clearing her mind of Peiter Wiersma, clearing it of Jenny, clearing it of her past. She looked around her new home slowly, taking in the walls, covered with a sort of whitewash with a small brown fleck in it. She was sitting on a very thin foam mattress covered in blue plastic on top of a low wooden bench about two feet high. In the corner of the cell was a three foot high concrete partition not very neatly tiled in white, behind which lurked a porcelain toilet bowl with two pieces of wood bolted to the rim intended to be the seat. There was no chain or visible means of flushing it. There was a sunken window high in the side of one wall, glazed with a dozen four inch panes of mottled toughened glass. Two very dim lights were let into the high ceiling next to a pair of six inch air vents which were covered by metal grills securely screwed into the ceiling. On the wall by the door was a small red button, like the sort found on buses to attract the driver's attention, under which some previous inmate had scratched *ROOM SERVICE* in large letters into the paintwork. This was the only graffiti in the whole cell.

She had not spoken a word since she left the hospital in the custody of two policewomen. The duty sergeant had tried desperately to get her to give him her name but she seemed not to hear, just stared wide-eyed at him. Eventually he had given up and sent her to the cells to await DI Milne's arrival. He had taken what few possessions she had on her and placed them in a clear plastic bag, making a note of every item and left the WPC to take her to the cells. She had been sitting on the thin mattress for about half an hour when the small hatch in the door opened with a crash and the duty sergeant looked in. He was just finishing his shift and was on his way home. It was customary for every prisoner to be checked up on at least every half hour and, as he was on his way out anyway, he took it upon himself to do the check, leaving a constable guarding the desk until the relief sergeant turned up.

As the sergeant closed the hatch and made his way down the corridor away from the cells, Marjan's eyes slowly came back into focus. She turned her head towards the locked door and, seeing and hearing nothing, stood up. Still in a dreamlike state she carefully removed all her clothes, folded them individually and placed them neatly on the mattress. She squatted and put her hands between her legs. After a certain amount of probing she stood up holding a condom between her fingers. She sat down, naked on the cold mattress holding the condom almost lovingly in her hands. Delicately she made a slit in the side with her thumbnail revealing the white powder within. She sat for a few seconds staring blindly at the cocaine in her hands. Quite suddenly Marjan brought the condom up towards her mouth and swallowed a large amount of the powder. She walked towards the concrete partition and sat on top of it. Partly deliberately she started to bang her arms violently against the tiles. The edges of some of the tiles were chipped and as Marjan slid her wrists across them, dark red blood spurted against the bright white of the cell walls, leaving them looking like some sort of Jackson Pollock artwork.

By the time the new duty sergeant had heard the commotion and made his way to the cell to quieten his prisoner down, Marjan Smits life had ebbed from her body and she lay in a pool of blood on the cold concrete floor.

DI Milne had been called from his bed. It was the first sleep he'd managed to fit in for several days. Finally he had thought he was at a stage where nothing more could be achieved and had thankfully retired home for a few hours. He'd decided to leave Marjan alone for the night, let her stew, let her get over Jenny's death. She was in no state to give him any useful information. The news he heard over the telephone woke him up immediately. He really didn't need this! There had been enough cock-ups on this investigation as it was and the dead body of a suspect in the police cells was serious trouble. Wearily he dressed himself and headed for the police station.

By the time he arrived there was quite a crowd at the door of Marjan's cell. The news had spread throughout the station and every officer on duty had come to see the gory mess the attractive Dutch captive had made of herself and their cell. Milne pushed his way through sending the errant officers back to their respective duties as he went into the cell. His anger was boiling up inside him. The duty sergeant was sitting on the edge of the blue plastic mattress looking suitably apprehensive. He stood up as Milne appeared.

'I'm sorry, sir. She was fine when Sergeant Rogers left and then, twenty minutes later, this happened. I just heard some banging but they all do that, sir. When I arrived, well, it was too late, sir. She was just lying there. Dead. Blood everywhere.'

Milne looked at the sergeant. He was a young man, probably with a wife and a kid or two, and he was very worried. He knew his job was on the line, as was Milne's probably. He didn't speak to the sergeant and transferred his attention to the body still lying on the floor. The body of the girl who, just a few hours earlier, he had been comforting by the side of another lifeless young body. He so hated this job! The police photographer had just finished his business and the pathologist was writing up his report in his notebook. Two constables were waiting with a long black PVC bag with a zip up the side ready to remove the body. Milne bent down and touched the already cold cheek of Marjan Smits. He gulped down the bile rising in his throat. Marjan's naked body was a mess. There were blood streaks along her arms and chest. Her wrists showed jagged tears on them, the muscles and sinews white against the red-brown blood. Milne signalled to the constables to wrap the body in the bag and take it away. He didn't want to see it any more. He crossed to the pathologist.

'It wasn't just the bleeding that killed her,' he said. 'I suspect some sort of overdose but until the post-mortem I'm not prepared to say.' He held up the remains of the condom in his gloved hands.

'Thank you.' The pathologist put the condom in a clear plastic bag.

Milne turned to the duty sergeant. 'Was she searched?'

The sergeant looked at Milne. 'Yes, sir, she was, I believe. I wasn't actually on duty myself, you understand.'

Milne leaned in towards him, very close to his face. 'Get the officer who was, then. I want him here as soon as possible!' He all but shouted into the sergeant's face.

'He's on his way, sir. I…er…took the liberty of calling him in. I thought you'd want to speak to him, sir, seeing how he was the one on duty when she came in and the last one to check on her before he left.'

Milne hated crawlers. He could see what the young sergeant was trying to do. Pass the buck; acquit himself of all the blame. Milne didn't think he'd be very successful. 'Thank you, sergeant,' he said. 'Find me an office and send him to me there as soon as he steps through the door. I'll see you with him at the same time. Also, keep this quiet. I don't want the press or anyone else asking questions until I have some answers myself. Do you understand?'

The sergeant nodded and led Milne to one of the station's interview rooms.

*

Han was waiting for Greg outside Denis' flat. He paid Greg's taxi for him and led him back up the stairs to the first floor flat. Denis had made some strong coffee and was sitting in the kitchen that was annexed to the living room. Greg had updated them on the news of Jenny's death. Denis was extremely worried and concerned for Greg and sat like a mother hen fretting in the kitchen until he arrived.

Han and Denis had not slept much the previous night. A lot of coffee and brandy had been drunk as they sat up discussing the last few days. Denis' life had been changed beyond measure. His normally dull routine had only been interrupted by theatrical parties before and he avoided them if he possibly could. Han, although living a slightly more exciting lifestyle than Denis, had also been thrust into situations he could quite happily never experience again.

They were pleased to see Greg comparatively safe and well. The last time they had seen him was at the hospital. Greg now proceeded to fill them in on what had happened at the old station in Maldon and how he had come to find out about Jenny's demise. Greg was completely honest with them when he came to why he wasn't with Jenny during her last hours. Denis was shocked and upset that Greg could even think of spending the night with a stranger while Jenny lay there dying.

'I didn't know she was dying. Cathy was a nurse and she told me I couldn't help Jenny by staying there. She was right I couldn't. I was confused. I just couldn't help myself.'

'You never can if there's a chance of getting into someone's knickers, Greg. And that's just one of your problems.'

'I know how you feel, Denis and you're no doubt right. Sleeping with Cathy was not on my mind. I needed out of the hospital, that's all. Where were you? Why weren't you there looking after two of your clients?'

'I didn't know! No-one told me what was going on! If I had that Inspector wouldn't have allowed me to come anyway.'

'How do you know? You didn't even try and find out what was going on!'

Han intervened before the two of them came to blows. 'Hey! This isn't getting us anywhere. We have to stick together. Come on!'

Greg sat on a kitchen chair. 'I'm sorry, I'm so, so sorry.' He burst into tears, deep, heartfelt sobs. He knew Denis was right, he'd had the same thoughts himself many times throughout the last few hours. He hadn't come to any conclusions other than knowing he shouldn't have done it.

Han asked if there was any further news about Marjan or Wiersma but all Greg knew was that Marjan was under arrest and Wiersma had fled the country. Greg said he was tired and Denis took him through to the bedroom and let him lie down. He went back to the kitchen and he and Han tried to make some sense of things.

Two hours later Milne telephoned requesting Greg Driscoll's presence at the police station.

*

Greg sat in another small office DI Milne had been allocated at Scotland Yard. He could feel the tears welling up inside him. He was tired, confused and very emotional. He couldn't say that he'd been particularly fond of Marjan, he still blamed her for Jenny's death. However, hearing the way in which she took her own life, the senseless waste of yet another young woman, brought a lot of the emotions he had been trying to keep in control to the surface. He cried uncontrollable sobs from the depths of his body. He shook with each breath he tried to inhale. He was crying for Jenny, for Marjan, for himself and for the world he had unwittingly got himself involved in. This was not a drama, not in the sense he knew it. Not fiction. This was real life and he didn't like it.

The desk sergeant came in with a cup of tea and placed it on the table next to Greg's heaving shoulders. He turned to speak to Milne but was ushered away with an impatient wave of the hand. Milne had had about enough. Most of his time seemed to be taken up dealing with incompetence and it was none of his doing. Or was it? Wasn't he supposed to be responsible for his sub-ordinates? Wasn't that why he was a Detective Inspector?

He had been very ambitious when he first joined the force. He had risen quickly through the ranks, quite a high-flyer. He had given up a lot to get this far but recently he started to think more about his life, other people's lives, people's lives he had destroyed in getting his convictions, no matter what? That was what was important. Get the conviction. Anyone in the way only got what they deserved! Was that true? What about the others? What about Jenny? What about that poor Dutch girl who was at that very moment being cut to pieces in the mortuary in order to find something incriminating inside her? They would find something, of that he had no doubt but was that the reason she killed herself? Because she'd been caught? To avoid a drugs conviction? Not long ago Milne would have accepted that without another thought. One less piece of scum to have to deal with! Now he wasn't so sure. Was he turning liberal in his old age? He kept repeating why. Why had this young girl become involved with all this? And what about this man in front of him? This actor he had never heard of until less than a week ago. He had been a bit arrogant, true, but that wasn't a crime in itself. How did he get involved? Milne wished he'd left him locked up when he'd first been arrested.

He tried to push these thoughts to the back of his mind. Now was not the time to consider the whys and wherefores of his job. He still hadn't got his conviction yet. That had to be the most important thing. That was his job. Much as he wanted to reach out and put a comforting hand on Greg's shoulder he knew he couldn't. Instead he stood up and paced around the room for a few seconds before turning his frustration on Greg.

'Pull yourself together, Driscoll. You're no use to me like that.'

Greg swallowed hard, gulping back his tears. Milne put a handkerchief on the table in front of him, walked to the corner of the room behind him, folded his arms and leaned against the wall. It was a few minutes before Greg finally dragged himself into a sitting position.

'I'm sorry,' he said. 'It's a shock. I never thought…she seemed so together…so sure of herself. You may be used to all of this, Inspector but to me it's difficult to deal with, OK?'

Milne sat back at the table opposite Greg. 'Come on! We have work to do. No matter how difficult it is for you, I need you to go through everything again, right from the start.'

*

The news of Marjan's demise had been a shock to Han, too. His reaction had been different to Greg's, though.

No tears; just anger. An intense anger. Denis had been frightened. Han didn't speak when Greg gave them the news over the phone he just paced up and down in Denis' flat. Suddenly, without warning he stormed downstairs and out of the flat. Slamming the front door with such force that Denis could feel the vibrations upstairs in the living room. He wasn't the only person in the block to go to the window and watch the tall Dutchman striding down the road, fists clenched in front of him.

Han leaned against the wall of a railway arch a few hundred yards from Denis' flat. He was breathing heavily. He put his head in his hands and tried to think. Something warm trickled down his cheek. Opening his eyes Han noticed that his hands were bleeding. He stared at them unable to understand. The knuckles were torn as were the sides of both palms. There were small pieces of grit in the wounds. He turned and noticed blood on the wall behind him next to his head. He had no recollection of pummelling the wall with his fists just seconds earlier. His hands were starting to sting. It was painful and yet it felt good. It was like a punishment but he felt no absolution, he felt guilty and he felt frustrated. Why had he left Marjan on her own in that hotel? He should have kept her with him. He wanted to get to Wiersma, he was the real villain! But how to get to him? No-one knew where he was apparently. No-one? Someone must know. Marjan must have known but he couldn't ask her now. He trudged slowly back to Denis' flat. He didn't get far before he saw Denis racing towards him. He stopped dead when he saw Han's bloody fists.

'It's OK, Denis,' said Han. 'I...er...hit the wall. I think. Stupid, eh?'

Denis took his arm and led him back to the flat. Helen Clarke was standing outside the door.

'Everything OK, Denis?' She was eying Han closely, especially his bleeding hands. 'Do you want me to call the police?'

'No, Helen, it's OK. This is a friend of mine. He's just had a fall, that's all. Cut his hands.'

'Oh. I'll come in and help you clean him up if you like.'

'No, Helen we can manage, thanks. Look, are you still OK to cover the office for a while. I'm still trying to sort out this contract problem.'

'Yes, I think so. I might not be able to do Wednesday, though. I don't have child care.'

'Don't worry, Helen. Just leave the answerphone on. I'd better see to my friends hands.'

'Did you find Miss Gulliver?'

Denis paused. It hadn't occurred to him that Jenny's death was not common knowledge. Han answered for him. 'Yes we did. Thank you for your help Miss Clarke.'

Han and Denis went upstairs to the flat leaving Helen feeling quite pleased that everything seemed to be sorting itself out and that she had another weeks work, she needed the money.

Back in the flat Denis fussed over Han's hands, bathing them in disinfectant before tearing up an old towel to make bandages. Han thanked him but declined the bandages. He took some analgesic in the form of the remainder of the brandy they'd drunk the previous night.

'Are we under any form of arrest, Denis?'

'I don't think so. We haven't done anything, have we?'

'No, we haven't,' Han said, thinking that was part of the problem. They hadn't done anything at all. He went to the phone, lifted the receiver and waved it at Denis. He nodded and said, 'help yourself,' adding as an afterthought, 'who are you ringing?'

'The airport.'

Denis sighed, 'I do have to go back to the office sometime.'

'It's OK. I'm going home. I want to be on my own for a while.'

'What about Milne? I don't think he'll be too happy if you just up and leave.'

'What has it to do with him? We're not under arrest.'

'Well, not strictly but…'

'Well then.' Han could see the worry on Denis' face. 'Don't fret. I'll leave you with my address. I'll be there if anyone needs me.'

*

Greg Driscoll and Roger Milne were still sitting in the small office in Scotland Yard. Greg had always imagines Scotland Yard to be a flash up-to-date place with all the latest technology. If it had any of that it wasn't in this room. He'd expected screens full of information from across the world. He'd expected there to be photographs of himself, Marjan, Jenny, Wiersma, Han even Denis pinned up all over the walls, but not here. This was just a plasterboard partition, a room like any other he seen in offices around London when he'd been forced to do some unskilled temporary work to pay his rent (or bar bill!). The two of them sat on the increasingly uncomfortable chairs. They had eaten sandwiches sent in by the Sergeant, they had gone through two glass jugs of coffee already and were waiting for a third to filter through. Nothing new had come from their deliberations. They had gone over and over the last few days in intricate detail. The police needed to find Peiter Wiersma but Milne was getting little help on that front. The Dutch police had no record of him, they knew his name as an eminent businessman but he was cleaner than clean as far as crime was concerned, donating to police charities, a well-respected member of the community etc. They had promised to question him if he returned to The Netherlands but as yet they didn't know where he was and had no reason to find him. The German police had given the same response. There was little more information on Rob Vanderlast. He had been picked up on a soft drugs bust in his youth but the Dutch police didn't seem to regard that as a serious offence. If they came across him they'd have a chat with him but that was all they were prepared to do without any strong evidence from the British police that he had committed a crime. As far as Milne knew the only offence Vanderlast was guilty of was enticing Greg Driscoll to unwittingly smuggle drugs and they had no conclusive proof of that. In fact the only person he could hang any criminal offence on was sitting in front of him. Roger poured some fresh coffee and handed it to Greg.

'Can't we just go and look for him?' Greg couldn't understand why Milne was sitting here questioning him while the real villains were being given a chance to get away. 'I mean, someone must know where he is? He must keep in touch with his companies.'

'Apparently he does little 'hands-on' work these days. He has people running the companies for him. He sometimes doesn't even go to board meetings it seems. He just lets the companies run themselves. As long as they're profitable he doesn't seem to care.'

'So what now?'

'You may as well go home. Or better still, go to your friend Young's flat. And Greg, I'm relying on you not to do anything silly, OK? I don't want you to leave the flat at all, except to go to the police station. You are still on bail, remember. If I find you defying me I'll have you locked up before you can think.'

Milne wasn't sure what he expected Greg to do. He wasn't sure whether he actually wanted him to go out and try to find Wiersma, Greg may have more luck than him. He knew it was unlikely. He had already been castigated by the Chief Inspector for not banging up Driscoll, especially after what happened in Maldon but Milne knew that Greg was just a patsy in this whole scenario and that he was his best chance of finding the real villains. But he was running out of time. They were going to pull the plug on the whole investigation unless he came up with some results soon. It was too expensive, apparently. It was only on-going because of PC Weston. They were prepared to extend things for one of their own. Jenny Gulliver and Marjan Smits, not to mention Brian Carter, were just expendable, unfortunate consequences. Without a conviction they'd close the case.

Greg was standing at the door. 'When you say I can't leave the flat does that mean not at all or am I allowed to go to the pub?'

Milne smiled at him. 'I didn't hear that. Just make sure I can get hold of you. Ring me on my mobile if you think of anything. Here's the number. It's the one that starts 07.' He handed Greg his card and walked with him to the door. 'Remember if you think of anything, however trivial it may seem to you, ring me. Day or night it doesn't matter. And get some sleep. You still look awful.'

***

CHAPTER TWENTY-ONE

There was an inquest into Marjan's death the following Friday. The Establishment was not happy when someone passed away whilst in the custody of the British Police Force. Their way of dealing with it was to try and make sure everybody knew that everything had been done to avoid the situation. Then they could wash their hands of any responsibility.

Greg had asked to attend the inquest to give what evidence he could only to be told that the inquest was solely about Marjan's death and the manner in which she died and unless Mr Driscoll had been present in the cell there was no evidence he could give. He could sit in the public gallery if he wanted to as it was an open enquiry but would not be allowed to speak. It seemed to Greg there were a lot of things he was not allowed to do these days. He'd spent the last few days in a deep depression. He had stayed at Denis' flat as Milne had suggested, leaving only to report to the police when required. There was a suggestion that any charges against him could be dropped soon but there had been no movement along those lines as yet. Wiersma was still being sought without much success and apparently this had a bearing on whether Greg's bail conditions could change or not. In the meantime he had to carry on reporting to the police station regularly. Greg had not left the flat at any other time, he had not been to the pub as he didn't feel very sociable in his present state of mind and didn't want to be the saddo in the corner getting drunk on his own. Instead he remained a saddo on his own in Denis' flat, gradually working his way through Denis' stock of alcohol, including the strange liqueurs Denis' had brought back from various trips abroad only to find that obscure beverages that were wonderful in the sunny climes of a holiday resort were not so palatable in the cold light of a London flat.

Denis had returned to the office. Helen Clarke was still helping him out there but he needed to get back to normality and normality for Denis was sitting in his office trying to find employment for his clients. Not for Greg, though. Greg did not want to work. He did not want to do very much at all other than remain in a numbed alcoholic stupor. Denis had tried hard to pull him out of his depression, even trying to convince him to do a very small part in a TV play – a request to a director he knew who owed him a favour. Greg did not need this! He understood that Denis was trying to help but all he was doing was destroying the little bit of confidence he still felt he had. He didn't even know if he wanted to be an actor any more. He didn't know what he wanted to do. He was in Limbo.

Denis, on the other hand was starting to get fed-up with Greg's attitude. He couldn't understand why he didn't want to just go and work, forget about all the problems. That's what he was doing and it was starting to bear results. He was feeling much more relaxed now he was back in his office, where things were as they should be. No more running round the country. No more running up huge bills on his credit card. Of course he was still upset by Jenny's death, he even felt sorry for Marjan but really thought she had brought her own downfall upon herself. He couldn't understand why Greg couldn't pull himself out of this by doing what he did best, a bit of acting. He didn't see what else he could do to help him. He'd got him an offer of a TV job. Greg had to help himself if he was to get over this and get back to normal.

Denis had tried to persuade Greg not to go to Marjan's inquest to no avail but, as he seemed determined to go, he spent the evening before sobering him up with black coffee and hiding the small amount of alcohol left in the flat. Greg looked a mess. Unshaven and unwashed. Denis had to force him to have a bath and a shave. He had been verbally abusive, calling Denis all sorts of names and blaming him for many things that were nothing to do with him. He feared Greg could get physical as well so he left him to bathe and shave while he made some pasta with a tomato and chilli sauce. Greg had calmed down after his bath, he was also starting to look human again. He remained very quiet while he forced down the pasta. Denis sat and talked throughout the meal, telling what he thought Greg should do; how he was always there for him if only he could explain what he was going through. If he didn't want to listen to him that was OK but he couldn't help unless Greg wanted him to. Greg said nothing throughout the meal but managed to eat it all. He put his cutlery down and pushed the plate across the table. For a moment he sat quietly listening to Denis wittering on. All of a sudden he grabbed hold of him, hugged him and sobbed uncontrollably onto his chest. Denis put his arms round him and let him cry. They had talked late into the night, Greg apologising, Denis consoling until, exhausted they went to their beds. Greg did not want Denis to accompany him to the inquest. He'd also decided that he wanted to go back to his own flat before the squatters moved in. Denis thought it was a bad idea and he should stay with him a bit longer. They came to a compromise; Greg would stay at Denis' till Marjan's inquest was over and he would let Greg go to the inquest on his own but would meet him outside the coroner's court as each day finished.

Clean-shaven and sober Greg, breakfasted and dressed in one of Denis' suits, was being fussed over by Denis. He broke away from the 'lint-remover' thing that Denis was waving at him menacingly.

'Does Han know about the Inquest, Denis? I suppose he ought to be there really.'

'Haven't heard a thing from him. Left messages. No reply. Could be anywhere for all I know.' Denis wanted to add and for all I care but stopped himself. He was actually quite pleased that Han seemed to have disappeared from the scene. He would like to have turned back the clock and never sent Greg for that commercial audition. He just wanted to forget it all and get back to work.

*

Greg thought it ironic that the sun was shining brightly on such a day of darkness. He left the dim atmosphere of the Coroner's court and squinted in the brightness. He felt hot and uncomfortable in the suit and tie that Denis had insisted on lending him. Marjan's death had been entered into down to the minutest detail. The results of the autopsy were revealed and noted down along with the verdict that Marjan Smits had taken her own life and that there was nothing the authorities could have done to prevent it. It hadn't taken very long. A whole life and death dealt with to satisfy the bureaucrats.

Greg stood on the steps outside the court and thought for a while. He couldn't see Denis. He could do with a drink. He was nervous about going back to his flat on his own, maybe Denis was right and he should stay with him for a bit longer. Someone flashed a camera in his face, thanked him and left. It made him jump and he looked around a bit confused for a moment. He felt a hand on his shoulder and was relieved to think that Denis was here to look after him. It wasn't Denis. It was Roger Milne.

'Press,' he said, referring to the photographer. 'You should be used to that as an actor.'

'Yes, I was a bit surprised that they'd bother.'

'Get at the police time, I suppose. The press are probably disappointed that the coroner didn't place any blame on us but I doubt they'll even bother reporting the result, let alone use any photographs. Do you fancy a drink?'

Greg did fancy a drink but not with Roger Milne. 'Thanks, Inspector but I'm waiting for Denis.'

'Well, I'll be in that bar across the road,' he pointed to a trendy bar that really did not appeal to Greg. 'If you still fancy one when your friend arrives, come and join us.'

'Celebrating, are you?'

'I'm not, Greg, believe me. I dare say some will be but not me.'

'I'm moving back to my own flat, by the way. Is that allowed under my bail conditions?'

Milne looked at Greg. 'Are you sure, Greg? You might be better staying with your friend for a while.'

'I'm a bit too old to be treated like a child, Inspector. I'm fed up with not being able to do anything without it being judged as my inability to cope. I'm coping fine and I haven't been to my flat for a long time. I want to be at home.'

'I understand and I won't stop you. I have your home number?'

'Yes you do. You have every number I've ever known. If you haven't I'm sure you could find it if you really needed to.'

'Don't push your luck, Greg. Just make sure you report to the local police station. You're still on bail.'

'Yes, sir.'

They shook hands and Roger Milne sighed and walked slowly over to the bar to reluctantly join his subordinates drinking the health of the coroner who seemed to have let them off all the blame that they should have been carrying.

Greg looked around for Denis. He still wasn't there so Greg walked to the nearest tube.

An hour later he was slowly walking up the stairs of the tenement block that housed his flat. His legs were shaky. The last time he'd been on this staircase he was going down unconscious on a stretcher. He gingerly put his key in the door, turned it and gently opened the door, pushing the small hillock of post out of the way, before closing it securely behind him. The flat was tidy, tidier than it had ever been. He knew Denis had been in after he'd been taken to hospital. Good old Denis. Maybe he should have waited for him, let him know what he was doing. He was standing in the hallway about two feet from the door when the letter box rattled violently, Greg nearly jumped out of skin. He turned and looked at the mottled reinforced glass in the top half of the door. There was a dark figure outlined against the fading sunlight.

'Who's there?' he said.

'Is that Greg? It's Olive. From next door.'

Olive was the only neighbour Greg had ever spoken more than a hello to. She was from the Caribbean, used to be an actress, she'd said. Greg suspected 'actress' was probably a euphemism but she had always been reasonably friendly. He put the chain on the door and opened it a little way. Olive was smiling her big white smile.

'Hello, Greg,' she said, beaming. 'I saw you in the paper. How are you? Terrible thing to happen. I brought you some of my special rum.'

Greg had had some of Olive's special rum before. It was dark rum laced with all sorts of herbs that Greg had thought better not to ask what they were. He undid the chain and opened the door, asking Olive in.

'Oh no,' she said handing him the bottle of dark spirit. 'I just wanted to give you this. Welcome home.'

'Thanks. Much appreciated.' Greg replied. Olive stood there for a few seconds, smiled her big smile and went back to her flat next door. Greg closed the door and went into the kitchen. He looked at the bottle. There were a number of odd looking bits of plant life floating about just visible through the dark liquid. Hanging from the neck was a label saying 'Black Olive's Special Rum'. Greg smiled, from the first time he'd met his neighbour he always felt a warmth inside. She called herself Black Olive, she'd said, because her name was Olive and she was black! She liked to see people's reaction, it made her laugh. Olive laughed a lot, something Greg rather envied. He went to get a glass from the drainer by the sink only to find Denis had put the few remaining unbroken ones away in the cupboard. He poured himself a large measure of black Olive's rum. There was evidently a lot of ginger in the concoction and it burned as it went down but it felt good. It felt good to be in his own flat drinking out of his own glass, sitting on his own chair at his own kitchen table and drinking his kind neighbour's gift. He wanted to phone Jenny, invite her to join him but he couldn't. He'd never properly invited her before and now he'd never be able to. He choked back the building tears and poured himself another glass of rum. He looked around the kitchen. It really was very tidy. He picked up his glass and walked round the flat. The living room was pristine, even the bedroom was neater than it had ever been. The table that had been in the hall had gone. The answerphone was on the floor, the lid open and the tape missing. He walked to the front door, picked up the mail and took it through to the living room. Putting his glass down on the coffee table, he sat on the sofa and went through the pile of letters and free magazines. It was mostly junk, a couple of bills all of which he put straight in the bin. There were a couple of letters from the dole office asking why he hadn't signed on and assuming he was now working they were informing him that has claim was closed. Amongst all the envelopes was a picture postcard. Greg didn't need to read it to know it was from Jenny; *Having a great time. Hotel is brilliant. In the middle of filming. I love it. See you when I get back. Jenny xxx.*' He put the card with the rest of the mail in the bin, picked up his glass of rum, downed it in one, felt the burn and went back to the kitchen for a re-fill.

*

The phone ringing woke him up. It was nearly nine o'clock. He wanted to let the answerphone pick up but without the tape it didn't function. He picked up the receiver.

'Where the hell are you?' Denis was very angry.

'You know where I am, you just rang me.'

'I know where you are now, yes. Where have you been and what are you doing there?'

'Denis. I told you I was going back to my flat once the inquest was over.'

'I didn't expect it to be over today.'

'Well it was, Denis. It took no time at all to go through Marjan's life and death and the authorities were completely absolved of all responsibility. DI Milne even offered to buy me a drink but I refused. I need to be on my own for a while, Denis. In my own space.'

'You could have let me know.'

'I'm sorry. I should have. I meant to ring you when I got home. I fell asleep. I'm sorry.'

'Shall I come over?'

'No Denis! I want to be on my own.'

'But Greg, in that flat after everything that's happened?'

'Yes Denis. In my flat.'

'Well, fine. I'll be here if you need me.' Denis hung up.

Greg sat there feeling guilty. Denis had been good to him but he couldn't stand being mothered. Denis wouldn't let him do anything for himself. He was forever fussing. Greg went into the kitchen. Black Olive's bottle of rum was on the small table. It appeared to be half empty. Greg smiled. It had done the trick, relaxed him, helped him to sleep. Thank you, Olive. He thought about going next door to thank her personally but he knew she was a single mum with two youngsters who would be needing their beds. He went over to the bin, fished out Jenny's postcard and pinned it to the noticeboard on the back of the kitchen door. There was no food in the house and Greg was hungry. He looked in his wallet and found the twenty pound note Denis had insisted on giving him as he left for the inquest. Intending to go to the local curry house he somehow found himself at the door of The Suffolk Arms and almost without realising he was in the pub sitting at the bar. It was quiet. Only a young courting couple in the corner. Greg was pleased to note that he didn't know them; he needed a quiet return to the drinking scene. The landlord came over and greeted him warmly, even buying Greg a drink. They chatted for a while, Greg was not sure whether he was pleased that the last week or so didn't come up in the conversation or not. He didn't really want to talk about it and yet he thought other people would show an interest. After two or three pints, several regulars had entered and he thought he was ready to spin some yarns about his exploits but something kept getting in the way. Memories of Jenny in the hospital; guilty feelings about the affair with Cathy, confused thoughts about Marjan all made him steer clear of the subject.

Being a week night, by ten-thirty the pub had emptied, even the courting couple had got tired of their public tonsil hockey display and gone off to somewhere more private. Greg was thinking of heading home himself when a young man came into the bar and sat on the stool next to Greg's. He was wearing a brown leather jacket with tassels hanging from the sleeves and black Levi jeans tucked into tan cowboy boots. He removed his jacket and hung it on a hook on the front of the bar revealing a red check lumberjack shirt. Greg smiled into the end of his beer thinking he looked like a refugee from a very bad amateur production of Oklahoma.

'Hi.' The stranger leaned over towards Greg. 'Can I get you a refill?'

Greg postponed his journey home. It would be rude to refuse a free drink.

'It is you, isn't it?' said the stranger as the drinks were being poured.

Greg looked round the empty bar. 'I guess it must be,' he said.

The cowboy took a copy of the Evening Standard from his pocket and pointed to a small picture on an inside page. There in glowing black and white was a reproduction of Greg standing on the steps outside the coroner's court. There wasn't much of an article, just a brief report on the verdict and the acquittal of the police. Milne seemed to be right that the press would not show a great deal of interest.

'Ah,' said Greg. 'Fame at last.'

'David.'

'No, Greg. Greg Driscoll.'

'I meant my name is David.'

'Yes, I realised that.'

David had a deep voice and spoke very slowly and deliberately as if speaking was a bit of an effort. Greg did not think he was in the company of a MENSA member here. He admonished himself quietly and tried not to let his smile look anything other than amiable. 'So what do you do, David?'

'I'm a teacher,' he said. 'I teach karate.'

Greg tried to imagine this rather thin young man in a karate suit; he gave up and finished his drink. 'Can I get you another?'

'I'll have a half, Greg, thanks.'

The two of them sat at the bar drinking and chatting. David didn't mention the newspaper article again, they chatted about football and the state of the country and all those things that men sitting at a bar talk about. At eleven-fifteen two uniformed police officers came into the bar and chatted with the landlord.

'We'd better go,' said David. 'Look at the time.'

'It's Ok, I'm sure we can get another once the law has left.'

'No,' said David, a little too emphatically. 'Not here, I know a little club down the road, we could go there for a few more. There'll be no worries there.'

'Not a disco, I'm a bit old for that, thanks.'

'No, it's a drinking club.'

'I've lived in Hackney for years and I never knew there was a drinking club here. I'd have joined ages ago, if I'd known. Is it legal?'

'Sort of,' whispered David. 'It's a Greek restaurant really. You're supposed to have something to eat but the guvnor doesn't mind as long as you spend money, if you know what I mean.' David winked at Greg. It was weird. One whole side of his face seemed to distort as if the muscles working his eyelid controlled his cheek and jaw as well.

Greg leapt off his stool and slapped his new friend on the back. 'Come on, then. I'm game. I could do with something to eat.'

*

The Casablanca Greek Restaurant was hardly a restaurant at all. There were only three tables, covered in plastic red gingham tablecloths and a bar at which sat three or four rough-looking characters and a beautiful, dark-haired, olive-skinned girl. The proprietor, a thick-set man called Spiros, greeted them warmly and, as Greg was introduced he was proffered a tiny glass of colourless liquid.

'It's a sort of initiation,' said David. 'You have to down it in one. Here sit on this bar-stool.'

One of the men stood up and offered Greg his stool. Greg thanked him and sat down. The bar stool was next to the girl, who looked at him with her dark brown eyes and smiled. Aware of her and the rest of the company watching him, raised the glass in the air, drew it to his lips and threw the spirit down his throat. Apart from a slight burning as the drink reached his midriff, the tasteless liquid appeared to have no effect. What effect Greg was expecting he didn't know but there was no reaction at all.

'Excellent,' he said, because he thought he should show his appreciation. 'Any chance of a lager now?'

There was a round of applause from the assembled customers who then carried on with their previous conversations, ignoring the newest member of this not-very-exclusive drinking club in the back streets of Hackney.

'Don't try and stand up for a few minutes.' Greg looked at the girl next to him.

'I'm sorry?'

'Your legs won't feel as though they're working, believe me. It's a Greek spirit that's about 100% alcohol. I'm Gina, by the way.'

'Well, hallo Gina. I'm Greg.' Choosing to ignore Gina's advice he tried to move his stool a bit nearer to Gina's. As soon as his feet touched the ground his body followed as if his legs did not exist. There was another round of applause and a lot of laughter from the rest of the customers, followed by the quiet murmur of them returning to whatever they were talking about before Greg provided the floor show. Gina offered him her hand and helped him back to his stool.

'Thanks. Can I buy you drink?'

'Thank you, I'll have a dry Martini.' Greg dug into the pocket of his jeans looking for what was left of his twenty pound note.

'It's OK,' said Spiros. 'It's on the house for you tonight.'

'Really? Are you sure?' Greg wasn't going to argue when he only had two pounds forty pence in his pocket.

'New member privilege.'

Greg looked round to offer David a drink but he didn't seem to be there. Spiros suggested he must have gone to the loo.

'I wouldn't worry, Greg. I'm sure your friend will be back soon and if not...?' Gina smiled again, showing her too perfect set of teeth. 'If not, I'm sure we can manage without him, don't you?' Gina had a voice like velvet with a touch of a Mediterranean accent. Which part of the Mediterranean, Greg couldn't work out but he didn't care. He was happy just to soak up the dulcet tones. He ordered the Martini and another bottle of lager for himself and sat securely on his stool.

In an hour's time David had not returned. Greg had discovered that Gina was a language student at Hackney College. She was Italian, from a large family, not the Mafia she pointed out but part of a small farming community in the region of Puglia. Her mother was a great cook and her father was a bum. Her six brothers were all bums and only her and her sister were ever going to make anything of themselves and only then if they got away from the oppressive male-dominated atmosphere of home. She had done a runner three years ago, worked her way through Europe and ended up in London the previous year.

How much of her autobiography was true, Greg neither knew of cared. He could have listened to her voice all night – which was now his intention! Besides, most of what he'd told her about himself was more than slightly embellished. Well, in fact most of it was untrue! He'd made himself out to be one of the most sought after actors in the country, turning down major films in Hollywood, refusing to be tempted by huge pay deals in order to bring theatre to the people in small village halls and pubs. Through his drunkenness he could see she was impressed.

As the night went further into the morning the Casablanca gradually emptied until there was just Greg and Gina left, Spiros was making it clear he wanted to close up and Gina took hold of Greg's hand.

'Do you think you can stand yet?' she said.

'I'll have a go.' He put his feet to the floor. His legs seemed strong enough to hold him up although a little unsteadily.

'My room's upstairs. I think Spiros wants to close.'

'You have a room here?' Greg felt a little worried.

'Spiros rents me a room at reasonable rate and I waitress for him occasionally. It's very expensive for students to rent a flat, you know. You don't have to come up, though. I wouldn't want you to think I was a prostitute or anything.' She laughed.

Greg returned her laugh, a little embarrassed. That was exactly what he had thought. He followed her up the dark staircase at the back of the restaurant into a small room on the second floor. There were two dining chairs and a small wooden coffee table. An old electric kettle and a couple of chipped mugs sat on a dirty tray on top of the table. The only other furniture was a single bed under a small window set into the sloping ceiling. A light bulb hung from the middle of the ceiling. Gina unplugged the kettle and left the room. Greg sat on the bed, his head beginning to swirl. It was times like this he wished he knew when to stop drinking. He stood up and shook his head. A mistake! He waited for the room to stop spinning and went gingerly over to one of the hard chairs by the coffee table. He sat and waited for Gina to return. He needed some coffee.

Gina came in with the filled kettle and plugged it in to an extension lead that ran from the wall socket to the table. She knelt at Greg's feet, rested her head on his knees and looked into his eyes. They didn't speak, they just looked into each other's eyes, Gina rubbing her hand up and down Greg's leg, he in turn caressing Gina's long dark hair. The kettle boiled. Gina stood up and started to unbutton her dress, it slid to the floor revealing her naked body. Greg stood looking at her for a moment before undressing himself. She walked slowly towards him, put her arms round him, pulled him close and they kissed for the first time.

The door suddenly slammed open banging against the wall and three figures entered the room. The first grabbed Greg from behind, prising him away from Gina. She threw her dressing gown round her shoulders and strode up to the other two.

'About bloody time,' she screamed at them. 'Any longer and I'd have had to do it with him, you bastards!' There was no longer any trace of the seductive accent. She left the room slamming the door behind her.

'That would have been a shame, wouldn't it, Greg?'

The man holding Greg turned him round bringing him face to face with David who was accompanied by a small weasel-like man with a thin moustache, making him look like a comic spiv from some old British movie.

'What's going on?' Greg stammered.

'That's what we'd like to know.' The weasel had a high-pitched nasal voice.

'Gina asked me here. I'm sorry. I didn't know…'

'I know she did,' whined the little man. 'We told her to. We'd like to have a little chat with you. If you tell us what we want to know we might tell her to come back. Would you like that?'

Greg was suddenly cold. He was aware that he was naked and was embarrassed. The large man was holding his arms behind his back, displaying everything to his captors. 'Look. I'm sorry. I think there's been some misunderstanding.'

'Indeed there has, Mr Driscoll. Somebody has taken us for a ride and we don't like it, do we, David?'

The cowboy answered in the negative.

Greg tried to struggle free but the grip from behind just got tighter.

'Are you uncomfortable? Perhaps he would like to sit down. Why don't you help him, Grace?'

Grace pulled him down onto the nearby dining chair, he could feel his hands being tied tightly behind him. David moved forward and tied each of Greg's ankles to a chair leg. He had no strength to fight. His feeble attempts at kicking David just resulted in the thin nylon ropes being tied tighter, cutting in to him. He sat there naked and trussed. Grace moved round to the front of him. Greg could see why he was called Grace. Nothing to do with charm or refinement; there nothing either charming or refined about this monster. He must have been six foot five inches tall and nearly the same width. He had a huge black beard that looked like it had never seen a comb or a pair of scissors. He was also wearing cricket flannels and waving a cricket bat.

'What is all this about?' Greg was scared. The weasel-spiv pulled up the other chair and sat opposite him.

'Where is he?'

There was a pause before Greg replied. 'Who?'

There was a loud guffaw from W G Grace. The weasel shot him a glance before reverting his gaze back to Greg.

'Where is he?'

Greg paused again before answering. He was trying to think. What was he supposed to say? Was this some sort of game? Was this some sort of sex club for playing perverted games?

'Look,' he said. 'I'm not into this sort of thing, I'm sorry there must have been some sort of mistake.'

'Where is he?'

'I don't know what or who you're talking about!'

'Where is he?'

Greg sat there silent. He didn't know what to say. He wanted to cry.

'Grace? Show him your spinning finger. Do you like cricket, Mr Driscoll?'

Grace was holding his middle finger up in front of Greg. 'I like cricket,' he grunted. 'Do you?'

'Yes,' said Greg quietly.

'Where is he?' The weasel was persistent.

'I don't know,' Greg tried, not taking his eyes off the fat finger waving in front of him.

'Grace?'

The large man put his hand between Greg's legs and took hold of one of his testicles. He rolled it around in his fingers gently increasing the pressure before taking the whole scrotum in his hand. The pain was intense as he twisted and squeezed Greg's balls. Greg screamed. The room started to swirl again. 'Please let me pass out,' Greg prayed silently. All of a sudden the pressure lessened. Greg didn't pass out. Some water was thrown in his face. Grace's hand remained, caressing, not squeezing.

'Where is he?'

'Who?' Greg sobbed.

'Who do you think?'

'Please, really, I don't know.'

'Grace?'

Grace squeezed again.

'I don't know,' Greg screamed. 'Please! I don't know!'

The weasel touched Grace on the shoulder. He released his grip. The weasel whispered in David's ear. David nodded and turned to Greg. 'Greg,' he said. 'Where is Herr Wiersma?'

The name sent a shiver down Greg's spine. 'Wiersma? I don't know.'

'But you work for him, Greg. Come on. None of us is enjoying this you know.'

Greg looked at Grace and thought that at least one of them was. 'I don't work for him. I don't know where he is. Ask the police.'

The mention of police seemed to press Grace into action again as he squeezed Greg's scrotum. Weasel touched his shoulder and the pressure was released. This did not make a great deal of difference to the pain seething through Greg's lower body.

'You shouldn't say things like that,' the weasel grimaced. 'Grace doesn't like the mention of the boys in blue. It makes him nervous and when he's nervous he loses control and sometimes he forgets his own strength. Now why don't you just tell me where he is?'

'Please, I don't know,' Greg's voice was weak and as high-pitched as his tormentor. 'I think he might be in Holland. Please leave me alone.'

The weasel stared hard into Greg's face as if he were trying to read his mind. He turned to Grace. 'Let him go.'

Grace removed his hand. Tears were streaming from Greg's eyes. The weasel spoke quietly to David again who walked behind the chair in which Greg was being held captive. He put his hands gently on Greg's shoulders and then suddenly pushed down hard and pulled towards him. Greg fell heavily onto the floor, his head bouncing on the threadbare carpet. Pain shifted momentarily from his crotch to his head and then, as if realising the damage was greater down below, shifted back again. Greg wanted to hold himself but his arms were tied and trapped beneath the chair. The weasel sat on the edge of the upturned chair between Greg's knees with his back to him. The pain shifted once more to Greg's crushed arms.

'Now,' the weasel said calmly. 'I ask you again. Where is he?'

'Fuck off!' Greg managed to get the words out in a whisper. The weasel took hold of Greg's big toe on his right foot. He slowly wiggled the toe in a circular motion before pulling it sharply and strongly to one side. There was a crack and the intense pain almost made Greg pass out. Water was thrown in his face again to make sure he didn't stop suffering.

'Where is he?'

'I don't fucking know! Please stop!' Greg's voice was little more than a hoarse whisper.

'His mouth sounds a bit dry, David. Why don't you give him a drink?'

David went over to a holdall by the door and took out a bottle of scotch. Removing the top he held the bottle above Greg's open mouth. He let a drop fall into the back of Greg's throat, Greg choked a bit before swallowing. Grace held Greg's mouth open while David proceeded to pour a large amount of neat scotch down his throat. Greg spluttered and gagged.

'Now,' persisted the weasel. 'I shall ask you once more. Herr Wiersma owes me a lot of money and I would like it. Do you know where he is?'

'I've told you, I don't know.'

The weasel took hold of Greg's other big toe and broke it.

'He doesn't know. Let him have a drink. Give him a few and dump him.'

Greg heard the little man leave the room as David poured most of the rest of the whisky into Greg's mouth. Greg didn't feel anything more. He was vaguely aware of booted feet slamming into his side and something colliding with his face but felt no pain as he slowly slipped into oblivion.

*

It was just after four-thirty in the morning when the security guard at Homerton hospital was roused from slumbering in front of the television by the sound of a speeding car skidding to a halt outside the front doors of the hospital. He looked out of the window in time to see a figure wrapped in a blanket being ejected from the back of the car before it sped off again. Two staff orderlies had arrived on the scene before he reached the doors. They started to unwrap the blanket to reveal what looked like a Michelin man, all puffed up and out of proportion. What could be seen of the face and hands were dark blue and blown up, there were drying streaks of blood to be seen on the flesh and the blanket had wet patches all over it. There was no immediate sign of life. One of the orderlies found the wrist and looked for a pulse. It was there but very faint. Two male nurses had joined them with a stretcher. Together they lifted him onto the stretcher and carried him straight to the operating theatre.

***

CHAPTER TWENTY-TWO

There was a small corps of press already outside the front of the Homerton hospital when DI Milne arrived at six-thirty. He had no comment for them and, for once, he could say that with complete honesty. He didn't have the faintest idea what had happened. He'd been called at home and told to go to Homerton hospital where, he'd been told, Greg Driscoll had been admitted in a serious condition.

After the inquest into Marjan Smits death he'd immediately put in for leave. He was contemplating an option on early retirement. He had completely lost any feeling of vocation towards the police force. He was disillusioned and couldn't continue to operate in an efficient manner at present. His superiors had been understanding and offered him a period of leave with full pay until he felt able to cope again. Roger Milne thought it unlikely he'd ever be able to cope again. He'd been told this would happen when he was made a DI. A retiring officer took him to one side, asking him if he knew what he was getting in to. At the time Roger was ambitious, this was the next step on what he had been working towards. Promotion, power, importance. These were what were important to him then. Now ten years later, having risen no further, having not kow-towed to the powers that be, having lost his wife and family to someone who was there for them, it all seemed such a waste. And once the drive had gone there was no way back. Early retirement seemed the best way out. After all, he had a good pension and at last he would have the time to do all those things he'd always wanted to do. Like what? All he'd ever wanted to do was be a policeman.

Now, here he was back in the firing line. As far as he was concerned he'd seen the last of Greg Driscoll on the steps of the coroner's court the previous afternoon. There had just been a few formalities to tie up before the case was closed and Milne started his leave. Peiter Wiersma had done a good disappearing act, apparently, and the authorities did not want to rock the European boat. The powers in Holland had done all they could, as had the Germans, supposedly but Roger Milne suspected it was convenient for them not to be able to find a big European entrepreneur. The advice from high-up had been to drop the case against him as the evidence was flimsy against a well-respected European businessman who had always conducted himself immaculately. Rob Vanderlast had been found and taken in for questioning in the Netherlands. He had convinced them he'd been duped into helping to run drugs unwittingly, claiming he knew nothing of the operation before being arrested and that he was under the belief he really was filming some commercials. He claimed no knowledge of anyone called Jenny Gulliver. He was fined and let off.

Interpol had had a cursory glance but were unable to find Wiersma anywhere. It was this sort of co-operation that was helping Milne to make up his mind about retirement.

He was greeted by Denis Young in the waiting area who was sitting on one of the brown plastic seats amongst the sprinkling of patients suffering from mostly minor cuts and bruises, the result of over-enthusiasm whilst under the influence of an over-indulgence of alcohol. It was eerily quiet in the waiting area. A few groans as people sobered up and the pain started hitting them, apart from that the most noise came from the vending machine that seemed to be doing a very good business in black coffee.

'How is he?' Milne asked.

'I don't really know. They won't let me see him. Do you know what happened?'

'I was hoping you could fill me in a bit on that.'

Denis sighed. 'I don't know any more than you, I'm afraid. I was phoned at about a quarter to five, they'd got my number from his hospital record apparently. Who'd have thought there could be an advantage to repeatedly visiting hospital? They had my office number it seems and the answerphone in my office gives my home number. I came straight away.'

A man in a flapping white coat, carrying a clipboard came up to Milne. 'Are you the Inspector?'

'Detective Inspector, yes.'

'Good. Your colleagues are through there.' The white coat pointed to an office behind the reception desk and went on his way. Milne and Denis went into the office. There were two constables in the office who stood up as Milne entered.

'Do we have any news as to what happened here?' Milne asked the constables.

'Badly beaten up, sir, looks as though it was a professional job,' said one of the men.

'What makes you think that?'

'The doctor, sir,' said the other constable. 'He said there was very little serious damage other than broken toes and bad bruising.'

'Gang torture, sir,' said the first constable emphatically.

Milne sighed and asked the constables to leave him alone with Denis. 'See if you can find some decent coffee and find me the doctor who's dealing with Driscoll.' The two constables, grateful for the excuse, left the room.

'Gang torture?' Denis' face had gone white.

'I would think's that's probably a bit strong.'

'But he said broken toes!' Milne said nothing. 'What do we do now?'

'Sit and wait for the doctor's report.'

*

It was several hours later that DI Milne was allowed in to see Greg. He was in a sorry state. The flesh around his eyes was a deep purple colour; his cheeks looked as if they'd been filled with cotton wool. His arms matched his eyes and cheeks, swollen and purple. He was propped up on three pillows, the rest of his body covered by sheets and blankets.

Roger Milne asked how he felt, realising it was a stupid question. Greg tried to smile. He was sedated up to a point but could still feel a deal of pain. Roger sat on the chair by his bed.

'Can you give me any information, Greg?' Milne asked, adding as an afterthought, 'Can you speak?'

Greg's swollen mouth moved slightly and a low groaning noise could just about be heard. He tried to clear his throat and pain shot down his sides. He winced.

'Shall I come back later?'

Greg thought about shaking his head, thought better of it, and slowly lifted his hand.

'Can you write?' Milne looked at Greg's swollen fingers and added, 'sorry.'

Greg managed another whisper. Milne leant close to his lips.

*

Han Koolhaven walked up the steps to the middle flat rented by Rob Vanderlast. Rob's family rented the top three floors of the tall town house in Amsterdam. His sister had lived on the top floor before she had married and moved to Rotterdam with her minor-oil-magnate of a husband. No-one had been sorry to see her go. In Rob's words 'she had become a snob' refusing even to admit that her family existed. Rob's parents had lived in the floor below Rob until they died, both within a few months of each other. Rob had retained the middle floor but the others had now been let. He had never really got to know any of his relatively new neighbours and had never bothered to visit the flats where he had spent so much of his youth and he'd never been asked. He was quite happy in his own place.

Han knocked on the door. There was no reply. He reached up and ran his fingers along the top of the door-frame. As he expected he knocked a brass key onto the floor. He stooped, picked it up and let himself into Rob's living room.

Rob was there, in a manner of speaking. He was stoned. The room was ripe with the sweet smell of marijuana; there were small bits of paper and tobacco strewn across an old LP record sleeve lying on the floor next to the sofa where Rob sprawled. He raised his head slowly and looked towards Han standing in the doorway. His face cracked and he giggled.

'Hello, man. What you doing here?' he croaked as his eyes tried to focus on his friend.

'Thought I'd look you up,' said Han. 'How are you?'

'Hey, I'm fine, man. You didn't bring anything to eat I don't suppose?'

''Fraid not!'

'See what's in the kitchen, will you? I'm starving to death here.'

Han went into the kitchen and returned with some bread and cheese. Rob had managed to sit up and was rolling another joint. Han sat on the floor opposite him and accepted the finished product. He lit it and took a deep lung-full of hazy smoke. He hadn't had a smoke for a while and it hit him, his head becoming light almost immediately. It felt good. He looked at Rob and realised just how different they were. Han enjoyed getting stoned occasionally but with Rob it was a way of life. That, no doubt, was how he got so mixed up with Peiter Wiersma's little project. Rob Vanderlast would have provided such easy pickings for someone like Wiersma, all he had to do was offer more and more drugs and a little cash and Rob would be hooked. But what now? How was Rob coping with Wiersma off the scene? If he was off the scene, of course. That was what Han needed to find out. He still had a few things to settle with Herr Wiersma and he intended to settle them, whatever the cost. He owed it to Marjan, if nothing else. But for now that could wait a while. He needed to relax and re-charge first. This is the way it was done in Amsterdam. He took another deep drag on the joint and passed it to Rob.

*

Greg Driscoll and Roger Milne had a sort of discussion for over an hour before the medical staff insisted, against Greg's will, that the patient needed some rest. Greg had told Milne about the weasel, WG Grace and David the cowboy. Milne knew them. It was Charlie Frank's mob. What Roger hadn't known was they seemed to have moved from protection rackets to the drugs trade.

Milne left the room. He reported back to Scotland Yard who subsequently discovered that the Casablanca restaurant was owned by a 'friend' of the Franks' gang. The police had visited the restaurant but it was closed, there was no sign of Spiros or Gina and no-one could be found admitting to ever having been in there. The owner was out of the country, apparently. The locals, when questioned said they thought it was disused.

Roger Milne told Denis that he didn't want Greg to press charges; something that Denis took a lot of persuading to agree to. He pointed out that although they knew it was the Franks gang there'd be great difficulty in proving it. Besides, if they were involved with Wiersma, they'd far rather get them for that than for a beating which would command a lesser, if any, sentence. Denis found this attitude appalling and would have taken up Greg's right to a private prosecution but for Roger's insistence that if the Franks gang were convicted on a non-custodial sentence the re-percussions would be far more dangerous than if he could get them put away on a more serious charge. Denis eventually conceded that Milne, probably, knew what he was doing.

*

Rob Vanderlast and Han Koolhaven had passed out. Han had spent the best part of the previous night plugging Rob for information about Peiter Wiersma. Rob either couldn't or wouldn't give any information. Every time Wiersma had been mentioned he'd burst into fits of giggles, it was very infectious and, especially as he was now stoned, Han found himself unable to speak about Peiter without exploding into near apoplexy.

Han woke early the next morning with no hangover but feeling terribly hungry. He looked at his friend still asleep on the sofa and wondered how the two of them got mixed up in this mess. He stood up and went to the kitchen in search of some food and coffee. Under the kitchen table was a holdall half packed with Rob's clothes, Rob's passport and an airline ticket. Han bent down and picked up the ticket. It was a scheduled return from Amsterdam to Corfu. It was dated for later that day.

Han calmly made some coffee and found some cake. He took them through to the living room and shook Rob violently. Rob slowly came to.

'Going on holiday?' Han asked, waving the airline ticket.

'What? Oh, no. I have a bit of business. Give me some of that cake, will you?'

Han kept the cake out of Rob's reach. 'What sort of business? Filming? Shouldn't I know about this, we are supposed to be partners in this company?'

'It's not filming. Give me a bit of cake, I'm starving!'

'If it's not filming,' said Han, finishing the last piece of cake, 'what sort of business is it?'

Rob started to get up. 'I've got to find something to eat.'

Han pushed him back onto the sofa. 'We have some talking to do, Rob.'

***

CHAPTER TWENTY-THREE

The sun shone brightly on the blue-green Ionian Sea. The weather had been beautiful for some weeks now, not a cloud in the sky. The large figure leaning on the pulpit of the chartered yacht took another swig of gin-fizz and tried to relax. He looked across the bay to Albania. How things had changed there since his last visit. He remembered stories of holiday-makers sailing the short distance from the north of Corfu to the beautiful and, more inviting, deserted sandy beaches of the communist country, only to find the beaches not deserted at all but populated by members of the Albanian armed forces. They weren't too keen on tourists in those pre-Republic days, tending to hold them prisoner on spying charges or worse, if they tried to flee back to the safety of Greece, shoot them. How true these stories had been were difficult to ascertain now. It had been quite a long time since Peiter Wiersma had been on holiday in Corfu.

The small bay and village of Agni had changed a lot since then too and so had Peiter Wiersma. He was not on holiday now, he was on the run. How had he managed to make such a mess of such a simple operation? Why had he been so greedy? He didn't need the money from the drugs. His business wasn't in any financial trouble. People would always want groceries! It had all seemed so easy when Rob

Vanderlast had told him of his little project that needed financing. He should have left it at that instead of suggesting bigger and bigger deals. Trying to co-operate with the Franks gang was also a mistake. They were dangerous. He should have kept clear of them.

His contemplations were interrupted by the sound of a small motor boat heading towards his yacht. He leaned over the pulpit rails so he could see the boat.

'About time!' he exclaimed and went towards the side of the yacht. He undid the rail and helped Rob Vanderlast onto the boat. Rob thanked him and sent the boatman away before joining Peiter Wiersma on the deck.

'Have you brought the money?' Wiersma demanded.

'In time, Peiter,' said Rob, clutching the holdall beneath his arm.

'Just give me the money and go, if you know what's good for you.'

'No!' Rob moved away from the side of the yacht and went onto the foredeck. Wiersma followed slowly. He was irritated. He only needed Vanderlast until he'd given him the money he'd asked him to bring out from Holland. After that Rob Vanderlast could go to hell as far as he was concerned and he had every intention of giving him a helping hand to send him there.

'I think we need to sort a few things out first, Peiter, don't you?'

'Whatever you say, Rob.' Wiersma moved towards the small bridge of the boat. 'Maybe this isn't the best place, though. Let's take a little cruise.' Peiter Wiersma started the engine and put it into gear. The yacht moved steadily round the north of Corfu into the Ionian Sea. Rob Vanderlast sat calmly on the deck as Wiersma steered the yacht south towards the Mediterranean Sea.

Neither man had spoken after their first interchange. Rob had helped himself to a gin and tonic from the cabin and returned to the deck, never letting go of the bag. Wiersma had lit himself a large cigar which he smoked as he sat at the wheel. There was no sense of amity between them. They both had a job to do.

After about an hour Peiter switched the engine off. They were somewhere between Malta and Crete, there was no sign of land. The odd fishing boat could be seen in the distance; apart from that they were probably as isolated as anyone could possibly be. The sea was calm and the boat bobbed gently as the waves lapped the side of the hull. Peiter left the bridge and went into the cabin.

'Would you like a refill,' he asked the tall Dutchman as he descended the stairs.

'I'm fine, thank you.'

'Come down and join me, then. We can talk in private in here.'

Rob looked around at the vast empty sea. 'It's a nice day and I don't think anyone will overhear, I think I'd rather do business out here.' He leant against the pulpit rails.

'Whatever you say. I'll just be a moment.' He went below, reappeared a few moments later with a large gin fizz and a neat black leather shoulder bag. They stood looking at each other, the length of the foredeck between them. Rob walked towards Peiter but stopped as he saw him draw his hand from the leather bag. It was holding a small pistol.

Rob clutched the holdall tighter. 'You can't be sure I've got what you want yet, Peiter. Don't you think we should talk a bit first?'

'Put the bag down and go back to the pulpit.' Wiersma was looking directly into Rob's eyes. Rob didn't move. Wiersma paused. He wasn't sure what to do. He'd asked, or rather ordered, Vanderlast to fly out to him with a large amount of US Dollars in used notes and some banker's orders made out to Georg Veidt. That was the name Wiersma had now assumed. That was the name he'd hired the yacht under. Georg Veidt had been a client of Wiersma's, supplying various grocery products, it was easy to get money orders from his company made out in that name. By the time anyone discovered that they never reached the real supplier, Wiersma would be in a safe haven somewhere.

He looked at Rob Vanderlast standing defiantly in front of him. Surely he must realise he was the only person to know the new identity and location of Peiter Wiersma which put him in a very vulnerable position. Wiersma had promised him money and drugs for bringing the cash and banker's orders to him. He'd also promised him a great deal of torment if he refused. Vanderlast must have known the potential danger he was in from various sources anyway just from being involved with the business. Vanderlast had set up the deals in England with the Franks mob and although the Dutch police didn't think they had anything on him at the moment, they wouldn't have to look too far if they wanted to. And then there was the unofficial police force employed by villains the world over, they wouldn't be far behind once they realised the main man had done a bunk. Vanderlast would have far more difficulty getting away from them, so surely he'd see that helping was best for him. Vanderlast had to believe he would give him enough money; then he could go and start a new life in some obscure country. But then he'd got the pistol out. He'd done it too soon. He should have waited till he'd got the holdall from him.

'Put the bag down,' he said again.

'Wait,' said Rob. 'I have a proposition.'

'I don't think you're in a very strong position to make deals right now. Put the bag down and step away!'

The tall Dutchman took a step towards the pulpit and held the bag above the sea.

'Stand still, you fool,' yelled Wiersma. He raised the gun and pointed it at Rob.

'You need this money, Peiter. If you shoot me the bag will go over the side. Would you like to talk?'

Wiersma slowly lowered the gun but kept his finger on the trigger. 'Well?' he said.

'If you fire that gun, those fishing boats over there will hear it, even at this distance. They will inform the authorities. How will you explain to them?'

'Self-defence!'

'And how will you explain your presence here when you are being sought throughout Europe?'

Wiersma slid his free hand into his bag and pulled out a length of metal tubing. Still staring into his adversary's eyes, he screwed the silencer onto the end of his pistol. 'OK?' he said.

Rob's long thin arms were beginning to ache. 'You still won't get the money. It's a long way down.'

'What do you want?' Wiersma pointed the gun again.

'Safe passage as agreed.'

'Put the bag down, then.'

'Not until you put the gun down.'

Peiter Wiersma lowered his arm.

'On the deck, Peiter.' The holdall hovered above the sea.

Wiersma thought for a moment and then squatted down and placed the gun on the deck by his foot.

The two men stood there for a short while, not speaking, not moving before the tall man brought the holdall slowly back towards the relative safety of the yacht's foredeck. He unzipped the top of the bag and put his hand inside. He noticed Wiersma's legs bend slightly. 'Don't move, Peiter. How do you know I don't have a gun in here?'

Peiter Wiersma paused for a second, then quickly bent down and grabbed the gun, at the same time throwing himself onto the deck. A noise rang out as the bullet hit the rail next to where the Dutchman had been standing. He too was now on the floor. The holdall was on the deck between the two men. The bulky Wiersma took aim again as he lay on the floor. The slimmer and more agile of the two, rolled and lunged towards the other man as three more shots dully rang out in quick succession from the silenced pistol. He felt no pain as one of the bullets winged his arm. He landed on the fat man and knocked him flat on the floor. The gun fell from Wiersma's hand and slid across the deck. A fist connected with his chin. Wiersma felt the pain. He wasn't in the physical condition for fighting and the other man was considerably younger. He was starting to panic.

'OK,' he spluttered. 'You can have what you want. Just leave now and you'll be safe, I promise.'

'Safe? What? Like Greg Driscoll and the others?' The younger man was now sitting on Wiersma's ample chest, his knees pressing down on his shoulders.

'Driscoll's a meddling fool. He would have been safe if he hadn't tried to be clever.'

Rob's fist connected with Wiersma's face again.

'What do you want, Rob?' Wiersma was spitting blood. 'Come on. I'll give you anything.' He was whining and whimpering now.

'You can't give me what I really want. It's too late!' The fist landed again. Wiersma felt his head and shoulders being lifted by the lapels of his suit. His head smashed heavily onto the deck and was lifted again. He was only vaguely aware of a voice in the distance.

'That's for Greg!' said the voice. 'And that's for Jenny; that's for Brian Carter and the police officers; all the people you've murdered.' Wiersma had drifted into oblivion by the time the Dutchman finished the list. 'And most of all, that's for Marjan!'

A gasp of air burst noisily from the large man's lungs, followed by a short wheezing sound, then silence. The Dutchmen's tears were streaming from his eyes long before he stood up and looked at Peiter Wiersma's prostrate body. There was a small trickle of blood dribbling from Wiersma's mouth and a larger pool of blood spreading from underneath his head. The tall man kicked the side of the body hard several times, screaming 'Bastard!' through his tears with every kick. Wiersma was past feeling or hearing as his ribs cracked and splintered.

*

There was no-one within sight of the yacht as the large, lifeless body tumbled over the side. The splash, as it hit the water, rocked the boat. The body floated for a while, eyes staring, before rolling over and slowly disappearing into the Mediterranean Sea. The yacht's engine started up and she sailed back towards the little bay of Agni. It was dark as the rubber dinghy was lowered quietly into the water.

***

CHAPTER TWENTY-FOUR

Greg was getting used to leaving hospitals. However, he wasn't too happy about his latest undignified exit from Homerton. Apparently the bed he'd been occupying was required for someone more seriously ill than Greg. There was no press; no well-wishers, apart from good old Denis, who was pushing his wheelchair from the front doors to the waiting taxi. There wasn't even a solitary nurse to give him a kiss, they were all too busy it seemed. He was wearing pyjamas, a rare occurrence at the best of times, and a silk dressing gown borrowed from his agent. Once again he was to be a house-guest in Denis' flat and this time the mother-hen was not going to let him out! Greg hated the loss of his independence but, as Denis repeatedly pointed out, he was lucky he had someone as kind as him to take care of him.

Roger Milne had been in to see Greg two or three times during the week he'd spent lazing about courtesy of The National Health Service. Charlie Franks had been tracked down and was being watched, whatever that meant; there was no news from anywhere regarding the whereabouts of Peiter Wiersma. One piece of news he had been able to relate was the discovery of Rob Vanderlast's body in his flat in Amsterdam. Apparently he had taken a lethal cocktail of drugs and alcohol and had been dead for at least two days by the time his neighbours found him. Greg felt a certain amount of sadness. Rob had, after all, only been caught up in this mess by default, the same as him, hadn't he? It wasn't as though it had all been his idea, was it? It was Wiersma who should be lying in some mortuary. On the other hand, Han had said that Rob knew what was going on and didn't try to stop it. Greg was confused. He'd really like to forget all about it but he didn't think that would be likely. This was going to haunt him for the rest of his life. He had enjoyed his brief working partnership with the Dutchmen, although the scripts were terrible, the shots had been good. And what had happened to Han? Nothing had been seen or heard of him since he left Denis' flat weeks ago. Maybe he was lying dead in some flat, another casualty of Wiersma's greed.

Greg was sitting quietly in the back of the black cab. He had no choice really. Denis was wittering on like an old woman about what they were going to do. He had a whole itinerary set out for Greg's welfare over the next few weeks including going to the gym! Greg thought it highly unlikely he would be going there unless they had bar that sold more than fruit juice. There appeared to be no time set aside for visits to any local hostelries, everything was healthy; the menu; the drinks; the lifestyle. If Denis thought he was going to change Greg he really was off his head.

Greg wanted to visit his flat before going to Denis', pick up a few clothes and some records that he wanted to listen to, rather than the stuff Denis liked. Denis reluctantly asked the driver to stop outside Greg's block.

'We'd better be quick,' he said. 'I'm not hanging round here long.'

Greg had wanted to ask what was wrong with 'round here' but thought better of it. Unable to climb the stairs to his flat, Greg had to be content to sit in the back of the cab listening to mostly racist comments from the taxi driver as he observed Greg's neighbourhood, while Denis went to get what Greg wanted. He came back with Greg's holdall and a plastic Sainsbury's carrier bag holding half a dozen LPs. He also had a few items of post in his hand which he handed over to Greg. They were mostly junk mailshots, Greg gave them a cursory glance and put them in the holdall.

'I can help you out if you're in trouble, Greg.' Denis was speaking quietly so the cabbie couldn't hear.

'What do you mean?'

'Financially, I mean.'

'I'm not. Well, no more trouble than usual in that department and I think I've a good enough excuse for not paying any recent bills, don't you?'

'Of course, it's just that I noticed one of those letters was from a solicitor. Don't just ignore it, Greg. Debts won't just go away.'

Greg looked in the bag for the letters. He hadn't noticed a solicitor's letter. He didn't think there was anything he hadn't paid that would warrant being sued. He searched through the small pile of post and came across a long envelope with Burns & Stallworthy printed across the top and his name and address across the middle. It was postmarked South London. Greg opened the envelope and took out several sheets of paper, all but the top one stapled together.

'I'll get Graeme on to it if you like. They can't sue you in the state you're in!' Denis was indignant.

'It's not a summons, Denis.' Greg put the sheets of paper back in the envelope and replaced that in the holdall. He sat very quietly, staring at the floor.

'Well, what is it?' said Denis.

Greg didn't answer. Denis went to take the letter from the holdall but Greg stopped him.

'Leave it, Denis!'

Denis, surprised by Greg strong reaction, took his hand away from the bag, folded his arms and stared out of the window.

'Don't sulk, Denis. I'll tell you about it later.' Greg was aware that the taxi driver was watching them in his rear-view mirror and listening in to everything they were saying. He reached forward and closed the glass partition between them. 'It's a letter from Jenny's solicitors.'

When they arrived at Denis' flat they decamped to the kitchen, where Denis started making coffee whilst Greg studied the letter from Burns & Stallworthy. Denis, although desperate to know what the content of the letter concerned, could see that whatever it was it was having an adverse effect on Greg. His head was visibly drooping as he read through it and tears were starting to flow from his eyes. He walked over to the table with Greg's coffee and put in on the table.

'You're dripping on the letter, Greg.'

Greg wiped his eyes with his left hand and handed Denis the letter with his right. Denis sat at the other side of the table and started to read. It was a difficult read. When he finished the letter he picked up the form that had been placed in the envelope.

'It could be good news, Greg.'

Greg lifted his head from the table. 'Good news! Good news! How do you make that out?'

'Well, as I read it Jenny's solicitors want to pay you a sizeable sum of money.'

'As I read it they want to pay me money to hush up the fact that Jenny's dead!'

'Well, not really…'

Greg picked up the letter. '*Burns & Stallworthy are handling the estate of the late Jenny Gulliver. As you are mentioned as a beneficiary we feel obliged to inform you of several conditions that must be conformed to before you can make any claim on the estate.* I don't want to make any claim on Jenny's estate. I don't know what they're talking about.'

'Did you know you were a beneficiary of Jenny's will?'

'I didn't even know she had a will.'

'It says here that her mother doesn't know that Jenny's dead.'

'Apparently she's been in some home in America for years. Never had any interest in Jenny.'

'Apart from paying her a very nice allowance.' Denis pointed to the long legal form. 'You have to fill this in, Greg. You are about to inherit £250,000.'

'I don't want it, Denis. It's not right. I have to agree that Jenny's mother doesn't ever know about her daughter's death. I can't do that.'

'According to the solicitors, she's not well enough to be told. Look, Greg, I know how you feel but this is obviously what Jenny wanted, you owe it to her to accept these terms.'

'Oh don't talk bollocks, Denis. This isn't what Jenny would want. She wouldn't want to be dead!'

'That's not what I mean and you know it.'

'Why would Jenny want to pay me off for keeping quiet about her death? No, this is the lawyers and solicitors

wanting to hang on to Jenny's fortune. And they can have it!
All of it! I don't need their hush money!'

'Well, strictly speaking, you do. This would clear all
your debts and you could buy yourself somewhere decent to
live.'

Greg looked at the letter again then screwed it into a
ball and threw it across the kitchen. Denis grabbed the form
from the table and put it in surreptitiously into a drawer.

'Give that back, Denis.'

'No! It'll stay in there for the time being.'

*

The next morning a postcard arrived at Denis' flat.
Who it was from was a mystery. There was no name and
neither of them recognised the writing. It had been sent from
the Greek island of Corfu and showed a picture of a small
fishing port on the front. On the back, apart from the address
was printed "It's over! The fat man has sunk!"

'What's this rubbish?' said Denis. 'Who do we know
who's gone to Greece?'

'No-one I know,' said Greg studying the card closely.

'What does this mean? Who's the fat man?'

'It ain't over 'till the fat lady sings!'

'What?'

'That's the expression, isn't it?'

'I don't know what you're talking about. Who's the
card from?'

'I'm not sure, Denis, but I think it's from a friend.' Greg studied the printing. It was written in capital letters. 'A friend who wants to remain secret, by the looks of things. I think we should respect that.'

'I think we should take it straight to DI Milne.'

'No, Denis. What do you think this means?'

'I haven't got a clue!'

'I think it means we won't be hearing any more from Herr Wiersma.'

'Well, I think this should definitely go straight to the police then!'

Greg held the postcard in his hands for a moment, seemingly studying the picture and then tore it into small pieces and threw them in the bin.

'Greg!' yelled Denis.

'Don't be such an old fart, Denis. Get me a beer from the fridge.'

'I'll put the kettle on!' Denis went into the kitchen.

'I'll maybe drop a few hints if I see Milne but I don't want you to tell anyone about this postcard.'

Denis turned to Greg, kettle in hand, and sighed. 'Greg, I've had enough of all of this. I'm not going to tell anybody anything anymore!'

'Good. Now stop waving that kettle around and put it on to boil. If I'm not allowed a beer the least you can do is make some decent coffee. If you're supposed to be looking after me again I want to be treated a bit better than last time. Letting me go off and get beaten up again, what on earth were you thinking?'

Denis' shoulders rose as if he were about to explode in a fit of rage until he saw Greg's bruised face grinning at him.

'Just a joke, Denis. I'll tell you one thing, I don't intend to be much trouble this time. I actually feel better than I have for some time, apart from a swollen face, a headache, sore feet and extremely tender genitals.'

'Well, at least that'll keep you out of strange girl's bedrooms.'

'For a while, maybe.'

*

Roger Milne's superiors couldn't understand his interest in Georg Veidt, whose chartered yacht had been found abandoned off the north coast of Corfu. Milne wasn't sure himself. He'd spent a long afternoon on the phone talking to Greg, seeing if he could get any more information from him. Milne had threatened to arrest Greg and take him to a police station and question him there but Greg knew he wasn't serious. All Greg would suggest was that Milne looked into any boating accidents off the coast of Corfu. Milne wanted more details but Denis claimed that Greg was tired and needed some rest and that DI Milne was provoking a sick man and he would report him unless he left him alone.

The description of Georg Veidt from the Greek police sounded familiar to Milne, very familiar, as did the description of a man who had hired a local fisherman to take him out to Georg Veidt's yacht moored off the coast of Corfu. His description bore a strong resemblance to a man who had recently been found dead in a flat in Amsterdam. Was there a connection? Of course there was. Milne thought he may at last be closing in on the end of this case. A few days later a bloated body had washed up on the beach at Syracuse on the coast of Sicily. The authorities had eventually assumed this was the remains of Georg Veidt. However, further inquiries led to the realisation that Georg Veidt was actually alive and well and living in Germany and still trading across Europe. He insisted, also that he had never been to Corfu, a statistic borne out by the German passport office, and that as he suffered terribly from sea-sickness would not dream of chartering a yacht even on a duck pond! From there it hadn't taken long for the authorities to work out the identification of the bloated body in Sicily. Herr Veidt's past business associations with Herr Wiersma led to inquiries about the missing Wiersma. Tests on the body proved the theory to be right and the conclusion was reached that Wiersma had travelled to Greece under Veidt's name, had some sort of altercation with Rob Vanderlast which had resulted in Wiersma's death. Vanderlast had returned home, couldn't live with the knowledge that he had caused the death of, or murdered, Wiersma and had taken his own life.

'A pretty tidy ending, don't you think, Greg?' Milne was on the phone to Greg.

'Oh definitely, Inspector.' Greg didn't even try to keep the sarcasm out of his voice.

'The file has been closed and there won't be any proceedings against you, Greg. I'd like to know how you made the Greek connection, though.'

'Flash of inspiration, I guess.'

'You do know it's illegal to withhold information, don't you?'

'I certainly do, Roger. Thanks for letting me know. We must meet up for a drink sometime.'

'Maybe. Take care, Greg, and good luck with your acting career. Try and make sure that agent of yours is a bit more thorough when choosing jobs for you in the future.'

'Oh I will, Roger. 'Bye.'

'What did he mean more thorough!' said Denis coming out of his bedroom.

'Where you listening in on the extension, Denis? That was a private conversation with one of Her Majesty's Inspectors of Police!'

'How was I supposed to know that commercial was just a cover for a drugs run?'

'I thought that was your job, Denis.'

'My job, young man, is to get you work opportunities, not to research every company that is foolish enough to want to employ you.'

'Never mind, Denis. I think he likes you really. Put the kettle on. Oh, and I'll have a large Cognac with my coffee, please, if that's OK.'

'It's not OK!' Denis huffed off to the kitchen but popped his head round the door a few seconds later. 'You can have a small one!'

The phone rang again and Greg picked it up before Denis could get to it. Greg was amazed to hear Han Koolhaven's voice down the line.

'Er…Hi, Han. How are you? You sound really close. Ha, ha. Modern technology, eh?'

'I am close. Well, Stansted Airport, actually. I'm glad I got you, I tried your flat but there was no reply.'

'No. I'm staying with Denis for a while and I haven't re-connected the answerphone yet.'

'Well, I'm about to start a new job over here at a film school in London. They've offered me a teaching job but I've nowhere to stay and I wondered if you could put me up for a while. Just 'till I find somewhere, you know.'

'You've heard what's happened, I suppose?'

'What? Wiersma and Rob? Yeah. I had to make a statement to the police. Isn't it terrible?'

'I suppose so. I don't know, I'm still a bit confused about the whole thing. Look, why don't you come over here and have a drink and we'll talk about it all. My flat's not being used, so if you want to stay there, I can let you have a key. OK?'

'Sure, thanks a lot for this, Greg. I feel a bit guilty, to be honest. I was part of getting you involved in all this, even if I didn't know what was going on.'

'Han. I don't blame you for anything. I believe you were as innocent as me. Just come round and have a drink.'

'Great. See you when I get there. 'Bye'

Greg replaced the phone as Denis came out of the kitchen. 'Who was that?' he asked.

'Han Koolhaven. He's on his way round here.'

'Oh no! Just look at the mess.'

Denis went for the Hoover.

*

It was about two hours later that Han Koolhaven entered Denis' now pristine flat. It was a bit of a shock for Han, seeing Greg's swollen face but a bigger shock for Greg. Instead of the long blonde pony-tail, Han's hair was cut short at the sides, leaving it floppy on the top. It also had the remains of a dark-brown wash-in dye showing. If he hadn't known better, Greg could easily have convinced himself that it was Rob Vanderlast who had just come in.

■■■

THE END

If you enjoyed this first part of the Greg Driscoll trilogy, you may like to read the beginning of the second part – THE PLAY.

THE PLAY

PROLOGUE

LONDON 1995

'You've done what!'

'I've bought a house in the country,' Greg replied. They were sitting in Denis Young's office in Oxford Street in the West End of London discussing Greg's next career move, when he'd brought up the subject of his physical move out of London.

'You can't move!' Denis was emphatic. 'Everything happens in London; auditions, castings, everything.' Denis was Greg Driscoll's theatrical agent.

'I'm not moving to Outer Mongolia, Denis. You're the one that said I should use Jenny's money to buy somewhere.'

Jenny Gulliver had been a friend of Greg's, an actress. They had both become unwittingly involved in a drug-running operation that was passing itself off as an advertising agency two years previously. Jenny had been duped into being a 'mule', carrying parcels of cocaine inside her body. The consequences had been fatal for Jenny. Having come from a rich but very difficult family, Jenny had named Greg as her next-of-kin along with a legacy of £250,000.00.

Greg had wanted nothing to do with the money and had left it sitting in a bank account, despite Denis' advice that he should invest it in 'bricks and mortar'. Somehow it felt wrong to Greg, he felt he'd let Jenny down and was in some way culpable and compliant in Jenny's death.

'I meant buy a flat somewhere in London and get yourself out of that hell-hole you live in in Hackney!'

'I like my flat in Hackney,' protested Greg.

'It's a council flat, Greg. It's not yours and, let's face it, it's not in a very nice area.'

'I've lived there for years. I've grown very fond of the area and the neighbours.'

'You never speak to the neighbours, Greg, apart from when 'Black Olive' delivers some of her suspicious mixture to you.'

'It's just Jamaican Rum, Denis. And anyway, I know my neighbours are there and I know them enough to say hello to. I like my flat.'

'So why are you moving to the ends of the earth to get away from it?'

'I'm not. I'm moving to Essex.'

'I thought you said you were moving to the country.'

'I am, Denis. I'm moving to the Essex countryside. By the coast. You've been there, Denis, remember?'

There was a long pause. Greg watched as the colour drained from Denis' face. Eventually he said, 'Please tell me you're joking,'

'No, Denis, I'm not. I have bought a house in Maldon on the Blackwater estuary, about a dozen miles from Chelmsford…'

'…Yes! I know where it is. I just don't understand why you would ever want to go near that place ever again.'

Maldon was the place where Greg had last held Jenny as she slipped into the coma from which she was never to properly wake. It had happened in the remains of an old railway station where the drug dealers were making their drop. Greg had burst in on them when he'd heard Jenny screaming. They had got away, Jenny had become unconscious and the police were livid. Denis had been there in Maldon at the time, trying to help Greg, Jenny and the police. He too felt guilty. He had become Jenny's agent and was unknowingly involved in her getting the job with the druggies who were posing as a legitimate film company. Both Jenny and Greg thought they were acting in TV commercials, when all the time they were just acting as couriers.

'I've been there a few times, Denis, since…well…since the incident. I like the place, believe it or not. There's something tranquil about it, even though the memories of Jenny are all around. In some ways it keeps

Jenny close. It's like she's there with me. I like to walk along the river, watching the birds, listening to the silence – that's something you never seem to get in Hackney, silence. Anyway, the last time I was there I saw this little terraced fisherman's cottage up for sale. I enquired at the Estate Agents and bought it. There and then. On a whim, maybe, but it's very sweet.'

Denis sat back in his chair. 'Is this just a sort of weekend retreat sort of place, then?' he said hopefully.

'No, Denis. This is a move. I've handed my notice in to the council and I'm moving within the month.'

CHAPTER ONE

MALDON 2003

The flash of light broke through Greg's Driscoll's sleep and woke him with a start. It was cold. He threw the duvet off and picked his dressing gown up from the floor, walked over to the window and looked out. He hadn't drawn the curtains the previous night, he rarely did. He peered through the grubby window panes but could see nothing. It was still very dark. He turned and looked at the clock by his bed. 6.48am it informed him. It was as he started back to the warmth of his bed that he heard the distant rumble from across the estuary. He turned back and looked out of the window. Roughly twenty seconds passed before the horizon lit up again, followed by darkness. Greg was always amazed at the number of times there was thunder and lightning round here unaccompanied by a single drop of rain. It was the difference between living in a built-up metropolis and out on the coast, he supposed. Here you could see a storm in the distance. He drew the curtains and crept back under the duvet.

Despite his agent, Denis Young's, protests that moving out of London would prove to be the end of Greg's acting career, it appeared to have made no difference at all. He still worked as much, or as little, as he had when living in

Hackney. The advantage of living here was that Greg was never bored. No more sitting in his council flat, broke, unable to afford to even go to the pub. No more looking at the dank walls he'd painted with dregs of paint left in old tins. Now Greg only needed to look out of his window and see a landscape with Thames barges, mud-flats and sea-birds. An added advantage was he could also see all these things from the terrace of The King's Head which was less than fifty yards from his front door. Plus, he still had money in his bank account

*.

The door-knocker's persistence forced him to rise from his bed and quickly throw some clothes on. The clock read 8.30am.

'Alright, I'm coming,' he yelled as he hurried down the stairs. He knew who it was at the door. He'd ordered a book from one of the larger London bookshops. One of the disadvantages of living in 'the back of beyond', as Denis liked to call it, was the difficulty of going out to a shop knowing they would have exactly what you wanted – or if they didn't, there'd be another shop within a stop or two of the Underground that would. In Maldon there was an extremely good second-hand bookshop but to get anything published recently meant ordering from the local WH Smith, which entailed a lot of details like ISBN numbers and publishers and loads of stuff Greg didn't know or have time for. By far the easiest way was to ring up a shop in London and get them to send it. He hadn't got used to using this thing called the internet yet, even though just about everybody was telling him it was the best and cheapest way to buy books.

The knocker rapped the door again just as Greg reached to open it. Sure enough, there stood the smiling face of his local postie – post lady he should say – wrapped up in a Royal Mail fleece to shield her from the cold.

'Been ordering books again, Greg?' she asked, as though it was a bizarre, even disgusting thing to want to do.

'I suppose I must have been,' replied Greg, taking the brown paper covered parcel from her. 'Want a cup of tea? You look freezing.'

The post lady looked around to see if anyone was watching before stepping through the door into the relative warmth of Greg's house.

The front door of the cottage opened straight into the living room. Through a door at the back of this room was the kitchen, a small kitchen but big enough to just fit the table and two chairs Greg had procured from a local second-hand junk shop in the town. The postie, Wendy Jenkins, went straight through to the kitchen and filled the kettle for Greg. She'd been here many times since Greg had moved in. She had been instrumental in helping Greg to settle and meet people. She'd been impressed by a large envelope that had arrived for him from the BBC and had wanted to know what he'd ordered from that Corporation. When Greg told her it was a script she all but invited herself into his house to talk about Greg and his acting career. Greg had been astounded by her nosiness and cheek but soon came to realise that people in the country behaved very differently from those in the big city and they could quickly become good friends. Wendy was married to Alan who did something in the city – not very high-powered, he was always quick to point out. He constantly boasted how he was a very experienced amateur actor. If this was intended to impress Greg it didn't! He had seen enough amateur dramatics in his time to realise that it had very little in common with the profession he followed. So far he'd always managed to be busy when Alan invited him to see their latest effort at 'Whoops! There go my trousers!' or whatever the production was.

'What's the book, then?' Wendy was sitting on one of the chairs fingering Greg's parcel.

'Isn't there some law that says you're not supposed to show an interest in the things you deliver?'

'No. Not as far as I know. I always want to know what people get in the post I shove through their letterboxes.'

'You're a postal voyeur, aren't you?

'Oooh! That makes me sound exciting. What's the book?'

'It's a book about the joys of smoking.'

'What?'

''How tobacco seduced the world.' It's a reference book about smoking from the earliest days, when it was considered a healthy pastime to the present day when it is rapidly becoming an abhorrent activity, sadly.'

'You can't say smoking is a healthy activity.'

'I don't know. Could be. Keeps me sane and all that.'

'Well, I think it's disgusting. Why would you want a book on it?'

'Research. I'm thinking of writing a play about smoking.' Greg opened his parcel and showed Wendy the book. Wendy, having no interest in the joys of smoking didn't even bother to open it but put it on the table. She reached into her sack and pulled out a couple of letters with Greg's name and address on them.

'Nearly forgot, you've a couple of letters as well. One's from the council. Not been paying your council tax again?'

'I pay my council tax by Direct Debit.' Greg opened the other letter first. It was from a company wanting to sell him life insurance. 'Where do these people get my name and address from?'

'Companies sell your name and address. If you order something you often agree to do that automatically if you don't look at the small print.'

'It ought to be illegal.' Greg turned to the letter from the council.

'Probably a parking fine,' said Wendy, sipping her coffee.

'You know I don't have a car, Wendy.' Greg put the letter unopened on the table. 'I'll look at it later.'

'You're joking,' said Wendy. 'You're not going to leave it there without me knowing what's in it?' She picked up the envelope and looked at it. Greg knew she would do this, it was a little game he liked to play with her. He was waiting to see how long she would wait before she opened it herself.

'Shall I open it for you?' It was less than a minute!

'Why not. You're only going to sit there until I do and then snatch it off me to read it anyway. I'm an open book, Wendy. I have nothing to hide.'

Wendy opened the envelope. 'At least it's a white envelope. I wouldn't open it if it was a brown one. That would be a fine or something.' She took the letter out of the envelope and started reading. 'Oh I say! How exciting! Did you know Shakespeare came to Maldon?'

'No. Probably before I lived here.'

'Well obviously. He's been dead for four hundred years.'

'Not quite. He died in 1616. That's only three hundred and eighty seven years ago.'

'Pedant!' Wendy carried on reading the letter. 'Oh, that's nice. It calls you an esteemed local professional actor.'

'I'm probably the only local professional actor.' Greg tried to take the letter but Wendy jumped off the chair and started reading it out loud.

'*Dear Greg Driscoll. We have recently discovered evidence that William Shakespeare's company of actors, The King's Men' visited Maldon in 1603 as part of a tour of the provinces. As an esteemed local professional actor I thought you might be interested in being part of a proposed Shakespeare Festival we are planning for this summer. I am sure your input would be greatly appreciated by the council and the community as a whole. Please ring me at your earliest convenience to discuss any involvement you could offer. Yours sincerely...*Ooh! It's from the Mayor.'

Greg took the letter from her and re-read it. 'No mention of money, I note.'

'What are you going to do?'

Greg put the letter to one side. 'I'm going to read my book on smoking until the pub opens and then I'm going to have a pint and read my book on smoking.'

'No.' Wendy sat down again. 'About Shakespeare?'

'I don't know, Wendy. I'm not a Shakespeare expert. I'm not sure what I could do for a Shakespeare Festival. Read some sonnets or something, I suppose. If they paid me.'

'You could do a production.'

'What on my own?'

'No. With the local community. A community production of Hamlet, with someone really good as the leading actor.' She pointed at Greg.

'Oh no! I'm not acting with a bunch of amateurs!'

'Oh well, if you're too grand...'

'I am. Amateur acting is different from professional acting, Wendy. We rehearse during the day, every day, not just at weekends. And we get paid for it. Have you any idea what it would cost to stage a production of Hamlet or any Shakespeare play?'

'Well, it wouldn't cost much if you just used amateur actors. You wouldn't have to pay them so if you could get the council to cover your fee...'

'...no, Wendy. I'm too old and decrepit to play Hamlet anyway.'

'True! Alan would be a good Hamlet.'

'Wendy.'

Wendy stood up and started for the front door. 'Oh well, I thought you'd like to help out on a community project. Alan would love it. I'd probably even get involved myself but if you're too busy reading about smoking yourself to death, that's up to you. I have the rest of my round to finish. Thanks for the tea, hope it wasn't too much trouble for you. Bye.'

'Wendy!' She was out of the door, sack on back and hurrying up the hill.

Greg sat down and looked at the letter again. He thought about what Wendy had proposed. There was something that appealed, he had to admit, in playing a leading Shakespearean role, even if it the rest of the cast were amateurs. They would only make him look better presumably. He poured himself a cup of coffee and opened his book.

■■■

Printed in Great Britain
by Amazon

74038111R00234